I0654321

"Knock – Knock!"　　*"Who's there?"*
"The Christmas Boogie Man!
You better run and hide!"

Christmas
Comes
Knocking

Jo Hammers

Paranormal Crossroads & Publishing

Christmas Comes Knocking © 2013 by Jo Hammers

All rights reserved. No part of this book may be repro-
duced or transmitted in any form or by any means without
written permission of the author. For information, address
Paranormal Crossroads & Publishing, Po Box 5056, Bella
Vista, AR 72714.

ISBN 978-0-9911540-0-5

www.paranormalcrossroads.com

This work is fiction. All of the characters, organizations,
and events portrayed in this novel are either products of
the author's imagination or are used fictitiously.

The publisher does not have any control over and does not
assume responsibility for author or third-party Web sites
or their contents.

The scanning, uploading, and distribution of this book via
the Internet, or via any other means without permission of
the publisher is illegal and punishable by law. Please purchase only authorized electronic editions and do not par-
ticipate in or encourage electronic piracy of copyrighted
materials. Your support of the author's rights is appreciated.

Image copyright Jo Hammers, 2013.

Table of Contents

"Knock – Knock!" *"Who's there?"*
"The Christmas Boogie Man!
You better run and hide!"

Christmas
Comes
Knocking

Jo Hammers

CHAPTER ONE

NO SNOTTY NOSED ELVES FOR ME

Edmond Marsh, a Jewish bachelor from California, has flown home to Chicago for the holidays. A taxi has just dropped him off in front of his sister Maxi's upscale, Chicago toy store. Christmas time is Maxi's busiest season in the toy store business. She milks the pagan, protestant holiday for all it is worth. Toys purchased by protestant parents, for Santa to deliver, net her most of her profit for the year.

Edmond Marsh is starchy Jewish and finds the Christmas season a bunch of materialistic nonsense, although he has always supported his sister in her choice of a business. Every year, Maxi has suckered him into playing Santa Claus on Christmas Eve for her customers. Maxi is the oldest, dominant, and wealthier of the pair of fraternal twins. Edmond has always played second fiddle to Maxi, as well as let her have her way in most everything. Playing Santa Claus once a year is a concession on his part to her dominance.

Edmond lives from pay check to pay check in California, working in a fast food restaurant. He is college educated, but just can't seem to get his foot in the door of his chosen field. He has always lied to his sister, telling her he works for a private detective who owns an agency named Zeke's Feet. He doesn't want his sister to see him as a complete failure in life. Fast food work is all he has been able to land in California. Monty, as he is nicknamed, has a teacher's degree in History. However, he dreams of being a detective. His teacher's degree was his parent's idea. They were both educators. When he landed his current job as counter help in a burger joint, he stated on his application that he was simply a high school graduate. He needed the job and didn't want to be turned away for being over-qualified.

Once upon a time, Monty dreamed of opening up a detective agency in Chicago. That dream died when his fiancé dumped him after he graduated college, two weeks before their wedding date. His fiancé shattered his heart. He had been truly in love with her. The West Coast, California, was where he and his broken heart fled to, in order to survive. The fast food burger place, he now works at in California, is next door to Zeke's Feet Detective Agency. Edmond (Monty) does work for Zeke in a way. He serves him his lunch each day at 'The Burger Stop.'

Until the current holiday season, Edmond had always welcomed the extra money Maxi paid him for playing Santa on Christmas Eve. A dollar was a dollar. Why not deep six some of the money thrown away by the Protestants on their pagan holiday frivolities. Being Jewish, Christmas Eve meant nothing but dollars to him and his twin sister, Maxi. Christmas was just another day to them. Money was money.

Once more, the Christmas season had rolled around in Chicago. Edmond was not in the mood to play the big fat guy in red for his sister. He had secretly made plans for a quiet Christmas Eve far away from the city and Maxi's toy shop. He was ditching his sister and his yearly Christmas Eve Santa gig.

Edmond, or Monty, had just made his way to the toy store from the airport. After a round of hugs and greetings with his twin in the toy store, the two made their way to the back storage room to discuss what was up for his visit and eat ordered in Pizza for a quick lunch together. Monty was waiting for just the right moment to spring it on his twin sister that he was not going to play Santa on Christmas Eve for her. After the pizza arrived and they had settled down to eat with two chairs pulled up to a couple of storage boxes, Edmond patiently waited till his sister had her mouth full. Maxi had always dominated him and conversations. He felt it would be best to spring his abandonment of her and the Santa gig when she couldn't get in a word edgewise. The time was right.

"I hate to spring this on you on such short notice, but I am not doing the Santa bit for you this year." He stated wading into conversation with his sister.

Maxi Marsh, caught off guard with a mouth full of pizza sputtered, "You what . . . ?"

"I have had my fill of holding snotty nosed, Santa crazy brats on my lap on the Eve of a holiday that I don't observe. They wipe their snotty noses on my beard and cough germs in my face. Every year, that I have done the Santa bit for you, I have ended up catching strep throat, the flu, a cold, or mono from holding one of them. I have never understood why protestant mothers insist on dragging their sick kids down to see Santa, with no regards as to the health of others. I am not doing the Santa bit for you this year, Maxi! It doesn't matter how much money you offer me. I am going to spend this Christmas Eve with a cup of spiked hot cider and a good book. I have worked hard all year as a detective out in California. I need a little kick back time, free of illness."

"Edmond, you have always played Santa for me. I depend on you." My sister replied trying to make me feel guilty.

"Save the Edmond bull crap. My friends call me Monty. Only you call me Edmond, and that is when you want something from me. I am not doing the pagan Santa bit this year." I spit out firmly, giving her a starchy, raised eyebrow look while I took a sip from the straw in my Pizza delivery soda.

"How can you do this to me? Where am I going to find a Santa on such short notice? It is Christmas Eve and Santa is supposed to be in his sleigh in an hour." She shot back trying to make me feel guilty.

"Get your stock boy to don the suit." I replied not giving in to her.

"Some of my customers' kids have come to sit on your knee ever since they were babies. That kinky haired, college girlfriend of yours is bound to show up with her little niece in tow. You wouldn't want to disappoint her niece, would you?" Maxi asked with an annoying, whiny, voice. "I seem to recall you being madly in love with that college girl, whatever her name was."

"College romances don't always survive in the real world, Maxi. Jen hasn't been my girlfriend in years. In case you have forgotten, we split up two weeks after graduation. She went her way and I went mine. I just imagine she is married and has a couple of kids by now. To be honest, I don't recall what I saw in her." I lied. I had been madly in love with Jen. She had dumped me for someone else two weeks before we were to be married after college. "I haven't seen her in years, Maxi."

"Oh . . . !" My sister answered with a surprised, far-away look on her face. "Has it been that long since you dated her?"

"You have been too busy making money, Maxi. I haven't seen or dated Jen for years."

"I guess time and life has gotten away from me. I have had my nose buried in my business."

"You have been like a dog with a bone, sis. Once you sunk your teeth into the business world after college, you became oblivious to time, space, and me. Jen is married to someone else."

"I have definitely been in a time warp on that one. Why did the two of you break up?"

"She wanted things I couldn't possibly give her." I replied not going into details.

"I tried to get you to invest in the toy shop and real-estate with me. Your minimum wage detective income is not my fault." Maxi replied, digging at my meager finances. She didn't have a clue that I was just a burger flipper.

"A detective is who I have always wanted to be." I replied, ignoring her 'I told you so' remarks.

"Are you seeing someone out in California?"

"I am a confirmed Jewish bachelor, thank you." I shot

back. "Marriage is for fools."

"I would give my eye teeth to marry and have kids." Maxi replied with a far away short stare into nowhere.

"Marriage is an outdated custom, Maxi, one that I never plan to embrace. I have spent too much time following cheating spouses for the detective agency I work for." I replied, lying about the detective part and my desire to be with someone. I had reasons for not dating.

"Don't let our Rabbi hear you talking like that. He will think you are gay. I have hard enough time explaining myself to him and why I won't go out with his son, Levi. Homosexuality is not exactly embraced by our religious homophobic community."

I grabbed another piece of pizza from the box. Some things about home I missed. Chicago pizza was one of them.

"I am not gay, Maxi. My reasons, for choosing a solitary life, are my business."

"One day you will meet a woman and your confirmed bachelor ideas will be gone in a sudden poof, like our father cutting a wind."

"Sorry Sis. I am committed to my embracement of bachelorhood. I am not like dad."

"You may say that now, but just wait till you meet my new, blonde, sales clerk. She is Jewish, educated, your age, and single. All the good, going somewhere, Jewish girls will soon be taken. You don't want to end up with a horse face old Jewish hag, or a divorcee with seven kids, do you?"

"Let me tell you once more, I never plan to marry. Secondly, I will never consider a woman with snotty nosed elves in tow." I huffed. My sister didn't have a spouse to nag at, so she picked at me.

"You need to get with the program and settle down, Edmond. I could let my new blonde sales clerk be your elf, and assist you on Christmas Eve. She could help kids on and off your Santa lap. I would even turn my back, should she choose to take a turn on your lap." My sister shot back. "You could check out her pretty legs while she is doing the sitting. In my thinking, one look at her charms and you will be singing, here comes Santa Clause-Clause-Clause."

"Forget it Maxi! I am not playing Santa Clause, or hooking up with your Santa crazy, going nowhere, blonde bimbo, register running, sales clerk. Educated girls don't run cash registers." I spouted while being a little, secretly embarrassed. I had a college degree and was flipping burgers, as well as running a register in a fast food joint in California.

"I work in this toy store, and on the cash register when needed. Do you see me as a going nowhere sales clerk?" My sister shot back asking, with a perturbed look on her face.

"You own this store. That makes the difference." I replied, rolling my eyes at her.

My sister Maxi had a bachelor's degree and masters in business and finance. She had purchased the building she was in, and had converted the second floor of the building into five apartments. She kept them leased out, so she could dabble around on the ground floor in the toy business. Some women dabbled in quilt making, or flower arranging. My sister's passion was toys.

13

"My bimbo sales clerk may own a toy store someday!" She huffed, while pausing for a moment or so. She then continued. "Have I mentioned that she has twin boys?"

"Enough is enough, Maxi. I will never date anyone that has kids as long as I live. I have gotten my fill of brats every Christmas Eve, while playing the white bearded, fat guy for you. I am not the father or stepfather type." I replied, as I offered her the last piece of pizza, which she turned down.

"You have always played Santa for me on Christmas Eve, Edmond. Now, be a sport and help me out. I am your sister, not to mention being your twin. You owe me! After I was born, I took the time to reach back, grab your foot, and drag you out of our mother. You were one screaming little sissy. They had to slap my bottom to make me cry. You came out screaming like a girl."

"You have been a royal pain trying to grab and guide my feet ever since." I shot back, as I bit into the last piece of pizza. After chewing a moment, I continued. "I have plans for Christmas Eve this year, Maxi. I intend to embrace the Protestant's Christmas Eve sanely, with a good book and fifty miles from the nearest snotty nosed kid and blonde bimbo."

"Just where does my Jewish, stick in the mud, confirmed bachelor brother plan on finding fast food and a place fifty miles from snotty nosed kids for the holidays?"

"I went in on the internet and found a woman named Wanda, who owns a rustic cabin north of here. She and her extended family have all moved to the South West and California, to escape Chicago's severe winters. They no longer use the cabin. Wanda has sentimental attachments to the cabin, and is unwilling to let it be sold. So, she rents it out to pay for upkeep and taxes on the property." I replied, reaching for my soda to wash down the one too many slices of pizza. I belched. "Excuse me, Maxi. I guess my stomach can't handle pizza like it used to."

"Squandering money and paying rent for mountain cabins will never make you a financial success, Edmond. If you want a cabin, buy one! Then rent it out during the parts of the year you are not using it. Make money, don't waste it. Someday you will wise up and want a wife and kids. You need to be thinking ahead and saving for your future, not squandering every penny you make renting mountain cabins. You should also get out and get yourself a real job. You are not going to get rich playing super-snoop."

"As I told you before, I have no intention of every marrying, Maxi. I make plenty of money to pay my rent and afford my weekly trip to a book store. I am a happy, contented, super-snoop and don't need a fat bank account, or a wife to spend it. I am a successful detective who just happens to live on a lower scale of life than you would like." I retorted, knowing that being a detective was a step up from who I really was. I was ashamed of being a burger flipper. I had a college degree, just like Maxi.

"A successful detective owns his own agency. You are a register man, just like my sales clerk. She works for a toy store for minimum wage and you do the same for your detective agency."

"Ouch sis . . . ! You sure know how to hurt a guy." I stated, watching the door of the toy store open and a bleached blonde bimbo walk in. She did have pretty legs. However, she had hips that almost didn't make it thru the door. My sister had to be desperate, wanting to hook me up with her. The blonde was at least a head taller than me. I shook my head and took another bite of pizza.

"You have worked for that cheap ass detective agency since you graduated college. Also, you have squandered your meager wages on books. Use the library, Edmond. You are twenty seven years old, and don't have a pot to pee in. In my opinion, you should have gone into the diamond trade with Uncle Eli. You would own your own jewelry store by now and a cabin in Switzerland."

"I am happy with my detective life, thank you!" I retorted lying. "Yes, my current savings account is depleted, but it is due to my buying a plane ticket to come home to visit you. However, when I get my taxes back in a month or so, I will have a little stash again. Renting a mountain cabin for the Christmas season probably does seem frivolous to you. However, it is not the end of the world, or financial disaster nipping at my heels."

"I know you better than you know yourself, Edmond. In case you have forgotten, we are twins and have spent our entire lives in each other's shadow. Are you still in love with your college sweetheart? I seem to recall the two of you planning to buy a cabin and raise a clan of little back-woods men, scouts, or something."

"Not all youthful dreams become reality, Maxi. Kids in college dream foolishly. The reality is that Jen has married someone else. I am now pursuing what I really want out of life, being a private detective." I replied once again lying. I actually hated my secret life as a burger flipper, but would never admit that to my domineering sister. Jen had walked out on our shared dream, not me. She had dumped me two weeks before our wedding for a rich, older dude.

"Do you know what I think, Edmond?"

"Lay it on me, Maxi. You are going to tell me anyway." I huffed. She was starting to ruffle my Jewish feathers. She was prying into my personal life.

"I think you still want the cabin and the simple life that goes with it. Why else would you want to dump me on the busiest day my toy store has all year? Are you meeting Jen there? Are the two of you getting back together?"

"Jen and I are history. Cut me some slack, Maxi. You are no different than me. You aren't married or have a significant someone."

"I would marry a significant someone in a heartbeat, if the opportunity crossed my path. In case you have forgotten, I don't have the options you do." She returned in a sarcastic voice.

"I am sorry I have stepped on your toes, Sis. However, the difference between us is, I have faced reality and know that I will not get everything in life I want. A cabin in the woods, a wife, and kids are no longer on my wish list. A pair of binoculars and a new camera to do my snooping with is." I retorted, lying about the binoculars and camera.

"You are a college educated man, Edmond. You are capable of having anything you want out of life. You just have to put your nose to the grindstone and pursue it. Out there somewhere is a mountain woman who will be more than willing to birth a dozen or so kids for you and live in a cabin on Po-dunk Mountain. You are off your path, Edmond. Do your California detective agency a favor and quit. You should be a forest ranger or a fishing tour guide, not a detective. Get back to who you once dreamed of being. I have always known I would pursue a career in the toy store business. As a kid, camping, fishing, and the out of doors were your forte."

"Get off my case, Maxi. You may have money, but I don't see you having a husband and kids to share your success with. You are confirmed single just like me."

"In case you have failed to tune into my life, Edmond, I am openly a lesbian. Marriage and kids are not an option for me. "

"Sorry . . . I wasn't thinking." I replied, seeing the hurt expression in my fraternal twin sister's eyes.

"Reconsider, Edmond. Rent your mountain cabin after Christmas. My toy store needs its Santa. I will pay you double what I paid you last year."

"Sometimes, you drive me crazy, Maxi. You don't listen to what I am saying and trying to make clear to you. You and I are Jewish. I do not believe in the Christian's fairy tale St. Nicholas. He is a myth. Furthermore, I am not sure I even believe in our Jewish God. I have never seen or experienced him." I stated, thinking how he had not been there when my ex-fiancé, Jen, dumped me and broke my heart. My Jewish God had not caused her to change her mind and return to me. "If God does exist, Maxi, He is probably going to rain hail and brimstone on you and me for embracing the protestant pagan's holiday. I want to cut all ties with religion, Santa, and my past and move on."

"I am a smart business woman, Edmond. Our Jewish God has made me so. I am Jewish eleven months out of the year, and a believer in Santa Clause during the month of December. In January, I give the temple their share of my December profits from good old St. Nick. The Rabbi never turns down my hefty check."

"You are pathetic, Maxi! You kiss the red, fat guy's backside for the almighty dollar."

"Santa Claus is a money maker, as is the Tooth Fairy and the Easter Bunny. You will be staying upstairs in my apartment, and sleep on a king size bed paid for by commercializing good old St. Nick."

"Don't you think it would be a little more appropriate to push Hanukkah?"

"Hanukkah is not where the dollar bill is. It is in the pocket book of the mothers who sit their kids in my huge red sleigh to ask Santa for expensive toys. Jewish mothers are practical. A spinning top is all their children are going to get."

"The dollar bill has become your God, Maxi!"

"Squandering a dollar bill has become yours!" She retorted, raising an eyebrow at me.

"I don't squander. I live for the moment and enjoy my life."

"We are twins and have had the same educational opportunities, Edmond. I am well on my way to retiring before the age of thirty-five. You are a renter who doesn't even own the furniture in your apartment. Might I also point out that you have wasted your education and work at an occupation that pays minimum wage. Penniless white trash is not who our parents have raised us to be."

"You may have money, Maxi, but your life sucks just as bad as mine. You play with children's dolls and toys, instead of adopting children and playing with them." I shot back annoyed. She always told me just like it was.

"When I meet my special someone, Edmond, I intend to share my wealth and life with her. Instead of carrying her over the threshold of a dump apartment with rented furniture, I plan to buy her one of the biggest damn houses in the suburbs she has ever seen. When my right someone comes along, I plan to make sure she has anything she wants, including enough money to adopt kids if she desires them. I may not be able to marry her, or give her biological children, but she will never want for anything that the almighty dollar can buy."

For a moment, I got lost in thought thinking about my college girlfriend and fiancé, Jen, who had dumped me. Instantly, I relived the shattered heart pain of losing her. I had been madly in love with her. I quickly let the thought of her go. I had tortured myself one too many times over our break up. Having kids was the issue that had come between us.

"I don't share your material views, Maxi. First off, I don't want a wife or kids." I huffed, knowing that I was lying.

"You are going to die old, alone, and with no one to care about you or attend your funeral." She returned, rolling her eyes at me. Maxi was a definite body language person.

"I won't have to share my rented coffin or borrowed burial spot with anyone." I retorted, secretly cringing on the inside at her words. No man wants to sleep alone or die old and not have arms to hold him. I couldn't find those arms, because I was still in love with Jen.

There was a secret I had never shared with my sister Maxi.

Some men have low sperm counts. I was a dud with almost no sperm count. A physical I took in my senior year in college had shocked me with that information. I was newly engaged at the time, with plans to marry my kinky haired fiancé two weeks after college graduation. Jen, my betrothed, dumped me before our wedding, when I told her about my diagnosis. I was madly in love with her and she dumped me over a zilch sperm count. She informed me that she wanted children more than she wanted me. Inside, I was still struggling with the breakup and her making me feel less than desirable as a man. At the time of our breakup, I made up my mind to never be up front and tell another woman I was half a man. In survival mode, I became a confirmed bachelor deciding to never put my heart out there for another woman to trample on.

"What if I die before you, Edmond?" Maxi replied interrupting my thoughts. "You will have no one to watch out for you, when you are old. Even worse is the fact that, you might end up living with me and my special someone when your hair is gray and your Jewish teeth have fallen out. Two oldsters is company, three is a crowd."

"If it will make you happy, if you go before me, I will marry your gray haired special someone when I am eighty and she can use your wealth to take care of me in my old age." I stated. Suddenly I stood, grabbed my sister, picked her up, and swung her around like she were still five or six. When she begged for mercy, I let her feet down.

"You are awful, Edmond." She laughed, punching me in the shoulder. If I was in a male body, you wouldn't get by with that. It would be me roughing you up.

"I have got to go, Sis. Have one of your register people

don the Santa Suit. I have already rented my cabin and a four wheel drive to get there in. My rental vehicle has been delivered to the curb out front. I am going to spend a quiet pagan Christmas, free from snotty nosed elves. I don't plan on speaking to a single soul till New Years. Don't try to call me! I don't have a cell phone. All calls are going to my answering machine in California."

"Just what are you going to eat in that remote cabin? I don't recall you being a hunter, or much of a cook lately."

"I am a detective who carries a gun. If the occasion occurs, I will shoot a rabbit or something. I have had plenty of target practice in my business in the pursuit of criminals." I lied. She didn't know that I worked in a fast food joint. Also, I didn't own a firearm. "I will just be gone five, maybe six days Maxi. I am going to take three man-sized, chicken TV dinners, a dozen glazed donuts, and a can of coffee. I won't starve in that time. There will probably be a convenience gas station within driving distance, if I need more food than what I am taking. The cupboards of the mountain cabin are probably stocked with staples. Someone occupies the cabin spring, summer, and fall."

"Might I suggest you take along a can opener, crackers, and a few cans of soup just in case? If you get snowed in, a hot bowl of soup could taste pretty damn good. I also suggest you take some toilet paper. I have never stayed in a mountain cabin that had a decent supply of the necessity. It is not like you are renting a motel room. There won't be a desk clerk to run you down a roll if you need it. Wiping on dried oak leaves is not my style. I am sure it is not yours, either."

"Don't over think my trip, Maxi. Three TV dinners, a

dozen glazed donuts, and a can of coffee will suffice. I put on a few pounds at Thanksgiving. Dieting a little will be good for me."

"You are going to regret not staying here and playing Santa for me!" My sister stated, folding her arms across her chest and shaking her head in a know-it-all attitude, which was typical of Maxi.

"I am not going to regret getting some much needed solitude." I replied standing my ground, a rare action on my part with my sister. She had been the dominating force in our sibling relationship since we were born. "I am thru with the Santa nonsense. Four or five hours from now, I will be breathing unpolluted air in the mountains, settling into a rustic cabin in front of a fireplace, preparing to drink a cup of hot coffee, and settling down with a good book."

"Well, at least do something constructive with the time. Take along a book on planning for your financial future and think over your life choices. You need to crawl out of your California gutter life and do something with your education to make me and our parents proud. Being a snooping Peeping Tom is not exactly classy."

"I am who I am, Maxi, a simple man who works five days a week and spends his weekend reading a good book. I am a confirmed bachelor who never intends to marry. I don't need to stash money back for a future someone special. As long as I am able to pay my rent and cash for the books I buy, I am successful in the life I have chosen." I replied and then added. "Every year I come to visit you and you stick me with playing Santa to a bunch of snotty nosed, sick, protestant kids, who infect me with the flu, strep throat, measles, chicken pox, ear infections, and other related illnesses. Their Santa loving mothers don't think twice about sitting their sick kid on my lap and leaving behind germs and viruses for me and the kids coming after them to catch. Enough is enough, Maxi. I am thru playing Santa. I am Jewish, for God's sake. I don't believe in him."

"Please reconsider, Edmond. You might not get sick this year. As many years as you have done the Santa bit, it is possible that you have built up immunity to kid's illnesses."

"My wearing the fat, red suited guy's pants is not happening this year." I stated, suddenly yawning. Eating two thirds of a Chicago pizza apparently was making me really sleepy. I had eaten way too much.

"Just so you know . . . I am putting the Marsh, Jewish, evil eye curse on you Edmond. Your fifty miles from nowhere excursion, abandoning your one and only loving sister, will turn into a Christmas Eve nightmare." My sister stated, pretending she was a gypsy placing a curse on me with her hands and a harsh stare from her eyes with one eyebrow up. Then she held out her hand to me. "Cross my palm with twenty and I will remove my evil eye curse."

I took the palm of her hand and kissed it, grinning. She never failed to amuse me with her antics. That was probably what made her successful in her toy business. She could imitate any cartoon or super hero character. She should have been an actress. "I have got to go, Sis. Fifty miles from nowhere is calling, and I have a long drive ahead of me. I need to get moving. Eating too much pizza is making me sleepy. I need the cold air outside to revive me. Do you have the heat turned up in here or something?"

Our lunch was interrupted by a sales clerk sticking her head around the corner, requesting Maxi to come help her with some problem at the register. Not waiting for her to return, I left the toy store and got in my rented four wheel drive. Once again, I yawned and blinked my eyes. After sitting there relaxing for a moment or so, I pulled away from the curb and headed out toward the interstate to begin my journey. Even though it was winter and cold, I cracked my window and left the heater off to combat my sleepiness. I just didn't understand why I was so sleepy. I had slept on the plane to Chicago.

CHAPTER TWO

FIFTY MILES FROM NOWHERE

After three hours of driving, I ended up in the North Woods, fifty miles from nowhere. I pulled onto a long, narrow, winding, snow covered drive that led to a small, deserted, log cabin. The little, rustic hideaway looked cold, desolate, and free of any living man or beast. On one side of the cabin were woods, and on the other was a small field, white with snow. The rocked path and rough, gray, wooden steps leading up to the cabin were snow covered and untouched by human boots or snow shovels. I was definitely in the middle of nowhere. I understood why its occupants went south for the winter months. There was not a gas station or convenience store within twenty miles or so. In the back of my mind, I could hear Maxi say, "I told you so!"

After parking near the door, I got out and walked up the un-shoveled path to the cabin. The silence was eerie. A black bird's excited squawk in the distance seemed to be trying to warn me that there was something wrong in the strange quietness.

"I am too used to city sounds and traffic noises," I muttered, stopping for a moment to breathe in the cold air and enjoy the silence.

Starting to feel the effects of the bone chilling, seventeen degree temperature, I looked under a huge planter where the female owner had told me the key would be. Sure enough, a painted door key was there. I was amused as I picked it up. It looked like someone had painted the entry key with red nail polish. Standing up, I thought I heard voices inside the cabin. Fearing, I was somehow at the wrong cabin, I decided I had better knock before using the key. I gave the door three hearty knocks. Too my surprise, the door just swung open on its own. What I assumed were voices ceased. The cabin was empty. I then decided I had watched one too many horror flicks, and read one too many books of Sci-fi fiction to fill my lonely bachelor, Saturday nights in California. My mind was playing tricks on me. I closed the door, preparing to settle in for some quiet time.

I was a little shocked as to how rustic the cabin was. The cabin's door was in disrepair. The interior appeared to have been built at least two hundred years before. The bed, two rockers, and small kitchen table with chairs were handmade and very old. I had desired a rustic retreat, but this place was a little too back woodsy for me. The one thing I was pleased with was its isolated location, fifty miles from the nearest town.

I wandered about for a few moments checking out the amenities of the one room. A full size bed loomed in one corner, pushed up against the wall. A couple of unpainted, handmade, slat board rockers sat in front of a fireplace on a second wall. On the third wall, a kitchenette with white cupboards loomed. The fourth wall had the entrance door and a door to a tiny lean-to bathroom. There was nothing pretentious about the twenty foot square, one room cabin.

After retrieving my overnight bag and meager food supplies from the four wheel drive, I scrounged up firewood from the back side of the cabin and proceeded to get a fire going in the fireplace. It wasn't long before flames started mysteriously dancing. Too my horror, the place was lit by kerosene lamps, and the only source of heating food was on a wood stove. There was no microwave, refrigerator, or other modern conveniences. I decided that I would have to store my three TV dinners outside in the cold to preserve them. The dozen glazed donuts had been a good choice on my part. They didn't need cooling or heating. I hoped I could manage making coffee on the wood cook stove. Cooking was definitely not my strong point. I had expected at the very least, a microwave. My choice of a hideaway was a little too extreme, even for a hermit like me. I could have sworn the owner in California had told me that the cabin had a small modern kitchen, electric lights, and propane heat.

It was late evening. The sun had dipped in the horizon and it was getting eerily dark outside. I settled into one of the two rough rockers in front of the fireplace, to enjoy the heat and think about my life. Maxi was right. Being a fast food worker was not getting me anywhere in life, neither was my lying to her about working for Zeke's Feet Detective Agency. I was a miserable Jewish failure, who was running away from my sister's success, women in general, and life. Living in California kept me and my deceptions safe.

Jen, my former fiancé, had done a number on my psyche. She had dumped me just after college graduation and two weeks before we were to be married. Even though it had been several years now, I had never gotten over it or her. Maybe it was time to let her go, and try to recapture the happy guy I once was in college. I wanted to live again. What I knew I couldn't do, if I lay my hermit life down, was to tell another woman that I was a dud, and could never father children. Jen had just walked away from me like I meant nothing to her, when I told her. I was like a broken toy. She tossed me in the trash and just went on with her life and married someone else six weeks later. She told me that she wanted children more than she wanted me. I was single, sperm-less, and afraid to fall in love again. I was haunted by my break up with Jen and her demeaning words pointing out the flaw in my manhood, my lack of sperm. She had done a definite number on my psyche. I definitely now had an inferiority complex, when it came to my maleness.

As I rocked, watching the flames dance in the fireplace, sleepiness overcame me and I dozed off. When I woke up several hours later, the fireplace logs had disintegrated into ashes and my fire was about to go out.

A knock sounded at the door. I immediately rose from my rocker and made my way to the door to see who it was. The harsh, rapping sound was a little shocking. I was fifty miles from nowhere. Opening the door, I was shocked to see a cross eyed guy, wearing an aviator cap with fur ear flaps, standing there. He was thin, tall, and had a nose that was visibly running from being out in the cold. He appeared to be in his twenties and my age.

"May I help you?" I asked, hoping he didn't want anything. I wanted to get back to my rocker, the red dancing flames, and my thoughts.

"I am looking for my mother and my dog." The cross eyed man replied, wiping his nose on the back of his glove. "Are they here?"

"No . . . I am the only one here." I replied, while eyeing the guy's World War II aviator hat with flaps that came down over his ears. "Is there a reason you think they might be here?"

"My dog was born out back in the barn. This place is home to him. Mama is probably wherever he is."

"Oh . . . you are a neighbor and you are looking for a lost dog." I replied, assuming that was what the odd guy was talking about.

"I am looking for my dog, Ace! However; I will take mama, if she is here. I lost her when my dog fell out of my back seat. Mama followed him."

"You lost your dog and your mother from your back seat?" I questioned a bit amused.

"No I didn't lose her. She should have had her seat belt on. Dogs don't know any better. She just went flying out over the back."

"What were you driving, a convertible?" I asked sarcastically, wanting to get rid of him. Glancing beyond the stranger out into the night, I could see that there was a heavy snow falling.

"Yea . . . something like that . . . !" The cross eyed guy replied, speaking slowly. "If you see my dog, will you let him in for the night? It is really cold out here. I have got to go find my mama. Santa won't come tomorrow night, Christmas Eve, if I don't find her."

At that point, I realized the man was mentally challenged, probably a neighbor. He had said his dog had been born in the small barn out back.

"If I see your dog, I will let him in." I replied, wanting to be rid of the odd, fruitcake man who was intruding on my 'fifty miles from nowhere' down time. "Your mama is probably back home by now, and baking cookies for Christmas."

The icy wind blowing in the cabin's door, as I talked to him, was not pleasant. I had stripped down to my boxers, sweat shirt, and socks once the fireplace had warmed the cabin's one room. I was roughing it, not embracing entertaining a stranger. The wind from the door was giving my bare legs goose bumps. It was snowing hard outside. My rented four wheel drive had four inches of snow on top. All the windows were covered over. The Santa loving Protestants prayed for snow for Christmas. My Jewish God was delivering.

Suddenly, there was the sound of whistling in the distance.

"That is my mama's whistle." The aviator capped guy stated with a huge grin crossing his face. He quickly turned and then bounded from my snow covered, cabin porch. He was gone in a flash and disappeared into the white night. I gladly closed my rented cabin's door.

"Fifty miles from nowhere . . ." I muttered, returning to the fireplace to warm myself and get rid of my goose bumps. My fire was down to embers and ashes. I immediately put my jeans back on, knowing I was going to have to fight the snow to get another arm load of logs. "Next time, I will make sure my rented cabin has a gas logs fireplace and a microwave."

Returning to the door, I put on my boots, coat, stocking hat, and gloves in preparation to go outside. When I opened the door, a gust of harsh, icy wind blew a white dusting of snow on the front of me. I looked like a powder sugar covered donut.

"It looks like the Protestants and good, old St. Nick are going to have a white Christmas!" I muttered, leaving the warmth of the cabin to retrieve wood. I was surprised to find that the snow was way above ankle level. It had been a skiff when I arrived. Treacherous, whiteout, blizzard conditions were setting in. I had not considered that possibility, when I had driven to the cabin earlier in the day. In my excitement abandoning Christmas, Maxi, and my yearly Santa gig; I had not checked the weather forecast.

As I rounded the back of the cabin, I heard a voice in the near distance yelling, "Help . . . !"

I looked about in the semi-darkness to see where the voice was coming from. About twenty feet behind the cabin, I spotted a short, female figure fighting deep snow, trying to walk toward the cabin. I quickly fought the new fallen snow and made my way to the red clad, snow covered human. When I neared the individual without a coat, I realized it was a short, frail, elderly, white haired woman who, in my opinion, had no business out in a blizzard. She had to be at least eighty years old. I instantly wondered where in the world she had come from. There was not supposed to be anyone living within fifty miles of the cabin.

"It is okay, I have got you. Who are you?" I asked slipping my arm around her waist to help her trudge toward the cabin.

The elderly lady, dressed in red sweats and house shoes, was shivering and scantily dressed for snow country. She wasn't wearing a coat, cap, scarf, or mittens. Her worn out house shoes and men's gray tube socks were visibly wet. I was alarmed. She looked like death warmed over, like she was about to succumb to the elements.

"My name is Kr . . . Kr . . . Kristina. I . . . I fell out of an airplane." She stated thru chattering teeth,

"You fell out of an airplane?" I asked in shock, as I helped her up the cabin's steps and then thru the front door into the cabin. I helped her make her way to the fireplace and then eased her into one of the two rockers in front of the glowing red embers

"Yes, I am an airplane builder, mechanic, and sometimes a test pilot." She replied. "I was riding with another pilot who was taking Old Faithful out for a test flight. I had just repaired its wing. The plane went into a tail spin, and I fell out."

"Great . . . ," I muttered under my breath. "Am I jinxed or something? Not only have I encountered a crazy guy who has lost his dog out of his vehicle, now I am stuck with a crazy old girl who thinks she is an airplane mechanic."

I realized in that weird, holiday moment, the frail white haired woman had to be suffering from dementia. My rented cabin, fifty miles from civilization, was nowhere near an airport, or repair hanger. In my opinion, there was no possible way she could have fallen out of a modern day air craft and lived to tell it. I saw no visible cuts, scrapes, or bruises on her. The question now was; who was she? How had she managed to make her way to the back of my cabin? There was nothing but a forest of trees in the direction she had arrived from.

"My name is Monty Marsh, Kristina. Did you just say you are an airplane mechanic?" I asked hoping she would give me some sort of clue as to her identity.

"My full name is Kristina Nicholas. You can call me Kris." She replied, holding her hands out in front of the fire, in the fireplace, to warm her-self. "Yes, I am the only airplane mechanic in these parts. My husband used to be the area's mechanic. One night he flew away and never returned. He was a fly by night, you might say."

"Do you have other family?" I asked, pumping her for information as to who she was.

"I have one grown son who is a pilot. I wanted more children, but was afraid to have more. My grown son was a handful as a child, and still is. He is passionate about airplanes. However, in my opinion, he is a somewhat reckless, daredevil of a pilot. I worry about him constantly."

I sat down in the second rocker and removed my dripping boots and socks. Then, I draped my socks, which had their tops wet from the deep snow, on the hearth in front of the fireplace to dry. Afterward, I stooped down in front of her and removed her wet house shoes and men's gray socks. I placed them next to mine to dry. She didn't resist my efforts to help her. She was an old woman. A woman my age would probably have slapped the fire out of me. I told myself that I hated women, due to Jen dumping me. Maybe I would retract that thought and exclude grandmother types.

"Keep your feet stretched out to the fire, till I get your socks and house shoes dry." I stated returning to the second rocker. This time, inside the cabin, I didn't strip down to my boxers to get comfortable. I had company. I didn't think an eighty year old woman would enjoy looking at my knobby knees, or my boxers. My hairy legs weren't my best feature in my opinion. My Jewish nose was. At least I thought so.

"You are very kind. Thank You! Did you fly here?" She asked while holding her bony, frail white hands out to the fire to warm them.

"No . . . I drove here from Chicago in a rented, four wheel drive." I replied stretching my bare, sun tanned feet out to the fire. I was a California, sun tanned, beach bum, confirmed bachelor who was taking some days off. "Where are you from?"

"Beyond the woods in back of this place a ways . . ." She replied. "I boarded my son's plane for a short flight around the area to listen to his engine. He flew over a snow bank and I fell out behind your cabin."

"What did you say your name was, again?" I asked wanting to get a handle on who she was.

"My name is Kristina Nicholas." She replied in a frail elderly voice. "My son may not be able to find his way back to me. He may have reached the Canadian line by now. He usually has a co-pilot that does the navigating. He can't read a map or instrument panels."

There was no way that she could have fallen out of a commercial jet, with pilots on board. She was definitely suffering from dementia. I decided that I would be nice, till the snow storm was over, and then drive her down off the mountain. I would turn her over to an ER somewhere and let them figure out who she was. In my thinking, she had probably walked away from a nursing home somewhere beyond the woods.

"I will help you find your way back home, after the snow stops." I stated, as the fireplace embers cracked and popped beneath the dancing flames. "You don't have a cell phone on you by any chance?" I asked, thinking I might call the sheriff and tell him that she had wandered into my place. I was sure she had to have nurses or someone looking for her somewhere.

I had purposely not brought a cell phone, due to my desire for some peace and quiet. If I had one with me, I would return every call that went to my answering. I didn't like untidy ends to things. I had been devastated at how Jen had dumped me and left me dangling just a week or so before our wedding. Left dangling was not a good thing for me. Non-answered phone calls were not a good thing to me. I now tried to keep all the ducks in my life in order for my sanity. I made choices. Leaving my phone behind to have a peaceful holiday was one of those choices.

"My son carries our cell phone." She replied, wiggling her old, bony toes in front of the fireplace's dancing flames, basking in the warmth.

I thought about the raging storm outside, and then the fact that I had brought provisions for one person, not two. Maxi had been right. I should have brought more than I needed, just in case. I had two mouths to feed now, not one. It might be days before I could get her off the mountain.

"Do you know where you are?" I asked, as I marveled at how blue her eyes were.

"It doesn't matter where I am, as long as my son makes it back to me for Christmas Eve. Home is where family is. My son and I always go to the city and visit Santa on Christmas Eve. Home is that brief moment when my son sits on Santa's knee and tells him what he wants for Christmas. Home is being with the ones you love. Wherever they are." She replied glancing over at me and flashing me the most charming smile. When my Jewish mother flashed me a smile like that, she wanted something.

"What do you want?" I asked, thinking she was like my mother and had to want something.

"I want to kiss Santa beneath the mistletoe on Christmas Eve, and for my son, Snicker Doodle, to make it back to me without a navigator." She replied. "What do you want?"

"Right now, I would like enough food for you and I for several days. I think I have miscalculated the severity of the storm that is raging outside. I should have brought much more food. Three TV dinners, a dozen donuts, and a pound can of coffee is the total sum of our food supply. I wasn't expecting a monster snow storm, or company."

"Don't worry! I will carry my weight around here till someone finds us. I make a mean apple cobbler."

"I am sure you do." I replied grinning and then biting my lip for a moment. She hadn't caught what I had said about my having so little food in the cabin.

"Don't worry about food, Edmond. My son will find us and take care of us. He is a good boy. He knows how to hunt, trap, and ice fish."

Within myself, I was sure that there was no son coming for her. She had, undoubtedly, wandered away from a nursing home in the area. I would just let her sit happy in her rocking chair and enjoy her delusions by the fire, till I could get her off the mountain.

"Will you settle for a glazed donut and a cup of black coffee before we retire for the evening? I will need to stretch our food till the storm is over."

"A donut and coffee sounds really good, Edmond. However, my son Snicker Doodle will find us by tomorrow, Christmas Eve. He never misses going to see Santa with me."

I broke out in a snort. "Your son's name is Snicker Doodle?"

"He was the cutest little cookie when he was born." She replied, ignoring my snort.

"Do you have other children with cookie names?" I asked.

"No . . . it is just Snicker Doodle and me. My husband left us years ago. He ran off with a neighbor woman, one who didn't want kids. My husband never wanted children. Snicker Doodle was a happy accident that my husband was ashamed of. I did not make a mistake having Snicker Doodle." She replied, looking like her mind was in a far off place of not so happy memories.

"I know all about mistakes, Kristina." I replied thinking about falling head over heels in love with Jen and then of her dumping me.

"Call me Kris." She replied.

"You may call me Monty." I returned, showing Jewish respect for her, an elderly, confused woman. "How old is your son?"

"My Snicker Doodle is special. He is thirty-nine, but looks like he is in his twenties. It may be a good thing I fell out of his airplane. Perhaps it is time for my mama's boy to fly away from me and become a man. Maybe, I fell out of his plane for a reason."

"I see . . . ," I replied casually, letting her talk. Apparently, her son was a thirty-nine year old wimp of a guy who was still living at home and mooching off of his mother. That was probably the reason she had on gray men's tube socks. She couldn't afford women's hosiery.

I got up from my rocker, walked over to the tiny kitchenette along one wall, and retrieved two donuts from the white pastry box. I carefully placed them on two donut shop, paper napkins. Then I prepared to make coffee in an old fashioned, boil type, coffee pot. That was when I realized that there was not a water faucet in the kitchen. There was a sink to do dishes in, but no in-cabin water supply. I immediately walked over to the bathroom door thinking I could get the water from there. To my shock, there was a shower stall with no faucet. Then, I looked at the toilet. It was an inside outhouse. There was no inside water supply in the kitchen or bathroom. It was at that point, I felt panic set in. I couldn't survive a blizzard without water to drink, or make coffee with. Bathing hadn't crossed my mind yet.

In a panic, I thought about the elderly woman I now had to look out for. I couldn't let her get dehydrated or go hungry. I had to get water somewhere. A boy scout, I wasn't. My idea of roughing it was wearing three day old dirty shorts and eating molded leftovers when you were between paychecks and hadn't been to the Laundromat. I was a confirmed, city bachelor, burger flipper. I definitely was not a survivalist.

Glancing around in the tiny lean to outhouse of a bathroom, I saw that there was only a half roll of toilet paper on the roll next to the outhouse hole. Maxi had been right. I should have listened to her and brought more supplies. With no toilet paper to speak of, my shorts were not going to be pleasant to wear or smell; if I was confined to the cabin for too many days. There was no complimentary resort washing machine to throw them in, much less water to put in the machine.

In my panic, I recalled my Jewish mother saying, "Change your shorts, Edmond. What if you get in an accident and die on the way to Temple? Do you think God will let you in Heaven's gate with soiled shorts on?"

I returned to the fireplace and handed Kris a donut on a napkin, and then sat down next to her in the other rocket to eat mine, trying not to show my panic.

"I'm sorry Kris. I couldn't make coffee. There is no water in the cabin. I will find some tomorrow morning when the sun comes up. I haven't figured out where the water supply in this cabin is, yet." I stated, taking a bite of my glazed donut which had to be my dinner. I was trying not to alarm her by showing emotions of how concerned about our situation I was.

"Water is all around you, Monty. Fill your coffee pot with clean snow and melt it down. All dwellers in the North Woods do that when there is a blizzard, or when their water pipes freeze."

"You are brilliant, Kris." I laughed, with my panic subsiding a little. City snows were too polluted and dirty to use for consumption.

"It will take one large dish pan of snow to make a small pot of coffee for two cups." She replied nibbling at her donut. Then she continued in her elderly, frail, charming, feminine voice. "Do you want me to go outside for the snow?"

"You are the survivalist brains in this cabin at the moment. I will go for the snow." I replied laughing. There was something about her that intrigued me. She was not only sweet and kind, but was also a very beautiful older woman in her eighties. I could see the beautiful younger woman she once had been. Her husband had been a fool for leaving her. Snicker Doodle was lucky to have her for a mother. My own Jewish mother was short, round, and waxed her upper lip. She was beautiful to me her son, but to the world about she was probably considered obese and pretty ordinary.

"Be careful on which side of the house you get the snow, Monty. If you have relieved yourself on the lower south side of the cabin in the snow, you will want to get our coffee water on the north upper side." She stated, wiping sugar glaze from the corner of her mouth. The sticky glazed donuts were messy to eat. The heat from the fireplace was making their sugary glaze melt.

"I get your point. Which side of this cabin do you suggest I make our water supply side?" I didn't have a clue which side of the cabin was north and which was south.

"Water runs down hill. Designate the high side as our water supply. If you use the high side for your relief spot, the yellow stuff will run down hill and become part of our water supply. I am not much into yellow coffee." She replied with an amused, but serious look on her face.

"I share your sentiment." I replied, once more snorting. "I am not a connoisseur of yellow coffee, either."

"You will probably find a huge metal dishpan beneath your sink. Everyone in the north keeps one for emergencies." She added. "Do you want me to get up and look for it?"

"No . . . you sit still. Carrying in and melting our water supply will be my job." I stated, as I walked over to the kitchenette and dug beneath the cabinet for a dish pan. Sure enough, there was a huge, round, aluminum one. Then, I proceeded to put back on my coat to go scoop snow for coffee.

"There is one more thing you should do, Monty." The frail, elderly, white haired woman stated turning in her rocker to look at me.

"What would that be?" I asked.

"Tie a rope between this cabin's porch and the small barn like shed out back. There is probably firewood and other things we may need that are stored there. When the blizzard turns into a white out, you can hold onto the rope when you go for firewood. It will prevent you from getting lost in blinding snow. Many city men have died in white-out conditions in these woods."

"I hadn't thought about that. Do you have any suggestions where I might find a rope?"

"It is probably hanging by the cabin or shed's door." She replied turning back around to bask in the warmth and glow of the fireplace flames.

I stepped out into the snowy night to fight an icy wind and harsh, blowing snow.

Kris was right. I could barely see as I found the rope and managed to get it tied between the two structures. After accomplishing that task, I scooped up a pan of new fallen snow on the high side of the cabin and returned inside to melt it down and make coffee. Kris showed me how to start a fire in the wood cook stove. I was a little embarrassed to have her do so. It was as though she was taking care of me.

Over the next couple of hours, we basked in the glow of the fireplace's flames, laughed, and told stories to amuse each other. We shared the snow coffee, as well as a magical evening in a less than perfect, one room cabin fifty miles from nowhere. When she started to yawn, I insisted that she take the one bed. I made myself one on the floor in front of the fireplace. I fell asleep listening to Kris snore, as well as watching the yellow and red flames of the fire dance.

CHAPTER THREE

ELOPING ON A SNOWMOBILE

It was about midnight when I was awakened by the sound of a banging on the cabin's door. I quickly jumped up, wondering for a brief moment if it was a grizzly making the pounding noise. The thought raced across my mind that one had possibly smelled our donuts. Then, I dismissed that idea when the knocking sounded again. Leaving the warmth of the fire, I went to answer the door. Being a city dweller, I didn't open the door, but asked who it was first.

"Who is it?" I half yelled thru the door.

There was no answer. However, I thought I could hear the chattering of teeth on the other side. I cracked the door.

"Is anyone out there?" I asked, peeping out into the night and blinding snow.

Two snow covered individuals were standing on the tiny cabin's porch, who looked almost too cold to speak.

"Please let us in." A male's voice begged. "We have lost our way in the storm, and are at the point of freezing to death. Our snow mobile crashed a short ways from here."

I opened the door wider and cautiously peeked at the two. As my eyes adjusted to the night, I saw that a teen boy, possibly sixteen, and a young girl, possibly fourteen or fifteen, stood shivering with their teeth chattering. I quickly pulled them inside, seeing that they were indeed about to succumb to the elements.

"What in the name of my Jewish God are the two of you doing out in this blizzard, at midnight, and on a snowmobile?" I asked helping the girl off with her snow covered coat, boots, mittens, and stocking hat.

"We were eloping!" The young, very obese girl stated shivering.

"You were eloping on a night like this?" I questioned, rolling my eyes and shaking my head in a negative manner.

"It was tonight or never." The teen boy stated. "Our baby is due in two days. Her mother won't let me marry her. We slipped out while her mother was busy watching a Christmas special on TV."

I took another look at the girl as she headed for the fireplace to warm herself. Obesity was not her problem. She was indeed very much pregnant, and looked like she was about to pop at any moment.

"Your baby is due in two days, and you have the nerve to put her, in her condition, on the back of a snowmobile?" I asked, eyeing the bulging front of the girl. She was way too young to be having a baby.

"We have grown up on snow mobiles and would have made it to town, if we hadn't collided with some nut on a red snow mobile with ironing boards attached. He ran into us and didn't even stop to check and see if we were okay. Our snowmobile went over a little embankment into a crevice of rocks and got stuck."

"How old are you?" I asked, turning to the girl.

"Fourteen." She replied, while wrapping her arms around her big belly which seemed to be moving somewhat.

I shook my head in disbelief. "How old are you?" I asked the boy as he removed his winter wear and headed for the fireplace.

"Sixteen . . . ," he replied thru chattering teeth, as he assumed a position in front of the fire next to the girl.

Once again, I shook my head in disbelief and then returned to the warmth of the fireplace, myself.

After giving the eloping pair twenty minutes to warm them-selves in front of the fireplace, I returned to the cabin door to put my coat and stocking hat on. It was time to get more firewood. I now had three people plus an unborn child to watch out for. I said a quick inner prayer, asking my Jewish God to prevent the teen girl's baby from coming till the pair of teens was out of my cabin, and off the mountain. Delivering babies was not my expertise. Flipping burgers and reading detective novels was.

Down deep, I had a selfish reason for not wanting to help deliver the girl's baby. Since learning that I was a sperm-less dud, and being made to feel that I was not a man because of it, I avoided babies. Jen, my former fiancé, had wanted a houseful of babies. She had dumped me because I couldn't give them to her. The sight of babies always brought her de-meaning dumping words rushing back to knife my psyche. Jen and her devastating words were my life's nightmare that played over and over again in my head when it got the chance.

"Where are you going?" The girl asked, as she stared at me with her backside turned to the fire to warm it.

"I am going out back to get more wood for the fire. We will need it before morning." I replied, continuing to dress myself in my winter wear.

"Do you want me to go with you and help?" She asked, with her huge belly visibly moving about.

"You stay here in front of the fire. You have your hands full holding your belly. There is no place in your arms for firewood. I want you to sit down in that rocker in front of the fire and not move till I get back. Your boy friend and I will carry in the firewood." I stated motioning for the six-teen year old to return to the door and get his coat on.

"Believe me, I won't move." The girl replied with a look of relief on her face. "I want this baby to settle down in my belly and go to sleep. It has kicked and given me belly aches off and on all day."

Her words didn't really sink in with me. After all, I was a single man. What did I know about early labor pains?

"Just sit down in that rocker and rock that belly baby to sleep." I replied, as the boy put back on his coat and stock-ing hat.

In my thinking, I was going to give the sixteen year old kid a serious lecture on the use of protection as well as recklessness. "What is your name?" I asked him, as we headed out the door and closed it behind us.

"My name is Joe." He replied, following me off the little

cabin porch. "Her name is Mary."

"That figures." I retorted, shaking my Jewish head. "I assume you are both Christians and will name your male child Emmanuel, Christian, or some other manger name."

"Nah . . . we are having a girl. Mary had ultrasound a few months back. The baby definitely is not a boy." He replied. "We are going to name the baby Merry, like in Merry Christmas."

"That figures." I muttered, shaking my head and pointing for him to hold to the rope that I had tied between the cabin and the shed out back where the firewood was. "I suppose you and Mary believe in the big guy who wears the red suit and white fake beard?" I sarcastically asked.

"We are a little old to believe in Santa Claus, if that is what you are referring to." He replied, as we held to the rope making our way thru the deep, new fallen snow and whiteout conditions to the shed like barn. The structure holding the firewood was no longer visible.

"I don't understand why Protestant parents lie to their kids, encouraging them to believe in a fairy tale being." I retorted, marking my Jewish territory. "Tomorrow night is the fat guy's big night. However, I know he won't be stopping at this cabin. I am Jewish, and definitely do not embrace St. Nicolas or all the Christmas crazy madness that surrounds him. I do hope you are not going to lie and teach your baby to believe in him, someday."

"I said we were a little too old for Santa to bring gifts to. That doesn't mean we don't believe in him." The boy replied, as we reached the small barn like structure behind the cabin, opened its door, and stepped inside to escape the blowing snow. "We will hang up a sock for our baby tomorrow night."

"Will you hang a pink or blue one?" I forced myself to ask in a sarcastic voice. I was running away from Maxi and her Chicago toy store's Christmas craziness. I wondered why my Jewish God was cramming Christmas crazy, Santa loving, Protestants down my throat in my secluded cabin that was supposed to be fifty miles from nowhere.

"I told you before that our baby is going to be a girl." The teen boy replied, shaking the snow from his coat and stocking hat inside the barn. "May I use your phone to call for help after we return to the cabin? I am sure that one of my buddies will tow another snow mobile over here, when the snow stops."

"I hate to tell you this, Joe. I left my cell phone back in California. The cabin doesn't have a land line. However, when the snow lets up tomorrow, I will shovel out my four wheel drive and go down the mountain for help. Till then, you and your girl are going to have to stay with me and Kristina. You are not putting your pregnant girlfriend back on the seat of a snow mobile."

"Who is Kristina?" The boy asked, mulling over the name.

"She is the elderly woman wearing the red sweats, occupying the cabin's bed. She wandered in here last evening, wadding thru a snow drift. She claims to have fallen out of an air plane. When I rescued her in the edge of the woods, she was almost frozen to death. She didn't have a coat, boots, hat, or gloves on. She was wearing house shoes."

"That is crazy man . . . No one falls out of an airplane and lives to tell about it. She has to be pulling your leg. If I were guessing, she is someone's visiting grandmother who has wandered away from some cabin around here. "

"She says she has a son named Snicker Doodle." I replied, loading the boys arm with logs. "Maybe he will follow her tracks in the snow and come for her."

"There won't be any tracks in the morning, not in a snow like this." Joe replied, as I put one last stick of wood into his arms and turned to fill my own. "It is sort of like playing 'Finders Keepers'. You have a keeper, till the storm passes." He further stated, shifting his arm load of logs to a comfortable position.

"Finders Keepers," I replied laughing, being suddenly amused with the teen who was just a kid.

"Maybe she is Mrs. Claus!" The boy replied snorting. "Maybe she fell out of Santa's sleigh."

"It is my understanding that your Protestant fairy tale Santa makes his rounds on Christmas Eve. Yesterday, when I found her, it was the 23rd, not Christmas Eve."

"Well, maybe she is an early valentine. You did say that she was dressed in red. Maybe cupid dropped her into your world."

I rolled my eyes seeing that the witty kid had gotten the best of me in the conversation.

"Did you and Mary, by any chance, pack food to snack on as you eloped, something we could possibly retrieve from the snowmobile when the snow stops?"

"We didn't need food. We both had been saving our allowances to elope on. We planned to get some burgers after we got into town. Mary does have a bag of lemon drops stuck in her coat pocket. She has craved them from day one of her pregnancy. We have considered naming our baby Lemon Drop."

"Lemon drops . . ." I replied, rolling my eyes in disgust. That wasn't much to add to the food supply. The kid didn't realize that we were possibly in a survival mode and could be stuck on the mountain for days with no food. Three TV dinners, ten donuts, and a bag of lemon drops wasn't much too work with. Now, there were four mouths to feed.

After returning to the cabin, I woke up Kris. She took Mary and made her comfortable in the one bed with her. Joe joined me for the night in front of the fireplace. In whispers, after the women fell asleep, Joe and I discussed his future as a father. I gave him the lecture I thought my Jewish father would have given me, had I brought a fourteen year old girl home that was nine months pregnant. Joe just listened and eyed the dancing flames in the fireplace.

When conversation ceased between Joe and I, my thoughts wandered to my college fiancé who had dumped me because I could not father children. I envied the sixteen year old boy and his pregnant girlfriend. I would never experience the moment they were having. As I fell asleep, my thoughts were bitter sweet. The sweetness was that my love for my former fiancé was finally dulling a bit. It had been five years. The bitterness was that she had permanently damaged my view of myself as a man. She had destroyed my self esteem, calling me a dud. I had decided to never reveal to another woman that I could not father children. It was safer to resign myself to living the rest of my life as a confirmed, non-dating bachelor. I was not putting myself out there again.

CHAPTER FOUR

THE PREGNANT GIRL'S CANDY BAR

The following morning, Kris woke up first. Hearing her feet on the wooden floor, I blinked my eyes open to see who was moving about. I watched as she slowly made her way to the wood cook stove, remove a black round cook top, and drop a small stick of wood down in along with a piece of old newspaper and a match. She then replaced the black iron burner and seated herself at the tiny kitchen table. I supposed she was waiting for the range to heat up. I rose from my position on the floor and stretched my weary bones. Sleeping on a hard floor was not something I was used to. After doing some serious stretching, I made my way to the table and joined her.

"I am afraid we are going to have to settle for a donut and a cup of coffee for breakfast. I didn't bring much food with me." I stated, watching her as she reached over from her seated position and felt the side of the wood range to see if it was heating up. "I didn't expect to have visitors. Also, just so you know, I am Jewish and do not embrace Christmas Eve, which is today. I assume you are Protestant and Christmas Crazy."

"Food will not be a problem Mr. Marsh. Christmas Eve is a time of miracles." She replied ignoring my Christmas Crazy and Protestant comments. "Wise men will knock on our door bearing food as gifts. Perhaps they will not be Jewish or Protestant. There is a parallel universe where all men's Gods dwell. All Earth men are children of the stars, my Jewish friend. My star cluster of beings, that I travel Earth with, just happens to have embraced Protestantism. They are indeed crazy about Christmas."

'Nut Case . . .' I thought, rolling my Jewish eyes in disbelief. There was only one God in the universe and he was Jewish. Kris was definitely embracing old age dementia. Star Children was apparently, a fantasy she embraced to cope, or it was a dementia hallucination. I embraced a life as a hermit in California to cope with my own personal problems. I didn't need fantasy, such as Santa Clause or Star Children, to complicate my miserable hermit existence. What I wanted, I could not have . . . children and a life with Jen. Jen wanted children, more than she wanted me. I had lost the woman I was in love with, as well as my dream of having a big, traditional, Jewish family.

Kristina continued, ignoring my disrespect and drifting thoughts.

"I am a believer in peace between all Star Children and their religious persuasions. Now, go get the three chicken TV dinners that you have stored in your four wheel drive ice box. I will heat up the fried chicken in a skillet, and then make water graving from the greasy, flour coating on the fried poultry pieces. You and I, plus our sleeping guests will savor a hot, Christmas Crazy breakfast. We will save the donuts for tonight. You have to have sweets to eat on Christmas Eve, not to mention providing a treat for Santa

Claus." She replied, eyeing my disheveled, slept in appearance. Then she asked, "Have you ever eaten water gravy? Santa and I used to eat it all the time. Possum fat makes really good gravy."

"You and Santa eat possum fat gravy?" I returned in shock and disgust.

"When hard times hit, carnivorous man will eat anything." She replied. "Santa, my son, and I have eaten a lot of things to survive in this northern environment."

"My sister Maxi is a Jewish vegetarian. She would die before she would eat an unclean animal such as a possum. I share my sister's sentiment concerning a possum. Furthermore, I don't eat gravy whether it is Jewish or Protestant made. I am a steak or a fried chicken and fries man. Furthermore, I don't embrace the belief in your toy toting old fart of a man dressed in red. I see no need to save one of my donuts for him."

"Your limited outlook on things is too bad. Gravy could put a little fat on your skinny, steak eating frame. A donut left for Santa could return as unexpected goodies in your stocking tomorrow morning. The only thing a non-believer in magic will find in his sock on Christmas morning will be his foot." She stated, holding up Mary's bag of lemon drops.

"How did you get those?"

"I traded Mary my pillow for them. Babies can make you feel really uncomfortable when you are lying flat. Pregnant ladies need pillows."

"Don't you think you should throw the lemon drops in on the community food stash? It might be days before we can make it down the mountain and find food?"

"No, I traded for the lemon drops. They are mine. I intend to put them in everyone's socks tonight. If you want your share, you will have to hang your sock."

I gave her a dirty look and returned, "You don't look like St. Nick to me."

"Maybe Santa is wearing a disguise this year. Everyone wears masks and costumes on Halloween. Maybe I am Santa wearing a left over Halloween costume of an old lady." Kris retorted in a firm, feminine, elderly woman's voice.

"I have had my fill of nut cases like you pretending to be Santa. I am Jewish and refuse to be a part of your Christmas Crazy madness. I want nothing to do with St. Nicolas, his snotty nosed elves, or Christmas Crazies like you."

"Too bad!" She stated, pulling a huge iron skillet from beneath the tiny cabinet that was almost too heavy for her to pick up.

I grabbed the bulky black iron skillet from her and placed it on the wood range.

"You do know that my three TV dinners is all the food there is? If you and our guests consume the three, we may go hungry tomorrow."

"Go get the dinners . . . you Jewish man of the stars, and of little faith!" She demanded, shaking her head side to side in seemingly disgust with me.

Somehow, the previous night, I recalled her as being older. This morning she looked ten or so years younger. However, even at that she had to be in her seventies. Rather

55

than argue with her, I did as she asked. I left the cabin and retrieved the three fried chicken TV dinners from my four wheel drive, which was now my refrigerator. The cabin didn't have one. Once back inside, we resumed our conversation.

"Everyone will have to suck on Santa's lemon drops and pretend it is Lemon Pie after the fine meal you are insisting on preparing. Just so you know, since you are hoarding the lemon drops, I will be keeping the donuts for myself." I huffed, as I watched her tear off the cardboard containers from the dinners and then remove the clear film wrappers from the little black trays of food.

"We are not going to go hungry, my donut stashing friend. When the snow stops, I will go out back and trap a raccoon or a possum for Christmas dinner tomorrow. Fried chicken and gravy are a treat to me. I thought about your chicken TV dinners all night. I don't recall the last time I have had fried chicken. I only go to town once a year." She stated with a sigh.

I lifted one eyebrow, while taking a serious look at Kris. Who in the hell went to town only once a year? I shook my head, feeling she had to be lost in some state of on-coming dementia.

"Why haven't you been to town?" I questioned, watching her stoke up the fire in the wood stove in preparation to cook.

"Snicker Doodle and I have stayed away from town folk. They don't cotton much to his daredevil, reckless antics as a pilot. He has a tendency to fly a little low sometimes, doing dipsy-doodle spins and roll overs. Sometimes, he gets a little too close to people for their comfort. They get irate and annoyed with him. I was a little upset myself when he lost me out of his plane. I keep him away from town folk, and insist he only fly northern, less populated, routes."

"I might be annoyed with a man who is careless enough to let his mother fall out of his airplane." I huffed sarcastically. "The least he could have done was to see that you had a seat belt on."

"Personally, I am glad I fell out. Fried chicken and gravy is worth it!" She replied, as she arranged the pre-cooked chicken pieces in the skillet.

"Might I ask what you plan to serve the water gravy on? I didn't bring any bread with me."

"I will make potato cakes from the instant mashed spuds in the three dinners. We will eat the gravy over them." She replied, turning the chicken pieces in the hot skillet. They started to sizzle. "Go scoop snow to melt for our breakfast coffee, Monty."

"Mission accepted." I replied, seeing that she had appointed herself as head chef of my kitchen that run along one side of my single room, cabin hideaway. I had to admire the old gal. She was a feisty little woman. The one thing I didn't like about her was the two piece red sweat suit and gray men's tube socks she had on. Dressed in red, she reminded me of Maxi's red Santa suit that I was running from. In-spite of the fact Kristina was a little Christmas crazy, I liked her. My Jewish mother, who recycled everything, would have liked her repurposing of the three TV dinners into somewhat of a feast. My mother would have also liked the way she saved the three plastic containers the dinners came in. She had placed them in the sink, instead of pitching them in the trash. I could hear my Jewish mother saying, "Waste not – want not . . . !"

"After you return with the snow for coffee, check the upper cabinet to see if there are enough coffee cups and plates for all of us. I am too short to reach the upper cupboard doors. Afterward, set the table. If there are not enough plates, I will wash the three plastic trays the TV dinners came in. We will use them."

I said nothing further. Amused with her, I took the ancient, dented, 1950's, aluminum dishpan and headed outside to scoop up snow. I shivered as I stepped off the cabin's porch to tackle my assignment. The snow was now knee deep and still falling. I could barely see. It also took a lot of effort to trudge thru the knee deep snow to the high-ground side of the cabin to scoop clean snow for coffee. We were definitely stranded in whiteout conditions. My four wheel drive in front of the cabin looked like a small snow covered hill. You couldn't tell that there was a vehicle beneath the white stuff that had drifted around and over it. Also, you could no longer tell where the road was. Mother Nature had dumped what looked like twenty to thirty inches of snow. The landscape, with its snow covered pines and mountains, was incredibly beautiful, a pristine, picture postcard moment.

As I was finishing scooping my pan full of snow, I heard whistling in the distance. It gave me an eerie feeling. I was supposed to be fifty miles from any sort of civilization. I then decided that it possibly had to be the crazy cross eyed guy who had knocked on my door the evening before. Maybe he was still out whistling and looking for his dog. I slowly scanned the landscape looking for him. Turning in a circle, I spotted what looked like a hunter in the distance, who had a white, wolf-like dog with him. The very short and stocky hunter was dressed all in white. Apparently, he was trapping or possibly rabbit hunting in the field beyond the high side of the cabin. I could tell that he was older. He had a heavy salt and pepper beard.

"Over here . . ." I yelled, waving my arms frantically at him. I needed a phone and help to get the Christmas crazies out of my one room cabin. He had to have a phone, as well as a moving vehicle somewhere.

The very obese, short hunter and his albino wolf dog started making their way thru the heavy snow towards me. In spite of his weight, the robust red cheeked hunter walked easily on top of the snow. He was wearing snow shoes. The wolf dog, however, was struggling as it leaped thru the deep snow that was as high as its body. After a minute or so, the white dressed hunter reached me. I set my dishpan of scooped snow down.

"What's up?" The hunter asked, as he held out his white gloved hand to shake. His vicious looking wolf dog sat down in the snow next to him, at his command.

I shook the man's extended hand and immediately entered conversation.

"I got snowed in here last night. Unfortunately, I have three unexpected strangers for guests. They knocked on my door last night seeking shelter. Do you have a cell phone on you by any chance? There is a teen pregnant girl inside whose baby is due tomorrow, Christmas Day. She and her boyfriend were eloping on a snow mobile last night. Their poor choice of a vehicle slid off the road and down into a rock crevice. My other guest is an elderly woman who says she fell out of an air plane yesterday behind my rented cabin. I rescued her, and now fear she has a screw or two loose. I think she might be suffering from some sort of dementia. She speaks of eating possum with Santa. Anyway, I really need to let someone know that the teens and the elderly woman are here. I need to get the three off of this mountain before they may be in need of food or medical attention."

"I am sorry, young fellow! I don't carry a cell phone when I hunt. The ringing scares away game." The hunter replied with his warm breath making clouds in the icy air.

"Are you camped out and possibly heading back into town later today?" I asked, hoping I could send my three unwanted guests with him.

"I am indeed camped out. About three miles north of here, I have a tent pitched. I won't be heading back to town for at least a week. I spend every Christmas Eve, and the week after, camping and hunting." He replied pulling a round, green can of chew from his back pocket. He then opened the little container, took out a pinch of the nasty stuff, and stuck it beneath his upper lip. "Want a chew?" He asked, extending the tiny can to me.

"Thank you, but no thank you! That stuff will rot out your teeth, or give you cancer of the mouth." I shot back not thinking. Insulting him was not going to get me any favors.

"You are probably right on that one. My woman quit kissing me when I started chewing the stuff. However, that is a good thing. She is a cancer I wish I could get rid of. The chew keeps her at bay." The hunter replied laughing.

"You wouldn't have any extra food at your camp that I could buy?" I asked, trying to further control my tongue.

A man who demeaned his woman to a stranger wasn't much of a man in my book.

"Sorry man. I trap and shoot my breakfast, lunch, and dinner. Whatever is left each night in my campfire pot, I feed to my dog. How desperate are you for food?" He asked, chewing and then spitting a black slime into the white snow.

"Breakfast is covered. Kristina, the elderly snow drift woman, is turning three, fried chicken, TV Dinners into what she calls water gravy, and plans to serve it over potato cakes made from the instant potatoes. After that, we are down to donuts and a small bag of lemon drops."

"Man . . . I haven't had a good plate of water, chicken gravy in years. Invite me in to stay for breakfast, and I will return later in the day and share whatever I trap or shoot. It could be a ground hog or maybe a rabbit."

"Man . . . there is barely enough food inside to feed my three unexpected guests, much less me and you." I sputtered, insulted at his fishing for an invitation to breakfast.

"You get out of life what you put into it." The hunter retorted. Then he turned, called for his wolf dog, and walked away. I was sorry I had wasted my time talking to him.

Suddenly, the hunter stopped, turned back around and returned to face me. He then pulled a chocolate bar from his pocket.

"This candy bar is for the pregnant girl only. If I return and find that you have eaten it, I will take aim on your balls. Believe me man, I won't think twice about shooting them off. You will not be fathering any children when I get thru with you. Do you understand me?"

"My identity as a male was shot down years ago. A cancerous woman named Jen beat you to it." I muttered, sticking the chocolate bar in my jacket pocket. "I will see that the pregnant girl gets it."

I then felt so guilty. Not only had I run down Jen in front of a stranger, I had turned down the hunter's request to eat with us. "Damn it!" I muttered.

As he walked away on his snow shoes, I reminded myself that he had a means of hunting and feeding himself. Arguing with my conscience, I convinced myself it was okay to preserve what food was in the cabin to feed those in my care. After all, I wasn't Santa Claus and the hunter was not on my Jewish gift list.

As the short, round hunter walked away in the distance, I yelled after him, "If you run into anyone with a cell phone, send us help?"

The hefty, short, white clad hunter just raised his hand in a gesture and walked away on his snow shoes into the whiteout.

I then picked up the dishpan of snow and headed back to the cabin. I was shivering. The time spent in my encounter with the hunter had left me chilled to the bone.

In my head, I could hear my Jewish mother saying, "A cold act becomes an ice cube in man's soul. Multiple cold acts turns man into a walking refrigerator."

CHAPTER FIVE

THE CHRISTMAS CARD MAN

Back in the cabin, I set the dishpan of snow onto the stove top to melt it into water for coffee making. Kristina was about finished making breakfast on the cast iron, wood range. An unexpected knock sounded at the cabin door. I went to see who it was, leaving the coffee making to Kris. It was unbelievable, in my thinking, that anyone else could possibly be stranded in the now howling blizzard that was playing havoc with my cabin fifty miles from nowhere. However, the knocking was a good thing. Maybe the hunter had sent help. I definitely needed a means of transportation to get Mary, my pregnant teen charge, into town for medical attention. She had started holding her belly as though the baby was moving about too much. I was sure that she could possibly go into labor at any time. That I didn't need. I knew nothing about delivering babies; much less had milk and provisions for one.

Opening the door, I saw a snow dusted mail man, wearing a Klondike hat and heavy winter clothing, standing there. Like any postman during the holidays, he was carrying a handful of what looked like Christmas card envelopes.

"Boy . . . , am I glad to see you!" I stated in a voice of relief. "I have a pregnant girl in here needing to go to the hospital. Do you have a cell phone I can use to call for help, or can she ride with you into the city in your mail vehicle?"

Not waiting for him to answer, I took him by the arm and pulled him inside the cabin. Then, I shut the door to keep out the icy wind and blowing snow.

"I am sorry on both counts, Buddy." The mail man stated, as he stomped his boots sending snow flying from them. He then dusted snow from his jacket sleeves onto the floor. "A kook, riding a flying bob sled like contraption, caused me to lose control of my mail wagon. I slid off into a deep, straight down ditch about a quarter of a mile from here. My cell phone went flying off my dash and out my open door. It hit a bolder and shattered into hundreds of little parts. I was hoping to use yours to call for a tow truck. I guess I will have to get my snow skis out of my wrecked van and ski cross country to make it home for Christmas Eve."

"Will you send us help when you reach town?" I asked. "I am sure the pregnant girl, seated over by the fireplace holding her belly, is going to go into labor at any moment. Tomorrow is her delivery date. Her baby is moving and kicking like crazy."

"You should have known better than to hole up with a pregnant woman in a place like this in the dead of winter and with a whiteout moving in." He retorted harshly. "Are you nuts?"

I bit my tongue. "The pregnant girl is not holed up with me. She and her boyfriend knocked on my door last night seeking shelter, just like you are now."

"I am not seeking shelter, just a phone." He replied walking over to the wood cook stove and sniffing the pan of chicken and water gravy. "My skis will get me into town in plenty of time to hang my sock by my fireplace and wait for St. Nick while lying in my own, Christian, bed bug free bed. I am not taking home any Catholic, Buddhist, or Jewish bed bugs."

"What . . . ?" I questioned in a huff.

"You heard me. How old do you think that mattress is on your cabin's bed, not to mention the sheets? Did you know that motels don't wash the pillows, quilts, and bedspreads every day? They only wash the sheets and pillow cases. When you sit butt naked on a motel or cabin bedspread, you are sitting where some other human has sat butt naked. If they had a bed bug, you will have a bed bug. You are Jewish and I am Protestant. I prefer not to share bed bugs with you. I will ski home to sleep in my own bed. My wife washes everything regularly."

I was insulted. It wasn't my choice to have his Protestant butt in my cabin. However, he had made a good point. I would not sleep in the cabin's bed no matter what. I had never given it a thought, as to what items got washed daily in motels and hotels. I shivered thinking of the numerous hotel and motel rooms I had stayed in over the years. Jen and I had spent a few casual weekends on motel sheets. I shivered thinking who might have sat butt naked on those bedspreads before us.

"Well, just take your Christmas Cards, and bed bug free, Protestant backside, and be on your way." I replied annoyed. "When you reach town, I do hope you will send help for your fellow Protestant bed bug buddies here!"

The mailman didn't reply for a moment. "I would be on my way, in a Protestant heartbeat. However, I have a little problem. I was hoping you might have a cell phone, or a roll of duct tape to loan me."

"What in your bug free world do you need duct tape for?" I retorted, totally annoyed with the man who was causing a puddle of water to form where he was standing. The snow covering him was melting.

"My skis were snapped in my mail truck mishap. I was hoping you might have a roll of duck tape that I could use to mend them temporarily with."

The idea of him mending his Protestant, bug free skis with my Jewish duct tape hit my funny bone and I began to laugh. Maxi was more outspoken than I was. She would tell the Protestant jerk to stick his skis where the sun doesn't shine. I wanted to, but I desperately needed help for the strangers that were in my charge. I bit my Jewish lip and sucked up my pride for the good of all those sheltered in the cabin.

"What did you say caused you to wreck?" I asked, controlling myself.

"A nut on some sort of a flying bob sled contraption ran me off the road. If you don't have any duct tape, I am afraid that I am going to need to stay with you till the white out is over and the snow plows come thru. I can catch a ride to town with one of them. You do have some duck tape, don't you?" He asked, pulling out a Christmas card envelope and handing it to Kris. She broke out into a big smile.

I was so annoyed with him and his bed bug insinuations, that I missed the fact that he and Kris seemed to know each other. If he hadn't known her, he would not have delivered to her a personal piece of mail. Afterward, he placed the other cards and letters in the inside pocket of his jacket, which he then proceeded to take off. What else could go wrong? I definitely did not have a roll of duct tape. My car was a rental, as well as the cabin. I just stood with my mouth open and watched as he walked over to the wood cook stove and held his cold hands over the cook top to warm them. Kris gave him room to do so, sticking her Christmas card envelope down the top of her red sweat-shirt into her high pocket for safe keeping.

"That gravy sure does smell good. I will trade you a hand-ful of other folks' Christmas Cards for a plate."

"There is just enough food for the four of us . . . Kristina." I butted in, making it known in a harsh voice that I felt the obnoxious, Protestant, mail man was intruding.

"You are welcome to eat with us, Mr. Shepherd." Kristina stated in her charming, feminine voice. "He can have my share, Monty."

"What . . . ?" I resounded in shock. "You are giving up your chicken. You just got thru telling me that you haven't had fried chicken in over a year."

"It will taste twice as good the next time I am privileged to have it." She replied sweetly.

"Great," I muttered, knowing I was going to have to share our food supply with a fifth person. There was no way I would let Kris do without her fair share of the fried chick-en. I would give her my share. I was a Jewish man who tried to show respect for the Jewish women in my life. Kris wasn't Jewish, but she currently was part of my life. If she didn't eat, no one ate.

So, in a matter of minutes, my four stranded, Christmas Eve guests (Kris, Mary, Joe, and the mailman named Mr. Shepherd) took their place at the kitchen table. There were only four chairs. I would have to stand at the cabinet to eat. Remembering Moses and how he and my ancestors had eaten manna in the desert, I gave Kris my plate, of chicken, gravy, and potato cake. I pulled a day old donut from the box and had it, with a cup of steaming hot, boiled, black coffee. The smell of the chicken and gravy drove my senses wild. I did my best not to show it. Maybe I was a gravy man!

"A hem . . ." Kristina mumbled loudly to get my attention. I had a mouth full of donut. "This is Christ's birthday! I think it would be appropriate, if we thanked him for having us at his pre-birthday feast."

"I am Jewish." I instantly retorted, annoyed that she would force me to listen to her Protestant ramblings. "If you want to thank God for Moses and manna in this frozen white-out desert, that is different."

Ignoring me, Mary and Joe bowed their heads. The mailman and Kristina followed pursuit. I felt a little guilty, but I kept my eyes open and peered harshly at them in disgust as Kris said her version of a Protestant breakfast prayer.

I liked Kris, even if she wasn't Jewish. She had stood her ground and prayed in spite of me. My sister Maxi always stood her ground and won most battles with me. I secretly liked Maxi's strong will and the fact that she bossed me around. It made up for my not having a wife to answer to. Now, I had found Kristina, and she was standing her ground with me. The old girl pleased me, but I would never tell her so. I was a dud of a man who was lucky to have any woman tell him where to jump and how high.

Three of my stranded guests started to eat. Mary, however, just stared at her plate big eyed and bit her lip. Then she ate her share of the peas from the three TV dinners, leaving the chicken and gravy smothered potato cake.

"What is wrong?" The mailman asked, as he eyed her plate of food. "Do you have morning sickness or something?"

"No . . ." Joe replied, pausing and giving Mr. Shepherd a dirty look. "Mary is a vegetarian."

Taken off guard, I snorted. Here we were, in a life and death starving situation, and one of my uninvited guests was a non meat eater. Taking a donut from the box, I placed the day old pastry on a deli paper napkin, and handed it to her. I then said, "Happy Chanukah."

She looked up smiling and replied, "Merry Christmas to you."

Immediately, Joe offered his peas to Mary. Kristina followed pursuit. The postman had already downed his. It was a Christmas Eve breakfast I would never forget, even though I was Jewish.

"I ate my peas, but you can have this to add to your vegetarian breakfast," The postman stated, pulling a small apple from his pocket and handing it to Mary. "As long as you are Protestant, being a vegetarian is fine with me."

Once again, I was put out with the postman. I felt he was digging at me, because I was Jewish. I eyed the red apple as Mary bit into it. She didn't offer to share it. I blamed that on her being a fourteen year old kid. Much to my annoyance, Kristina took Mary's plate of the chicken and gravy and divided it between Joe and the postman, ignoring the fact that a donut was all I had eaten. The bed bug Protestant was eating my food, with no thought as to who had paid for it and provided it. I bit my Jewish tongue to keep from telling my group of unwanted, stranded house guests to go to Protestant hell.

My one consolation, in my rented, mountain cabin, fifty miles from nowhere, was that there weren't any snotty nosed elves to annoy me. A Mary, Joseph, Shepherd, and Santa loving Kris was all I could handle.

CHAPTER SIX

THE TOILET PAPER MIRACLE

After breakfast, I was about to pick up the aluminum dish pan to go outside and scoop up snow to melt for dishwater. A healthy knock sounded at the door. I just about jumped out of my Jewish skin, not expecting the noise. I was accustomed to people knocking in the city, but fifty miles from nowhere was a little eerie.

"Do you want me to answer it?"Kristina asked, putting down a stack of dirty dishes into the sink that she had just gathered from the table. Joe and the postman had left the table and were seated in front of the fireplace on the hearth talking. Mary had returned to the bed to lie down. Her belly was moving all around.

"It is my cabin, I will answer my door." I replied adamantly and sarcastically. My desired, peaceful, Jewish hermit holiday had turned into a Protestant, Christmas crazy, social event. None of my unwanted guests were Jewish, or seemed to respect the fact that I was.

"Well, open the door before whoever is outside freezes to death." Kristina demanded and then quickly added asking, "Do you have any more toilet paper anywhere? I used the last of the roll in the inside outhouse just before breakfast."

"Great!" I replied, rolling my eyes as another round of knocking sounded at the door. My intestines were unexpectedly rolling. I was sure that I was going to soon be in need of toilet paper.

Walking over to the door, I opened it. A skiff of snow blew in. To my surprise, a woman wearing a church dress, nylons, and hi-heels stood there. She wore no coat, boots, mittens, or other winter wear. I eyed her for a moment. She was very inappropriately dressed for a blizzard. In one bare hand, she carried a black Bible. In the other she carried a tote bag of pamphlets. Her teeth were chattering.

"It can't be," I stated to myself in disbelief. "Not fifty miles from nowhere, on Christmas Eve, and in whiteout conditions."

"Have you heard about the144 thousand who will populate God's new Heaven and Earth?" The door knocking, literature toting, Jehovah woman asked as she shivered and her teeth chattered. She was visibly about to freeze to death. Her fingers and lips were blue.

"No . . . but I am sure you are going to try to force me to listen." I retorted in annoyance. "Don't you door knockers know what a coat and hat are? Don't you usually travel in pairs?"

"My Kingdom friend and I started out together this morning. However, some crazy kid on a snow mobile came flying along and knocked her down. She went back to town to have a sprained foot looked at, and hasn't returned. I am alone spreading the news of the new Heaven and Earth, till she sends someone for me."

"Well, go work elsewhere and spread your news. I am Jewish." I retorted, wanting to rid myself of her. Door knockers were nightmares to deal with. Only suckers let them inside.

"Would you just take one of my pamphlets and read it?" She asked thru chattering teeth.

Suddenly, my stomach loudly rumbled and gave a big gassy roll in my gut. I knew I was toilet stool bound. At the same time, I recalled Kristina's words telling me that there was no toilet paper. The pamphlet suddenly took on a whole new meaning.

"Yes, I will take one." I replied, suddenly smiling. "Come in and warm yourself by my fire. I am sure all of my holiday guests would love one of your Kingdom pamphlets."

"You may have one, after I read you a scripture." The door knocker stated thru chattering teeth. Shivering, she opened her black Bible and quickly read a New Testament verse to me. I bit my lip and told myself it was worth listening to, in order to get a hold of that paper pamphlet for toilet paper.

"The old shall pass away and everything will be made new . . ." she finished reading.

I grabbed the pamphlet from her, forgetting about the open door. In desperation, I made a run for my rented cabin's, inside outhouse. I heard Kris behind me greeting and making the doorknocker welcome, as I closed the bathroom door.

When I returned to the main room of the cabin, after my body function explosion, the door knocker had my four guests gathered around her feet in seated positions, with the exception of Mary who was now seated in the second rocker. The door knocker was reading one of her pamphlets to them. Annoyed, I walked up to the group and said to the door knocker, "Isn't it time for you to move on and knock on the next cabin's door before the blizzard worsens."

"I am a Kingdom missionary. I go where the need is and where I am invited in. I am in and I am staying till all of you sinful heathen in this cabin see the light. I must not leave here, till I have done my best to show you God's righteous path. There is a pregnant girl here who is not married, a perverted teen boy who has forced himself on a fourteen year old, a foul mouthed full of himself postman, an elderly woman who believes in Santa, and you are a heathen who doesn't believe in Christ. Your Jewish ancestors murdered my Christ. You are my mission field. I cannot in good conscience leave, at least not till the Kingdom Hall sends someone to relieve me."

Mary, Joe, the postman, and Kristina, all grinned and pointed to her bag of literature when her attention was turned to me. They all lip synched "Toilet paper."

My stomach gave another roll. I knew that I was going to have to make another run for it. I had already used the pamphlet I had been given.

"Forgive me, Miss Jehovah Missionary! You are absolutely right. All of my house guests are Protestant heathen. You may stay and do your missionary thing to show them the light." I replied forcing an 'ear-to- ear' fake smile. "What is your name anyway?"

"Angelica . . . ," she replied. "My friends call me Angel."

"That figures!" I mumbled. Now, I had a Protestant Joseph and Mary, a Shepherd who watched letters, and now a door knocking angel. "Where are you, Moses and Elijah?" I asked in a mumble, turning my face upward.

My guests spent the rest of their Christmas Eve morning reading the door knocker's literature in order to receive and keep a pamphlet. I read a second pamphlet myself, for good reason. I had the trots and needed toilet paper. I blamed my condition on the prune Danish donut I had eaten for breakfast.

Just before lunch, the harsh reality set in that the blizzard was getting worse. What remained of our food supply was eight, day old donuts and Kris' small bag of lemon drops. Sitting on the hearth warming myself, I suddenly realized that I hadn't asked Angel if she had a cell phone.

"You don't by any chance have a cell phone on you?" I asked, interrupting her Kingdom ramblings. "Mary's baby is due tomorrow. We really need to call for help, in order to get her off this mountain before she goes into labor."

"I have one, but it is in the vehicle I arrived here in this morning. I was afraid the ice cold winds might cause my cell's battery not to function. It went back to town with my sprained ankle friend this morning. However, Jesus didn't have a cell phone on his three year journey of ministry. I am no better than him. It is not necessary to have a cell phone to work in God's Kingdom. Also, just as Mary gave birth to Christ, it is not necessary to have modern medical help to birth a Kingdom child."

"Well, do you have any sort of food stashed in your bag of literature?" I asked, realizing I had one more mouth to feed.

"I have a peppermint candy cane. A heathen Baptist lady handed it to me early this morning when I knocked. I do not celebrate Christmas. I intended to throw it away after leaving her door. I forgot."

"A peppermint candy cane . . . ," I replied in disgust while once more rolling my eyes. "Well, hang on to it. We may need it before this blizzard is over. We can make hot peppermint tea or something from it."

I motioned to Kristina to follow me to the kitchen cabinet. Once there, I whispered, "What are we going to feed all of these people? I need to save the sack of donuts for breakfast tomorrow."

"St. Nicholas, wearing a door knocker's face, has brought us a gift of much needed toilet paper." She replied in a smug voice. "When we are in need of food, it will come knocking."

"Right . . . ," I retorted. I wondered what my Jewish mother, always the perfect hostess, would do in my foodless situation. Then I snorted, my Jewish mother would have gone to each of her neighbors on the block and borrowed a cup of this and that from each, and then made soup. I wasn't so fortunate. In my cabin, fifty miles from nowhere, I had no neighbors to borrow a cup of macaroni, a cup of chicken broth, or a pack of crackers from.

Kris was somewhat different from my mother. She wanted her borrowed cup of macaroni and crackers hand delivered to her door. My Jewish mother always said you had to put legs on your prayers.

CHAPTER SEVEN

WISEMEN ARRIVE BY PLANE

About eleven in the morning, I heard a sputtering loud sound from a much too low flying aircraft above the cabin. I had been sitting at the kitchen table, trying to ignore the door knocker who was still spouting her beliefs and trying to push them down everyone's throat seated by the fireplace. I jumped up from my kitchen chair, realizing that the plane had just missed the top of the cabin. I told myself that it was possibly a search plane looking for all of us. Maybe the pilot had killed his engine on purpose.

"Thank God . . . help has come." I yelled, as I run to the door to watch the small plane land on the snow covered road below. Just as I opened the door, I heard the way too low plane's engine start and stall a couple of times and then reluctantly run again. Instantly, I knew it wasn't help coming for us. Whoever was in the airplane was in trouble. It would be a Jewish miracle if the plane landed safely. In my opinion, the aircraft was about to crash, and I was about to witness a Christmas Eve disaster. I could picture myself pulling dead bodies from a burning plane.

"Grab your coat and boots Joe!" I yelled. "Whoever is flying that craft is in serious trouble!"

I quickly put on my boots, jacket, and stocking hat. Joe did the same and we were out of the cabin in a flash, fighting the blowing snow and icy wind. I could barely see. I admonished Joe to stay close to me. We didn't want to get separated in the whiteout conditions. We could barely see the plane that was gliding just a few feet above the snow on the road below. Joe and I hurried as fast as we could toward the inevitable, crash spot.

As we ran, there was a sudden thrashing, crashing sound. The snow ski plane had set down on the snow covered road, but then suddenly twisted and turned into the mountain's snow covered trees and brush, like it was trying to avoid hitting something. It disappeared off the road into a ravine. Joe and I ran like crazy to where the plane had gone over the side. It wasn't easy in knee deep snow. The plane had come to a crashing halt about fifty feet down in the sloping ravine. It was upright, but both wings had been clipped off by tree branches, and the glass was out of the cockpit.

"Are you al right?" I yelled, hurrying to the aircraft's door and knocking harshly. I could smell fuel spilling out somewhere from the plane.

"Help . . . ," muted voices yelled from the inside.

"We have got to hurry and get them out, Joe. This plane is going to go up in smoke."

About that time, the plane door flew open and the smallest man, I had ever seen, peered out. He couldn't have been more than thirty inches tall. He was dressed in a colorful, purple, silk, circus costume of some sort. "Jump . . .

I will catch you!" I yelled, seeing he was too short to climb out. The plane's stair steps were gone, as was part of the underbelly.

Immediately, the little man jumped, due to someone behind him giving him a rough push. I caught him vicariously, and then stood him down on the snow covered ground. Immediately, the snow swallowed him to his chest. I looked back up toward the plane. Joe was helping out another short little man who looked just like the first, except he was dressed in a gold silk swami pants and turban. His shoes were pointed like the ones Maxi made my yearly elf helper wear, when I played Santa for her.

"Don't forget me!" a voice yelled from the plane.

Too my shock, a third little man, identical to the first two, was preparing to jump. He was wearing burgundy, swami clothes. I immediately smelled the scent of smoke and a fire catching. "Jump . . .," I cried. He immediately did and I caught him.

"Take one and run, Joe. They are too short to escape on their own."

I already had the third burgundy clad little man in my arms. I immediately picked up the first one, who was dressed in purple, by the waist and made a dash to get away from the plane. Seeing a huge pine tree, I ducked behind it with them, as did Joe. Immediately, the plane blew up and pieces of the plane and flames shot about fifty feet in the air.

"That was a close one!" The little purple costumed man stated, freeing himself from my grip.

"You have got that right." The burgundy suited little man

stated, joining him.

"I know we always do things together, brothers. However, this is a little much." The third in gold silk stated.

"Who are you?" I asked in a shocked voice. Joe and I had just rescued three little elf like men in silk turbans, pointed shoes, and silk clothing.

"We are the Wise Brothers." All three chimed in at once.

"That figures . . . three wise men." I mumbled, while rolling my eyes. Now, I had an angel, Mary, Joseph, a shepherd, and three elf size wise men. I was cursed. My quiet Jewish holiday 'fifty miles from nowhere' had turned into a protestant nightmare.

"Are you Trolls?" Joe asked the little men. "We have no bridge for you to troll."

I could tell by the look on Joe's face that he had never seen a dwarf or a little person before. He was relating them to some fairy tale he had read as a kid.

"We are circus performers. Thanks for coming to our rescue." The little man dressed in gold stated, as he straightened his silk turban.

"You landed safely. Why did you veer off the road into the trees?" Joe then asked.

"Some nut on a snow mobile flew out in front of our plane, just as we were skimming the roadway to emergency land. Our engine was stalled. We couldn't pull up the nose and climb. The crazy guy on that snow-mobile ran us off the road. If I eve r get my hands on him, he is dead meat!" Stated the burgundy clad, little man, as he pounded his right fist in the palm of his left hand.

"The plane ride down the embankment into the ravine was as good as any roller coaster ride I have ever taken." The little man, in gold swami circus clothes, stated excitedly while smiling from ear to ear.

"I am cold." The purple clad little fellow stated, rubbing his arms.

"Hurry, Joe. Pick one up and head for the cabin. He will never be able to walk in this snow. I will carry the other two."

Joe immediately picked up one of the little fellows and started climbing up out of the ravine. I picked the other two up like they were three years old; one in each arm. Then, I followed Joe in a laborious climb up out of the ravine and then thru the heavy snow back to the cabin. The cabin could not be seen from where we were. The whiteout had worsened. We followed what was left of our tracks in the snow, the ones we had made running to help the survivors of the crash. Once inside the cabin, the shivering little men huddled up to the fireplace to warm themselves. Everyone, big eyed, scooted out of their way, giving them access to do so, as if they were the bearers of some sort of Christmas magic.

"What are your names?" Kris asked, as she wrapped the three little men in bath towels, which were Afghan size to them.

"My name is Gold," Stated the one dressed in gold silk.

"My name is Frank," Stated the one dressed in red.

"My name is Merve," Stated the one dressed in purple.

"Do any of you have a cell phone on you?" I asked interrupting.

"We all had one. They are back in the plane, and surely barbecued now to a crisp." Frank in red stated.

"Here today . . . gone tomorrow!" Merve in purple echoed.

"All of my lady friend's numbers were stored in my cell phone bank. Irreplaceable . . . ," Gold added in a sad voice, as he wrapped his towel afghan tightly around himself.

There was a shortage of quilts in the cabin.

"Do you see our Christmas Eve miracle, Monty?" Kristina stated excitedly. "We have three Wise Men who have dropped in on us for Christmas Eve. They are Gold, Myrrh, and Frankincense."

"Gold, Frank, and Merve . . . ," I shot back. "However, they can be your Gold, Myrrh, and Frankincense if you wish to see them as such. There are no three wise men in my holy book, The Old Testament. I am Jewish, just in case you care. I would prefer a visit from Moses or Elijah; if I had a choice. Hanukkah is my holiday, not your fairytale Christmas with its Santa and wise men."

"We empathize with you, our hero rescuer!" Gold piped up. "We are American born Hindus. Our parents are naturalized Americans. We do not celebrate Christmas either, although we are not objectionable to joining in with you drinking hot chocolate, eating gingerbread cookies, and licking candy canes for the evening. We have traveled a lot and have learned to adjust in our encounters with many religious persuasions and traditions."

"You are Hindu, yet you lower yourself to embrace Christmas?"

"We embrace anything that feeds us or will turn a dollar. When you are a little man, you don't have many job or life options."

"What do you do in the circus?" I asked, pointing to their pointed toe shoes.

"The circus we travel with is wintering in Georgia. During the off season, we pick up extra work playing Santa's elves, etc. We were on our way to the huge mall up in Canada, when our plane went down. We were going to play elves for Santa. After Christmas, we had a bit part in a Canadian movie being shot about some famous quintuplets. We were going to play three of the five."

Once more, I rolled my eyes. "The famous Canadian quintuplets were girls!" I shot back sarcastically.

"We are not opposed to wearing girl wigs." Merve retorted. "We are actors."

"Well, I hope you eat like a girl. We are short of food around here." I threw out in disgust, knowing that I was now stuck with three more mouths to feed. Where was I going to get food to feed them, not to mention Mary, Joe, Shepherd, Angel, and Kris?

"We may be little, but we have healthy appetites." Gold replied, crossing his arms across his chest.

"Do the three of you, by any chance, have any food tucked away in your turbans and little pointed toe shoes?"

"I have a pack of fruit flavored gum." Gold stated.

"I have a small can of tomato juice." Myrrh stated pulling it from his pocket.

"I have half a cheese sandwich." Frank added.

"Well anti-up. We are sharing food in common till this

blizzard is over. There is no cupboard filled with food here. All the people you see here are stranded."

Reluctantly, Frank handed me his half of a cheese sandwich that was preserved in a little, zip up, plastic sandwich bag. The half of a squashed, cheese sandwich looked like it had been sat on for the last fifty miles. I carried it over to the kitchen and handed it to Kris. Then I smiled from ear to ear. "We have a lot of mouths to feed. What can you make from this Hindu, butt pressed sandwich?"

"I will keep it for Mary."She stated, giving me a flirtatious, elderly grin. I will make her a grilled cheese sandwich from it, when the time is right. Santa eats a lot of cheese at the North Pole. I used to tell my son that when he was little. My Snicker Doodle always loved hearing about Santa eating a grilled cheese sandwich, just before leaving out on his sleigh to deliver toys."

"Well . . . don't get too excited about your fairy tale, cheese eating Santa stopping here tonight. I am Jewish, in case you have forgotten. The doorknocker doesn't believe in celebrating holidays, and the three Wise men brothers are Hindu." I retorted sarcastically. "You, Mary, and Joe are the only believers in your fairy tale Santa."

"There will be more Santa believers arrive here for Christmas Eve, including my Snicker Doodle. He is probably searching for me, as we speak. He may be a grown man and a pilot, but he definitely is a believer in Santa Claus."

"Your pilot son is probably in Canada by now, and not looking back. He is probably glad to be rid of you." I retorted. "He is probably tired of being a mama's boy. Not only that, only an idiot would let his mother fall out of an airplane and not send help to rescue her. You are hallucinating, Kris. People falling out of planes are flattened like a swatted bug on impact. There is no way you could have fallen out of a plane yesterday. You don't have a scratch or a bruise on you."

"Thank God for snow drifts!" She replied simply. "Snicker Doodle didn't mean to lose me."

"I didn't mean to find you!" I shot back.

CHAPTER EIGHT

POSSUM FAT AND DUMPLINGS

I t was approaching noon on Christmas Eve. My stomach was growling. The prune flavored donut hadn't filled me up. I was about to suggest to Kristina that we all eat half of a donut and wash it down with a cup of hot coffee, when another knock sounded at the door.

"What is this . . . Grand Central Station of the North?" I muttered, rising from my chair at the table and going to see who else could possibly be out in such miserable weather.

Once more, Kris followed me to the door. She had settled in and was acting like my rented cabin was hers and she was greeting holiday guests. That really annoyed me. When I was a kid, Maxi always beat me to the door when a knock sounded. Stepping past Kris, I opened the door slightly to keep the icy wind and blowing snow out.

"Are you Jewish, Hindu, Christian, Kingdom door knocker, or a follower of some other Great Spirit?" I sarcastically asked the stranger at my door, who had a runny nose and a gun slung over his shoulder. "Who are you and what do you want?"

"My name is Johnny Appleseed." He replied, as he inhaled a deep breath of the icy Christmas Eve air. In doing so, he sucked dripping snot back in his head.

I wanted to gag, but I cleared my throat and let it go. It was apparent that the cold air was making his nose drip. Anyway, I hoped that was the problem. Every Christmas Eve, when I played Santa for Maxi's toy store customers, I caught all kinds of nasty ailments from their little runny noses.

"Well . . . Johnny, cut to the chase. What do you want?" I asked with Kris peeping around me.

"I was doing some trapping across the road, and saw that you have a really large crowd gathered in for Christmas Eve. Could you use this fat possum I shot at day break? I have too much game to carry back out when my hunt is done. This fat old possum is excess baggage for me."

"A fat possum . . . ," Kristina squealed, pushing past me. "Would you like to stay and eat him with us? It won't take me but an hour to clean him, throw him in a boiling pot, and add dumplings."

"Well, that is nice of you. However, I have a rabbit roasting on a spit back at my campsite." He stated, handing her the possum by the tail. At the same time, he sucked more running snot back up his snout.

I wanted to barf. Between the visibly bloody, dead possum and the snot, my weak Jewish stomach was turning. Then again, I told myself, it might be another round of the trots coming on from the prune flavored donut I had eaten for breakfast. My gut was churning.

"If I didn't have so many guests here to cook for, I would

make you an apple pie, if I had apples. Then I would join you at your campsite to share your rabbit feast." Kris stated, holding up the possum by the tail and taking a good look at him. "This fat, little fellow is going to render down and make some great fat. I need fat to fry with. I am out of lard. Thank you Johnny! This is a much needed Christmas gift."

"Merry Christmas," The tall hunter stated, as he bent down and kissed Kris on the cheek. "I would lay a good one on you, but I don't see any mistletoe hanging above your door. Do you want me to find some and bring it to you? Christmas Eve just isn't Christmas Eve, without mistletoe."

I was a little more than annoyed that the hunter, with a disgusting, drippy nose, had taken the liberty to kiss Kris on the cheek. She was elderly. Did he want to pass on his possible head cold to her? I wouldn't dare kiss Maxi or my Jewish mother if I had a runny nose. I respected them and their health too much. Johnny Appleseed was totally disrespectful of Kris in my book.

"Find me some mistletoe, Johnny, and I will save my Christmas Eve kiss just for you." Kris replied smiling, turning the dead possum around and looking it over.

I could have sworn that dead possum opened one eye, stared, and then winked at me.

"Kiss her beneath the mistletoe over my dead body . . ." I muttered, as he ignored me and discussed possum rendering with her. I didn't know why, but I was suddenly a little territorial when it came to Kris. What was that all about? I hadn't let any woman, other than Maxi and my mother, into my life since Jen. I was suddenly seeing Kris as belonging to me.

Interrupting their conversation, I asked the runny nosed hunter, "Would you let me use your cell phone? We have a pregnant girl inside who is about to pop. Her due date is tomorrow. We really need to let someone know she is here, and get her into the city in case she needs medic al care."

"Is she in labor?" The hunter named Johnny asked, as he wiped his running nose on the back of his glove.

"Well, not yet. She could be at any time!" I replied.

"I don't have a cell phone. They are useless here in these mountains. Your cabin is in a pocket. You couldn't get reception to use one, even if you had one." He replied, as Kris headed for the cabin's kitchenette with the disgusting possum.

My stomach was rolling. There were some things edible in my book, opossum was not one of them. I lived by Jewish traditions. You didn't eat unclean animals. They didn't come any un-cleaner, in my book, than a possum that would eat any rotten thing, including other animal's excrements. I wanted to puke. I tried to control my views that wanted to come spilling out of my mouth. I needed the hunter to send back help for us.

"When you hike out in the morning, will you contact authorities and send us help?" I further asked, trying to control my gag reflex as he once more sucked snot back in.

"I will, if anyone can see me." He stated grinning, once more wiping his nose's runny green liquid on his glove.

"What do you mean, if anyone can see you?" I asked in annoyance at his answer.

Ignoring me, he returned his attention to Kris who had returned to the door after placing the possum in the kitchen sink.

"I have a Christmas gift for you Miss Kris."

"Really . . . ?" She asked with sudden excitement in her eyes, while completely ignoring me. She stepped in front of me, pushing me out of the encounter.

My fiancé Jen had dumped me. Now Kristina was dumping me as her host. He had a gift for her. I did not. Jen's new husband had given her children. I had not been able to give her children. Jen had traded me in for someone with sperm. Now Kris had traded me in for a dead possum and a snotty nosed hunter named Johnny. All my old hurts, concerning Jen dumping me, had just resurfaced. I ached inside, just like Jen was dumping me all over again. It had been a long time since I had let any woman in my world. Now the woman, who had fallen into my life out of an airplane, was also sticking it to me. Annoyed as I was, I could see the excited anticipation in Kris's eyes as she eagerly waited for the hunter to present her with a gift.

"Make sure you plant this gift in the spring." Johnny instructed, as he removed one glove and then reached his hand in his coat pocket to pull out something. He then held out a closed hand to drop something in Kris'. "My gift is an ever-bearing one that you will remember me by for years."

Kris's eyes twinkled as she held her hand beneath his extended one. Then, he opened his closed hand and let five small brown seeds fall into hers. "Apple pie is a must for Christmas. Plant and nurture these seeds. You will have Christmas apples for many, many years. I give to you, what you do not have."

"I am sure this will be the most treasured Christmas gift I will receive this year." Kristina stated, reaching up with her free hand and patting the hunter's cheek that had dried snot on it, from the continuous wiping of his nose. "Thank You, Johnny!"

"Oh . . . one other thing . . . ." He replied, sticking his hand inside of his jacket. Could you use these to go with the possum?"

My eyes got big. Johnny Appleseed, the snotty nosed hunter, handed Kris what looked like a cup or so of dried apples and raisins. The two fruits were probably his version of trail mix. My mouth was watering.

"I will soak the apples and then bake them into a pie for Christmas Day. One piece I will cut and leave for Santa tonight. I am sure he will be quite pleased. He gets served too many cookies on Christmas Eve." Kris stated in a charming voice and appreciative words that I wished were for me.

Guilt swept over me, knowing that the hunter was providing my household, or cabin full of strangers, meat and fruits. Looking at Kris' gleaming eyes, I could see that I had let the snotty nosed man become the man of the hour. It was time to suck my pride up and reclaim my position as head of my house, and perhaps the twinkle in her eye.

"I am sorry I have been so rude to you, man." I quickly stated. "You are welcome to eat lunch with us, especially since you are providing it."

"A power, greater than I, provides. I am just a deliverer of what he has entrusted me with. I have apple seeds. You have a cabin. Give what is given you. What you have must flow out, in order for new good to flow in. We are all children of the stars. We are all bearers of gifts, like Santa. We all come from the same divine source. Your Jewish God is my God of the Orchards." He replied winking at me. "You go to Temple to pray. I sit beneath an apple tree and pray. Kris prays when she falls out of airplanes. We are all one and the same. It is the praying and belief in our source, the creator of all star children, that is important. Merry Christmas Keeper of this cabin, your Christmas gift to strangers.

"Another Christmas Crazy nut," I muttered as he turned, wiped his runny nose once more on the back of his glove, walked down the cabin's porch steps into the blinding whiteout, and disappeared from sight.

"Help me get the possum skinned and cleaned." Kris requested, as I closed door. "Take the dish pan and go scoop snow. We will need water to clean the possum. I plan to make a huge pot of possum and dumplings for lunch. The apples, I will save for Christmas pie. The raisins, I will save for Mary."

"Me . . . help you skin and clean a possum? Why ask me?" I huffed, as I stepped to the kitchen sink and looked at the bloody, dead possum. Once more, I wanted to barf. There was no way I was going to eat her possum and dumplings. Possums were scavengers. They would eat anything, right down to a dog's poop. My stomach was doing some serious churning. I was definitely about to puke. The thought of Kris saving the fat off of the possum to fry things in, equally repelled me. "Ask one of the others to help you clean and butcher that disgusting animal."

"If you were an invited dinner guest to my home, would you want me, as your hostess, to insist you clean the turkey or goose for the meal?"

"Well ... err ... uh ... no!" I retorted in annoyance. She was just like Maxi. She liked to put me in my place and point out my social flaws.

"Well, don't be a rude host. We are all your guests and this is your home. As guests of yours, we should not be asked to butcher, clean, cook, or do dishes." Kris stated with her hands on her hips. "I am your guest, just as the others are. You are lucky that I am willing to help you in your kitchen."

"Have you ever heard of uninvited guests?" I retorted in annoyance. I then raised one eyebrow and gave her a dirty look. Grabbing the aluminum dishpan off the kitchen cabinet, I headed out to scoop snow, as she had asked me to do. I was only in my twenties, but I wondered if my and Kris' relationship was what it would be like to be married. She was telling me what was what, where to go, and how high to jump.

Although she was an elderly woman, Kristina was everything I had always dreamed a woman could be. She was witty, could cook, and didn't care to stand her ground with me. Her only flaws were that she was not Jewish and she was at least fifty or more years older than me. In retrospect, I told myself that an older woman wouldn't expect to have children by me. I now judged my position in life's grand scheme by the fact that I was a dud, not a man. I was sure that no woman, in her child bearing years, would ever want me. Jen had done a number on my psyche.

"How many dishpans of snow do you want?" I asked, as

I carried in the first one and presented it to her. In spite of the fact I had no intention of eating any of the possum, I would carry in as many pans of snow as she needed. I suddenly wanted her to respect me. At the same time, I could hear my Rabbi speaking and saying, "Touch not the unclean beast!"

CHAPTER NINE

THE WOLF PUP

For a late lunch, Milky Way did indeed serve possum and dumplings. Miraculously, Kris had found flour, salt, and sugar in the upper cabinets of the cabin. The staples were stored in some out dated, three pound, metal, coffee cans. She had also discovered a fourth can, filled with a few basic spices. She was so thrilled. I was not so thrilled, and wondered how old the spices and staples were. The metal coffee cans were ancient. Plastic coffee containers had been used by manufacturers for years. I guessed the metal cans to be at least twenty or thirty years old. I feared I would die, if I consumed the outdated items. Kris didn't seem worried at all.

When the possum and dumplings were done, my uninvited guests all eagerly took their places at the table, all except Mary. Kris served her the dwarf man's half of a cheese sandwich, Johnny's raisins, and a cup of my hot coffee by the fire. Mary's belly was moving everywhere. She was trying to sit still and not cause herself to go into labor. I felt she understood the seriousness of her stranded position in the cabin, with no medical help to call.

The butt pressed half of a cheese sandwich had been contributed by one of the Wise brothers. I had to admit that God had provided a meal for Protestant, vegetarian Mary. My Jewish God had not come thru for me yet. I was still stuck with day old donuts and coffee. Down deep, I resented my house full of strangers who had eaten my chicken TV dinners, with no respect for me the hungry man; me, who had paid for them.

As everyone sat down to eat lunch, I stood at the kitchen counter and pretended once more not to be hungry. I could tell from Kristina's facial expression that my act annoyed her. In defiance of her glare, I opened the day old donut box and took out for myself a caramel covered cake donut. I was Jewish. I did not eat unclean food. In my thinking, the possum was such. Then, I watched as everyone ate slowly. They all realized that the possum and dumplings was all the food there was in the cabin. Also, they knew how serious the snowstorm was outside. There was every possibility that we might all be in the cabin for days without food.

~   ~   ~

Mid-afternoon, the door knocker's pamphlets had run out. It seemed that everyone but Mary now had the trots. I verbally blamed their problems on eating the fat of the possum. Kris took my words as an insult against her cooking and had ceased speaking to me. The door knocker, without pamphlets, was just one of a crowd of hungry, bowel sick, Christmas Eve strangers.

Mary was the only one that had not taken the trots. Vegetarian, she had not consumed the possum and dumplings. I was sure that my Jewish God, who demanded that

I eat only clean animals, was pleased with her and me. My morning round of the trots had ceased. I also decided that my Jewish God was telling me not to eat deli made, prune flavored donuts. Perhaps, the grease the donuts were deep fried in was not clean. My Jewish traditions and my desire to be a private detective were all I had to make my life worthwhile. Jen had destroyed the other side of me, the man who wanted a home, wife, and children.

~   ~   ~

It was my rented cabin and I gave Mary permanent seating rights in one of the two rockers in front of the fireplace, due to her pregnancy. Everyone else took rotating turns sitting in the other rocker. Between turns in the chair, the only seating was at the kitchen table or on the floor in front of the fire place. The wise brothers had replaced the door knocker as the center of entertainment. They kept everyone amused with stories of their adventures as circus performers. Joe and Mary, being so young, seemed to be those most interested in the three little men's stories and antics. One of the Wise brothers could do back flips, the second could stand on his head, and the third could juggle coffee cups. Kris kept her distance from me for the afternoon. Mr. Shepherd, the bed bug phobia guest, took a nap on the floor, covered with his coat, as far away from the cabin's one bed as he could get. The door knocker read her black Bible in silence. I was sure that she saw the three Wise brothers as little devils.

Everyone fell into somewhat of a routine for the afternoon. Between short cat naps, Mr. Shepherd seemed to be content keeping the fire going. After an initial trip accompanying me to the barn for dry firewood, he took over that chore. Joe was young and used to having a father tell him what to do. Whatever I told or asked him to do, he obliged. Mary, being just fourteen, also did as she was told. Charming Kris was all about making everyone feel comfortable, and controlling the kitchen. She had her turf, and I currently was not welcome on it, even though it was my rented cabin kitchen. I guess I was the cabin's self appointed butler. I answered the door.

My main concern for the afternoon on the Protestant's Christmas Eve was finding a way to get everyone safely out of my rented, holiday hide-away and my life. My few days of tranquility fifty miles from nowhere, to ditz Christmas and my Santa gig at Maxi's Toy Store wasn't going as I had planned. I couldn't believe how many people had knocked on my isolated 'fifty miles from nowhere' door. It was also inconceivable that none of them had a cell phone. It was as though I was cut off from the outside world and had taken up existence in some sort of strange time warp.

Sitting at the kitchen table listening to Mr. Shepherd snore, I thought about the kook with the runny nose who had knocked bearing a gift of a dead possum. To me, he was the eeriest and the strangest of all. I was still trying to figure out what he meant when he said, "I will, if anyone can see me." From my extensive obsession, reading detective novels, I knew that kooks sometimes turned out to be perverted, demented, murderous villains. In my opinion, possum man was definitely a mental case. For one thing, he believed he was invisible and no one could see him. Second, he believed he was the mythical pioneer day character, Johnny Appleseed. I was glad he had not asked for shelter. I didn't need a Christmas Crazy who might knock off my guests one by one. Mr. Shepherd with his bed bug phobia was all I wanted to deal with.

As I finished off the last sip of a leftover cup of cold black coffee, a slight scratching sound at the cabin's door pierced the air.

"What is that?" Kristina asked, while motioning for everyone to hush their talking.

"It sounds like a dog wanting in!" Mary piped up. "My dog back home scratches the door to get in."

"I will check it out," I stated, stopping Joe from stepping past me and going to the door to open it. "It could be a wolf or a bear that is attracted to the smell of the possum, donuts, and apples."

"Get a life . . . Monty!" Kris stated pushing past me. She then hurried to the door and opened it wide.

To everyone's surprise, a full grown, white wolf like dog sat in the snow on the porch with one small, frisky, white pup between her legs. The mother dog barked. Immediately, the small white pup waddled into the cabin and immediately headed for the fire where it sat down and eyed the dancing flames. Joe seemed thrilled and stooped down to pet it.

"Come in . . . ," Kris greeted the mother wolf dog.

The big dog just gave a friendly bark, rose from its seated position, licked Kris' hand, and then lumbered off the porch and disappeared into the white out.

"What was that all about?" I asked, while eyeing the white wolf pup that was now being petted by Joe and Mary. I was not in the mood to add housebreaking a peeing and pooping pup to my list of cabin duties.

"Mamas always know what is best for their babies. I have

always known what was best for Snicker Doodle. The mother wolf probably needs to hunt. She feels her pup will be safe and warm with us. In my opinion, she has probably been a sled dog somewhere, sometime. She may be lost, or her owner has died and left her to fend for herself."

"I am not a dog lover." I huffed. "It is abominable to take the price of a dog into the temple. Dogs are unclean, and rate right up there with pigs and possums in my book. The pup has to go. I am not cleaning up after him."

"All creatures, great and small, were created by God. That includes Jewish jerks like you, dogs, wolves, pigs, and possums." Kris retorted. "I am sure that my Snicker Doodle will love finding that wolf pup in his sock tomorrow morning. On the other hand, no one is going to be thrilled about finding you in their stocking."

Her comment hurt for reasons she would never know. It was true no woman would ever want me in her stockings, as Kris put it. I was a dud as a man.

"This is my rented cabin," I huffed. "There will be no Christmas stockings hung in it. You are all lucky that I have given you shelter. Putting up with all of you is not how I planned to spend my time."

"Tell them like it is!" Piped up the door knocker. "Like you, I do not celebrate Christmas. Participating in decorating this cabin with stockings could get me thrown out of my Kingdom hall?"

Mr. Shepherd, the postman cut her off, "My Mrs. says it is okay to read and consider, but not agree with what you have read or the circumstances you find yourself in. This Christmas Eve gathering is one of those tolerance times for me. I am tolerating you, Miss Doorknocker, and your need to push your views down everyone's throats. Shouldn't you show a little tolerance for the idiots in here who believe in Santa. Personally, I am Catholic and believe in St. Nicholas. He actually existed. It is just the Protestant's Santa Clause that is a fairy tale. If I want to hang a sock in St. Nicholas' honor, it is my business. When I pray to St. Nicholas each December, my rewards are golden."

"Your Catholic St. Nicholas will bless me with gold, if I hang my sock in his honor?" Hindu Gold piped up questioning with a big smile.

"Yep . . . that is what a saint is for. We pray to them and leave them gifts. In return, they give back. Tonight, I will hang my sock in his honor, and I will tolerate the idiots who hang theirs in honor of their Christmas Santa. Furthermore, if my sock offends you Mr. Marsh, that is your problem. I haven't seen you trying to convert any of us to Judaism. Aren't the like of us good enough for you and your religion?"

It was at that point that I realized that a religious war was about to break out. It was time to suck it up and make peace. Spending multiple days with stranded strangers, who were at odds with you, would not be a good thing.

"Peace to you, Mr. Shepherd." I stated, while wanting to take him by the seat of his mail man's pants and toss him out the door of my cabin into the whiteout. "May the lion lay down with the Lamb . . . !"

"I am not lying down with any lion, if he has bed bugs in his cabin." Mr. Shepherd replied. "Thank God that Christ wasn't born in an infested rat trap like this."

I rolled my eyes. My house full of uninvited Christmas Eve guests were all crazy, demented in their own ways.

"The Messiah hasn't even come yet!" I stated harshly, throwing my own Jewish beliefs into the Christmas Eve melting pot. "Peace won't come to Earth, or this cabin of religious fruitcakes, till he arrives. Your Christ was a great teacher, but not the Messiah to us. Peace will come when my Jewish Messiah arrives on the scene."

Then Mary jumped in speaking with a charming, young feminine voice. "The lion is man and the lamb is the animal kingdom. When man quits killing and eating the animal kingdom, then there will be peace."

Then Kris waded in. "Man is a snarling animal. We need to cut each other a little slack, and not devour each other with words. If we want peace on Earth in this cabin for this holiday season, which we will all be sharing, I suggest we quit gnawing on each other. Some people like chocolate cake, others like white or yellow. Cake is cake. Men's relationships with the creator are all cake, just different flavors."

"I have a right to state my beliefs." I sputtered at Kris in annoyance. "My cake is unleavened bread."

"Apologize, Monty, for your share of the gnawing." She demanded, putting her hands on her hips and giving me a serious don't mess with me look. She reminded me of my Jewish mother who took her wooden spoon to me, if I did or said something she felt was inappropriate. I eyed the big metal cooking spoon that Kris had been washing and drying. One look at it, and I was a child once more in my mother's kitchen. I knew that spoon would leave one heck of a whelp. I cringed, even though I was in my twenties. I was in some sort of déjà vu and my mother was about to let me have it again.

"Shalom!" I yelled to all in my cabin. Then, I headed for the door to put on my coat, hat, and gloves. I needed to put a little distance between Kris and I. She had just made me cower to her. As I opened the cabin's door to exit and get a breath of fresh air, I wondered if my little run in with Kris was what married life was like. I secretly wanted a woman in my life, even if she did tell me when and where to jump, and how high. I was so lonely. At the same time, I knew no woman would ever want me. I was a dud, as my ex-fiancé Jen had cruelly pointed out to me.

As I stood in the heavy drifted snow on the cabin's tiny little porch, I thought about my job back in California. I worked as a burger flipper next door to Zeek's Feet Detective Agency. The guy who owned the agency had it going on. Every detective he had on his staff was a gorgeous woman. They showed up for work wearing four inch, open toe spikes and dressed to kill. I was sure that Zeke was not a dud. His female snoops adored him. I think they had knockdown, drag out, cat fights to see which one could snag him and a night in his bed. I listened in on the female detectives' conversation when they were in the burger joint grabbing a quick meal on the go. I had filled out several applications trying to get on as a male detective with Zeek's agency. Working with his gorgeous girls had to be a good substitute for not being able to have one. I was afraid to open up to another woman and tell her that I could not father children. Jen had put me in my place.

As I was standing there on the cabin's porch, I thought I saw movement of color in the blinding whiteout that was fiercely blowing sheets of snow. As I stared into the blinding snowstorm, a familiar crossed eyed guy walked out of the white and then up my cabin's steps. He definitely was not lost in the whiteout.

"Did my dog and mama make their way here?" He asked, while dusting heavy, clinging snow off of his clothing. It was the cross-eyed guy I had encountered earlier who had been whistling and looking for his dog in the neighboring field.

"No . . . I haven't seen your mama or your dog." I replied. "Why are you still out in this weather? Shouldn't you go home and wait for her and your dog there? She has probably already returned there, and so has your dog."

"My home is wherever mama is." The cross eyed guy replied. "I will not be home till I am in her arms again. I must find her. Santa won't come tonight till she reads me the story about Santa and the night before Christmas. I have got to find her. Christmas won't come until I do."

"Well, what does your mother look like, just in case she does come knocking at my door?" I replied, wanting to get rid of the guy. I already had too many unwelcome stranded strangers as guests to invite him in and add him to the Christmas crazy bunch. I figured he would leave after giving me a description of his mother."

"Everyone knows what Mama Claus looks like." He replied looking seriously at me with his crossed eyes. "She is Mrs. Santa Claus!"

"Great . . . ," I muttered to myself, ". . . one more Protestant Christmas nut case to annoy me."

At that point, the odd guy seemed to be distracted by a wolf howling in the distance. He turned and left me, just as quickly as he had appeared out of the whiteout storm.

"Enough is enough!" I yelled, looking up into the whiteout sky. I shook my fist at my Jewish God who had to be somewhere up there ignoring me. Then I asked, "Why have you cursed me with these Christmas lunatics? They are driving me crazy in my Jewish, rented, 'fifty miles from nowhere' cabin?"

About that time, Joe opened the cabin door and stepped outside to join me for a breath of fresh air.

"There are too many women in there. I need a little air." He stated, pulling his jacket around himself, to protect himself from the icy wind.

"You have got that right." I stated, amused with him. "I am heading out back to get more firewood. Do you want to come along?"

"Lead the way." Joe stated. "Anything is better than listening to Mary groan, that door knocker preach, Mr. Shepherd snore, and your Kris sing the same Christmas song over and over."

"She isn't my Kris." I repeated, annoyed.

"Well, you couldn't prove it by me." Joe shot back. "She has had you jumping thru hoops all morning. I figured the two of you were one of those May-December romances. Usually, it is the man that is older. I don't see why it can't be the other way around."

"Don't get too excited about your theory. I am Jewish and I would not dare think about dating a Protestant Christmas Crazy woman, much less one that is old enough to be my grandmother." I huffed.

"Sorry man. I didn't mean to crawl under your skin. Kris isn't as old as you think she is. Life has weathered her."

"Life in this cabin is definitely weathering my patience." I muttered, stepping from the porch. "My hair will probably turn gray, before I get you all out of my cabin and my life."

Earlier, I had tied a rope between the cabin and the small barn like shed out back. It was a safety line, enabling me to traverse the whiteout conditions to our wood supply.

"Hold on to the rope." I demanded, speaking to Joe.

The barn behind the cabin could not be seen due to the whiteout conditions. Joe took hold of the rope behind me and followed me.

When we were midway, between the house and the shed, a snow mobile sped out of the snowstorm and hit the rope just behind Joe, breaking it. Joe was knocked down and our rope safety line was whipping in the air. I quickly grabbed it and secured it to my belt as I helped Joe up. The end connected to the cabin was gone. My rented, mountain cabin could not be seen by us. We had to proceed to the wood shed. Joe and I were on our own. There was no going back, without a safety line.

"What are we going to do now?" Joe asked with a hint of fear in his voice. "I cannot see a thing!"

"Hold to what remains of the rope. We will follow it to the shed and take shelter there till we decide what to do. If we have to, we can stay there till the whiteout, snowstorm stops." I replied. "We have to consider our safety first."

"What about Mary and those in the cabin? They won't have enough firewood to make it thru the night." Joe yelled at me over the howling wind.

"We will look for another rope in the barn that we can tie to the end of this one. If we walk in a circle, holding to the end of the two tied ropes, we will eventually bump into the cabin. Then we can reattach our safety line. For now, we have to go on to the shed."

Holding on to the rope, we made our way to the barn. Once there, we fought the fierce howling wind to get the gray, wooden plank door open. Once we were inside, we let out a sigh of relief. I brushed the snow off myself, as did Joe. I looked up in a panic when Joe spoke to someone.

"Who is he?" Joe asked in a startled voice, while pointing slightly upward and to one side.

I quickly looked in the direction he was pointing. Seated on a rickety stall gate was the cross eyed guy who was looking for his mother.

"Who are you?" Joe asked him.

"I am an airplane pilot. This is my hanger." The cross-eyed fellow replied, while fiddling with a pair of ancient, aviator goggles that were hanging on a strap around his neck.

"Oh crap . . . ," I muttered, thinking I was going to have one more mouth to feed, as well as a fruitcake to put up with. "Where is your airplane?" I asked in total annoyance.

"Which one?" He shot back.

I eyed him as he stood up and then jumped down from his seated position on the stall's gate. He was half a head taller than me and Joe, and skinny as a rail. His combat boots were old and full of holes; as were his Jeans and jacket. His aviator cap, with pull down ear muffs, looked like a rat had slept in it for thirty years. I was sure that he was wearing the only clothing he had, and had worn it for years.

"You cannot take up residence in this barn? I have this place rented for the holidays. You are trespassing." I stated feeling a little threatened by the odd man who was taller than me, possibly a pervert, and maybe an escapee from some mental institution, or family who was keeping him hidden in the North Woods. I wondered if he were dangerous. I did have women in the cabin to protect.

"This is my barn. I live here." He stated pointing to a door in the small shed like barn's floor."My planes are down there."

Joe looked at me and whispered. "Don't antagonize him. A sociopath escaped from the nut house up north, about a week ago. Law enforcement has not caught him. The TV news said he was a tall, skinny killer who had slashed the throats of two orderlies in the nut house before escaping. He was in the facility for six rapes, five murders, and the butchering of a family on the Canadian line. When Mary and I left out to elope last night, he had not been caught yet."

"It can't be this guy. He has the mind of an eight year old. He knocked on the door earlier looking for his mama." I retorted, as I studied the odd cross-eyed fellow from head to toe.

"If he can show us his airplanes, I will let my guard down." Joe retorted in a low voice, while continuing to eye the cross eyed man in alarm. "I have Mary and the baby to think about."

"We would like to see your planes." I replied, keeping my distance from the cross eyed man. Joe now had me spooked. Even if I was a dud as a man, I still wanted to live to see another day.

"One is parked behind the barn at the end of the landing strip." The odd cross eyed man replied.

Then I knew he had a screw loose. All that was behind the barn was a fence, snow drifts, and a snow laden pine tree forest. There wasn't room for a landing strip or an airplane. "Show me!" I demanded in disgust, knowing that I had one more Christmas crazy to look after.

The tall, skinny man put on his aviator goggles and buttoned its strap beneath his chin, securing his aviator cap flaps. He then walked to the rear of the small barn. There, he pushed open a rear plank door. Joe and I followed him. To our surprise, parked beneath a snow laden Pine tree was a cherry red snowmobile. On the sides of it, two portable, round ended, ironing boards were attached like airplane wings. To an eight year old, lost in his imagination and play, it would be the real thing, an airplane.

"That is your airplane?" I asked in shock.

"Isn't she a beauty? My mama built her for me." The cross eyed guy with a runny nose replied. He then wiped snot on the sleeve of his coveralls. He and the hunter had the runny nose thing in common.

Joe and I stepped outside of the back door of the shed to look over the snowmobile airplane. Joe seemed to be really intrigued. He was just a kid him-self. I had built a car from a cardboard box when I was a kid. My dad had put on four pot lids for wheels. The cross eyed guy was lucky. He was still living in those magical moments of childhood.

"Does it get fuel mileage?" I asked, trying to think of something to say, as Joe circled the vehicle admiring it.

Joe didn't give the cross-eyed guy a chance to answer. He

suddenly turned to me with an angry look on his face.

"What is the matter?" I asked.

"He has to be the damn guy who caused Mary and me to wreck our snowmobile. I am going to kill him." Joe stated, while balling up his fists.

I grabbed Joe by the shoulder and held him back. "He is a kid of eight in his thinking, Joe. He probably didn't know what he was doing. Mary is okay. His snowmobile plane may be our way, our only way of getting Mary out of here. Cool it." I whispered harshly.

Reluctantly, Joe backed off.

"I would sure love to have a ride in your plane." I then stated.

"You will have to wait till mama goes to town and fills my gas can again. I just ran out of gas." He replied all smiles. I am the pilot. She is maintenance."

I could tell from the twinkle in his eye, that he was pleased with the attention we were giving him. His family had probably kept him in the northern mountains and away from people on purpose. Perhaps, they were ashamed of him.

"Have you been a good boy all year? Santa comes tonight." I stated, stepping back from my Jewish self. I stepped into my Maxi toy store, Santa personality, like putting on a familiar pair of shoes. It was imperative that I refrain from being the Jewish pain in the butt that I knew that I had been all day. It was time to let the lion lay down with the lamb, for the overgrown kid's sake.

"I have been very good. Mama says I am the best boy

ever. She will help me hang my sock tonight, and get it just right for Santa. My papa will come home tonight for a visit. He will fill my sock with goodies, and maybe leave me new wings for my air plane. Last year I got two new wings that were unpainted. Mama bought a can of red paint and painted them to match the body of my plane. Papa never paints my wings before he leaves. He is too busy. "

"Where is your mother?" I asked, remembering he was looking for her and his dog earlier in the day.

"I lost her, and have been looking all day for her."

"What does your mother look like?" I asked, realizing the guy could be miles away from his home and in play fantasizing that the shed was an airport-hanger.

"She looks like Mrs. Santa Claus!" He replied.

"A slow in the oven Fruitcake . . . ," Joe whispered. "He can't stay out here in this cold shed; neither can we. There is no heat. We will freeze to death."

"Give me a minute," I whispered back, as the cross eyed man closed the rear door to the shed.

"You had better make that minute speedy! I am cold." Joe replied, rubbing his arms.

"What is your name?" I asked the cross eyed guy.

"S . . . D . . . Clause." He replied.

"Well, S.D., You wouldn't know where there is a long piece of rope that we can use. Our safety rope broke as we made our way here to this shed to get firewood." I stated, while biting my lip. The kid in a man's body was definitely delusional as to who he was. He also posed a problem for me. How was I going to take him back to the cabin with me? He had to be the culprit on the snow mobile who had ran everyone off the road and caused everyone's individual Christmas catastrophe. My group of hungry, starving, uninvited house guests might turn vigilante and kill the cross eyed snowmobile flyer.

"Sorry . . . , "S. D. stated. "I have no need for rope. I am a flyer, not a cowboy calf roper."

Amused, I snorted at his reply. Joe looked at me and broke out in a grin. He was warming up to the guy in his thirties, who was just a kid.

"When the whiteout is over, how about you giving me a ride in your red plane?" Joe asked good- natured, forgetting his and Mary's mishap. "I have always wanted a pilot for a friend."

I was pleased with Joe's response. He was having compassion on the odd, slow guy, and befriending him.

"I will have to ask my mama if it is okay." S. D. replied with a serious look on his face. "I don't want her to stand me in the corner or ground me. I have to have permission to have anyone ride with me. She would tan my backside, if I took you for a flight and let you fall out of my plane."

It was at that point, my suspicions were confirmed. S. D. Claus had the mind of a seven or eight year old. He was definitely mentally challenged. Grown men didn't get their backsides tanned.

"After the whiteout is over, I will help you find your way home to your mother. Do you have an address, or know your way home from here?" I asked.

"Mama will find me. She always finds me when I am lost." The cross eyed guy stated wiping his running, snotty nose once more on the sleeve of his coveralls. "I have been looking for her all day. She must be out hunting meat for our dinner. We always have baked possum on Christmas Eve. They are easy to trap. You throw a little garbage out your door, and they will be right there to eat it, no matter what it is. Most of the time, I just grab one by its tail and mama takes an ax to its neck."

I wanted to barf. It was bad enough that Kris had stewed one inside the cabin. A 'live off the land', hunter's life was definitely not for me. I wasn't sure why I had thought roughing it, in a cabin, fifty miles from nowhere, would make a great holiday.

"Where is your father?" I asked, as Joe walked around the inside of the barn looking for something to use for a rope to connect to our broken, very short, safety line.

"Papa is always at work! However, he will be home sometime tonight. I am really excited. He always comes home on Christmas Eve."

"I always look forward to my dad coming home from the town's bakery." Joe replied, accepting SD as the child he was. "My dad used to bring me leftover donut holes. He is a baker in a pastry shop."

"I like donuts. Mama makes them on special occasions. Tonight is one of those special occasions. Before I go to bed, she will treat me to an apple fritter and hot chocolate. Then we will put one on a plate, and leave it out for papa, to surprise him. I am usually asleep when he comes home. It would be nice if papa and I got to eat our Christmas Eve fritters together. However, it never works out that way."

"Your papa works late every Christmas Eve?" Joe asked,

as he continued to look about the shed for rope.

"Papa works year round. Mama says he is a very hard worker. Once a year, on Christmas Eve, he comes home and brings me new wings for my air plane. Beneath this shed are two air planes that I have worn out. The one out back has a wing that keeps coming off. I lose it all the time. People get annoyed with me, when it flies off and knocks them down, makes them crash, or runs them off the road. They stand and shake their fists at me. I never stop. Mama has told me about stranger danger. I go back later for my broken wing, when they are gone."

I snorted and broke out into laughter. It was S.D.'s wing that had played havoc with all of my uninvited guests. In his mentally challenged state, he was oblivious to the fact that he had caused so much chaos, including Mary and Joseph not making it to town to be married. Controlling myself, I thought about Maxi. She was a child at heart, and would love S.D. She went out of her way to treat the special kids in her Santa line with respect. She always made sure their experience with the red suited guy was a good one. I know that from experience. Until this year, I had been Maxi's Santa. Till now, all the kids (smart and challenged) had just been snotty nosed little nuisances, climbing on and off my lap. Playing Santa had been something I survived every year, in order to stay in the good graces of the only person who loved me, Maxi. I could hardly wait to tell her about SD.

"I found something . . . ," Joe yelled, pointing to a box on a high shelf.

I left S. D. to see what it was Joe was so excited about. The cross eyed boy, in a man's body, was hot on my heels.

"Will that do?" Joe asked, pointing to a shelf where there was a huge ball of Christmas tree lights. "It looks like there might be a couple hundred feet of outside lights in that ball."

"The strands of wiring will work." I replied, helping Joe retrieve the ball from the high shelf.

Suddenly, S. D. became agitated.

"You can't take . . . you can't take . . . you can't take my lights. They belong to me and papa!" He stated grabbing the huge ball from us.

"We are not going to take them and keep them. We need to just borrow them, and string them between here and the cabin to make a safety line. Joe and I can't journey back and forth tonight getting firewood for the cabin without a safety line in this whiteout. Our rope was broke by a flying red airplane."

S.D.'s face was suddenly red and flushed. I had heard that the mentally challenged could be dangerous when they were full grown and angry. I backed up a little bit. Neither, Joe or I, were in the mood to get kicked or bit by him. Suddenly, Joe stepped in front of me.

"It is okay, S.D. No one is going to take your lights." Joe stated, gently picking up a fallen bulb and handing it to the cross eyed guy. We will only use them if you say it is okay.

"These are my runway lights." S. D. stated, holding the ball of Christmas lights to himself and wrapping his arms securely around them. "Papa will be coming home tonight. I must string them due north so he can see where to land. If they are attached to the cabin he will fly right into it."

I was stunned for a moment. S. D. was living in a fantasy

world, possibly one that his mother had created for him. He lived in a mystical place of make believe runways and snowmobile airplanes. His mother had possibly convinced him that his father was Santa Claus. I felt sorry for the guy. He was living a delusion. His mother had to be one of the worst kinds of Christmas crazy, lying to him about who his father was. Perhaps his mother was single, and didn't know who S.D.'s dad was.

"I am so glad to know that you are in charge of Santa's runway on Christmas Eve." Joe piped up, keeping the guy's attention. He knew that I was Jewish and didn't go in for the Santa fairy tale. "Would you agree to create a runway toward the cabin, so we can take flight and make it home for Christmas Eve? There is plenty of time. It isn't dark yet. After we fly away, you can then stretch the runway lights due north for your papa's incoming aircraft. It is Christmas Eve and you have a bigger job to do this year. We need to fly to the cabin, and then on to Chicago."

"I have been to Chicago. My papa lives there." S.D. suddenly stated, smiling from ear to ear. "I used to go every year on Christmas Eve, to see him. Mama took me. I would sit on papa's lap and he would always promise me new wings for my plane. Mama says I am a big boy now. I have to share papa. All the little boys and girls in his line are his children by a second marriage. Mama has always told me that I can't be selfish. I have to take my turn and give my little step brothers and sisters their turn on papa's lap. He just has one night off from work, Christmas Eve, to visit all of us. Now that I am too big to sit on his knee in Chicago, he stops off here on Christmas Eve."

"What a line of bull crap . . . ," I whispered to Joe. "I bet his mother doesn't know who his father is, and has made up this outrageous lie to satisfy his curiosity, while she hides him away from the world here in these woods."

"As of this moment, I do not intend to ever tell my child that there is a Santa." Joe whispered back to me. "Should anything ever happen between Mary and me, I definitely wouldn't want my baby thinking some dude in a red suit was his father."

"Will you help us string the run way lights to the cabin, so we can fly home to Chicago?" I asked, trying not to antagonize him.

"Okay," He replied simply and headed for the door carrying the ball of Christmas lights.

So, the three of us unrolled the huge ball of Christmas tree lights. I then tied the socket end of the strand to the end of our rope. Then, Joe and I stretched out the lights in the direction that we felt the cabin was. The blizzard conditions had turned into a total whiteout. You couldn't see one foot in front of you. Easing our way out into the whiteout, holding to the rope and then the strand of lights, we maneuvered side to side at the end till we bumped into the cabin. Then we kept one hand on the cabin, and walked around it till we came to the front steps and the tiny porch. To our surprise, there was a pile of firewood on the front porch. We wondered how it got there. However, we immediately entered the cabin with our arm loads and placed them in the corner by the fireplace. Then, we hurriedly took a position in front of the fire to warm up. Joe and I had been outside a long time, our teeth were chattering.

"Do you think he will be okay?" Joe asked me in a low voice, as we stood side by side shivering in front of the fireplace.

"These woods are his home. Survival is a way of life with him." I replied between shivers. "I am sure he will be fine."

"We should have asked him to eat Christmas Eve dinner with us." Joe replied. "He could be that stranger that knocks on your door, the one no one will let in. I have heard my church pastor speak about the stranger who knocks at your heart's door. You can either let him in, or turn him away. Judgment comes if you turn him away. He could be Christ in a Halloween costume."

Caught off guard by his Halloween remark, I snorted and then replied, "I am Jewish. I am sure that if your Christ comes knocking, it will not be on my Jewish door. He is a character in your New Testament. Moses and Elijah are in my Bible, The Old Testament. If Moses wants to return tonight and knock on my door in a new body, a stranger's body, I will be fine with that. I would love to ask him how he managed to part the red sea and then get all those people across without killing all of them for their idiosyncrasies. The quirks of all of you are driving me nuts."

"Our quirks . . . ?" Joe replied, with a look of disbelief on his face. "You are the Christmas Eve Fruitcake."

CHAPTER TEN

THE FLYING GOOSE

Night shadows fall early in December. It was about five in the evening on Christmas Eve, yet it was dark outside. It had been a long day and I was getting really agitated with my uninvited guests' never ending chatter about Santa and Christmas. I decided to step out on the tiny front porch to catch a breath of peaceful, silent fresh air. As I stood outside, with my hot breath making clouds in the cold air, I thought I heard voices somewhere out in the whiteout.

"Is anyone out there?" I yelled.

"What the hell are you yelling about?" A male voice yelled back at me from somewhere out in the blinding snowstorm. I scanned the landscape to see where the voice was coming from. After a moment or so, I spotted a winter clad, older man heading my way, walking on top of the knee deep snow. He had a heavily bundled woman his age by the hand helping her walk. They both were dressed for the weather and had on snow shoes. As they approached me, I was surprised to see that the man was carrying a freshly killed goose by its legs.

"It is a lovely winter night for a hike." The man stated when he reached the porch. He didn't climb the cabin's steps or try to join me on the porch.

"Do you always hike in a whiteout carrying a dead goose?" I shot back.

"The poor thing was still alive, when we started our hike. We couldn't just leave it behind for the wolves to eat alive. My wife is an animal rights activist. I have learned to live with her quirks." The man in his sixties stated, turning and grinning at his wife who was standing next to him. "Sometimes, she drives me crazy with her little animal rights activist quirks, but I love her."

"I have Christmas quirky guests inside that are driving me crazy. I am not so sure I love them." I replied reaching out my hand to help the middle-aged woman up the steps and onto the porch to get out of the snow. The man followed carrying his dead goose by its feet.

"We should be so lucky, as to have a houseful of Christmas Eve guests." The woman replied, as she pulled down her muffler, which had been covering her mouth.

"We don't have any children or family anymore." The man added.

"We had a daughter, but she is deceased. No parents should outlive their offspring. It makes your older years very lonely." The woman interjected, with a sad faraway look in her eyes.

"Now, we spend our holidays RV-ing around the country. Tonight, our holiday routine has changed unexpectedly. We are hiking."

"You have chosen to hike in whiteout conditions like

this?" I asked in disbelief.

"Not by choice!" The man added, as his breath made clouds in the icy air. "About thirty minutes or so ago on the road below, a kid on a snowmobile, with a goose riding behind him, flew across the road in front of our RV. He couldn't have been anymore than twenty feet in front of us. I slammed on the brakes. His goose flew off and hit our windshield. Our luxury home on wheels slid off the snow packed road and into a ravine nose down."

"And you just happen to be in the vicinity of my 'fifty miles from nowhere' cabin," I muttered, shaking my head. Why was the God, of Jacob, Moses, and Elijah, cursing me?

"You wouldn't want this dead goose, would you? We have no use for it, but couldn't leave it behind. If cleaned and baked, it could provide enough meat for a large group of Christmas crazy guests. We are not English. We prefer good old American smoked ham for Christmas dinner. That is what we will order, when we eat in a restaurant tomorrow."

I snorted. They definitely were not Jewish. Pork, or ham, was considered unclean meat in my Jewish world. I bit my lip for a moment. Then I replied. "Thank you, but I am not sure the lady of this house will be up to cleaning and butchering a goose for Christmas. Helping Kris with the possum had been bad enough."

The man plopped the dead goose down on my cabin's porch in the snow.

"I am sorry about your accident." I stated, having nothing better to say, before biding them goodbye.

"The guy was so close, when I slammed on the brakes,

that I looked right into his crossed eyes and those of this goose. The guy didn't look a bit frightened. The goose was a different story. It was flapping wildly when it saw my windshield about to get it." The man stated as he watched his wife step back down the snow covered steps.

"So, you want me to feed my guests a goose that has been frightened to death?" I asked, thinking about all the times I was afraid to cross the street when I was little. The goose and I had something in common. I definitely would not have wanted someone to have eaten me, had I been hit by a car while crossing the road. Why should I eat the goose that was innocently crossing the road?

"No, the windshield got him. A piece of glass slit his throat." The man returned. "The kid on the snow mobile was luckier than the goose. He did a little dipsy-doodle and flew away from the moving nose of our RV unharmed. My wife and I were glad. No kid should have to spend Christmas Eve in a hospital. A hospital Santa always arrives with a bag full of hypodermic needles, bed pans, and clear liquid foods that aren't worth consuming. The kid, that we didn't hit, is probably eating cookies and drinking hot chocolate right now. That is the way it should be on Christmas Eve."

Two more Christmas crazies had wandered into my space. Thank my Jewish God they were not asking for shelter. I decided that I would refuse the dead goose.

"Shouldn't you use your cell phone to call for help, and then wait for your RV to be towed?" I asked, fishing to see if they had a phone.

"We ended up so far down in a ravine, that it took us fifteen minutes of straight up rock climbing to reach the road. There isn't a tow truck with a wench cable long enough to hook on to it. It will be spring before our RV can be retrieved. Our cell phone went flying off of our dash and out the broken windshield. It was getting dark, and the ravine was too steep down to look for it. The wife and I are too old to be climbing up and down a kid's steep slide the wrong way. The ravine was almost straight down. We were lucky to have retrieved our winter wear and snow shoes."

"How did you find your way here? I can't see more than a few feet out into this whiteout." I asked, knowing that Joe and I were using a safety line to retrieve firewood from the shed out back.

"We weren't heading for your cabin. We are headed south, following the hunter's compass on my survivalist wrist watch. Your cabin just happens to be on our route and south of where we were. Your cabin is not our destination."

"Oh . . . ," I replied. "My name is Monty Marsh. I have a pregnant teen girl inside who may need medical attention before tomorrow. When you reach civilization, will you call law enforcement and send back help to us? None of us here have a phone, and my rented vehicle is now a snowdrift."

"My name is Caesar and my wife's name is Augusta. We will attempt to send you help."

"Attempt to send me help . . . ," I muttered, as they walked away into the snowy night. "Who attempts to send someone help, you either do or don't."

"Wait . . . ," I yelled, considering the fact that the RV couple might need the goose to eat on their journey into the unknown. I had no intention of eating the poor dead thing.

"You have left your goose!"

"It is not our goose!" The woman yelled back. "It is now yours, Jackass."

Her remark struck me funny. I broke out into Jewish laughter. The Protestant's manger scene always had a donkey in it. I had just been appointed the Jackass for that scene, now taking place in my rented cabin fifty miles from nowhere. Now, there was a Joseph and a Mary, a shepherd, an angel, an older woman who saw herself as a Mrs. Santa, and now me the jackass.

The cabin door opened and Kris stuck her head out. "What is all the noise about?"

I reached down and picked up, by its two legs, the dead goose with a slit and broken neck. "Are you interested in Goose to add to your Christmas dinner menu tomorrow?" I asked, hoping she would say no.

"Oh my God, you have killed his pet goose! Are you crazy?" Kris asked, not smiling.

"I killed someone's pet goose?" I replied asking, in annoyance. "What do you mean?"

In a distraught voice, and wringing her hands, she continued. "How am I ever going to explain to him that you have killed his pet goose? He has raised that goose from a hatchling."

"I assume you know the crazy, cross-eyed kid who flies about the area on a snow mobile with ironing board wings?" Then, I regretted the remark, suddenly realizing who she was. It was the cross eyed guy's snowmobile airplane that she had fallen out of. It was her that he was looking for. She was his mother.

"Save your insults, Monty. I have a challenged son that I have spent years protecting ... protecting from prejudiced, supposedly civilized idiots like you. Give me his goose!" She stated, holding out her hand. "I suppose the only thing I can do now, is bake the goose for dinner tomorrow. However, you will not eat any of it. This goose was my son's heart. He has not been privileged to have playmates like other kids. Now, you go and kill the only thing he loves besides me and Santa. Don't you step one foot inside this cabin till I calm myself. Freeze your backside off out here, and then eat your donuts tomorrow. "

I was livid. Not only was she accusing me of killing the goose, she was denying me access to my own cabin. It was like a wife telling her husband to sleep on the couch. My mouth went into overdrive.

"I am tired of you making me jump thru hoops and ruling my house. You and all the other freeloaders inside are infringing on my goodwill and Jewish holiday. I didn't ask for any of you to knock on my door seeking shelter, or to fall out of kiddy airplanes. I have only put up with all of you, and your Christmas craziness, because of the storm. If this were the city, I would kick you all out and tell you to go check into a homeless shelter or hang out beneath an overpass somewhere. I don't need any of you. It is all of you that have needed me."

About that time, all my unwanted guests gathered around the open cabin doorway to witness my spat with Kristina. There were gasps, shocked faces that turned white, and then total silence. Kristina then slammed my cabin door in my face, and locked it. I was not a happy, Jewish camper.

Endless pounding on the cabin's door and yelling did not

125

gain me entrance. Finally, I decided to walk over to the little cabin window on the porch, and break it to gain entrance, if I had to. I was shivering. Taking a deep breath, I made my way to the window.

Before breaking it with a stick of firewood, I peeped in. Too my surprise, my cabin was empty. There was not a soul inside. I scanned the room thru the frosty glass, with my eyes wandering to the kitchen cabinet. On it sat three unopened, man size TV dinners, a sealed box of donuts, and an unopened can of coffee. What I was seeing was impossible. The TV dinners had been eaten, the coffee opened, and a third of the donuts eaten. I tried the window to see if it would slide up and open. It was locked. I forgot about breaking the window. I returned to the cabin's door and tried the handle one more time. The door opened immediately, and easily. I stuck my head in, hoping Kris would be there and throw a tea towel or something at me. There was no sign of her or any of my uninvited guests having ever been there. I quickly walked to the lean –to bathroom door and flung it open, thinking all my guests might be hiding from me there. The tiny, indoor outhouse was empty. On the back of the stool area sat the half roll of toilet paper that had been there when I arrived at the cabin. There was no evidence of door knocker literature in the room, its trash can, or down the outhouse hole. I returned to the main room and saw that the fireplace was clean, cold, and swept free of ashes. There were no red hot embers or logs dancing with flames. I glanced over at the bed. It had not been slept in. The two rockers sat idle. The cabin was just as I had found it, when I opened its door for the first time.

Panic set in. I considered the fact that I might have just experienced a mental break of some sort, and had imagined my encounter with Kristina, the cross eyed guy, and the others. I thrust my hand into my pants pocket. Too my surprise, I found my cell phone there. I quickly checked the time and date on it. I knew it was Christmas Eve. My phone said it was not. I grabbed the mantle of the cold fireplace to steady myself. It was December 23rd again, the morning of my arrival at the cabin and the day prior to Christmas Eve. I was at a total loss, as to how I had traveled back in time to over twenty four hours earlier.

I returned to the cabin's entry door and stepped outside to check for clouds indicating a snow storm was brewing. There were no clouds. It was icy cold, but the sun was shining. I then jumped from the little cabin's porch and run around the cabin to check the spot where I had rescued Kris, in her red knit sweat suit, from a snowdrift. There was no snowdrift and no Kris. I waited till noon at that spot. She did not fall out of a plane. Returning to the cabin, I made a fire in the cabin's fireplace, and then sat in one of the two rockers and watched its flames as they began to dance. I listened for knocks as I rocked. None sounded. None sounded. Late evening, I waited for Mary and Joe to knock on my door. They did not. At midnight, I reclined on the cabin's bed and fell asleep, thinking I was having a mental break. When I awoke, it was Christmas Eve morning and all was eerily quiet. I sat up, in hopes my unwanted guests would reappear. They did not.

I waited anxiously all Christmas Eve day for Kris, Joe, Mary, and the others to reappear. They did not. No whiteout snowstorm developed and my 'fifty miles from nowhere' cabin became my nightmare, one that I would not be able to explain. At midnight on Christmas Eve, I got in my rented four wheel drive and made my way back to the nearest town. Stopping at an all night restaurant, I ordered a sandwich and then called Maxi telling her I was returning early, but not why. How do you tell your family that you have had a mental break?

As I drove back toward Chicago, in the wee morning hours, I muttered, "Jen . . . you have finally done it. I am having a nervous breakdown." After replaying our breakup in my mind and beating myself up for not being a man, I returned my thoughts to Kris and asked in a mutter, "Why now, when I was starting to fall in love with someone new?"

Then I gasped at what I had said. I was in my mid twenties. Kristina was a much older woman. No young man in his twenties, in his right mind, develops feelings for someone old enough to be his mother or grandmother. I had indeed lost my sanity. How was I going to hide that fact from Maxi? How was I going to convince myself that I was not in love with Kris? Furthermore, how was I going to deal with the fact that in my delusional state, un-real Kris had dumped me just like Jen had done?

CHAPTER ELEVEN

SURVIVING A MENTAL BREAKDOWN

After spending a couple of days with Maxi, I returned to California and resumed my position as a burger flipper at the fast food place next door to Zeke's Feet Detective Agency. I had no further delusions, hallucinations, or déjà vu moments. I kept my mouth shut about my eerie experience at the cabin. The last thing I wanted was Maxi, or my acquaintances in California, to think I was nuts. I returned to my everyday routine of flipping burgers and trying to land a position as a private detective. I tried to forget about the mystical cabin experience that I could not explain.

Landing a position with Zeke's agency was my number one goal, even though he only hired female detectives. On more than one occasion, when asking his receptionist for an application, I was told that Zeke and his father filled the quota for male employees. I didn't give up. On breaks, at Burger Flippers, I would sit outside at a round table that was shaded by an umbrella. From that position, I would study Zeke's clients and female detectives as they came and went. Sooner or later, I would figure out what made Zeke tick, and then land a job with him.

On a couple occasions, I had thought seriously about asking Zeke to help me figure out my mystery, my disappearing Christmas Eve guests. However, I secretly consulted a psychiatrist instead. I was assured by my shrink that the stranded strangers, who had knocked on my cabin door seeking shelter, were not real. My psychiatrist had been very happy to point out to me that Johnny Appleseed was a character in a fictional tale from the 1800's. He also assured me that I could not have spoken with him at my cabin door, or fed my guests possum he had trapped. I never shared with him that I had fallen in love with a Christmas crazy woman named Kris, who kept looking younger every few hours; going from 80 backwards to 70, 60, and then into her late forties before she disappeared.

Almost eleven months had passed since my mental breakdown. It was a few days before Thanksgiving. I was doing my usual, flipping burgers in the fast food restaurant that I worked for in California. My sister, Maxi, believed I worked for Zeke's Feet Detective Agency. I had let her believe that lie for some time. She was so successful in her life. I didn't want her to be ashamed of me. I had a college education just like her. She had a successful business, real estate, and money. I had a rented apartment and a going nowhere job. Being a detective had a little more class to it.

I had never told my sister about my eerie experience at the cabin, or that I was seeing a psychiatrist as a result of it. After the time warp and disappearing people incident at the cabin, I caught a plane back to California and checked into a mental health facility. I had spent three months there, before being released to return to society and work. Now, I was just trying to act normal, think normal, and not think at all about Kris and the cabin.

Forgetting, or getting over Kristina, had not been easy. She and the others had become like family to me, for some reason. I disliked them when I had to put up with them in the cabin. Now, I secretly longed for just one more moment of their presence. They were like family members that had suddenly died, due to some tragedy. I had spent eleven months secretly grieving and agonizing over them. The loss of Kris bothered me the most. I had fallen in love with her in those brief moments we shared. She had replaced Jen in my heart. However, she had done a number on me, and had dumped me just like Jen. My self-esteem as a man was zilch.

Now, it was eleven months later and I was trying to move forward with my life. It was a couple days prior to Thanksgiving. As I sat beneath the outdoor umbrella, I realized that the Christmas season, with all its madness, was once more about to show its ugly head. Maxi had already called, demanding that I play Santa for her on Christmas Eve. She tried to make me feel guilty stating that her hired Santa, to replace me the previous Christmas Eve, had been a total flop with the customer's children. After much begging on her part, I agreed to fly to Chicago and help her out.

Haunted by my cabin experience, I wanted to return to the 'fifty miles from nowhere' place and hopefully find Kristina and the others there, waiting for me. However, I was fighting the urge to do so. My psychiatrist said that my desire, to relive my delusion, was my wanting to run and hide from my feelings for Jen. I didn't agree with him. Meeting and falling in love with Kris had nothing to do with Jen, even if she had dumped me like my ex-fiancé. My psychiatrist had made me promise not to revisit the cabin, for my own sanity. I didn't want to spend another three months in a psychiatric hospital, so I agreed.

My psychiatrist believed I wanted a family, to the point of fantasizing or creating an imaginary one. On more than one occasion, he had pointed out to me that Johnny Appleseed was the proof that my experience was a delusion. If Johnny wasn't real, Kristina and the others were not real either. So, I had spent almost a year taking prescribed pills, and trying to forget. The psychiatrist was right. Down deep, I did want someone to love. I was a family man and wanted a wife and children. At the same time, I knew it would never happen because, as Jen had pointed out, I was a dud. I was a man who was unable to produce children. I was sterile.

My plane ticket to Chicago for the holiday season was purchased. I would spend the Hanukkah/Christmas season with Maxi in her apartment above the toy shop. I would do the Christmas Eve bit playing Santa and then embrace my own Jewish traditions with Maxi. I did not intend to rock my mental boat, by even considering, taking off to another cabin, 'fifty miles from nowhere'. I had to be careful during the holidays, Maxi did not know about my mental breakdown the year before.

My sister had always seen me as the lesser, in our relationship. She had always dominated in our relationship as twins. I didn't want her to see me as less than less, a brother who was walking a fine line between reality and insanity. She was all the family I had, or possibly would ever have. When you are on a sinking ship with only one life line, you are careful to protect that life line. Maxi was all I had, the only woman who would ever love me. I didn't want to disappoint her, let her think I was on the edge of insanity. I had not told her about my cabin experience. After Christmas the previous year, she asked how my cabin holiday turned out. I told her it had been a lousy, cold experience, and that she had been right. I should have taken more food and toilet paper. She had retorted, "I told you so!" I never mentioned my cabin outing again, and she never asked.

As I sat outside beneath one of the fast food restaurant's umbrellas, I watched a very expensive, luxury, recreational vehicle pull alongside the curb in front of Zeke's place and park. Zeke had a lot of wealthy clients. However, few arrived for their appointments in RV's. I watched as the driver, with his back to me, put money in seven parking meters. The long RV took up that many parking spaces. I grinned. Only an eccentric wealthy man would do that. Zeke had lots of interesting people that came and went as clients. I wanted to work for him, and had filled out numerous applications. Zeke always turned me down, stating the same thing he always said, he only hired female detectives.

From the back, the male owner of the RV looked really familiar. However, I couldn't place where I knew him from. After a moment or so, his wife stepped out and turned in my direction eyeing me. She also looked familiar. She was wearing a sundress, sandals, big sunglasses, and a floppy hat which hid most of her facial features. The man was dressed equally as casual in shorts and a flowered summer shirt. As I stared at the woman, she spotted me, pulled off her sunglasses, and stared intently back. She then grabbed one of the meters, like she was trying to steady herself. I heard her half yell her husband's name, which also sounded familiar. She seemed to be in a panic, and I was the problem.

Feeling that my staring was causing her emotional distress, I rose from my chair and returned inside the fast food restaurant to go on with my day. My break was over. I decided the woman had possibly purchased burgers from me. Maybe her order had been wrong and she was holding it against me. People do weird stuff when they get the wrong orders. I had a lady come back once and throw her sack of food at me. I hoped she wasn't going to come into the restaurant and make a scene.

Resuming my counter position inside the restaurant, I took an occasional glance out the window at the luxury RV. I was fairly sure I knew the owners, but I did not recognize the RV. Turning to the guy working on a register next to me, I asked, "The couple out there with the RV that is parked in front of Zeke's place, are they customers of ours?"

My fellow employee replied, "What RV . . . what couple?" Then he got busy with a couple of customers that were in his line.

I ignored his reply, thinking he hadn't had time to take a good look due to having customers. I eyed the RV, in-between waiting on customers in my line. The couple had gone into Zeke's building. I wasn't sure what my fascination with them was. However, I felt I had to find out who the couple was and where I had met them. It was one of those little mysteries in life that drives you crazy till you solve it. My curiosity was getting the best of me.

"I am taking my next break early, Pete. Watch the counter for a few minutes. I have got to get a closer look at that RV and the couple driving it. I know I know them."

"Well, don't take too long. If the boss catches you taking a break off schedule, you are likely to get canned."

I took off my white apron and left the fast food restaurant by the side door, and then made my way to the rear of the RV, where it was parked along the curb. It was a beautiful day in California. However, as I approached the RV, a sudden icy wind blew across the landscape. I had an instant case of goose bumps. I rubbed my arms to warm them. "It is November," I muttered. "I should have slipped on a hooded sweatshirt."

Eyeing the rear of the RV, I read the license plate. There was nothing unusual about it. It was a California tag. However, the tag was expired. I decided I would point that fact out to the owner, as a conversation opener, when he returned from Zeke's establishment. I stepped off the curb into the street, and then walked down the driver's side of the luxury coach, looking it over. As I did, I spotted a name painted on the side. It wasn't unusual for people to name boats, air planes, and RV's. However, the name on this coach shocked me. Written in huge letters was 'The Flying Goose'. Below the name was painted a mural of a goose in flight, being chased by a man on a snowmobile. I gasped and instantly knew where I had seen the couple before. They were the couple wearing snow shoes, who were hiking off the mountain after sliding their RV off the road into a ravine. They had given me a dead goose, just minutes prior to Kris slamming the door in my face and disappearing. I placed my hand on the side of the RV in a panic, trying to steady myself, just as the woman had tried to steady herself. Were my delusions returning?

After a moment of trying to control sudden trembling, I walked to the front of the RV where the driver's seat was. Lettered, beneath the window, were the owners' first names, Caesar and Augusta. Once again, I placed my hands on the side of the coach to steady myself. It was definitely them. Forcing myself to let go of the side of the coach, I walked around and stood in front of Zeke's Detective agency door with rubber for knees. I knew I should be on the phone calling my psychiatrist. However, the RV and couple were real. I had to know if they knew me, and what part they played in my madness. What part did I play in the woman's panic? I needed to ask the couple if they had seen Kristina and the others, possibly thru the lighted window, when they had called me a jackass and yelled that the goose they had been carrying was mine. I wasn't crazy, if they had seen my guests thru the window, or a crack in the door.

As I stood facing Zeke's door trembling, I considered the fact that the RV behind me could be a hallucination. Maybe my mind was snapping again. If I went inside and demanded to see a non-existent RV couple, I might get laughed at by Zeke and his staff. I wanted to work for Zeke, not be seen as a lunatic by him. I waited with my knees shaking.

"Johnny Appleseed is not real . . . Johnny is not real . . . Johnny Appleseed is not real," I muttered, fighting my fears and memories.

About that time, Caesar exited the detective agency's door, stepping out onto the sidewalk, standing suddenly face to face with me.

Forcing myself, knowing he might tell me he didn't know me, I sputtered, "Thank you for the goose you gave me on Christmas Eve last year. I am Monty." I then quickly extended my hand nervously to shake.

"Holy crap . . . it's you!" The man replied with the blood

draining from his face. "Where did you come from? How can you see me?" He asked weakly, taking my hand to shake, but not releasing it.

"I work next door at the fast food restaurant. I saw you pull up and park the RV. Do you remember giving me a goose on Christmas Eve last year?" I asked, ignoring his odd question asking how I could see him.

"Holy shit . . . ," Caesar stated, releasing my hand, and then making the sign of the cross. "You are real . . . !"

"Are you real?" I asked in return, hoping he was not a hallucination on my part. I was sure that I would be admitting myself back into the psych hospital, before the day was over.

"What was I wearing last Christmas Eve?" He asked cautiously.

"Winter wear and snow shoes." I replied. "What do you remember about me?"

"I recall you complaining about having a cabin full of uninvited guests to feed. My wife and I gave you a goose that had flown in front of our RV, breaking our windshield." He replied with a face that was white as paste.

"Did you . . . Did you by any chance see any of my guests thru the window, or my cracked door last year?"

As I waited for his reply, my cell phone vibrated in my white work pants pocket. I knew it had to be my work buddy warning me the boss was back, and I was about to get canned if I didn't return immediately.

"No, I didn't see anyone with you at the cabin. I do recall a light streaming from your tiny window. After leaving you with our goose, we ran into a trapper who invited us to eat with him. Did you by any chance, encounter a trapper named Johnny Appleseed?" Caesar asked nervously.

"You . . . you met Johnny Appleseed?" I asked, realizing I was not as delusional as the psychiatrist had convinced me I was. At the same time, I needed to know if he had met the same Johnny I had. "Did your trapper Johnny have a bad habit that annoyed you?"

"Yea, he was always wiping his runny, snotty nose on the back of his gloves." Caesar nervously replied. "What do you remember about him?"

Gulping, I replied. "He gave one of my guests, apple seeds, dried apples, and raisins."

Caesar then got real fidgety.

"He gave my wife seeds too. One minute we were eating rabbit with him. He had it roasted over an open fire on a spit. The next minute, he just up and vanished. I recall that a wolf howled. My wife and I turned toward the sound. When we turned back, the apple seed man and his trapper's camp were gone and we were back in our RV, about to be rescued by paramedics. We have not known what to make of our shared experience with the trapper, or of one we had with a guy with crossed eyes."

At that point, I realized Caesar had encountered two of the individuals that had played major roles in what my psychiatrist insisted were a delusion. Was there a possibility that part of my delusion was real?

"You saw the trapper and the cross eyed guy?"

"Yes," He replied, as he eyed me up and down.

The trapper and the odd guy had never entered my cabin. I had spoken with them only on the porch of the cabin. Was the porch a dividing line between the real world, and the one that the psychiatrist insisted that I had made up?

"The cross eyed fellow that you met, was he looking for his dog and his mother?" I asked, seeing that the man looked a little spooked and in shock.

"I . . . We, my wife and I, have thought the apple seed man and the cross-eyed fellow were just part of a hallucination, due to the fact we spent two days in a wrecked RV, slowly dying. We were nose down in a ravine. I had two broken legs and a concussion. My wife had a broken hip and arm. We do not know who discovered us in the ravine, in the whiteout, and sent us help. We were flown by helicopter to a hospital, fifty miles away. The RV you are looking at is a replacement, paid for by our insurance." He replied with a hint of unease in his voice. "Neither my wife or I could have hiked to your cabin on snow shoes, which we did not have. We thought we share dreamed, or hallucinated the event. Our emotions were out of whack at the time. We were headed north in the other RV to lay our only daughter to rest. She had passed away the day before our accident. We were distraught with grief."

"Apparently, you entered and shared some type of psychotic break with me. My psychiatrist has repeatedly insisted that I imagined you, your wife, Johnny Appleseed, and the trapper."

"Augusta has always believed in paranormal states and parallel universes. She is a Wiccan. She could never convince me of her views till we shared the snowshoe hike experience taking us south to your cabin and then the trapper's camp. I always thought her ideas were a bunch of fairy dust. Now, I don't know what I believe, or how you are standing here and seeing me. You can't be real."

"I am real!" I replied. "I am a Jewish man who rented a cabin 'fifty miles from nowhere' to get away from civilization and its December Christmas Crazy madness. My sister Maxi owns a toy store in Chicago. I rented a vehicle and drove to the cabin from Chicago. The trapper and the cross eyed guy knocked on my cabin door, as did several other Christmas crazies. After finding myself in a situation I couldn't explain, I flew home here to California thinking I had a mental breakdown of some sort. Somehow, time stood still there and even turned backwards."

Caesar looked a little ashen. "Did you find yourself 24 or so hours backwards . . . back in time," He asked sheepishly, "After meeting us?"

"My stranded, unwanted, house guests disappeared on me, just as the trapper did on you. Instead of it being Christmas Eve, I traveled backwards in time somehow, and it was the 23rd, the day before Christmas Eve."

"We slid off the road and nose down into the ravine on the morning of the 23rd. We were not rescued till after dark on Christmas Eve, the 24th. A helicopter flew us to a hospital fifty miles away. When we landed on the roof of the hospital, I checked the date on my watch. It said it was December 23rd. I asked several different medical personnel what the date was. They all said it was the 23rd. I know it was Christmas Eve, the 24th when we were rescued. I did not hallucinate that. Our daughter was to be buried on Christmas Eve. Like you, we left Chicago on the 23rd heading north for her funeral, which was to be Christmas

Eve morning. We wrecked on the 23rd and were rescued after dark on Christmas Eve. My wife, in her injured state and fighting death in the RV, was distraught that she had missed her own daughter's funeral. The paramedics sedated her on the helicopter ride. Somewhere on the helicopter ride, we entered a time warp. I managed to get my broken body into a wheel chair and down to the lobby. I caught a cab, telling him I was a dismissed patient. I rode the cab all the way north, checked into a motel on the 23rd and then attended my daughter's funeral the next morning on Christmas Eve the 24th. I passed the deep ravine and my wrecked RV on the way."

"Are you telling me that you were injured and trapped in a crashed RV when you were speaking with me at my rented cabin? Was the goose real?" I sputtered.

"All I know is that my wife and I shared some psychic, mystical experience hiking on snow shoes and meeting you, the trapper, and Johnny Appleseed. Afterward, I was suddenly seated back in my seat in my wrecked RV with two broken legs. I was distraught over the accident, as well as missing my only child's funeral. While being rescued, I somehow entered a time warp and traveled backwards in time. With two broken legs and my wife in intensive care, I caught a cab north and attended my daughter's funeral, which had already taken place. I have not been able to explain the time travel event, or meeting you. So, I have kept my mouth shut about it, as has my wife."

"I am sorry about your daughter. Would you like to tell me about her death?" I asked, seeing the pain of grief in his eyes.

"My wife is Wiccan. I am an agnostic, or was. My daughter in her adult years embraced the religion of the Kingdom door knockers. Much to our dismay, she became one of those nuisances who knock on your door and try to stuff their pamphlets and views down your throat. She saw me and Augusta as heathen, two of the not chosen to be one of her 144,000 that were to live and reign with her Christ. She was handing out pamphlets and knocking on doors when she died."

"She died when she was knocking on doors handing out pamphlets?" I asked in a gasp, while thinking of Angelica who had shared all of her literature with us. We had used it for toilet paper.

"A freaky snowstorm blew thru. She was caught out without winter wear. She got lost in a whiteout and froze to death the day after Thanksgiving. We had to wait till after her autopsy to bury her. They kept her in the morgue for almost a month. No one should have to bury a loved one during the holidays. You always associate the day with it. Christmas Eve is not a time of giving to my wife and me. It is the day our daughter was lowered into the cold ground; the day I sat in a wheelchair in pain, with two broken legs, grieving."

I couldn't help myself, I had to ask. "What was your daughter's name?"

"Angelica . . . everyone called her angel." Caesar replied with a faraway sad look in his eyes.

"Did you catch a glimpse of any of my cabin guests that night?" I asked, wondering if I should tell him that one of them was possibly his daughter. The thought bothered me. For one thing, in my Jewish religion, it is forbidden to inquire of anyone who could speak with the dead. If my Angelica the doorknocker was his daughter, I had been entertaining a dead woman. I had to be on my Jewish God's hit list. In the Old Testament, he destroyed seers and witches. Caesar had openly admitted his wife was a witch, or Wiccan. A real witch had given me a goose in the mystical encounter that I could not explain.

"You did not invite us in to your cabin. We spoke with you only at the base of your steps and on your porch." Caesar replied. "You were not in a very sociable mood that night, as I recall."

"My plate was full that night. I did not know how to deal with it. I had guests and no food to feed them. I got very angry at my guests and told them that I really didn't want their presence. One, named Kris, slammed the door in my face. When I managed to get inside, a few moments later, they were all gone. They just disappeared. My psychiatrist has tried to convince me that I imagined you, your wife, the goose, and my cabin full of guests last Christmas Eve. Seeing you here is a shock." I replied, as once more my cell phone vibrated in my pants pocket. I ignored it. Finding someone to prove that I wasn't crazy was more important than keeping my job as a burger flipper.

"My wife and I were sharing a plate of sorrow and grief, when we somehow exited our broken bodies and walked on snow shoes to you. I was an atheist before the experience. Now, I am a believer in parallel universes and time travel. You must decide what the mystical experience means to you." Caesar replied, checking his watch. "My wife will be out in a moment and we must journey on. Perhaps, you and I will meet again someday, in another time warp experience that we cannot explain."

"May I ask why you have named your RV 'The Flying Goose' and have painted the image of a guy on a snowmobile chasing a goose on the side?"

"The man on the snowmobile, and the flying goose, were what caused us to wreck. The guy ran us off the road and the goose hit our windshield shattering it. We think the goose was a ghost. There is no other explanation. There was no goose found back at our crash site, in our RV. The goose hit our windshield, shattered it, and landed in the floor between Augusta and me."

"What about the cross eyed guy?" I asked, mulling over the word ghost.

"He and his snow mobile just disappeared after we wrecked. We do not know what happened to him. He did not come to our rescue. Like the goose, he may have been a spirit, a ghost. I do not know."

"A goose ghost . . . ," I muttered in a shocked voice. I had never toyed with the idea that I had encountered ghosts in my cabin. I didn't believe in spooks, especially Protestant, Door knocker, and Hindu ones. I was Jewish. Why would I be haunted by ghosts from other religions?

About that time, Augusta exited Zeke's Feet and stopped dead in her tracks seeing me standing with her husband facing her.

"Oh my god . . . it is happening again." She sputtered, grabbing for her husband's arm. "Do you have the cross-eyed man and the goose with you?"

"Augusta . . . ," Caesar quickly interrupted, getting his wife's attention. "Monty is human. He works next door at the fast food place. He was in Chicago last year the same as us. We both traveled north at the same time. He rented a cabin in the same area we crashed our RV. He is not one of our ghosts."

"Can he see us?" She asked.

"We are not snow shoeing spirits in a time warp, like we were when we took a hike last Christmas Eve. Monty here has been just as confused for the last year as us. He thought he had imagined or dreamed us and our goose."

"Oh . . . ," she replied and said no more.

My current encounter with the RV couple, and the discovery that Kristina and the others were possibly ghosts, was sending shivers thru me. I was now facing a new kind of crazy, a ghost seeing crazy. My Jewish religion said it was a sin against God to speak with the dead. I just knew I was going to get struck dead by lightning. My Jewish God was not a God of love. He was a destroying God, who demanded absolute obedience to him and his views on anything and everything. Free thinking was not part of his agenda. Embracing a belief in ghosts was definitely not of his liking, I was sure.

To my surprise, Augusta suddenly reached out and pinched my arm.

"Ouch," I yelled and jerked my arm back.

"Forgive me. I just had to make sure you are not a ghost." She replied big eyed. "We have lived in a sea of questions the last year, trying to find answers for how we exited our bodies and traveled back in time, taking with us a dead goose."

"I have been seeing a psychiatrist and popping pills for the last year, in order to cope." I shot back, while rubbing my arm where she had caused a whelp to rise.

"Well, throw away the pills, Monty. The three of us have shared a Christmas Eve time travel adventure that few men have ever experienced. We have gone where Scientists have not been able to go." Caesar stated, as he pulled the key to his RV from his pocket.

"We couldn't persuade you to return with us to your mountain cabin, and see if we might be able to inter-act with time travel and the other world again?" Augusta asked with big eyes.

"I am planning to spend Christmas Eve in my sister's toy shop in Chicago playing Santa this year. Last year, I fell in love with one of my guests, a woman named Kristina. I have had a hard time dealing with the fact that she dumped me just before she disappeared." I replied. "I don't ever want to experience rejection again. I never plan to return to the cabin."

"If you change your mind, meet us on your rented cabin's front porch on Christmas Eve, exactly at the time we met you last year, when we came carrying a goose. We have plans to retrace our steps of the night we exited our bodies. That includes walking to your cabin carrying a dead goose. We have one in the freezer inside the RV. Our daughter is gone. We want to try to enter the in-between worlds and see her once more." Augusta further added.

I bit my lip. I wasn't sure whether I should tell them I had encountered their daughter after her death. Had they stepped onto my cabin's porch, pushed me aside, and entered my cabin's door the previous Christmas Eve, they would have entered the in-between world where their daughter dwelt, if I wasn't hallucinating my in the moment experience with them discussing ghosts.

"It is time to go, Augusta." Caesar stated, taking his wife by the arm and starting to escort her toward the front and door of the luxury RV. "Did you complete your business with Zeke?"

"Yes . . . he is going to look into the mysterious circumstances of our daughter's death." Augusta replied as they walked away.

I stood watching them leave, even though my cell phone was vibrating like crazy in my pocket. I waved by to them, as they stepped up into the luxury coach. Then they pulled away from the seven parking meters.

Needless to say, my boss at the fast food place fired me for taking an unauthorized break.

CHAPTER TWELVE

MAXI FREAKS OUT

The following day, after being fired, I made a list of places I thought I might get on quickly. Fast food places were a dime a dozen and always short of help. Then I spent most of the morning filling out applications of everything that was within a couple of miles from me. I did not have a commuting personality. I liked to walk or bike to work. Close to noon, I decided I might as well fill out one more application for Zeke's Detective Agency. Sooner or later, the guy would get tired of my applications crossing his desk and hire me. Anyway, that was my opinion. So far, I think I had filled out a total of 49 job apps. Standing in front of the detective agency's door, I removed my sunglasses and ran my fingers thru my hair, in an effort to make myself more presentable. I reached for the door handle, when the door swung out and open, revealing a gorgeous young woman in hot pink spikes leaving the building with a key in her hand.

"Sorry . . . ," I stated, with my entering having almost collided with her exiting.

"May I help you?" She asked fiddling with the key.

"I was just about to go inside and fill out a job application. I am Monty Marsh." I replied, extending my hand to shake with her. She didn't return the gesture.

"Now, Sweetie, one thing you will learn, if you are around here long is that you don't shake hands with every Tom, Dick, and Harry that comes along, until you check out their aura and see if there are any holes in it. Men with holes in their auras usually have some sort of sickness, and it could become your community property; if, you know what I am talking about? Big holes in men's auras say they have cancer, aids, or sexually transmitted diseases."

I bit my lip to keep from laughing at her. I didn't want to antagonize one of Zeke's female detectives who might end up being my detective partner in the future, when Zeke hired me.

"What does my aura say?" I then asked, stepping back and admiring her gorgeous legs. She had it going on in her pink spikes. She was hot.

"Well, let me look . . . ," She stated, stepping back a short ways, tilting her head, and seemingly letting her eyes go out of focus for a moment. "Your aura has two lightning bolt shaped cracks in it for starters. That means that your heart has been broken twice. On the bottom of your aura you have a tiny hole, the size of a blueberry. I would say that sometime during the last year you have had the diarrhea due to eating something that didn't agree with you. I don't see any male diseases. I do see an odd man becoming part of your world. People are afraid of him. He is reckless and looks somewhat like a boogie man."

I was taken back for a moment. She had read me like a book, except for the boogie man. Jen and Kris had broken my heart, and I had gotten the trots last year at the cabin from eating a greasy donut.

"Am I right?" She asked, returning to the agency's door and inserting her key to lock the door.

"I would say you are probably a fairly good psychic, if there is such a thing. I don't know any boogie men, however. Maybe you should read the aura of my shaking hand. It is the part of me that you refused to shake." I replied, watching her as she tested the knob on the door to make sure it was locked. I wasn't about to tell a gorgeous woman like her that a donut had given me the trots last year, or about my mystical encounters with oddball ghosts. I held out my hand to her, palm down.

"Well, turn your palm up!" She demanded putting her hands on her very shapely hips. "Haven't you ever had your palm read before?"

"Err . . . uh . . . no!" I replied, as I quickly flipped my hand over to palm side up. She was just like Kris, making me jump thru her hoops. She was wrapping me around her finger. I liked it. I was definitely a man who longed to be henpecked.

Miss Pink Spikes eyed my palm, but didn't touch it. "You have filled out job applications all morning. God knows how many dirty hands you have shaken before trying to shake with me. I see from your dirty palm lines that you ride a bike. You are financially strapped from working a minimum wage job that you have been fired from. I see that you want more out of life than you are getting." She stated tracing the lines in my palm with her perfectly painted fingernail, but not touching my palm as though she were afraid something really bad might crawl off it and grab her. "Am I right?"

"You are right about the bike part." I replied not wanting to admit to gorgeous her that I had been a minimum wage burger flipper, or that I was a dud who wanted a wife and a houseful of kids. "I am looking for work. My name is Monty Marsh."

"My name is Milky Way." She replied. "There is one other thing your palm tells me."

"What is that?" I replied, amused with her.

"You will eventually be a doorman, not a detective. There are many doors to open, Monty Marsh. Not all of them are like this wooden one guarding the entrance to Zeke's."

I laughed thinking she was a little ditzy, and had perhaps read one too many books on palm reading. I had read one too many on being a detective.

"Did you say your name is Milky Way?"

"Yeah . . . like a path thru the planets." She retorted.

"Well, Milky Way, I plan to land a job and be one of Zeke's detectives some day. When that time comes, you have my permission to read my aura every day, before getting close to me, or shaking my hand."

"It won't be me checking your aura. I don't work for Zeke!" She replied. "I am a temp filling in for Zeke's receptionist till about one or one-thirty. She had a doctor's appointment or something this morning. Did you know that Zeke's female detectives are required to wear four inch spikes to work every day? It has something to do with his agency's image. Anyway, these stilettos I have on are killing me. There is no way that I would work for him full time. My feet, that normally wear sensible sandals, do not like being tortured. I dread the days the temp service hands me a pair of pink spikes and sends me here."

I laughed. "What is your dream, Milky Way? I gather that being a floating receptionist is not totally to your liking."

"One more month of temp work and I have my down payment to purchase the little dilapidated building next to Zeke that once was a little mom and pop store. I am going to open up a palm reading business there, and sell a few related knick knacks and books. Above the storefront is a tiny apartment. I plan to rent it out to make my payments. I will live in the back storeroom of the first floor. You don't need a stock room when you are in the palm reading business."

"You remind me of my sister Maxi. She started out in Chicago that way, and is now quite wealthy. She has made a business out of buying buildings, converting them into condos, and then renting them out. I dare say I am talking with one future, very wealthy woman."

Milky Way broke out in a ditsy, pleased grin. "I am heading over to the burger place next door for a quick lunch. Do you want to join me? Zeke's receptionist won't be back for an hour or so. You can only get a job app from her."

"I will pass on your invitation, due to my doing some serious job hunting today. This former burger flipper has got to find a new place to work his magic with a spatula. You were right on everything you said, just in case I never see you again."

"Well, may the Gods of the Astral be with you in your search." She replied, and then turned and walked away leaving me standing, drooling, and watching her go. Only my being a dud kept me from following her and asking her out. There was no use starting something I could not finish. Women wanted two things, marriage and children. I had learned my lesson with Jen. Don't put your heart out there. You will only get it stomped on.

About that time, my cell phone rang. I reached in my pants pocket and pulled it out to see who was calling me. I couldn't afford to miss any call that might be a job opportunity. I lived from pay check to pay check.

It was my sister, Maxi. I flipped my cell phone open.

"What is up, and why are you calling me in the middle of my business day?" I inquired, after putting my cell phone to my ear. Not giving her a chance to respond, I continued in a firm voice. "I am on a big case and stake out!"

Maxi believed I worked for Zeke's Feet and that I was a detective. I had lied to her for years telling her that was how I made my living. My fraternal sister was very successful and wealthy. She dabbled in the toy business, but had made her wealth in real estate. I was sure that she would be ashamed of me, if she knew that I had spent my years in California, since college, as a burger flipper.

"I am creeped out, Edmond! A weird guy entered my toy store earlier asking to see you. He was dressed very poorly and had multiple holes in his clothing. I thought I had better call you, and ask you about him. He was so odd, that I have taken my little pea shooter hand gun from beneath the register, and have carried it all morning in my pants pocket."

"Was the odd guy Hindu, Protestant, or Buddhist?" I

asked sarcastically. "Maxi saw anyone not Jewish as odd. We had been raised in a very recluse, strict Jewish family who did not socialize outside our Jewish community and temple. We grew up thinking that Judaism was the one and only true religion, as well as thinking that anyone not from our race was odd or a plague on Earth that God would one day destroy. As a teen and then an adult, Maxi was a little more tolerant than I was, due to the fact that she was a closeted Lesbian, a fact that she carefully guarded. Homosexuality was a forbidden, Sodom and Gomorrah sin in the tight knit Jewish community we grew up in."

"How shall I put it? The guy was challenged! He was wearing an antiquated aviator's cap with the funny flaps that pull down over the ears. His eyes were crossed and his nose was running like a faucet."

"What?" I sputtered, as my knees once more became like jelly.

"You heard me!" She huffed. "He was a cross eyed, runny nosed pervert. He asked me if I knew where you and his mother were. Have you been shacking up with some Protestant, low life, street woman out there in California? The guy was definitely a street person. He didn't look like he had bathed or brushed his teeth in a year. His teeth were green, not to mention the steady stream of green snot that was running from his nose."

"Is he still there?" I asked in a panic. There was no way I could get to her, or help him. I was several states away. He had to be Kris' son, Snicker Doodle; or SD as Joe and I called him. It was possible, that he was a ghost. That really would freak Maxi out. I decided quickly that I didn't want to suggest that to her.

My sister ignored my question and went on with her frightened rant.

"That is not all, Edmond. He was definitely mentally challenged, a boogie man if I ever saw one."

"Oh my Jewish God . . ." I replied feeling weak kneed. The ghosts and dwellers of my 'fifty miles from nowhere' cabin experience were invading my world and that of my sister. "Did the mentally challenged man say he would be back?"

"He hung around for awhile, and then approached me and asked me to tell you he would see you Christmas Eve at the cabin. He wants you to help him string his runway lights, because he can't find his mother to help him. Do you have a street person, older woman girlfriend who is missing, Edmond? I hate to ask you this, but have you and the cross eyed freak murdered his mother?"

"What have I done to make you feel that I would sink so low as to do something like that?" I replied mad. "I can barely swat and kill a fly in the summertime."

"That is a relief." She sighed. "Now tell me, how do you know this freak of a boogie man?"

"He is just someone I met casually last year on an airport runway. He was a cargo pilot. I apologize, Maxi. I may have told him about your toy store and how I had not wanted to play Santa for you." I replied stretching the truth as far as I could. "He is harmless, unless you let him in the cockpit of a plane."

"Well, from now on, refrain from telling freaks about me." She retorted.

"Did he happen to mention anything about a woman

named Kristina, or a teen boy we mutually knew named Joe?" I asked hoping.

"No he didn't mention anyone. I am not in the habit of holding conversations with freaks." She replied. "My register girl was freaked out too."

"Is he gone?" I asked, hoping he wasn't. I wanted to try to convince Maxi to put him on the phone.

"I had to run him out of my little boy's airplane section. He was taking toy planes out of their packages and playing with them. I told him, if he didn't intend to buy them, he shouldn't remove them from their packaging. I was interrupted and turned my back to wait on a paying customer. When I turned my attention back to him, he had just disappeared. I don't know what happened to him. I was spooked and checked all the corners of my toy store, and the storerooms, to make sure he wasn't hiding somewhere with plans to rob or attack me later. I am really freaked out, Edmond. If he contacts you, tell him to stay out of my toy store."

"If I hear from him, I will." I replied, to ease her mind. "Did he leave a message with you for me?"

"He only said for you to be the man at the door of the cabin on Christmas Eve, which you are not doing! You have promised to play Santa for me this year!"

Milky Way's words haunted me. She had spoken of me being a door man. The previous year, I had been the door man in my rented cabin, fifty miles from nowhere. Was she inferring that I would have repeat encounters with the dead? Like Maxi, I was a bit spooked. However, my previous year Christmas gift, (knock on Jewish wood) of

Christmas Crazy ghosts, was a once in a lifetime mystical moment that men only speculate about. Being Jewish, I had refused my Christmas Crazy Ghosts as a gift. I truly had been a jackass at the manger.

CHAPTER THIRTEEN

BOOGIE MAN IN A SANTA SUIT

Returning to Chicago by plane, on the 23rd of December, I dozed off mid-flight. To my surprise, in the land of dreams, I found myself back at the cabin. It was Christmas Eve, just prior to the moment in time and space when Augusta and Caesar had knocked on my rented cabin's door bearing a goose. I was standing in the middle of the cabin with my stomach growling from hunger. Kristina was making a pot of coffee and humming a Christmas Carol. My heart leapt with joy seeing her. I glanced around the room and also saw Joe and Mary sitting by the fireplace. Mary was holding what looked like a year old baby girl. Joe was stoking the fire. Mr. Shepherd, the mailman was reading Christmas cards to the door knocker. I now knew the Kingdom Hall woman was Caesar and Augusta's daughter. Lying in front of the fireplace was a huge husky dog. Somehow, I knew it was the pup the wolf had left the year before. A sense of family swept over me. They were my door knocking family, those coming to me from biological families that were not mine. In the dozed off state, I knew what it was like to adopt a child and love that child that is not biologically yours. I loved everyone in my mountain cabin; including the bed bug phobic Mr. Shepherd. I knew, in the dream, that I was not related to any of them biologically. However, they were my family.

I turned once more to look at Kristina. She was still reversing in age. She looked to be about 35 or 40. Her hair was no longer white like snow. She had salt and pepper hair and her skin was very pale, like she had never had a sun tan. She had no wrinkles to speak of, for her age. She was just younger than the previous year and still just as charming. In my sleep state, I zoned in on the red sweat suit she had on. I hated the red sweat suit. A soft pink or baby blue would have suited her better. Some people couldn't wear the color red, due to their delicate coloring. She was one of them. Even though Kris wasn't Jewish, I wanted her to claim me in the dream. I felt like an abandoned pup, that no one wanted. I was looking at Kris and all the others, but they were paying me no attention. I felt a little rejected and yelled at them, "I am sorry!" They ignored me and I felt rejected just like I had when Jen dumped me, finding out I could not father children. Somehow, I knew that I was asleep in the land of humans, but awake in the land of spirits. I wanted to stay there. Feeling that my time was short there, I walked up behind Kris and surprised her by wrapping my Jewish arms around her, and resting my chin on the top of her salt and pepper hair.

"I have missed you." I stated in the dream. "I am so sorry I said what I did. Please don't slam the door in my face, now that I have found you again. I want to be here with you and the others. I need all of you, Kristina. I am so lonely."

"I am not yours to love, Monty. I have a son and a husband who will one day come to join me. It is purely by accident that I am in this parallel world without them. I fell out of my son's plane and died of a broken neck in a snow drift. I fell out of my husband's heart because I was not the human bed partner he wanted. I must wait for them to come to me. My son loves me and wants to be with me. I will change and make my husband love me when he crosses over."

"You cannot make someone love you, Kristina. If your husband's heart loves another, you must let him go. I had to let Jen go. She wanted children. My body could not produce seed. I fell out of her heart. Waiting for Jen to return to me would be fruitless. It is time for me to love again, to choose another. I choose you, Kristina."

"One cannot tell another soul where, when, or how to let go of loving someone. You found me in a snow bank. By parallel world, treasure hunter's law, you have the right to say finders- keepers and hold on to me forever. However, can you keep something that is not yours? I am waiting in the in-between worlds for my husband and son to come to me. Do I abandon my wait and choose you instead? You still speak of your former fiancé. Have you abandoned your memories of her?"

"Jen is history, Kristina. You have to let your husband become history to. You and I are meant to be together. Why else would I be making my way back to you?"

"I have a husband, Monty. He went a little crazy, when my son was three, discovering other women. He will see the error of his ways here."

"A perverted crazy man will not return to you, innocent like he once was. He will be changed, a different man. You need to let him go, just like I am attempting to let Jen's painful words go. Jen is not the same woman I fell in love with. She has several children by another stud. Your husband is not the same either. What if he comes to this world of yours with another woman or wife on his arm?"

"I am the reason my husband left. I was imperfect in bed. Had I worked harder at being perfect, he would not have walked away when Snicker Doodle was three. The perfect women in town, where he had a part time job as a Santa Bell Ringer, replaced me. I am making myself younger so we can start all over when he gets here. He has been missing from my life for a long time. We are soul mates. Like you, I am lonely, but not lonely enough to take another. I will forgive him."

"Your pervert of a husband has probably dumped you for the tooth fairy." I spit out in anger. "I dare say he will reject you here, just as he did when your son was three. A man's soul is either black or white according to their accumulated deeds. When your husband returns here, he will be the same perverted man who abandoned you on Earth, bringing with him his accumulation of garbage deeds and possibly two or three other wives that he loves more than you."

"I am sorry you wish to jab me with your words, Monty. My husband left me for many reasons. However, the main reason he left me was that he was ashamed of me and our son. I birthed him a less than perfect son. My only baby was born mentally and physically challenged. My husband saw our less than perfect, cross eyed, mentally challenged son as an insult to his being a man. He said our unusual child was my fault, not his. He said he should never have married me, that I was a misfit, an ugly woman. He pointed out to me on many occasions that I was imperfect, and had

161

produced the imperfect. Now, that my husband is older, I am sure he will see the error in his thinking, and want to be with his son. Snicker Doodle needs his father, his bell ringing Santa."

"You are off the wall in your thinking Kristina. An abuser always try to convince the woman everything is her fault." I sputtered as I felt a drawing, like I was about to be sucked out of the dream. "Women do the same thing to men. My Jen is like your Santa. She called me a dud and refused to marry me because I was imperfect in her eyes. I couldn't father children. She was my abuser, the one who wanted a perfect man."

Then Kris started crying and wailing in my dream. I couldn't comfort her. Then everything went pitch black and I felt a hand on my shoulder. Startled, I opened my eyes.

"Are you okay?" A stewardess was asking me, as I blinked.

"Oh God no . . ." I sputtered. "Why did you wake me? I just found my way back to her."

Then I heard snickers and snorts around me, and realized that I had an audience.

"We know all about her!" The man next to me stated laughing.

"You have been talking in your sleep." A woman across the aisle interjected.

"I have tried several times to wake you!" The stewardess added, before she turned and walked toward the front of the plane.

Turning red, I got up and made a speedy escape to the

airplane's rest room in the rear. I guess I had been talking quite loudly in my sleep, and everyone in hearing distance had been amused. I stayed in the cubby hole of a John, till another passenger knocked needing the use of the facility. Then I returned to my seat hoping everyone around me had moved on to some other sort of entertainment.

As I sat down, the man seated behind me leaned forward and asked in a low voice, "Did Kristina choose you or the perverted Santa?"

Trying to be a sport about it, I replied. "She chose the Santa jerk."

He laughed, patted my shoulder, and then sat back in his seat.

~   ~   ~

I made the rest of my flight to Chicago in a depressed state. I now knew there were two worlds and somehow they existed parallel to each other. My world was a lonely one and I wasn't sure I wanted to exist in it. Down deep, I wanted to be where Kris and my cabin family were. I was tired of living my life that was going nowhere, and was somewhat of a lie. I was tired of lying to Maxi, telling her that I was happy in California and living my dream as a detective. If I had my choice, I would enter the parallel world and find Kris. I was sure that I could make her see the error in her thinking, and to love me, not her Boogie Man Abuser Santa of a husband. I wanted someone to love me. I wanted Kris to love me. I was willing to let my memories of Jen go.

Maxi didn't meet me at the airport. It was a weekday, and she had a toy store to run. Taking a cab from the airport was fine with me. It would give me a little time to muster up a happy face for Maxi's benefit. There was no way I wanted my sister giving me the third degree. If she sensed anything was out of whack with me, she would prod, snoop, and poke into my affairs till she got an answer. A Jewish man may be head of his house and rule it, but it is the woman who sets it in order. Maxi had always been good at seeing that my Jewish backside was well chewed on and kept in line. I don't know what I was thinking when I made the decision as a sperm, to be born a twin with her. She had dominated our twin relationship ever since that moment.

I wanted to be happy, but my happiness existed in a parallel universe somehow. I knew I belonged with Kristina. Perverted or not, I was in love with a seventy or eighty year old female ghost, and I was twenty-eight in human years. I had given up trying to explain my craziness to myself. I was in love with her, and that was that. It was something I could never tell Maxi or anyone about.

After retrieving my bags, and hailing a cab, I left the airport. Leave it to me, to get an eighty year old cab driver wearing a Santa Suit. I ignored his Ho-ho-ho and helped him load my bags into his trunk. Once inside the cab, I studied the back of his unkempt, white hair and the cheap red felt Santa hat he had on.

"Where too, Bud?" The cabbie asked. "This sleigh isn't making any money sitting still."

"Maxi's Toy Store." I replied, getting ready to give him the address. "It is . . ."

"I know where that expensive piece of crap, hole in the wall, toy store is." He interrupted. "I have driven a relentless stream of mothers there this year, and every year, so their kids can sit on Santa's knee and have their ugly little elf mugs photographed. Maxi's Toy Store is a hot spot this time of year with the wealthier class."

"That it is," I replied, recalling the long lines of kids that had sat on my knee every year, till I had rebelled and headed for my cabin 'fifty miles from nowhere'. "Do you take your grandchildren there?"

"I don't have any, and don't want any." The Santa cabbie replied, checking his mirrors and then speeding away from the curb.

"You don't have any grandchildren?" I inquired, thinking I had misunderstood him.

"No I do not, and glad of it!" He replied driving like a bat out of hell.

"How about your children, when you were young. Did you take them to see Santa?"

"My first wife presented me with a defect she called a kid. He was three the last time I saw him. He couldn't have been mine. He was the most stupid little sucker ever, and had to take after her side of the family, or whoever she slept with to get him. I dumped him and her ass years ago. She used to bring him to Chicago to see Santa back then. Maxi's wasn't Maxi's back then. The best I recall, it was called Snicker's Toy Store, or something like that. It has been a lot of years. My stupid wife named her kid after the shop. Old man Snicker, or whatever the owner's name was, might have been my wife's kid's dad."

I had temporarily forgotten that Maxi had purchased the toy store business from some old guy when we first graduated college. He made her a good deal, and owner financed it to her. I was thinking his name was Mr. Doodle. I bit my lip, suddenly realizing where Kris had gotten her son's name. I recalled Maxi referring to the man who had sold her the toy store as being named Nick Doodle. Nick had to be short for Snicker.

"Was the toy store's name, Snicker Doodles?" I threw out asking, as the elderly cabbie in a Santa suit drove like a mad man. I hoped I didn't get his cab, when I returned to the airport. He was dangerous with his disrespect of other drivers and careless traffic maneuvers. Then I thought of Snicker Doodle, Kris' son, who flew his snow mobile air-plane causing havoc with all vehicles in his presence.

"Yeah . . . that was the name of the place. Every year, my wife took the kid there to see Santa. I refused to go with her and the stupid little fart. He was a throw back. My wife must have been born with bad genes. I knew the lit-tle cross-eyed creep wasn't mine, the minute he was born. I stuck around for awhile, because her name was on my cabin's deed. Then one day, I decided the piece of a crap cabin wasn't worth sticking around for. I left when he was three and haven't seen her or him since. I divorced her, Chicago style."

"Do you ever miss her or him?" I asked, knowing that he had to be Snicker Doodle's dad.

"I am an old man now, and they are probably dead. Re-tards don't live to be old men. She should be in her eight-ies, if she is alive. Personally, I hope she was swallowed up in my cabin's outhouse hole and drowned in it. In order to get a divorce from her, I had to sign over the cabin to her. It was a choice of paying a lifetime of child support or giv-ing her the cabin. I got it stuck to me."

"I see . . . ," I replied wanting to strangle the obnoxious, Boogie Man in a Santa hat. I couldn't father children. At least he had one. Mentally challenged or not, I would have loved my son forever.

"The witch stuck it to me." The cabbie stated as he ran a red light, causing a car to skid in order to miss him.

"Is your second wife living?" I asked, trying to keep the conversation going and pump him for what information I could get from him. If I made it back to Kris, I could tell her what her Santa was really like.

"My second wife has never wanted children. She has chosen to keep her figure and look good for me. I had a right to find someone else. My first wife played around and presented me with a misfit. Those marriages don't count. My first wife was a dunce. She would iron my shirts and trousers. I would wear them to go see the gorgeous girl I really wanted to be with. She is this Santa's babe. To answer your question, we have six dogs and three cats. None of our animals are misfits. They are all pedigreed. I have insisted on it."

"Pedigreed . . . ," I repeated, rolling my yes. He had his back to me. "Your first son wasn't pedigreed?"

"Are you deft? I told you he was a throw back." The obnoxious man stated roughly.

"Define throwback for me." I replied.

"A throwback is a deformed, sick inside, or mentally challenged kid. I would never have married my first wife, had I known she couldn't produce healthy babies. She produced a misfit that wasn't mine and expected me to love the brainless, little deformed fart. I don't eat second day bread, drink stale coffee, or waste my time on useless throwbacks. She produced the broken cup. I left him in her hands to mend. It was her genes, not mine, that caused him to be the way he was. I am a pedigree man."

I was totally appalled at his words. However, it was his cab and I would be out of it in fifteen minutes time. I wondered what Kris had ever seen in him?

"What was your first wife's name?" I asked, wondering if he even remembered.

"Why bother remembering her name." He replied.

"How about your son, that you say is not yours, what is his name."

"Would you believe my idiot first wife insisted on naming him Snicker Doodle? You know where she got that name. I have already told you."

I grabbed for the cab's door handle, and steadied myself. He was indeed talking about my Kristina. I could feel my Jewish blood pressure rising. I wanted to kill the obnoxious sucker. At the same time, I was pissed thinking that this was the man she was waiting for. He was an egotistical jerk in a Santa Suit. I was about to explode, like a balloon popping, when he pulled over to the curb in front of Maxi's and stopped the cab.

"That will be Twenty –five dollars, bud." He stated.

I pulled out my billfold and paid him. What I really wanted to do was wipe up the pavement with him. After he opened the trunk, I retrieved my bags quickly. He then slammed the trunk closed, got back into his cab, and sped away, cloud covering me with exhaust fumes from his muffler. I coughed and hacked for a moment.

How was I going to tell Kris, if I ever managed to make my way to her again, that I had met her missing Santa husband? How was I going to tell her that he was definitely not returning to her? How could I tell her that he had traded her and Snicker Doodle in for a new wife, six pedigreed dogs, three cats, and a half ass job as a cab driver?

As I watched the guy drive away, it suddenly dawned on me that Kris was dead to human existence, but Snicker Doodle might not be. He had never entered my cabin that was 'fifty miles from nowhere' the previous Christmas. S.D. may have managed, somehow, to make it to Chicago looking for me. He may have been physically in Maxi's Toy Store, the morning my sister called me in a spooked frame of mind

~   ~   ~

Picking up my bags, I made my way to the toy store's door.

"Edmond . . . ," Maxi squealed, when I walked in the front door. She left the busy register she was on, and threw her arms around my neck. Then in Jewish fashion, she kissed me on the cheek and said, "Shalom, brother."

"Peace to you, sister."

"I am so glad to see you. I have some exciting news to tell you." She then stated pulling me toward the back stock room.

When we reached the stockroom, I replied, "Well, it must be exciting, if you are this happy to see me." I replied picking her up off the floor like she was a rag doll and swinging her around in a circle and then sitting her feet back down on the floor.

"I have met someone, Edmond. I know she is the one I want to make a commitment to. I have just got to catch her first." She spit out and laughed.

"Don't tell me you are off chasing some straight girl again?" I spit out. We were twins. I knew her like a book. We had grown up as each other's best friend. Maxi was a Jewish lesbian, a fact that she kept a guarded secret. Only I knew her secret. Our parents were oblivious to it.

"I quit chasing straight girls when we got out of college." She retorted, hitting me on the shoulder.

"Well, I am glad to hear that. What is this new Miss Right like?" I asked good natured.

"Well, she is not exactly like you and me, but I am just positive she is the one. I have known her for quite a few years. I just have never chosen to pursue her. Also, I have been a little too busy making my niche in the business world to ask her out, not to mention she married a straight guy and was off the grid for awhile."

"You don't want to get mixed up with some lesbian nit-wit with a bunch of baggage. You deserve better than that, Maxi. You deserve someone that thinks you and only you walk on water. Those types always go running back to their ex-spouses."

"Don't go using those Protestant phrases on me, Edmond. Christ walked on water. The children of Israel crossed the red sea on dry ground. We are one up on them. I have a few exes in my own background. Just because I, a Lesbian, couldn't marry them, doesn't mean that we weren't couples."

"Touché," I replied. "I have had my share of ex-girlfriends

too. I broke up with one last week." I stated lying.

"You didn't tell me you were going with anyone?" Maxi replied.

"You say the current focus of your attention is not like you and me. Are you saying she is a different color, doesn't speak English, or what?"

"Well, for starters, she is not Jewish. However, I am sure that I can convert her."

"What is she, a Muslim or maybe a Buddhist?"

"She . . . she is a divorced Kingdom door knocker." My sister quickly spit out, and then bit her lip waiting for my reaction.

I broke out in a snort and then laughter. "You have got to be kidding!"

"I am not kidding. My heart melted like butter when I laid eyes on her. She is hot."

"She has to be hot to attract the attention of your cold heart." I replied teasing her. "Wasn't it last Christmas you were seeing that iceberg lettuce girl from your food coop? What happened to her?"

"She was too picky of an eater. I got tired of eating iceberg lettuce salads and nothing else when I went to her place. You know how I like to eat."

"That I do." I replied grinning at her. She gave me another sucker punch on the arm.

"How long did you date the girl you just broke up with in California?"

"It was a short lived romance. It lasted a couple of weeks."

I replied lying. "I don't need a steady girl, Maxi. When I do need a female companion on my arm for social events, one of the girls at the Agency usually accompanies me."

"I swear, Edmond, you are hopeless. One night stands are not going to get you anywhere. You are going to need a woman to warm your big Jewish feet when you are old. They don't make water bottles big enough." My sister retorted seriously.

"Your Jewish feet are as big as mine. Your Kingdom door knocker will probably wrap yours in her pamphlet literature to warm them, and then go sleep in a different holier than thou bed."

"You have one coming for that dig, Edmond. You just wait."

"Forget my dating habits, Maxi. Tell me about your new heart throb, the one you haven't had the time to catch yet."

"She is a friend of yours. She just wandered in here when I first opened the shop this morning, looking for you. She said she knocked on your cabin door last year, trying to convert you. She said you used her literature for something that was in her book an abomination. She wouldn't tell me what the abomination was."

I gasped, knowing Maxi had a visitation from Angelica. She was the deceased daughter of Caesar and Augusta. Angelica was a ghost.

"I don't think you will be able to catch her, Maxi. She will be here one day and gone the next. It is who she is."

"If she is going to be at your cabin this year, I am going to the cabin and you can stay here and mind my business. She is the one, Edmond. I just know it. She made my skin tingle and I felt really cold. Every hair on the back of my neck stood up. I have never had that reaction with any woman."

"Well, I hope you asked her for her telephone number, because I don't have it. Furthermore, I didn't rent the cabin this year. Someone else has it reserved. You are stuck with me playing Santa for the holidays."

"Telephone number . . . ," Maxi slowly said and then turned to me asking, "You really don't have her number?"

"Sorry, Sis, she isn't in my black book."

"Damn it all to Protestant hell!" Maxi spit out.

Occasionally, my sister cursed when she was mad at herself for pulling some dumb stunt. I wanted to laugh at her, but I didn't dare. She hadn't asked for Angelica's phone number. I was totally amused.

"May my Jewish God have mercy on you for not getting her number, your foul mouth, and your current state of lusting insanity . . . ," I replied.

~   ~   ~

After our brief conversation, Maxi returned to her toy store customers, and I wandered upstairs to my sister's apartment to shower and make myself comfortable after the long plane flight. After showering, I sprawled naked across Maxi's guest room bed to relax and watch a little TV, till Maxi's Toy Store doors closed for the day. It was the 23rd day of December.

Relaxed from the hot shower, I suppose I dozed. Suddenly, I felt a hand nudging my shoulder. I jumped up quickly and grabbed the edge of the bed's spread to cover my naked manhood. I thought it was Maxi walking in unexpectedly on me. It was not Maxi. Mary, from my cabin experience, was standing at the foot of the bed staring at me with big eyes. I was embarrassed and blushed.

"I . . . I am sorry you have caught me with my pants down." I spit out holding the spread about me. Then fearing she would disappear on me, I sputtered. "Where is Joe?"

"He is watching the December 23rd portal entrance for me. He is afraid I won't make it back thru to him and our baby." She replied, while pointing to her belly which was no longer big or moving about.

"You had your baby . . . ," I stated grinning.

"Yes, it was a girl." She replied smiling. "I named her Eve. She was born just an hour or so after you left us."

"Eve is a good name." I replied, regretting not being there for the event. "Why have you chosen to visit me, Mary? How have you managed to do so?"

"You fed me last year and didn't eat yourself. I owe you a thank you. My Earth mother always told me a respectable girl always said thank you and wrote thank you notes. You are getting a thank you visit. Thank you for taking me and Joe in last year, in your cabin 'fifty miles from nowhere'. We actually died before reaching your cabin, in case you are wondering. We got lost in the blizzard, after wrecking our snowmobile in the middle of nowhere. We succumbed to the elements. Knocking on your cabin door was our first experience as ghosts. I was carrying a little ghost when we knocked. My unborn, human baby also died in the blizzard."

"I see," I stated, continuing to hold the spread about me.

"Is Kris and the others with you and Joe, beyond the portal?"

"Everyone but Kris is. She has unfinished Christmas business and has entered the December 23rd Christmas portal when it opened this morning."

"Where does that portal open at?" I asked, trying to figure out where Kris was heading.

"She has gone to look for her son, Snicker Doodle. Her human body died last year from exposure. She was riding a snow mobile with her son, when she fell off in a snow drift. He did not realize she had fallen off. He couldn't retrace his tracks in the snow to find her. He is alive and she is dead. She says he cannot survive without her. He has been wandering aimlessly for the last year looking for her."

I was suddenly extremely jealous. Kris had entered the Earth realm in search for Snicker Doodle, not me. I felt second class dumped, just like Jen had dumped me for someone else. My old pains of rejection surfaced. I ached on the inside with unbelievable, repeat performance, emotional pain. I tried not to show it, for Mary's sake.

"Will you give Kris and the others in your world a message for me?" I asked, feeling very hurt and in anger.

"Sure, what is it?" Mary asked sweetly.

"Tell them I want them all to butt out of my life. I don't want any more visitations. Tell Kris I am sorry I ever rescued her from the snow bank and took her in. She is just like Jen. I am not good enough for her." I sputtered.

"Does that include me?" Mary asked, with tears in her young, ghost eyes, as she began to fade away.

Hurting Mary had not been my intention. I was mad at Kris for choosing to visit Snicker Doodle, not me. Sometimes a person says things they don't mean. After Mary was gone, and I had cooled down, I regretted not using my visitation with Mary wisely. I should have asked about Mr. Shepherd, the wolf pup, and the three Wise brothers. I should have also sent word, by Mary, to Katrina that her husband was not returning to her. I had wasted my visitation.

I sat down on the bed and ran my fingers thru my hair. I had blown my opportunity. How could a Jewish man, like my-self, be so stupid? Jewish men were supposed to be leaders in trade, business, education, and wealth. Jen was right. I was a dud.

~   ~   ~

The Christmas season came and went. I played Santa on Christmas Eve for the patrons of Maxi's toy store. Down deep, I wanted to return to the cabin. However, I resisted the temptation. Kristina had gone seeking Snicker Doodle, not me. I had no further visitations.

Five Christmas seasons, after Mary's visitation, came and went. I had no further visitations. I continued to fly home to play Santa for Maxi. She continued her non-ending search for the perfect mate. I avoided women, in fear of being hurt again. In the second of those five years, I managed to land a part time detective position with a small detective agency that was one of Zeke's rivals. My secret plan was to work for the rival agency, while I continued to pester Zeke to hire me. Last count, I had filled out 257 applications and turned them in to him or his receptionist.

Zeke's Detective Agency was the most famous detective

agency in southern California. He worked for and intermingled with the rich and the famous. His lady friend, Jackie, was a hair dresser and did the hair of multiple Hollywood stars. I was determined to work for Zeke, sooner or later. In the meantime, I was busy following cheating spouses, the specialty of the agency I worked for. I was more of a motel window photographer, than a detective. However, it was better than flipping burgers. During the five years, I settled into my California life and didn't talk about my cabin experience. I pushed it as far down inside me as I could get it, the place where I had also pushed my memories of Jen. I moved on with my life.

CHAPTER FOURTEEN

THE GHOST CHILD

Five years had passed since my last visitation from my cabin ghosts. I had moved forward in my life, and had been a detective working for Zeke's rival several years. Once more it was the Hanukkah and Christmas season. I always took my vacation in December and flew home to Maxi for the holidays. This year was no different. I had my plane ticket purchased and my bags packed.

Since the cabin incident, I no longer argued with Maxi about playing Santa for her on Christmas Eve. My life was predictable, and I wasn't seeing a psychiatrist or ghosts. Little did I know, I was living in the lull before a storm! The two women I was running from were about to reenter my life, and open up all my old wounds.

On December 23rd, I once more boarded an air plane and made my way to Chicago and my sister's toy store. I entered my sister's life, as I always did, thru the front door of her business. Usually, she scurried, dropping whatever task she was doing, to greet me. On this particular trip, she was in her office shuffling papers, and didn't see me arrive. The girl at the toy store's register told me where to find her.

I walked in and sat my bag down in her Toy Store office, which also doubled as her real estate office.

"Ah em . . . don't I get a hug this year?" I asked getting her attention, leaning on the frame of her office.

"Edmond . . . ," She squealed as she always did.

From the time Maxi and I were born, she had squealed when excited. My Jewish mother said she never cried as a baby. She squealed and screeched line a Ban Chi. I was the good baby, according to mom, the one who never caused any trouble. We were twins, but oh so different. I was a straight guy, a dud, who couldn't father children. Maxi was a Lesbian who chased straight skirts, and wondered why I didn't. She was wealthy, I was not.

My sister, after giving me a squeal and a Jewish hug, poked my thin Jewish frame with her finger.

"You are as skinny as a rail, Edmond. What have you been eating out in California, a steady diet of tofu?" She inquired, looking me over.

"It wouldn't hurt you to eat a little tofu, sis. It looks to me like you have been eating maybe one too many Chicago pizzas." I retorted. "Or have you been dipping in your toy store's Christmas chocolates a little too much?"

"I started a diet yesterday. For your information, I met a skirt who turned out to work in a pastry shop. I am afraid I have eaten one too many trying to hook up with her. I got twenty pounds of fat out of the deal, and she married the bakery owner, Mr. Goldstein."

"You need to quit chasing straight skirts, sis. At your age, you should know better. They are not going to give you the time of day, much less go out with you."

"I am going to make a New Year's resolution to lose twenty pounds, and no more chasing straight skirts." She replied seriously. "I have different plans for my future. I have dated all the Jewish Lesbians in our community. I think I will give the Protestant ones a try."

"Have you got my Protestant, Santa Suit ready for tomorrow?" I asked, grinning at her. My sister never changed. She would be back to chasing Jewish straight skirts by Valentine's Day.

"Cleaned, pressed, and kid proof . . . ," She replied, motioning for me to sit down in front of her desk. She resumed her seated position in her desk chair, behind a mound of paperwork.

"I hope one of your snotty nosed little customers, doesn't give me the flu again this year. I have flown home to California sick every year that I can remember." I replied, doing my yearly complaining, which she had come to expect. It was almost like my complaining had become a holiday tradition. Since my episode in the cabin, 'fifty miles from nowhere', I just tried to slide thru the holidays and not make waves. Whatever Maxi wanted to do, we did. I didn't want another round of getting hurt by Jen, or a ghost named Kris.

"This will be the last year I make you play Santa, Edmond. I know you are going to be happy about that."

"Have you finally found a decent, Jewish replacement for me?" I asked sarcastically, and relieved. I had never enjoyed enter-acting with the long lines of Santa crazy mothers and their offspring. I was Jewish. I only played the part every year to please Maxi, and help her turn an extra dollar or two for her business. She was Jewish and so was I.

"Me replace you . . .? Never . . . !" She replied as she got up to answer a knock on the toy store's back door. She had ordered in Chicago, five cheese pizza. We were Jewish and didn't eat pork. Sausage was not an option for us as a topping. After paying and tipping the delivery boy, she returned to her desk which became our table. We simultaneously flipped open the box lid, chose a piece, and started to devour it. I hadn't eaten on the plane, and apparently she had not had lunch yet. As she was chewing, Maxi jumped back into conversation. "I am planning on making some drastic changes, after the Christmas toy season is over. I hope you will be pleased, Edmond."

"What kind of change?" I asked, finishing off my first piece and taking a drink of soda.

"I am not getting any younger, Edmond. In my opinion, it is time for me to close the toy store. I have made more than enough money off of it and my real estate holdings to last a lifetime. It is time for me to grow up, and quit playing with toys. As you have always pointed out, we are Jewish, not Protestant and Christmas crazy. I feel a need to get back to my Jewish grass roots, as well as visit some of the memorials and sites dear to our faith. Neither of us has seen the Holocaust memorial or the Wailing Wall. Neither of us has been to Israel. I realized this last year that I am off my path, and that is the reason I am not meeting that special someone. I want to meet someone, Edmond. I don't want to die having never loved, or been loved. Years ago, you told me that I wasn't going to meet someone, as long as I was obsessed with making a dollar, and playing with toys. You were right."

"You are going to close your toy store?" I asked in total shock.

"Yes, Edmond, I am. I am going to have a closeout sale after Christmas, and then convert the retail space into apartments. The blonde bimbo, I tried to fix you up with five or so years ago, has been a good employee. I am going to let her manage my 52 apartments. I am lonely, Edmond. It is time."

Until that moment, I didn't realize that Maxi and I had something in common. I was lonely due to being a dud of a man, and she was lonely due to being a Jewish lesbian. I never realized she was suffering some of the same emotional pains I was. I had been rejected because I was not a sperm producing male. She had been rejected by life, because she was a male living in a girl's body.

"Whatever you want to do is fine with me, Sis. You are right about the fact that it is time for us to abandon what is not working for us. Just like you, I am too busy being a detective, to meet a special Jewish woman." I stated to please her. Down deep, I was positive that I was going to die old and alone. No woman wanted a dud for a man. I had resigned myself to that.

"I am pleased to hear you agree with me, Edmond."

"I know I have been raised to think of you as my sister, Maxi. However, I am aware that you are a male like me. You just happen to be stuck in the wrong gender of body. Whatever you want out of life is fine with me, including a straight skirt if you can catch one."

"Thank you, Edmond. You have been a good brother. What would you like for a gift for the holidays?"

"I hope you are going to spend some of your wealth buying me, your poor brother, a new camera for a gift. My old one is shot. I dropped it in a swimming pool last week; or should I say a cheating husband shoved me and my camera in." I replied finishing off my third piece of pizza.

"A camera is nothing, Edmond. I will see that you have one before you board your plane returning home. I was thinking of giving you something more of a lasting nature that will go up in value. Remember when I told you five years ago that you shouldn't waste your money renting a mountain cabin?"

"Yeah . . . you informed me that I should buy one, and then rent it out the parts of the year that I didn't want to use it." I replied with all the memories of Kristina suddenly flooding back.

"Well, I have decided you need an annual break at the holidays, even if I am not always around to share the Hanukkah season with you. I want to buy you a cabin, Edmond. You can visit it once a year, and rent it out the other eleven months. If I don't meet someone special soon, I will meet you there every year as we grow older, for Hanukkah. I want to buy you that cabin you rented."

I choked on my pizza and gasped. Regaining control, after Jewish her slapping the hell out of my back, I continued. "You want to buy me that cabin?" I managed to spit out, while thinking of the misery the cabin 'fifty miles from nowhere' six or so years earlier had caused me.

"You seemed thrilled with it back then, when you rented it." She replied, returning to her pizza on the other side of the desk.

"I am glad you are choosing a future for yourself, Maxi. However, I just really am not interested in the roughing it, cabin experience anymore. Keep your money in the bank. I would prefer a really nice camera."

"A camera it is, I guess." She replied taking the last sip of her soda. "Maybe you will change your mind somewhere down thru the years. If you do, my offer stands."

"You are the best, Maxi. However, I will be happy if you just drop in on me out in California, between your jaunts here, there, and elsewhere around the globe. You have never been to California to visit me. Granted my studio apartment is tiny, but it is big enough for company. It is time for me to host you." I shot back.

"I guess we are finally growing up and facing life, aren't we?" Maxi replied asking. "I have enough money for both of us, Edmond. Would you like to go with me to Israel, and embrace our Jewish roots together?"

"Will your Jewish God approve of the fact that you will pay for airplane tickets to the Holy Land, with Santa dollars?"

"Oh you . . .," she laughed, grabbing the last piece of pizza, before I could take it. We had sparred with words since we came out of our mother's womb. It was who we were.

"Personally, I am staying away from any Jewish holy ground that our Jewish God might strike me dead on. I have shared in your money making abomination. I have worn the clothing of iniquity, the red Santa's suit."

Maxi laughed. Then, our impromptu meal was interrupted by Maxi's cell phone ringing.

As she spoke with one of her wholesalers, I silently faced the fact that this was my last Christmas Eve as a Santa in Chicago. My predictable world, and that of my sister, was changing; coming to an end as it once was. Our Jewish mother had died about eighteen months prior. Our father, a jewelry store owner, had been dead for three years. There was nothing holding Maxi and I from moving on to whatever lay ahead.

~   ~   ~

On Christmas Eve morning, I donned my dry cleaned Santa Suit and seated myself in Maxi's red sleigh to play Santa to her patrons for the last time. I would work a twelve hour shift, breaking briefly here and there for quick meals and trips to the store's rest room facilities. It was two minutes till nine. The store's door was about to open. A long line of mothers with kids were waiting outside. It was prestigious in Chicago to have your child's photo taken with Santa at Maxi's aloof, high end, toy store. Maxi catered to the wealthy of the city. Her photos with Santa cost three times what they did in the discount stores. Maxi had become a wealthy woman. She knew how to work the upper-class, and extract their dollars at Christmas time.

Taking a deep breath, when the toy store's doors opened, I shouted my yearly "Ho-ho-ho" and the madness began. Child after child climbed on and off of my lap. Cameras flashed, letters to Santa taken, and candy canes were handed out. Mothers were given a sprig of mistletoe, and told they could collect a kiss from Santa at the back door when the store closed, if they wished to return for the evening. I winked at the mothers and patted their darlings' heads. It was part of the charm of seeing Maxi's exclusive Santa. Mother's were given just as much attention, as their child. However, no mother ever returned Christmas Eve night, with their sprig of mistletoe, to collect on the promised kiss.

Mid morning, Maxi cut in between two children and whispered in my ear. "Just down the line, there is a little girl with no shoes on. No decent upper class mother would let her kid be seen here in winter, barefoot like that. I don't know who she is. She doesn't have a parent with her. Get her on and off your lap quickly. Time is money. Give her a cane and send her on her way. I have told the photographer to skip taking a shot of her. Beware, brother dear, she looks like the type who might be carrying this year's flu and strep throat bug. She is as washed out white, as any mono carrying child I have ever seen."

I glanced down the line and spotted the little girl. She definitely did look like some street person's kid who had wandered in. Her parents were probably waiting on the outside, not having money for the photographer. There was a seventy five dollar fee to have your photo made, as well as to see Santa. Maxi's Toy Store Santa was not free.

The line moved smoothly, and the little girl's time arrived. My assistant didn't help her on my lap, like she did the others. She just ignored her. That teed me a little. I wasn't wealthy like my sister. The pale little barefoot girl climbed on my lap, unassisted. Then she looked up at me sweetly with big eyes and grinned.

"What would you like for Christmas?" I asked her, not bothering to look at the camera. I knew that the photographer had been told to ignore her.

"Why do you hate me?" The little girl asked in a serious voice.

"I don't hate you." I replied, reaching over in my assistant's stash and getting her a candy cane. It was very evident that my assistant was not going to do so.

"Mama says you do." She retorted.

"What is your name?" I asked, trying to get around the mama comment.

"You should know me. I know you! I used to listen to you, when I was a baby. I remember you telling someone to save the half of a cheese sandwich for Mary. My mother says she was the one you saved the cheese sandwich for."

I know all the blood drained instantly from my face. No wonder my assistant was ignoring her. She probably couldn't see her. Joe and Mary's little girl was sitting on my lap. She was a ghost. At the same time, I wondered how it was possible that Maxi had been able to see her.

"Where are your parents?" I asked, scanning the line of mothers waiting.

"I don't know. When the between worlds, holiday portal opened yesterday, I got loose from them, ran, and made my way here. I want to know why you hate me and our cabin friends so much. You told all of us, years ago, to butt out and never bother you, ever again. Butt is on my no-no word list."

I snorted. Then, out of nowhere, a car backfired outside of the toy store's front door. I glanced toward the front of the store, as did all the mothers in line. When I returned my attention to my lap, the little girl was gone. I trembled, knowing that I had once more experienced a visitation. I glanced down my line of waiting mothers, to see if they had shared the experience. Apparently, they had not.

All day, I waited for another visitation. None occurred. I was disappointed. Down deep, I wanted to see them all again. However, only Joe and Mary's child chose to visit me on my last stint as Maxi's Christmas Eve Santa. Down deep, I was sad. I had loved all of them. I just hadn't realized it back then. My only sorrow with the cabin experience was that Kris, like Jen, had dumped me. I kept telling myself that years would eventually numb my feelings for Kris, as they had my love for Jen. I now hated Jen, and had mixed emotions concerning Kristina.

About fifteen minutes before the store was to close on Christmas Eve, I approached my sister about Joe and Mary's little girl. My line to see Santa was empty. Most kids were home and tucked in, asleep and waiting for Santa.

"Why did you let that sick, parent less, barefoot little girl get on my lap?" I asked, while pouring myself a cup of stale black coffee in her office. The coffee had been made early morning, before the store opened. I needed a shot of something stronger, but it would have to do in the moment.

"I have been too busy with satisfying last minute shoppers, to worry about your line."

"Do you at least recall her?" I asked.

"Hundreds of kids came thru this store today. They are all a blur." She replied, pouring herself a cup of the black, stale coffee. "You better get the lead out and return to your sleigh. I heard the front door bell sound. That Robin Steiner Jones is probably bringing her two brats to see you late again this year. She doesn't really want to bring them, being Jewish like you and I. I think her and her husband argue every Christmas Eve till she does, making her the last in the door. I told her when we were young, and in college, not to marry a Christmas loving Protestant. Mixed marriages do not work."

I gulped a swallow of the cold, stale, black brew and then returned to my sleigh for my last fifteen minutes as Santa Claus. I didn't pay any attention to who was in line. I had smiled and said my "Ho-ho-ho" for way too many in my twelve hour shift. This mother wasn't getting the smile, the wink, or the Maxi experience. I was on my last nerve, and running on pure adrenaline and black coffee. I didn't even bother to look up as my assistant picked up her basket of candy canes.

"Are you ready?" My assistant whispered, as I settled into my sleigh seat and took a deep breath.

"Ready as I ever will be." I replied.

A little boy stepped forward and my elf assistant helped him climb onto my lap. I patted his back with my red mitten and gave him a ho-ho-ho. Then, I forced myself to look up, so the photographer could snap our photo. While smiling for the photographer, I gasped seeing who the mother of the boy was.

If there was a Jewish God, he was getting even with me, as I spent my last few minutes as a Protestant Santa. A very pregnant, about to pop Jen was the little boy's mom. She had three other little ones in tow, ranging in ages from about five down to two. All my pent up emotional pains, concerning her dumping me and calling me a dud, swept over me in waves as her four kids climbed on and off my lap, having their photos made, and telling me what they wanted Santa to bring them.

"She has a lot of nerve . . . just get thru it!" I muttered in disgust, as Jen paid the photographer.

The last child who was about three climbed on my lap.

"What would you like for Christmas?" I asked, skipping asking her name. I had once dreamed of having a houseful of children with Jen. The one on my lap should have been mine, had not my Jewish God cursed my maleness.

"I want my daddy to come home." She stated with sad big eyes.

"Is your daddy in the army, or possibly away on business?" I forced myself to ask politely, just trying to get thru the experience with my mouth and emotions intact.

"He is in Heaven." The little girl replied. "Do you think you could fly your sleigh up there and bring him back to me?"

I bit my lip and glanced up at Jen, who had her arms folded across her very huge pregnant belly. I didn't smile.

"I cannot bring your father back in my sleigh. He is an angel now. God needs him to fly all over Heaven to do business for him. I could suggest to God that he send you a new daddy, one who will give your mother another six, big fat belly babies." I replied, not being able to hold my pent up anger at Jen. I knew she was listening intently. I had never got to express how I felt about her dumping me. I had never got to tell her what I thought of her and her opinion of me as a dud. Insinuating that she was fat was all that I could manage with her kid on my lap. Believe me, I wanted to explode and tell her off for even daring to get in my Santa line.

"Would you send me a daddy with six kittens instead? Mama says she can barely afford to feed us, now that daddy is gone. She says we are on welfare, whatever that is."

I glanced up at Jen. She was red faced.

"Welfare is a good thing." I stated with a hint of joy in my voice. "One gets out of life, what one chooses." I replied in a sarcastic voice, directed at her. Then I gave the little girl a candy cane and set her off my lap.

"I . . . I honestly didn't think you were still doing the Santa bit here for Maxi, Monty. The last I heard, you were out in California pursuing a life as a detective. I just got my check late this afternoon. This store is the only one near me with a Christmas Eve Santa. I haven't had the money till today, to bring them. I will know better next year."

I couldn't control my feelings or my mouth any longer.

"You are on welfare, and you take your four hungry kids to see the most expensive Santa in town?" I huffed in a disgusted voice. "I wasn't raised to be welfare trash and neither was Maxi. Apparently, you have taken a slippery slide down into the gutter of life."

"I am doing the best I can, Monty. My dead, jerk of a husband left me knee deep in debt and no life insurance. He claimed he was too young to need it. Now, I am on welfare and food stamps. Does that please you, Monty?" She yelled, and then burst into tears.

I did not rise from my sleigh to comfort her. However, I did eye the four children she had with her. They could have been mine, had I not been a dud. I really did not know what to say to her. She had destroyed me, when she broke up with me a week before our wedding. I was thirty three now, and still trying to deal with her painful words that had stabbed to death my feelings that I was a man. Was I supposed to feel sorry for her?

At that point, Jen grabbed her kids' hands and left the

store. I did not run after her. She was my nightmare. You don't chase nightmares.

"What was her problem?" Maxi asked, walking up to me with her register money bags and the toy store's front door keys in her hand. It was 9 P.M., closing time.

"That big bellied woman was Jen, Maxi. Those four brats are hers. Her husband has recently passed away. She is on welfare and food stamps. In case you have forgotten, she broke up with me one week before our wedding. She deserves the gutter hell she is living in." I sputtered.

Maxi knew about my being dumped by Jen. She just didn't know why. Maxi did not know that I could not father children.

"Is there any chance of the two of you getting back together?" Maxi asked, as she helped me remove my fake white beard, wig, and Santa cap. There were no customers left in the store.

"No . . . Sis. It was over between us years ago." I replied. "I hope she rots in her welfare state."

"What happened between the two of you that has caused you to be so angry, harsh, and cold towards her?" Maxi asked, fiddling nervously with her keys for some reason.

"She dumped me. Isn't that good enough reason?" I asked, biting my lip to control my emotional anger.

CHAPTER FIFTEEN

THE RETURNING NIGHTMARE

Waking on Christmas morning in Maxi's apartment, I rolled over and groaned. I had held one too many snotty nosed elves on my lap the previous day, during my twelve hour shift. My bones ached and my nose was running. Once more, the gentiles' kids had infected me with some sort of Christmas crazy virus. I felt awful, and was sure that I was running a fever. However, I dragged myself out of bed, in order to share a breakfast of hotcakes with my sister, a yearly tradition. Her Toy Store was always closed on Christmas Day.

Holding my head, and wiping my nose on the sleeve of my pajamas, I headed for the shower. I wanted to wash as many germs off of me as possible, before heading to my sister's breakfast table. I saw no need to make her ill, if I could help it. Naked as a Jay bird, I reached in the bathroom's shower stall and turned its water on. While I was waiting for the shower's water to warm, I turned to the lavatory sink and stared into the mirror. Letting out a sudden gasp, I grabbed for a bath towel to wrap around my nakedness. A woman was in the doorway staring at me. After covering my manhood, I spun around and then gasped again. It wasn't just any woman. It was one of the women from my 'fifty miles from nowhere" cabin, six years prior. It was the door knocker. She was dead, a ghost.

"What do you want?" I sputtered nervously.

"I don't want anything. I am on holiday from the in-between worlds, and have chosen to drop by for a visit."

"Don't you mean you have come with Je . . . ova Literature to annoy me?"

"I am sorry about that. I was quite annoying in my human life, wasn't I?" She replied as she looked me up and down. "You aren't bad to look at. Why didn't I notice that back years ago?" She asked ogling me.

Maxi's pink bath towel wasn't covering much.

"Maybe it was because it was your friend Kris that I was interested in." I returned, not really knowing what to say or do.

"Oh, I remember." She stated, looking like a light bulb had gone on in her ditsy ghost head. "I was still in my doorknocker mode. I hadn't laid my human life down yet. I was still under the impression that I needed to hook up with a male door knocker, if I had any chance at all of being one of the 144 thousand. My Christ was coming back to earth to live and reign. You were a Jew, one of a religious persuasion that had killed him. I remember now. Boy . . ., wasn't I a mixed up mess?"

"You are not a door knocker in the in-between worlds?" I asked, knowing I personally had killed no one.

"Religions are not necessary, when you reach the in-between world. The parallel worlds are full of personal Heavens." She replied. "In my Heaven, I am not tired from packing about heavy bags of literature and wearing pinching heels, while I knock on doors. In my Heaven, my feet don't hurt. I carry no heavy bags and wear no shoes. Heaven is different to each individual who goes there."

"Who else of our cabin friends has a Heaven where you are" I asked, not fully understanding what she was telling me.

"Mr. Shepherd, the mailman, lives in his Heaven next to mine. He sleeps on bed bug free sheets that are as white as snow. He receives mail, instead of delivering it. Every day is sunny in his Heaven. He always hated the rain, snow, and sleet that he had to deliver mail in." She replied.

"What is Kris' Heaven like?" I asked, hoping there was some mention of me in it.

"She cooks and bakes Christmas cookies in her Heaven, to occupy her time till her husband joins her, after laying his human body down. In her Heaven, her human husband is in love with her. In her Heaven, she plans to have a houseful of kids by him. Her Heaven is a place of planning." Angelica replied.

"I don't want to hear anymore." I retorted feeling hurt. I had been in love with Jen who dumped me. Then, I had been a fool and fell in love with Kris, who had dumped me for a man who did not want her. I definitely had a rejection complex.

"I gather you still want us all to stay out of your life?" Angelica asked, as her body started to fade from the feet up.

"Yes . . . , stay out of my life. You and the others only cause me unbelievable emotional pain. I spent a year on a psychiatrist's couch trying to get over caring for all of you. I deserve better."

"I deserved better than to pop out of my human body, and then watch it dying in a snow filled ditch. I was totally lost and needed all of you, when I knocked on your door in a confused, spirit state."

"I didn't know that back then. I thought you, Kris, and the others were alive." I shot back as she faded to her hips. "If I had known you were all ghosts, I probably would have pissed my Jewish pants, hi tailing it out of that cabin."

"Kris was the same as I. She fell out of an airplane in a snowdrift and had terminal injuries. She had just popped from her human body, and was in her spirit form. You rescued her spirit form, not her human one. It was in a snow drift, covered by blowing snow, and dying. Mr. Shepherd's human body was dying in his crashed mail truck, as were the three Wise brothers in their crashed airplane. We were all poppers!" She laughed as she continued to fade. Only her upper torso was visible now. "We popped out of our bodies, knocked on your door in spirit form, and stayed awhile till we got our bearings in our new existences. We waited for our human bodies to finish dying."

"Is Snicker Doodle a ghost?" I asked loudly. She was slowly disappearing.

"No . . . he is an abandoned, forgotten human, who is looking for a father to love him." She yelled back. Then, she was gone.

Where Angelica the door knocker had stood, in Maxi's guest bathroom, a piece of Mormon literature fell to the floor. I broke out in laughter. Apparently, Angelica had changed religions in her new Heaven.

~ ~ ~

After showering, I made my way to my sister's breakfast table. I heard voices as I walked down the hallway, and was in shock when I stumbled into her breakfast room and saw who the voices belonged to. I was speechless. Pregnant, about to pop Jen, was seated at my sister's table for two with a mug of hot coffee in her hands. Seated on the floor, were four red and blonde haired little kids, the same ones that had sat on my lap the previous night before. Jen's kids all had bowls of cereal, and were eating it on place mats on the floor.

Before I could say anything, Maxi stated, "I went and got them last night, Edmond. Jen needs us. She was once, almost family." she stated in a sharp, demanding voice that said I was to keep my Jewish mouth shut and do what she said. "Furthermore, Santa is going to deliver these kids toys here later. They are last on his list this year. They are still waiting for his arrival. Isn't that right?"

"Er . . . uh . . . yes; I think this apartment is his last stop, before going home to the North Pole." I replied, saying what my sister wanted to hear, but not what I wanted to say.

I wanted to tell my sister and Jen to go to Hell. How could Maxi do this to me? How could my sister try to cram Jen down my throat, like the door knocker had once tried to cram literature down her unsuspecting victims' throats? I was totally pissed, but tried not to show it. I took the mug of steaming black coffee that Maxi handed me, and sat down in the floor with the kids. My sister Maxi and pregnant Jen had the two kitchen chairs occupied. The kids seemed pleased to have me join them in the floor for breakfast. I wasn't at all pleased. Forcing a smile, I accepted a spoon from the five year old, who observantly noticed that I did not have a spoon for my bowl of cereal. She handed me hers, which was dripping with milk and goo. I was amused, even though I was going to kill Maxi when I got the chance. Not only that, I was looking forward to my traditional breakfast of hot cakes and Blueberry syrup. Maxi made her own syrup. It was to die for. Cold cereal was a real let down.

I tried to be polite for Maxi's sake. I was a guest in her home. However, I limited my conversation with Jen.

After breakfast, Maxi pulled me into the apartment hallway. In her dominating Jewish manner, she demanded that I slip downstairs into the toy store and put back on the dirty Santa Suit I had worn the previous day, Christmas Eve. She also instructed me that she had placed a bag full of toys next to the Santa's suit for Jen's kids.

"Why are you doing this, Maxi? Jen is Jewish like us. Remember, we celebrate Hanukkah, not Christmas? What makes you think she wants her kids to receive presents from the Protestant's fairy tale Santa?"

"Just do it, Edmond! These kids don't have any toys in their apartment, much less decent food and clothes. After Christmas, I will tell them that Santa isn't real. Besides, I think Jen has abandoned her Jewish roots. She was married to someone not Jewish."

I was totally pissed, but I controlled myself. How could my sister lie to the little kids in the floor, as well as betray me in such a thoughtless manner? Jen was my nightmare! She had made an emotional cripple out of me.

Rather than destroy my relationship with Maxi, I did as I was instructed, all the while making plans to end my visit as quickly as possible. I was sure that my sister thought she was doing good rescuing Jen and her welfare offspring. I was reminded how the door knocker had forced the guests in my cabin, years ago, to read her literature. She had crammed her pamphlet beliefs down their throats. Jen had called me a dud and dumped me, a week before our wedding; cramming the word dud down my throat. There was no way in Hell that Maxi was going to cram poor, penniless Jen and her food stamp kids down my throat now, and expect me to like it.

I did as I was instructed to stay in the graces of my Jewish, lesbian sister. I donned the Santa suit and then burst thru the back door of her apartment shouting ho-ho-ho and then handing out gifts to Jen's kids. Maxi was pleased, Jen cried, and the kids were delighted to have a personal visit from Santa. I was smiling and just trying to survive the morning. My plane back home to California left at two in the afternoon. After the Santa bit, I excused myself and returned to my bedroom to pack and get away from my nightmare, Jen. I was really pissed at my sister. When my bag was packed, I exited the apartment when no one was looking and caught a cab to the airport. Maxi and Jen could take what was left of Christmas and stick it where the sun didn't shine, in my book.

At the airport, I found a quiet spot in a corner, away from other passengers, and seethed. It was four hours till my flight left. Normally, I would have spent that time with Maxi.

As I was sitting in the airport lounge in a very sour mood, a man dressed in white, India type garb walked up and sat down beside me, as if it was the only chair available. I wasn't in the mood for conversation. That didn't seem to matter to the dark skinned fellow in white.

"Why are you sitting here by yourself?" The stranger in a turban asked. His voice sounded a little on the feminine side.

"This is just great," I muttered while rolling my eyes. "I am going to get hit on by a gay Hindu. Do I look like I am not a man?"

"Why are you choosing to bother me?" I retorted harshly, wanting to get rid of him. "I am not gay! Go pester someone else."

"Gay . . . , do you mean you are not happy?" He returned asking. However, he did not give me a chance to answer. He continued. "I am bothering you because you spent the morning with my wife. I think I have the right to bother you. You might be the father of at least one of my children."

"You have me confused with someone, dude. I spent this morning with my sister, Maxi. Now bug off!"

"You spent the morning with your sister and my wife." The man replied not flinching.

"I spent the morning with my sister and indulged a nightmare." I retorted.

"You ate breakfast with your nightmare, my wife." He replied, ignoring my repulsive behavior.

"I assure you that I am not having an affair with your wife, whoever she is. You have me confused with someone." I huffed. "Now, get lost!"

"I am not confused. You joined my wife Jen, my four children, the one about to be born, and your sister who is a man, for breakfast. All of you had cereal. You wanted hot cakes." He threw out shocking me.

"Oh crap." I replied disgusted. "Are you Jen's dead husband?"

"I want you to take my words of rejection and give them to my wife." He replied. "I wish to divorce her in the ever-after of the soul, on the grounds that she is an adulterer. You may also tell her that I did once love her."

"If you want me to go and tell your wife you love her, you can take your want and stuff it. You stole Jen from me, when I was at the lowest point in my life. She dumped me for you. Your four kids and the one on the way should have been mine, had I not been a dud, as she put it."

"Don't get so uptight, portal keeper. Five men stole her from me. None of her offspring are mine. I want you to tell her that I know. That is the message I want you to deliver to her."

"Jen's kids are not yours?" I repeated. I hated Jen, but I had never seen her as promiscuous or a cheater in the years I dated her in college.

"After we were married for six months, I went to the doctor and found out I couldn't father children. I had the mumps, a childhood disease, when I was in my teens. It destroyed my ability to produce live sperm. One by one, babies arrived, and kept arriving. My wife and I argued about each arrival, as to who fathered them. I demanded DNA testing, just before my death. The tests came back and I was right. We had a miserable marriage while I was alive. I blew my brains out, to escape her and the children who were not mine."

I lost it laughing. Apparently, Jen had spent just as many miserable years as I had. It was Jewish Karma. She called me a dud, and then unknowingly married a man who couldn't father children. My Jewish God had avenged me, or his Hindu God had. I almost rolled in the airport lounge floor with uncontrollable laughter and tears. The ghost of Jen's husband just sat and waited for me to get over my delight.

Drying my tears, I wondered where Jen got the sperm. I was now a detective. Cheating spouses were my specialty. If the Hindu man had not been a ghost, I would have taken him on as a client pro bono, just to see Jen get what was coming to her. I did feel sorry for the cute little girl who had given me her spoon with milk dripping off of it. I had found her to be amusing. However, she had a father out there somewhere that she might not ever be aware of. That saddened me. All children, in my book, had the right to know their parents.

"You think my death and bad marriage is funny?" The turbaned ghost with a feminine voice asked, folding his arms across his chest.

"I am sorry, man. I really am. You just don't know the whole karmic story. What is your name anyway?" I asked, trying to control myself.

"My name is Allie Rodpuh. My Hindu parents from India immigrated to the United States when I was a toddler. I met Jen a couple of weeks before graduating college. We met in the campus bookstore. I eloped with her a few weeks after graduation. All Hell broke loose, as you Americans say. My parents were not happy with my choice. They said

I had married beneath myself. My mother and my new wife were constantly pulling each other's hair out. My parents were right. My wife gave me four children and one on the way who were not mine. I married a . . . a whore."

The term whore shocked me. I was sure that Jen wasn't that.

"Are you sure you are not mistaken about not being the father of Jen's children?" I asked a little bit in defense of Jen. I never questioned her fidelity when I was with her. Perhaps, I should have.

"The children are not mine. I secretly took samples and had their DNA tested before I killed myself. I was not able to test the one not born. The four tested confirmed my suspicions. Did you know all four had different fathers?"

That was a shocker. My mouth fell open for a moment. Jen and I had dated for my sophomore, junior, and senior year. We became an engaged Jewish couple during Hanukkah, my senior year. Jen's problem with me came after college, when I found out I could never father children.

"Do your four children have dark skin and look Hindu like you?" I threw out, trying to give Jen the benefit of a doubt, even if I did hate her guts.

"Look at my hair! Do you see black hair?" The turban man stated removing his head covering.

"Yes," I replied. "You have jet black hair." I replied wondering where the conversation was headed.

"What color do you remember my wife's hair being?" He then asked.

"She has black, kinky curly hair like her Jewish parents."

I replied.

Suddenly, like a light bulb turning on, it dawned on me what he was trying to point out. One of Jen's four birthed children was a blond. Two had light brown hair. The little girl with the spoon had red.

"Their hair . . . ," I sputtered.

"Do you now understand my shame?" Allie asked with a 'know it all' attitude. "Two parents with jet black hair are not likely to produce blonde and red haired little bastards."

With that said, Allie rose from his seated position in the chair next to me. He walked away about eight feet and then turned to look back at me. I could see that, like my other ghosts, he was starting to fade from the feet up.

"What do you want me to do about your cheating wife?" I harshly half yelled at him. "She is not my problem."

"Save me from spending eternity with her." He yelled back. "I made a mistake marrying her. Help me get an eternal divorce. Save me from her."

After Allie had totally faded out as a ghost and disappeared, I muttered in disgust. "I couldn't save my own ass from being hurt by her. What makes you think I can save you from spending Eternity with her?"

CHAPTER SIXTEEN

INVADERS OF MY SAFE HAVEN

Six or so Christmas Seasons had passed, since my original 'fifty miles from nowhere' cabin event had taken place. Returning home to California, after spending the holidays with Maxi and my nightmare, I busied myself with my detective agency's high stack of cheating spouse cases, in an effort to once more forget Jen, as well as my latest ghost encounters. Maxi was leaving Chicago in a week and going to live for a spell in the Holy Land. I would no longer have a reason to return to Chicago, or be visited by the ghost named Allie Rodpuh.

Easter came and the California weather became beautiful and sunny. I had just closed a major, movie star spouse cheater case, and had collected my pay check. Grabbing a few necessities from the supermarket, I headed home to my apartment to celebrate. I was considering grabbing my swimming trunks and heading to the beach for a swim, some reclining in the sun, and maybe a steak at the beach front grill. My tan had faded from the year before. It was time to get with the program and renew it. I was slowly starting to forget my life as it once existed in Chicago with my Jewish parents and sister. It was Maxi in Israel that I now called home to. I was excited about getting some sun and watching a few non-Jewish bikinis walk by. They were safe to watch. I was Jewish and would never date one of them. Kris had been the only Christmas crazy protestant that I had ever considered. Jen had been Jewish.

I now had a car. Detective work had brought me a certain amount of prosperity. I was no longer flipping burgers for minimum wage. I had moved out of my studio and was living in the basement apartment of a very nice elderly landlord. I had rented from her for a couple of years. Parking along the curb, I got out and proceeded to enter the flower lined sidewalk leading to the bungalow and then circling the house to the back, where my door was. My landlady, Bette, was in her eighties. I tried to respect that and not play my stereo loud, or do other things to annoy her. Ms. Bette was standing on the entering sidewalk sweeping up what looked like dried cereal.

"Do you need some help?" I asked, sitting my bag of groceries down on her front step.

"You have got to do something about that rowdy, undisciplined, mouthy little girl that has come to visit you. She had driven me crazy for the last two hours or so. If she isn't throwing dried cereal on this walk for the birds, she is singing, 'Here Comes Santa Claus'. She is driving me crazy, Monty. You know the rules, no overnight guests or children in your apartment unless you tell me about it. Children get on my nerves." Bette spouted, visibly agitated.

"I don't know what little girl you are talking about, Bette. I have no family here and my golfing buddy at work has no kids. Are you sure your little nightmare said she was visiting me?"

"Oh yeah . . . , she told me this long winded story about you playing Santa Claus and eating cereal with her dirty spoon."

"Oh crap." I stated, closing my eyes for a moment and wondering how one of Jen's kids had managed to make her way to me. I prayed that Jen hadn't flown to California, and was downstairs waiting for me in my apartment. Maxi had a key to my place, in case she ever popped in for a visit and I was out on a case somewhere. I had always had a key to Maxi's toy store and apartment.

"Here, give me the broom, Bette. If my surprise visitor has made a mess, it is my job to clean it up. What else has she messed up?"

"Only my nerves, Monty . . . will she be staying long? I could go visit my sister till she leaves."

"I will get rid of her Bette. My sister from Chicago must have flown in, bringing her along. I will see that she doesn't make any further messes, or causes you trouble. I will send my sister and her on to a hotel for the night."

"Thank you, Monty. I do not think I can stand hearing her sing 'Here Comes Santa Claus' one more time. She sang it for two hours straight while she played on this walk scattering dried cereal everywhere. I am Jewish like you. I do not celebrate Christmas. Now, however, I have that stupid gentile tune in my head. It is driving me crazy."

"I understand, Bette. Think of a Barbara Stries' hit song and start singing it. She is a good Jewish girl. You sing her song long enough, the protestant's Santa Claus one will go away."

With our chat ending, I picked up my groceries and hurried down the sidewalk that circled around the bungalow, and then stair stepped down to a rear door that led to my apartment in the basement. I was not a happy camper. I had tried to free my life of all thoughts of Jen, children, and ghosts. Now, my own sister was once more rubbing Jen and her kids in my face, or at least I thought at the moment she was.

My door was locked. I quickly took my key and let myself in. It was dark inside, due to the lights being turned off. The TV was silent, as was my stereo, and radio. That was odd. Maxi loved noise. She always had her television and stereo blasting.

"Maxi . . . ," I yelled.

There was no answer. I walked back to the single bedroom and flipped its light on, after depositing my sack of groceries on my kitchen counter. Perhaps Maxi, and whoever she had with her, was cat napping. There was no one in my bedroom. The bed was how I had left it. I checked the bathroom. Its light was out and there was no sign of any one having been in there. The toilet paper was in the same position I had left it that morning. Returning to the main room which was both kitchen and living area, I flipped on the overhead light. Nothing was out of place. There was no sign of an open cereal box. My apartment was empty. There was no little girl in it.

Confused, I walked out of my apartment and into the tiny back courtyard. I looked about for any sign of a child being there. There wasn't any. I opened the door of a small lawn mower shed and peeped in. There was no sign of anyone having been hiding or playing in there. Then, as I was closing the little shed's door, I heard a baby crying and children's voices behind me. I spun around and there stood Jen holding an infant and three of her four children eyeing me. I was flabbergasted and did not know what to say. The blood drained from my face. Surely, Maxi would not send her to impose on me.

"Did Maxi send you here?" I asked in a cold tone, having no intentions of inviting her in.

Jen did not have time to answer.

"Looking for me?" Maxi asked, walking around the corner on the narrow little path that led to my basement apartment. She was carrying a diaper bag and three sacks of fast food. "Surprise . . . !"

"What the hell are you doing here, and with Jen and her kids?" I sputtered.

"Well, that is a great brotherly greeting." My sister replied, handing the sacks of food to me to hold. She then handed the diaper bag to Jen, who was holding the baby.

Jen whispered to Maxi. "I don't think we are welcome."

"I heard that. For your information, I cannot have kids here as visitors. It is in my lease!" I retorted, walking over and opening my door so I could get them all inside and out of the view of Bette, whom I was sure was now watching from her upstairs kitchen window.

"They are not Jen's kids anymore. I have adopted them." My sister spit out, as she ushered the group of snotty nosed little elves, one newborn baby, and one ex fiancé into my apartment.

I looked about for the little girl that I had shared a milky spoon with at Christmas, and Bette had complained about.

She was missing.

"You adopted what?" I retorted asking, thinking I had not heard Maxi right.

"April Fool . . . !" My sister then shouted to my annoyance.

All the kids laughed and snickered, as did Jen. I was really annoyed that my ex would dare laugh at me in my own apartment. She had a lot of nerve.

"Where is the little girl, the one who shared a milky spoon with me at Christmas?" I then asked, trying to change the subject.

"She is dead, Monty, a victim of a hit and run driver in Israel. We thought that sort of thing only happened in the United States. Anyway, Jen is really distraught about it. We buried her a month ago in Israel. For her other children's safety, we have returned home." Maxi half whispered to me.

I glanced over at Jen who was shuffling the baby from one arm to the other. She did have some serious dark circles around her eyes.

"This is just great . . . !" I muttered, knowing that the little girl on the front walk scattering cereal had to be my milky spoon's ghost. My encounters with ghosts had once more begun. Stranger ghosts were fine. I could deal with that. However, I wanted nothing to do with Jen, and that included the ghost of her little girl.

"Aren't you happy to see me, Edmond?" My sister asked as I put the sack of fast food down on my kitchen table.

"Jen is my ex, Maxi. I am not into hanging out with Jewish trash, ex-girlfriends and their little welfare, gutter rats." I sputtered in a low voice, hoping the kids didn't pick up on what I was saying. "Feed your entourage, and then get them out of here. I have no intentions of trying to explain to my current girlfriend, why my ex-fiancé is in my apartment. Do you want to spoil a good thing I have going? I am dating a socialite." I stated, lying about the socialite girlfriend. "You are welcome here! Jen and her snotty nosed, little welfare elves are not."

"Why do you hate Jen so much, Edmond? I rather enjoy her company, and that of her kids. Just so you know, she has been staying with me since our last Chicago Christmas. I moved her in Christmas night, and afterward toured Israel with her. Jen is a good person. She is just down on her Jewish luck."

I took Maxi by the arm, dragged her into my bedroom, and closed the door.

"Jen's husband didn't just die. She made him so miserable that he committed suicide. You just wait! The truth will come out about it." I spit out. "Furthermore, I don't understand why you are trying to cram her and her kids down my throat."

"That is beneath you as a Jewish man, Edmond." My sister replied in a stern voice. "Jen has told me why you hate her. She once upon a time called you a dud and dumped you, so what? Everyone says things in heated arguments. She dumped you because she was in love with someone else. She did you a favor, by not going thru with a marriage to you."

"She dared to tell you why she dumped me?" I asked, boiling mad. I had tried to keep that bit of embarrassing information under lock and key. Now, Maxi knew.

"She is sorry, Edmond. People do and say stupid stuff when they are young, and usually live to regret it. Forgive her and let the three of us be friends. Jen and I have bonded over the last few months, since Christmas. You know, as well as I do, that I am probably never going to marry, or have children, Edmond. Her three living children and the baby like me. I don't want to grow old alone. I make enough money to take care of them and me."

"Don't tell me that it is her skirt tail that you are now chasing?" I asked indignantly.

"What if I am?" My sister asked.

"She is using you for your money!" I spit out mad. "She will get you to buy her a big house in the suburbs, and then she will dump your lesbian ass just like she dumped my dud one. Look at her kid's hair, Maxi. A black haired Hindu and a kinky, black haired Jew do not produce blond, light brown, and red haired offspring. Jen is a tramp! She is playing on your sympathy and using you big time for your money. Let her get out and make her way in the world like other single mothers."

"When, Edmond, did you get so cold hearted? I recall that you were once madly in love with her. So madly in love with her, that you got me to sign loan papers for her an engagement ring."

"I made payments on that ring, long after she dumped me, not to mention that she didn't return it to me. Jen used me and abused me? Now, she has zoned in on you."

"I'm sorry about the ring, Edmond. I didn't know. However, it takes two to tango, and two to fight. You probably said something that made her angry enough to keep the ring." My sister shot back in Jen's defense.

That was just too much for me to handle. I exploded.

"Take Jen and her little bastards, and get them out of my apartment. Never bring them back here. This is the biggest insult you as my sister could possibly ever give me. If you truly loved me, Maxi, you would not have brought her here."

In a huff, Maxi gathered up Jen, the new born baby, and Jen's three living children and walked out of my apartment. I then slammed the door behind them. I was so angry. Maxi had chosen her over me, not to mention that my old emotional wounds were all sliced back open and bleeding again. What had I done to deserve such disrespect from my sister?

After slamming the door, I sat down in my silent, dark apartment and cried. Men weren't supposed to cry. I just couldn't help myself. My California sanctuary, my apartment, was no longer my safe haven. It had been contaminated, destroyed by my past. Jen had invaded my space, taking Maxi as plunder.

CHAPTER SEVENTEEN

THE JAMMED DOOR

After being invaded by my past in the month of April, I gave Bette notice that I was moving. She was in total shock. I assured her that it had nothing to do with her dislike of the little sidewalk girl, or anything she had said or done to me personally. How could I tell her that I felt my safe life had been compromised, and my apartment contaminated. I just did not feel free to tell Bette that I had been betrayed by my own Jewish flesh and blood.

While filling out my weekly job application at Zeke's Detective Agency, I was told by one of the female detectives that their temp receptionist, Milky Way, had purchased the building next door. I remembered what she had told me about renting out the top floor studio. To me, it was an opportunity to move on from Bette's place, and surround myself with a new, safe world adjacent to where I really wanted to be. Even though I was working for another detective agency now, I longed to work for Zeke. Renting an apartment next door was a step toward that goal and many steps away from Jen.

Milky Way was glad to see me, and rented me the loft studio, no questions asked. I was glad to discover that someone was getting what they wanted out of life. Milky Way had bought the building, just as she had said. On the first floor of the building, she had turned the stockroom into a one room apartment for herself. Renting the upper floor studio made her payments on the place. Even though Milky Way was a bit ditsy in my book, I admired the fact that she was a shrewd business woman. I was sure that she would one day be rich like my sister. I only had two goals in life. One was to forget about Jen's devastation of me. The other was to land a job with Zeke.

It seemed that my palm reading, new landlady had quite a following. The minute she opened her doors for business, she had a steady stream of customers. I was sure that she was making more in one day, than I was all week. Just like Maxi, I was happy for her. She had found her niche in society and was going for the gold.

In my opinion, palm reading was a psychic 'want-to-be' craft. Although Milky Way had read me like a book, when I originally had met her, I was sure that she was a fake. It was my guess that she had learned palm and Tarot card reading from books. Also, I was sure she had studied body language which helped her in her art. I studied people's body language myself, in the detective business.

As a Jewish man, I refrained from inquiring of witches and seers, fake or real. God destroyed men in the Old Testament for doing such. Even though I didn't attend Temple regularly, I did fear my Jewish God. My Jewish mother had taught me to do so. If anything had gone wrong in my childhood, my mother told me that it was God getting even with me. I broke my arm when I was eleven. My mother told me it was God getting even with me for riding a board that was not mine. "Neither a borrower or lender be . . . ," she had spouted to me. Pain from my broken arm and her words had convinced me. Once, she borrowed a measure of yeast from a neighbor to bake bread. When the bread didn't rise, she said God had done it. He was getting even with her for too much borrowing. Eating flat bread that night for dinner had made a believer out of me. I feared my Jewish God's wrath. He was not a God of love, in my book. He was a God who ruled you with an arm of wrath. I tried not to upset him.

My belief in a parallel universe inhabited by ghosts was walking a fine line, as a Jew. I wasn't sure how my Jewish God felt about a land inhabited by ghosts. He was a dictator type, with his own Kingdom and agenda to preserve. In the Old Testament, He destroyed anyone not thinking like him, or doing his will. Unintentionally, I had discovered a parallel universe that was not necessarily a Jewish place. Protestant Kris, as well as the Hindu Wise brothers, was there. Jen's Hindu husband was there, as well as Angelica the Kingdom door knocker. I had also been informed by Angelica, back on Christmas Eve, that there were all kinds of Heavens in the parallel universe. I secretly wondered if my deceased Jewish mother was there, and if her Heaven was one of having a fully stocked pantry, a place where you never ran out of anything. Also, I wondered if my deceased father was in the parallel world. Was his Heaven a giant vault of Diamonds? He had owned a jewelry store. My Heaven, if I were dead, would be to work for Zeke and have a woman who loved me enough that she didn't care if I was a dud.

In order to salvage some part of my sanity and dignity, I

did not give my new address to Bette or Maxi. I needed a safe haven to go home to at night that had no memories of Jen in it. Maxi didn't realize how fragile my emotions were concerning Jen. I decided that I would never give Jen or Maxi the pleasure of knowing their bonding and unexpected visit had just about pushed me over the edge into an emotional breakdown. Seeing ghosts over the years had just added to my secret fragile state. At least Maxi didn't know about my ghosts.

I made some very hard decisions, the week after Maxi and Jen invaded my space. I changed my phone number and didn't give it to my sister. If she was going to squander herself and her fortune on Jen, I did not want to know all the details. I decided to walk away, and try to forget I had a sibling. I informed my employer, a rival detective agency to Zeke, not to give my sister my new phone number or take messages from her or Jen. It was a harsh decision. Maxi and I, as fraternal twins, had always been joined at the hip. Jen, the meat cleaver, had separated us; just as she had separated me from my image of being a man.

I settled into my new loft apartment and resumed my predictable schedule of Saturday morning bookstores, golf, following cheaters, and living the life of a confirmed bachelor hermit. Milky Way, my palm reading land lady, was the new addition to my life. I was sure that she had reinvented herself, just as I had moved and started over. I was sure she was probably running from a life somewhere that haunted her. She had once told me that her name, Milky Way, was derived from watching the stars. I often wondered what her real name was. I was of the opinion that her parents had blessed her with a really bad name at birth, such as Gertrude or Roberta. Only people with bad first names changed them. Whoever Milky Way once was, she was no more. I was running from my past with Maxi and Jen. She probably had something or someone she was running from.

Spring and summer passed with no further encounters with ghosts, or my sister and Jen. I was very lonely and missing Maxi's weekly phone calls. However, I kept telling myself that I was okay. I was a grown man who had to make choices for my own sanity. Kristina was slowly fading into the past, along with the fact that I had once been in love with her. I felt a new sense of peace in my apartment above the Palm Reader. Little did I know; that I had once more entered a lull before an approaching storm. The quiet existed till the second week in the following December.

A knock sounded on my loft apartment door. I forced myself to get up and answer. I had been up most of the previous night following a cheating spouse. I had crashed on top of my covers in my boxers.

"Who is it?" I inquired roughly thru the door, running my hands thru my hair, and then feeling a really serious four o'clock shadow on my face.

"It is me, Monty." The voice of Milky Way called in somewhat of a panic. "Let me in."

"Great . . . ," I muttered, undoing the dead bolt and opening the door. I had only been asleep a couple of hours. "Come in, and forgive my boxers. This is the middle of my night." I stated, turning and walking back into my apartment with Milky Way at my heels. I spotted a pair of dirty jeans discarded on the back of a chair. I grabbed them and proceeded to put them on.

Milky Way was dressed in a peasant skirt which was swishing as she walked. Multiple bangle bracelets on her arms were jangling. She always dressed like a gypsy, even though I secretly felt she was from Texas or Oklahoma. She had a drawl in her voice.

"Zip your jeans and come on, Monty. Something has happened downstairs in my reading room that I cannot explain. I am a little frightened, and need you to tell me that I am not imagining it."

"Has someone broke in or tried to rob you?" I asked hurrying.

"It is my reading room door, Monty. Someone or something has jammed it. I was in my palm reading studio with a client who took a coughing spell. I exited by my personal door behind the reading table to obtain a glass of water for him. I walked out, filled a glass with water, and then returned to re-enter my reading room. The door to my reading room is different and jammed. I don't know how to explain it. I need you to come and tell me that I am not crazy. There are now voices beyond the door and they are asking for you."

I snorted, figuring that Milky Way was just trying to trick me downstairs for some reason. She had asked me several times to come down and eat with her. I had always refused, knowing I was a dud. There was no need to start a relationship that you couldn't finish. I never intended to have to explain to another woman that I was almost spermless. However, I couldn't refuse to un-jam a door for her. I liked my new, loft apartment and wanted to stay as long as I had with Bette. I wasn't the moving type. Not only that, my loft's building was next door to Zeke's Detective

Agency. I planned to eventually work for him. I had been pestering the life out of Zeke, by routinely, every Saturday morning for six or so years, filling out a Job application. I wasn't going to rock my boat with my landlady.

"Do you have some tools downstairs, to un-jam it with?" I asked, ignoring her comment about voices asking for me. I figured that was just part of her ploy to get me down stairs. I grabbed a T-shirt and pulled it over my head.

"Human tools won't work on this door. Just come on!" She replied grabbing me by the arm and pulling me barefoot toward my apartment door.

Figuring it wouldn't take me a moment or so to un-jam her door, I followed her barefoot down the outside stair case and into her apartment. She quickly ushered me toward the front where the entry door was to her tiny reading room. I pushed on the roughly hewn, wooden door and tried to open it. She was right, it was stuck, and missing its doorknob.

"See . . . ," She demanded, pointing to the rustic closed door to her reading room. "My door knob is gone . . . my door is gone. This backwoods monstrosity you are looking at is not my door. Mine was painted Milky Way white."

I gave up on my pushing on the door and gasped, suddenly recognizing the worn out door. Just as I gasped, snow started falling inside Milky Way's building. Instantly, I was standing barefoot in a winter snow storm. I held my hand out and let snowflakes fall into my palm. Snow was falling from nowhere and covering the carpeted floor in front of the rustic door. I was standing in front of the door to my rented cabin, 'fifty miles from nowhere'. I grasped Milky Way's arm to steady myself. I needed her for back up. I was frightened and panicked. It had been six or seven years since my starving, whiteout, cabin experience.

"I don't know how, but I fear I have somehow opened a door to a mystical in-between world. Just as I do not know how I opened it, I do not know how to close it. Hear the voices beyond it, Monty?" She asked nervously, while turning her right hand's palm up to catch snowflakes that were falling inside of her building. She then turned her face upward and let the snow fall on her face and eyelashes, like she was a two year old experiencing her first encounter with the white, falling fluff.

"Kris is beyond the door. I hear her voice." I muttered, after putting my ear to the door to listen.

"Who is Kris?" Milky Way asked, as she turned her attention from the huge, swirling, falling snowflakes to me and the mystical cabin door.

"I was once in love with her. She disappeared on me, you might say." I stated, not wanting to go into details. "What were you doing, to make this door appear?"

Recalling how my ghosts always faded from the feet and then upward, I glanced at the base of the door to see if it was starting to fade; it seemed to be stable for the moment.

"I was reading the Tarot for someone you know."

"Who . . . ?" I asked, still examining the mysterious door, my cabin door from many years prior.

"I was reading for your boss."

"You what . . . ?" I asked snorting, having been taken off guard by the comment. My burly, detective boss didn't seem the psychic loving type, unless he possibly had met and had a thing for Milky Way. I was amused.

"You don't have to be shocked or tell anyone. Your boss often comes to me for advise; asking how to become the number one detective agency in this area. Everyone should have a goal and get professional help with it. He wants to up Zeke. I am his professional advisor."

That was just too good to be true. I snorted again and then bit my lip, seeing how serious she was.

"You were shuffling cards and lighting candles. What happened after that?"

"I lighted my candles, shuffled my Tarot deck, and then placed three cards in front of your boss. I had this eerie feeling that the three cards were wise ones, like the three Wise men who delivered Gold, Frankincense, and Myrrh to the Christ child. When I told my client, your boss, that; he gasped, sucking spit down into his wind pipe. He lost it, like he had just had the shock of his life. He went to coughing and turning red in the face. I jumped up, slapped him on the back a few times, and then exited my private door to run and get him a glass of water. When I quickly returned with the glass of water, I was praying he hadn't choked to death while I was gone. I don't have liability insurance on my building yet. So, being a little superstitious, I decided to knock on wood to make sure everything would be okay. I knocked on my wooden, reading room door three times, with intentions afterward to immediately open it and hand the water to my client who could no longer be heard coughing. My white painted wooden door changed immediately after my third knock to this cabin one. Also, I was suddenly standing in a snow storm, inside this building."

"Kris . . . !" I yelled pounding on the door with my fist. There was no reply, however the door remained and the snow continued to fall. Milky Way was shivering. "You heard three voices, plus one identifying herself as Kris, who was asking for me?" I inquired, not wanting to believe that I was being haunted again.

"Three male voices first called to me from beyond the door. Then a fourth voice chimed in asking for you, saying her name was Kris. I was so frightened, not to mention I had a man who might be dying beyond my real door. I ran out the back door and then up the outside stairs to get help from you." She replied nervously, while wringing her hands. "I think there are elves or trolls on the other side of this door, Monty."

"Elves . . . ? Trolls . . . ?" I asked, in reply to my ditzy landlady.

"Their voices came thru the door down low, about the height of my belly button." She replied big eyed. "The short ones told me their names were Gold, Frank, and Merve."

"Gold, Frank, and Merve," I replied in utter shock. My past was once more returning to haunt me. "Pinch me, Milky Way. I need to know if I am dreaming this. This is the middle of my night!"

At that point Milky Way gave me a super serious pinch on my arm. I flinched and groaned. I knew that I was definitely awake. Then she held out her arm for me to pinch. I returned the favor and she squealed. We then returned our attention to the inside falling snow and the worn out cabin door.

"The snow is above my ankles, Monty." Milky Way replied lifting one of her sandaled feet off the floor to show me.

Immediately, I felt the sting of the cold snow on my bare feet. I glanced from her feet to my own, which were red from the cold. That is when I glanced at the bottom of the door and saw that it was starting to fade away, just as my ghosts always did. I was in a sudden panic, having an overwhelming desire to return to my ghost family. In a flash, I grabbed the door handle with the intent of trying to force the door to open. Too my surprise, it swung easily open. Just inside the door, Kris was standing with her arms crossed, like she was mad at me. I saw in her eyes that she was about to uncross her arms and slam the door in my face, just as she had done that Christmas Eve so many years ago. Not giving her a chance, I put my palm firmly on the door, holding it open. Then, I stepped thru; not really knowing what would happen. Perhaps I was crazy, sleep walking, or hallucinating. It didn't matter. I just knew that my heart was once more beating wildly for Kris, a woman who was much too old for me. Although, she appeared younger than she looked the last time I saw her. For some uncanny reason, Kris was in a reverse aging process.

At that point, Milky Way reached thru the door, grabbed my arm, and jerked me back out the door into her building. Poof . . . , my beloved Kris and the Wise brothers were gone. I fell to the floor on my knees in disbelief and tears. Milky Way placed her hand on my shoulder, but didn't speak. She was in a shocked state of her own.

Nothing remained to show that the cabin door portal ever existed in Milky Way's building. The carpet, that had been wet with snow, was perfectly dry. The private, gypsy, white wooden door once more hung on its hinges. Beyond the door, my agency boss and fellow detective sat coughing.

Milky Way was no longer interested in my boss' inhaled spit attack. She let him cough and hack it out. Instead, she pulled a tiny bottle of Vodka from her pocket, opened it, and downed it. In shock, I remained on the carpeted floor on my knees. My boss seemed oblivious to my presence just beyond his Tarot reading gypsy's private entrance door. The three of us had experienced the opening of a portal between worlds, just in different fashions. I was sure that my boss would only remember suddenly thinking he was choking to death.

After downing the Vodka, Milky Way muttered in a very serious voice. "I am now the real McCoy. I have seen between worlds, and thrust my arm between worlds. I am no longer a phony!"

In spite of my own distress, I was amused with Milky Way. She had just had a life altering experience. I had heard the Protestant's speak of a born again experience, when they met their Christ. I was sure that Milky Way's encounter had been a similar experience. The Protestants claimed to no longer be sinners after their Christ encounters. Milky Way had just claimed to no longer be a fake gypsy, or psychic.

Milky Way put her empty vodka bottle in her pocket, straightened her clothes, stepped thru her white reading room door, and nervously resumed business. I heard my boss immediately quit coughing. I got up from my knees wondering what the experience now meant to me. I wasn't born again. Angry better described me. Once more, I had been left on the outside of the mystical cabin door wanting in. Once more, I was left behind. I could not find anything in my Jewish theology to explain my encounter, other than I was a possible seer. My Jewish God was bound to send a devastating judgment on me, for joining forces with an occult gypsy fortune teller. I was doomed!

Feeling extremely sleepy, I returned barefoot to my upstairs loft apartment and crashed in a strange exhaustion. I did not know how to explain how Milky Way opened my portal door, nor could I explain why my heart beat wildly for Kris. It had been years since I had spent that fated Christmas Eve with her in the cabin 'fifty miles from nowhere'. Once again, I felt like a pervert. Why would someone my age be attracted to such an older woman? Was I in to grannies? That thought horrified me. In my thinking, I had always tried to be a decent, upright man. Until meeting Kris, Jen had been my only emotional rough spot. Then, I considered Bette, my former elderly landlady. I had felt no attraction toward her, or her elderly friend Pam who had lived next door. What was it about Kris that excited me, other than the fact that each time I encountered her she looked five or ten years younger? This time beyond the portal cabin door, she looked to be about forty or forty-five. When I rescued her from the snow drift behind the mountain cabin years before, she had been in her eighties.

Kris is safe! I told myself. She is too old to want children by me. That must be why I am obsessed with her. It is a Jen hang-up thing. I am afraid to fall in love with someone my age!

CHAPTER EIGHTEEN

RETURNING TO 'FIFTY MILES FROM NOWHERE'

Milky Way and I formed a bond in that incredible moment when she somehow opened my portal door between worlds. However, she could not repeat the mystical opening the door incident, even though she tried on more than one occasion. Developing an interest in psychic abilities, I began to sit in on occasional séances held by Milky Way for a chosen circle of believing friends. The dead did not come to speak at the séances, and the door did not open again. Milky Way and I both returned to our routines. She told fortunes and I followed cheating spouses.

Christmas and Hanukkah came and went. I did not call Maxi, or make any attempt to return to Chicago or the cabin. I wasn't sure whether Maxi and Jen were in Chicago, sailing around the world, or had returned to Israel. I had cut ties with my sister for my own sanity. Due to Jen, I no longer had anyone to go home to for the holidays. Jen had taken over my place in Maxi's life. I would celebrate the holidays alone, light my simple menorah, and feast in a restaurant with strangers.

The holidays were uneventful. Then, a year passed with no further mystical visits from my ghosts, or the appearance of the mystical cabin door. I assumed my ghosts had forgotten me and had moved on to haunt someone new. Milky Way had no further encounters either.

Once more the holiday season rolled around. It was December 23rd in California. I was crashed, sprawled naked on the bed in my loft apartment. I had just completed an all night stint following a cheating spouse. I had intended to shower before climbing in bed. However, I had reclined on the bed for a moment, and had fallen instantly asleep. Suddenly, I was floating in the land of dreams, in a crowd of unfamiliar faces. I was floating mid-air in the dream, like a feather flittering about on a breeze. The strange faces were whispering to each other, "Jen says he is a dud!" Their words were hurtful. That is when I spotted Kristina in the distance. I could just see the hair on top of her head, which was no longer white. Her hair was brown, with a wisp of white hair at the temples. Once more, she was younger. I didn't understand how she could de-age. She looked to be in her late thirties.

"Kris . . . ," I yelled.

Instantly, she turned and floated up to me. "Why are you yelling, Monty? Do you want to raise the dead? There are those of us, we do not wish to wake."

"Am I dead?" I asked, looking at my body which was naked. I was embarrassed in the dream like state. A white piece of cloth came floating by and I grabbed it and wrapped it around my hips and my manhood. I didn't want Kris to see my male parts. I worried that she might be able to tell that I was a dud. I didn't want anyone to know.

"You are not dead, Monty, but I am angry enough to make you so." She replied, folding her arms across her chest like she used to in the cabin, so many years ago.

"Why are you mad at me?" I questioned, seeing tears in her eyes.

"You have abandoned your post as the Chicago's Toy Store Santa. Do I mean nothing to you? Do the others mean nothing to you? Does Snicker Doodle mean nothing to you?"

"I am Jewish, in case you have forgotten. I used to play the Santa bit to please my sister, the toy store owner. That doesn't mean that I believe in him, or any other part of your Protestant Christmas craziness." I replied, as I fidgeted with the white cloth, trying to hide my manhood from her.

"Help me find my son, Snicker Doodle, and Christmas Crazy me promises to never return to you." She replied, not smiling. "He did not make it back to me for Christmas Eve to hang his sock, on the night you told all of us to get out of your life, so many years ago. He is wandering aimlessly looking for me and his father. He needs a father. I need his father."

"Why is it always about someone else's needs?" I huffed, as I realized that she wasn't interested in me as a man. She just wanted to use me to find her son. I was pissed.

"Maybe I am selfish." I yelled harshly back at her. "None of you appreciated me and what I sacrificed for all of you on that Christmas Eve so long ago. I gave you shelter, my food, my bed, seating in the rockers, and tolerance. I went hungry, slept on the hard floor, and put up with all your non-Jewish chatter. I fought a blizzard to keep a fire going to keep you all from freezing. I got nothing in return but abandonment, a year of psychiatrist's couches, and years of tormenting encounters."

"There are givers in life, and there are receivers. There are senders of gift messages from our world, and there are receivers in your world. Once you were a giver. Now you are a receiver. I have nothing to do with either. I am just one in a long line of those crossed over, who are trying to send messages back to those left behind. Snicker Doodle and my husband have been left behind. I need you to tell them that I am waiting for their crossing over."

"I fell in love with you in that cabin years ago, Kris. The others, whom I did not know were ghosts, became family to me. Was I nothing but a dud to you and them? Is that what a receiver between worlds is, just an unloved and unwanted dud, a mailman between worlds?"

"I have a husband. He will one day come to me here, as will Snicker Doodle. We are a family. You cannot be anything more to me than a friendly mail man, as you put it."

"You were something to me." I replied feeling totally re rejected by her. "I loved you! Doesn't that mean anything? The husband you are waiting for is a little, egotistical, piss ant of a man wearing a fake Santa's hat. He will come to your world, but it will be with a second wife on his arm. He doesn't want you or Snicker Doodle. You are lost in a fairy tale delusion. Santa is not coming home to you. He does not love you or his son. You are throw backs to him."

"Why do you want to destroy my Heaven with your words, Monty? All souls need a Heaven to survive in. You are not in my Heaven. You are a mailman who carries letters from my Heaven to the Earth Plane. I am not a cheating spouse. I am waiting for my family with forgiving open arms. Now, be what you are and take my message to my son wherever he is. Tell him that I am waiting for him."

"Take your letter and go to Protestant hell!" I spouted back in Jewish outrage. "It will be a cold day in your Protestant hell when I carry a message to your husband, or your lost son. It should be me that you are waiting for."

Ignoring my emotional pain at being a reject, she continued, "Snicker Doodle is lost somewhere on the Earth Plain. He is a special needs child. He needs a receiver to help him find his way to the portal door. I need you to find him, and care for him till a portal door opens that he sees and can return thru. I need you to give my son wings every Christmas till he crosses over."

"You want me to take care of your son, the airplane pilot?" I asked in bewilderment, ". . . the one who let you fall out of his airplane?"

"Snicker Doodle is not just any pilot. He is a special needs air plane pilot. Always keep two ironing boards on hand for repairs. You will need them."

"Two ironing boards . . . ?" I questioned, knowing that I had to be lost in a nightmare, one that I would soon awake from. I decided to just let the dream scenario play. When it was over, it would be over and I could go on with my life.

"Yes. They are a necessity in caring for him." Kris replied in her sweet, charming, female voice.

"How old is your pilot son, the one you insist I look for?" I asked, shaking my head in disgust in the dream.

"He is going on forty!" She replied simply. "How old are you?"

"Old enough now to know that you don't love me and that you are trying to use me for your own personal agenda. I am sorry that I have spent years loving you, Kris. It is time to let you go. I will not help you. As I told you years ago, on the porch of the cabin that was 'fifty miles from nowhere', butt out of my life. I have no intentions of dealing any longer with another version of Jen. She wanted children more than me. You want your perverted husband and your child more than you want me. I may be a dud, but I have no intentions of letting you make me feel like Jen did. Goodbye." I stated with tears welling up in my eyes.

"Do not say goodbye, Monty! I need you to find and rescue my son. Only Santa can do so! You are the only Santa he knows."

"I am Jewish and don't believe in the pagan, protestant fairy tale Santa character. Furthermore, any guy as old as me, who is smart enough to be a pilot, doesn't need a mother rescuing him. Let the poor mother's boy spread his wings and fly. He may not want to return to you and your Heaven. He may have his own ideas of what Heaven is."

I was at the point of being pissed in my dream-like state. She wanted to hold onto a grown son, older than me in human years, and a husband who had abandoned her for another woman who had six dogs and three cats. Kris was living in a very blind Heaven.

"Snicker Doodle needs me." She replied in a huff. "He is a special child who will always need his mother."

"Has your ghost world doctor bothered to tell you that you are suffering from dementia?" I shot back in pure annoyance. "Your husband is living it up on Earth without you, and your son is to. It has been years since you fell into the snow drift and I rescued you behind the cabin. Your Santa husband and your special pilot son have moved on without you."

"You don't understand, Monty. My husband's name actually is Santa. His mother named him that. Snicker Doodle believes his dad is the fairy tale Santa, as you call him. I raised him with the idea that the story character Santa Claus was his father, and that his dad was away all year at the North Pole working. He was a little boy who needed an explanation as to why his father was not around and never came home."

"There is nothing like lying to your kid." I huffed.

"There is nothing like lying to your-self about wanting a wife and a kid." She huffed back. "You secretly want a child, but you are not willing to accept one that isn't biologically produced by you. Your sister is one up on you. She is not a dud."

"That is low, Kristina." I replied with her words cutting me like a knife. Somehow, she knew that I was a dud. I could vacate and run from my old contaminated apartment and landlady Bette, but where do you run for safety from a ghost? "You have chosen to willfully stab me with your cutting words, Kris. You are just another version of Jen."

"Perhaps, Jen and I are alike. We know that we cannot live a life with a man that we are not intended to be with. My husband is the other half of me. You were not Jen's soul mate. It was a blessing that she chose to dump you. You have an Earth destiny, a special one that includes my son, but not me."

"You are naïve and prejudiced in your thinking, Kris. You claim a man can love and be a father to a child that is not his biologically. Shouldn't that apply to soul mates also? When your other half has abandoned you, are you not free to be adopted by and loved by another who does not have a soul mate for some reason? Snicker Doodle your son is basically up for adoption. His father has abandoned him. You are basically up for adoption. Your husband has abandoned you."

"He may have abandoned us on Earth, but he will want us here." She screamed with pain in her voice, like I had hit a nerve. Then, poof . . . , she was gone.

It was time for me to move on. Perhaps there was someone else out there for me. In the dream, I realized that Kris would never let her-self love me. She was lost in a delusion of expecting her ex to return to her. It was time to let her go. I had wanted her love. She had not been willing to give it. I would abandon her, just like I had Maxi and Jen, for my own sanity. Suddenly, the crowd of unfamiliar faces began to fade. I gave in to a force that was pulling me downward toward my bed. I could see my sleeping body laying there snoring. Then, I dove back in to my naked human body and got lost in the darkness and silence of sleep.

~   ~   ~

Sleeping soundly, I was awakened by repeated knocking on my loft apartment door. Reluctantly, I sat up on the side of the bed, and then ran my fingers thru my hair. As the knocking continued, I grabbed the bed's top sheet and wrapped it around my naked torso. Afterward, I headed for the door. Once there, I gave my sheet wrap a little extra tucking, before cracking open the door.

"Yes . . . ," I mumbled, thru my slightly opened door. Batting my sleeping eyes, trying to wake up, I saw that it was Milky Way.

"Let me in, Monty. I have made a decision that I need to talk to you about." Milky Way stated, pushing past me and wading directly into conversation.

"What kind of decision?" I asked, rubbing my sleepy face with one hand and securing my sheet wrap with the other. "Do you mind getting right to the point? This is the middle of my night."

Milky Way made her way to my tiny kitchen table for two and seated herself. I followed her and plopped down half awake in the chair opposite of her.

"The mystical door we both saw, haunts me, Monty. I have questioned myself over and over why it and its ghosts chose to appear to me. I am a fake, Monty. I pretend to read palms. Reading the Tarot cards is a learned skill. I also watch people's body language. The day I first met you outside of Zeke's place, I already knew all about you. I had read one of your job applications and saw your attached photo, while I was filling in for his receptionist. Since the door experience, I have tried to be a little more above board, as they say, with my clients."

"I understand where you are coming from. I read people's body language in the detective business. You are making yourself a living, I am doing the same. Cut to the chase, and tell me about your decision. I really need to go back to sleep. This is the middle of my night."

"I want to experience the opening of the door again. My problem is, I just can't figure out how to get it to open. You said you once experienced the same door at a mountain cabin you holidayed in years ago. I thought perhaps we might be able to get it to reappear, if we made a trip to the cabin where you first encountered it. I have a question for the ghosts that I must have an answer for."

"You have a question for the ghosts?" I asked, deciding to get up and put on a pot of coffee. This was not going to be a short conversation, and I needed a cup of the strong black brew to keep me awake and tuned in to her. Milky Way waited till I had the pot going to reply.

"I want to ask the ghosts, 'Why me?' I am a fake gypsy psychic. Why would they want to make themselves known to me? Why is the other world taking an interest in me?"

I snorted.

"Believe me, Milky Way. I have asked myself the same thing. I am a confirmed Jewish jerk who believes his Jewish God sends wrath and destruction on those conjuring up the dead. Furthermore, the ghosts I encountered were not Jewish. They were Protestant, Hindu, and Kingdom door knockers. After I first experienced the door and the ghosts knocking wanting in, I spent a year on a psychiatrist's couch asking why me."

After biting her lip for a moment, Milky Way continued. "Do you think you and I are latent, blooming psychics who speak with the dead?"

"You think I am a psychic?" I asked in a shocked voice. Then, I snorted and broke out in laughter. "Knock on wood, Milky Way, and may my Jewish God not be listening. I am already staying clear of him, due to my ghosts. A righteous Jewish man does not inquire of witches and seers, much less be one."

"Perhaps, the Deities, Heavens, and in-between worlds are not what we have been taught. I personally was brought up believing in a Great White Spirit and Kachina."

"You, a gypsy, have been taught to believe in a Great White Spirit and Kachina?" I asked in amusement, trying to dig her. "Aren't gypsies usually Catholic?"

The coffee had finished brewing. I poured us a mug of it.

"I was fifteen and a runaway when I hit this city. I slept beneath park benches and ate out of trash cans. A street woman, named Wanda, taught me how to read the Tarot. I taught myself how to read palms from a book I checked out of the library. Reinventing myself as a gypsy psychic gave me a skill to make money to feed and house myself. I was too young to work, and had no ID. The non-gypsy I am is a simple Indian girl who didn't want to live and die on a reservation in Oklahoma."

"I have always figured your life was something like that." I replied, finishing off my mug of Joe.

"The Cherokee have their psychic ones. They are called medicine women. I am beginning to think that I might be one. As a child, I was not pointed toward future occupations to pursue. My father was a janitor in a casino. My mother worked in the casino's restaurant as a waitress. The only expectation for me was to grow up, work in the casino like my parents, and turn over my paycheck to help pay family bills. Even though my parents were full blood

Cherokee, they did not hold to any of the tribes' traditions. I didn't attend any type of powwows or native ceremonies. I have tried to forget the life I ran away from. Now, I have experienced seeing the in-between worlds. In my Native American culture, medicine men and women go on vision quests to see such things. I have to be, somehow, a medicine woman."

I took a serious look at Milky Way. "So, what does your being a medicine woman have to do with the decision you are making?"

"I want to make a trip to the mountain cabin where you first experienced a portal door. I want you to go with me, Monty. I want to try to open your cabin portal and ask the ghosts, 'Why me?' I want to know positively whether I am a medicine woman."

"I can't go back to that cabin, Milky Way. I was in love with a woman beyond that door. She chose her ex and her son over me. I would be humiliated to face and be rejected by her again. I am afraid I will still be in love with her, should the door open. I am a dud, Milky Way." I sputtered. "No woman will ever love me or want me. I cannot give a woman what she wants."

"What do you mean you are a dud? Any woman would be crazy to not want to fall madly in love with you. Have you ever taken a good look at yourself in the mirror, Monty? You are an extremely handsome, Jewish man."

"Being handsome doesn't make me a man, Milky Way. Handsome is a mask I wear. Beneath that mask is a dud no woman will ever want. I am a reject or throwback in life."

"Maybe behind your mask is a special man with a calling. Being normal 'nine to five' wives and husbands is not in the destined cards for medicine women, psychics, seers, and mediums. I would drive a normal husband mad with my palm reading and mystical doors. A normal man sees me as a crazy kook. The word dud could describe me to. Perhaps it is time for you and me to forget the normals in our world and embrace the lives we are destined to lead. You are just like me, Monty, only a male version. If you were Native American, you would be a medicine man."

I was touched by what Milky Way said. Maybe, I was more than I thought I was. Perhaps, it was time to face the fact that my inability to father children was destiny, not a curse. I was free to chase mystical doors, if I wanted.

"When do you want to go to the cabin?" I asked, realizing it was December 23rd, the day before Christmas Eve.

"I would like to leave today, if you can free up your work schedule. You once told me that you rescued your first ghost, Kris, on the 23rd."

"My boss has closed down the detective agency for the holidays. However, there is no way we can get plane tickets, Milky Way. Tomorrow is Christmas Eve. There are probably lines of last minute travelers trying to get tickets that don't exist."

"Just tell me you will go. I will find tickets." She replied, with a sheepish smile crossing her face, which told me she already had the tickets. I didn't know how I knew that. It just popped into my head.

"Okay, I will go. However, I don't want you to be disappointed if we find the cabin empty. The last time I was there, I was angry. I didn't realize I was in a mystical cabin and interacting with ghosts. I demanded they all butt out of my life and never bother me again. It has been years since I was there, Milky Way. There is no guarantee the cabin portal even exists. " I replied, pouring us both a second cup of black brew. I was beginning to feel more awake. "As a detective, I have never been able to make sense of my cabin experience. I went to a psychiatrist for a year, thinking I had imagined my experience at the cabin."

"We must go, Monty. There is every possibility that you and I are late blooming mediums?"

"If I am, Milky Way, I will keep it a secret. Being a detective is who I want to be. A fruitcake who speaks with the dead will do nothing for my career. My goal is to work for Zeke someday. When I get on with him, I will be a success and somebody. My detective work is all I have that makes me a man."

"I left Oklahoma, and my tribe, because I was a no one. I was a fifteen year old girl who spent every waking hour beyond school being mom to nine brothers and sisters. My parents worked two low paying jobs to support all of us. They had no goals to do any better. I was an unpaid baby sitter who was just a child herself. I never had the spare time to discover who I was. My world consisted of changing diapers and seeing that my brothers and sisters were bathed and fed. I never took piano or dancing lessons like other little girls. I had no friends, because there was no time for me to play. I was a slave to my parents who were too dumb ass to know what birth control was. My mother announcing she was pregnant again on my fifteenth birthday was the event that pushed me over life's edge and sent me running. The thought of one more baby to diaper was too much for me."

"I always felt you were running from something. Now, I understand." I replied, offering her a third cup of coffee, which she turned down. I poured the final cup into my mug.

"I never plan to marry, or have children Monty. I have already done a forced stint in raising babies and being a slave housekeeper. I am free here in California to be me, and pursue whatever floats my boat."

"I understand needing space, Milky Way. Growing up, I always walked in the shadow of my twin sister. She was born kicking, screaming, and demanding to get her way. She was an outgoing, demanding, look at me person who sucked up all the air and space in a room. There was no room for me to breathe, act out, or exist as a normal child. I lurked about in her over powering shadow, not that I wanted to. Like you, my living here in California is my way of stepping out of her shadow. Here, I don't have to explain why I am not married, or successful like her. In my family's and Jewish community's eyes in Chicago, I should own a detective agency, not work for one."

"You are not destined to own a detective agency in Chicago, and I am not destined to be a baby butt wiper." She replied. "We have fled the shadows of what others wanted for us."

"I am free here. However, there is one thing I cannot free myself of, my religion. I am Jewish, and that I am not willing to run away from. Along with the embracing of my Jewish beliefs, comes a God of Wrath who sends wrath, devastation, and death on seers and witches. Proclaiming myself to be a psychic medium would get me ostracized by my Jewish community, and possibly destroyed by my Jewish God. I believe He exists and I fear him."

"I understand your wanting to hold on to your roots and religion, Monty. However, you will have to admit that when that mystical door opened downstairs in my reading room, three Hindu dwarfs and a white protestant Christmas crazy woman confronted us there. I don't think the in-between worlds are made up only of Jews or the Cherokee. I am now of the opinion that all souls return to the parallel worlds, including the dark ones. I think Earth life is a learning experience, sort of like a private prep school. We either pursue higher education, or enlightenment, or we become a life school dropout and settle for being normal. Men, who are normal, live in darkness. They do not have eyes to see the mystical, the paths to knowing all; the freedom to be portal walkers."

"I understand what you are trying to tell me. However, without my Jewish identity, I am no one beyond the door of the detective agency where I work."

"I will always be Cherokee. You will always be Jewish. Those are our Earth school identities. However, you and I are on the verge of graduating prep school and entering the higher realms of astral education."

"I get where you are going." I replied, giving it a moment or so of thought. "I am no longer a senior in life's college. The master's program awaits me, and then a doctorate. Being Jewish, Catholic, Hindu, Buddhist, or Protestant is like being a high school senior. There is a higher thought process, the possibility of being something that is far more advanced than being Jewish or Cherokee."

"I was told stories, as a Cherokee child, about special Kachina spirits who walked between worlds. The ordinary

Cherokee native feared them. Men always fear what they do not have eyes to see or understand. Apparently, you and I are both Kachina, the misunderstood ones, the portal walkers."

"If I am a Kachina, then I am definitely on my Jewish God's hit list. He does not approve of his followers inquiring of witches and seers, much less be one." I replied taking in a deep breath and letting it out with a long sigh.

"Perhaps you should convert to being a Cherokee. A medicine man is revered in my tribe."

CHAPTER NINETEEN

REVISITING THE CABIN

At lunch time on the 23rd day of December, Milky Way and I flew to Chicago. I was right! My conniving landlady already had the tickets purchased before asking me to accompany her. That was a little annoying, but I didn't have anything to do for the holidays. I just went with the flow, being used to Maxi dominating and getting her way. Milky Way was just filling some shoes that were missing in my life. Maxi and I were still not speaking to each other, because of Jen.

I did not call and inform my sister that I would be in and around Chicago for the holidays. She was probably off on some holiday jaunt with Jen and her kids anyway. There had been a cold silence between Maxi and I, since I had told her to get Jen and her snotty nosed elf brats out of my basement apartment at Bette's. In my thinking, my sister had betrayed me in the worst sort of way.

Sunny skies greeted us as we landed in Chicago. However, the ground was slushy from a snow that had fallen a week or so before. Milky Way and I rented a four wheel drive at the airport, loaded our luggage in to it, and then headed north for the cabin that was 'fifty miles from nowhere'. I was not able to come up with a telephone number for the owner of the cabin. After six or seven years, some things just bite the dust. I couldn't recall the owner's name and had lost the telephone number for her. Milky Way and I were winging it. If the cabin was empty, we decided we would just make ourselves at home and do our thing. If it was occupied, we would pretend our car had problems and ask for shelter.

We arrived at the cabin about seven in the evening, on December 23rd. It was vacant and looked like it hadn't been used in years, possibly since I had been there. That surprised me. Letting ourselves in, Milky Way and I found that the cabin was just a big, dusty empty space with no signs of life in it. It was icy inside. We could see our breath form clouds on the inside of the cabin. There was no fire in the fireplace. The 'fifty miles from nowhere' cabin was cold, dank, dark, and the bed linens had rotted. Otherwise, the cabin was just as I remembered it. I checked the kitchen cabinet and found the metal pan that I had scooped snow with. In the bathroom, to my surprise, was a half of a roll of toilet paper, just as it had been on my arrival many years before. I felt as though I had stepped back in time.

After looking about inside the cabin, I went outside and headed around back to gather some wood for a fire. It was already dark, due to it being winter time. I knew that a blazing fire in the fire place would be my and Milky Way's only heat for the night. I remembered the former, whiteout blizzard and how everyone had gathered around the fireplace to keep from freezing to death. It was nice weather outside for December. However, I wasn't taking any chances. I wanted a good supply of wood in the cabin, just in case the weather went to Hell, like it had on my first stay in the cabin.

Food was also a priority with me. On the way to the cabin, I had stopped at the last town and purchased two buckets of the Colonel's chicken and multiple side dishes. I was not going to starve this time. If I had uninvited strangers knock on my door, I would have enough food to share. Milky Way had done her thing at the last town, purchasing a couple grocery totes of goodies and a month supply of toilet paper. She was prepared, in case my ghost house guests knocked on my door seeking shelter. I had shared with her all the details of my former stay in the cabin, after her encounter with the cabin's door replacing her white reading room one. There was one thing I had forgotten to tell Milky Way. That fact was that there was only one bed in the cabin. I decided I would sleep on the floor in front of the fireplace, as I had done so many years prior.

After I got the fire going, Milky Way and I tore into our fast food containers of southern fried chicken and sides. It was December 23rd, the day before Christmas Eve, just as it had been so many years before. However, the night was different. Christmas crazy Kris and nativity Joe and Mary were absent. Neither, Milky Way or I made references to Santa or the next day being the Protestant's Christmas Eve. I was Jewish and Milky Way was Cherokee. We were just two friends of different religious persuasions, sharing a candle light, fast food dinner in a rustic cabin fifty miles from nowhere. We listened for ghosts knocking, our mission in being there. No raps sounded.

Our first evening in the cabin was uneventful. I made several trips to the back for firewood in hopes of finding Kris in a snowdrift, like I had so many years before. I was disappointed. Milky Way took the dusty bed and I made myself a bed in front of the fireplace about midnight. The cabin seemed extremely icy cold and drafty for some reason. I didn't remember it being that cold inside before. Maybe I was just getting older, and the north winds were causing my bones to ache. I had heard older people talk about bones aching due to weather conditions when I was young. I recalled laughing at them, assuming they were imagining their aches and pains to get attention. I wasn't laughing now. The cold was like knives going thru me. I also considered the possibility that my body had, over the years, adjusted to the temperature and sunshine of California. Getting older was something I did not want to think about. I was in my early twenties when I first made my way to the cabin to spend a quite holiday. Now, I was in my thirties. I was still a dud, with no hopes of ever being loved by a woman.

There were no knocks during the night at the cabin door. The only night sounds were the whistling of the northern wind outside, and the popping and cracking of the flames in the fireplace. Christmas Eve morning came. I got up first and put more wood in the fireplace. Then, I tried to start a fire in the wood cook stove to make coffee. I just didn't seem to have the knack to do so. It kept going out. That annoyed me. I wanted to at least look like I was a macho man to Milky Way, a mask to cover the fact that I knew I was a dud. To my annoyance, she pushed me aside and took over the building of the fire in the wood range and the making of the morning coffee. Just like Kris, she made me scooper of the snow.

Christmas Eve morning passed, and then the afternoon. Although there was a north wind blowing, the sun was shining outside. We both were disappointed at not having my uninvited ghost guests from years ago knock seeking shelter. With nothing happening, we became bored with our adventure. I went out back and chopped a lot of wood and Milky Way played a lot of solitaire on the tiny kitchen table to pass the time.

About four in the afternoon, on Christmas' Eve, Milky Way and I were getting restless in the drafty, cold, lifeless, cabin. There was no TV or other form of entertainment. There was no blizzard raging outside or strangers knocking, seeking shelter. What there was, were two California odd balls starting to get on each other's nerves, having drank one too many cups of black coffee. Milky Way put her cards down and walked over to the window to look out, like she was suddenly distracted by something happening outside. I remained at the table, considering the thought of kissing the cabin goodbye and returning to Chicago where I could check into a nice warm, hotel room and douse my aching body in a hot tub. The cold was really getting to me.

"Look . . . ," She suddenly demanded in a loud excited voice, as she pointed out the window.

I walked over to the window to see what had her interest. Too my surprise, it was snowing like crazy. The windshield on our rental car was covered, in spite of the fact that the sun was shining. The sky was white with snowflakes, but only in a circle around the cabin.

"Oh my Jewish God . . . , it is happening again." I stated, looking out the window in astonishment. "Only this time it is different, somehow! Before, the whole countryside was engulfed in the blizzard. This one only extends out a few feet from the cabin."

"It snowed like this on the carpet inside my building that day my white door turned into this one. What next, Monty? What do we do to get the ghosts to come to us?" Milky Way asked excitedly, as boredom was forgotten.

Even though we were standing at the window looking out, we did not see anyone walk up onto the cabin's tiny porch in the blinding snow. Suddenly, a knock sounded. I nearly jumped out of my skin. I looked at Milky Way and she looked at me big eyed.

"Shall I answer it?" She asked, seeming to sense that I had rubber for knees. The first time in the cabin, I did not realize my guests were ghosts.

"I . . . I had better answer it. That was how it was years ago." I replied, moving towards the door with Milky Way hot on my heels.

"Do you think it is one of your ghosts?" Milky Way asked, grabbing my arm for a moment, just before I was about to open the door.

"This is how they arrived before. They knocked, I cracked the door to look out, and Kris let them past me and in. If it is someone seeking shelter, Milky Way, just push me aside and invite them in." I muttered, preparing to open the door. "You have to play the role of Christmas crazy Kris."

"I understand, Monty. You have told me about her."

Then, nervously, I cracked the cabin door open and peered out. To our surprise, a black cat was sitting in the snow on the porch, meowing as though it wanted in.

Opening the door wide open, I looked about for a human ghost. None was to be seen. I was disappointed and I could tell that Milky Way was also. Rather than let the black cat freeze to death in the winter storm that was circling and snowing only on the cabin, I picked it up and welcomed it inside as a guest needing shelter. The last time, a mother wolf had left her pup to be cared for by Kris. I guess it was up to me to take care of the cat.

"I am going to step outside and get a breath of fresh air." Milky Way stated in disgust, after discovering our door knocker was only a cat who had probably been clawing at the door.

"I will join you on the porch in a few seconds. Let me find a piece of last night's chicken to give this cat. It seems hungry."

Milky Way exited the cabin door, leaving it open for me to follow her. Startling me, the door slammed violently shut, with me on the inside and Milky Way on the outside of it. I turned my attention from the cat and hurried to the door and tried to reopen it. The door would not budge. That is when I heard familiar voices behind me. I spun around and was shocked to see Mary, Joseph, the door knocker, Mr. Shepherd the mailman, and the three Hindu circus dwarfs all huddled around the fireplace for warmth, just as they had ten years prior. I also smelled dried apples and a possum baking. I turned my attention to the area of the wood stove. Kris stood there cooking, just as she had done so many years before. However, she appeared to be shorter and once more younger. She now looked to be about thirty. The door knocker was no longer pushing Je . . . ova literature. She was carrying a Mormon Bible. That amused me. I glanced at the kitchen counter. All the food and supplies, that Milky Way and I had brought, were gone. In their place was a partial box of day old donuts, a bag of lemon drops, and a candy cane. I quickly felt in my pocket. In shock, I pulled out the candy bar that the hunter had made me swear to give to Mary on my previous cabin adventure into the world of ghosts.

"You must let Milky Way inside. She will freeze to death beyond the door." I demanded, knowing that I could not open the door. I now knew it was a mystical portal door.

"She will wander off into the snowstorm and find something to amuse herself till our visit is over." Mr. Shepherd stated. "I had my fill of checking for bed bugs and head lice the last time we dealt with you. Humans are nasty creatures. I am just not in the mood to deal with another like you."

"I can assure you that Milky Way does not have bed bugs or head lice." I replied in annoyance. I had forgotten about his hang up.

"I don't know which is worse; Cherokee fleas, Jewish head lice, or all American bed bugs. I am being very careful to keep them out of my Heaven." Mr. Shepherd replied seriously. "You will understand someday. Heaven is only as good as you make it."

I turned my attention back to the wood cook stove. "Where did Kris go?" I demanded in a panic. Once more my heart was racing like crazy for her.

Grinning from ear to ear, Mary pointed to the door of the little lean to inside outhouse. In a panic thinking she was going to disappear on me, I walked over and flung open the door. Immediately, there was an outraged scream. Kristina then immediately picked up the half roll of toilet paper next to her and threw it at me. I immediately closed the door to give her some privacy. Then, grinning from ear to ear, I knew I was where I wanted to be; home with my Christmas crazy ghost family. My only concern was Milky Way, who was on the wrong side of the door. I wanted her to share my experience. However, I wasn't sure how I would explain being at the cabin with a woman other than Kris. I felt a little bit like a cheating husband, even if Kris had made it very clear that she did not want a relationship with me. I thought I had forgotten, or gotten over Kris. Apparently, I had not.

"What is today?" I yelled, asking those seated around the fireplace. I knew it was Christmas Eve, years in the future from my first encounter with them.

"It is Christmas Eve, Monty, and there is no Jewish mistletoe in the bathroom. If you ever fling a rest room door open on me again, in such a rude manner, I promise you that I will have Santa leave in your sock, every year, the worst case of Christmas hemorrhoids he can come up with at the North Pole." Kristina stated, exiting the little lean-to bathroom with fire in her eyes and a sharp edge to her tongue.

I grinned at her, and then threw my arms around her, hugged her, picked her up, and swung her about in a circle. She squealed with laughter. When I set her feet back down on the cabin floor, I grabbed the big metal pan from the kitchen cabinet and stated, "I have got to get us snow so we can make coffee. That possum and apples smell really good, Kristina."

"You smell like some strange woman's perfume." She replied unsmiling.

I quickly sniffed myself and realized that Milky Way's

perfume must have rubbed off on me. I blushed, almost like I was one of the cheating husbands I followed as a detective.

"I can explain the perfume. Honest I can!" I quickly spit out, as my other ghosts snickered and cleared their throats. It didn't matter to me. They were my friends and family. All families poke fun at each other. It is a sign of acceptance. There was no way I was going to tell all of them to butt out of my life this time. I was still Jewish, but I also had learned a lesson in tolerance. There was every possibility that people of all religions dwelt in the next life. I was now fully aware that there were many Heavens.

Just as I had the thought about tolerance, my family of ghosts all started to fade from their feet up.

"No . . . don't go!" I yelled, as the metal dishpan, I intended to scoop snow with, disappeared from my hands.

"We travel to you by portal, Monty." Joe yelled, getting my attention. "We are subject to its scheduled openings and closings, not our travel desires."

"I love and need all of you in my life. Take me with you!" I begged, suddenly realizing how lonely in human life I had been. My family of ghosts was faded now to their waists.

Then Mr. Shepherd piped up, "You are not dead yet. You have bed bugs to smash and stomp. Someone must rid mankind of cheating spouse bed bugs. I will be watching you from my bug free Heaven. You be a good exterminator, till we work something out sending you down a new path. We have a short little bed bug we are sending your way. We all think she is right for you. Kris is not your bed bug to have."

At that point, Mr. Shepherd totally disappeared. I turned quickly to Kris. In a split second she and the others were gone. Once more, I felt the sorrow of losing my family of Christmas crazy ghosts,

A fierce knock sounded at the door. I knew it was Milky Way, trying to get in. How was I going to explain my having an encounter without her? Then the door to the cabin opened on its own, and Milky Way half way fell into the cabin.

"You will never believe what happened to me!" Milky Way's voice stated excitedly. "I met a guy and we have been out joy riding on a snow mobile. I have had the best time. We just circled the cabin round and round and round in the circle of falling snow. It was like being on a winter wonderland carnival ride. His snowmobile was red and it had airplane wings on it. I think I might have just been on some sort of mystical magical journey. Snowmobiles don't have air plane wings."

"In our world they do." I replied biting my lip for a moment. I knew she had encountered Kris' son, who was still humanly alive.

The rest of our stay in the cabin 'fifty miles from nowhere' was uneventful. Late Christmas Day, we drove back to Chicago, turned our rental vehicle in, and then waited in the airport lounge to board our plane for California. I felt really guilty not calling Maxi. However, it was time for me to have a life of my own, one free of Jen.

CHAPTER TWENTY

MAXI'S NEW FAMILY

Returning to Chicago, Milky Way and I sat n the airport lounge waiting for our flight home. Our plane was late and I was restless and depressed. For Milky Way's sake, I put on a happy face. My cell phone suddenly rang. I pulled it from my pocket, and saw that it was my sister Maxi. I wondered how she had managed to get my new number. We hadn't spoken since I had told her to take Jen and get lost. Maybe it was time to make up with her. Hopefully, Jen had moved on without consuming too much of my sister's fortune, or emotions.

"What is up, Maxi?" I forced myself to ask, putting my cell phone to my ear.

"She is gone, Edmond." My sister stated, sniffling.

"Who is gone?" I asked, not really wanting to know the answer.

"Jen is gone." She replied.

"If she has run off with half your fortune, don't cry on my shoulder. I tried to tell you." I spit out.

"Don't start in, Edmond. Just because you had a bad relationship with Jen, doesn't mean that I did. Jen has not run off with my money; she died yesterday."

"I should be so lucky . . . ," I replied in a harsh voice. "If she is dead, the world is better off without her. I know I am."

"Well hang your sorry ass pettiness up. Jen is dead, and I need help."

"Help with what?" I reluctantly asked. Down deep, I wanted to make up with my sister. However, she was pushing all of my buttons forcing me to talk about Jen.

"Jen let me adopt her kids, just before she died. She wanted to make sure they would be cared for."

"Isn't that just great," I replied mad. "Take them to social services, dump them, and go on with your life."

"You are so heartless, Edmond."

"Only when it comes to Jen and her snotty nosed elves." I shot back.

"In case you have forgotten, Edmond, I am a Lesbian. The possibility of me ever having children of my own is not in the cards."

"Well, join the crowd!" I huffed.

"I see Jen as blessing me with children."

"She probably knew she was dying. You have money. She has scammed you to make sure her kids live well. Don't ask me to embrace her children. It is not happening. Jen ruined my life."

"Her six kids could have been yours, Edmond, had you

married her." Maxi interjected.

"That is the point, Maxi. I didn't marry her, they are not my kids, and you are a fool."

"I see myself as lucky, Edmond, not a fool. I have a family now. I want you to be part of it. My kids need an Uncle Edmond."

"Well, I don't need them, or memories of their mother." I replied harshly. "Now, tell me why you have called?"

"I am sorry that you have that much ill-will towards Jen. However, her kids are now my kids. You are going to have to get used to the idea."

"Cut to the chase, Maxi. What is it you are wanting from me?"

"I am going to reopen the toy store. I think it would be a great place for the kids to grow up. Chicago is a great city. I plan to open after the first of the year. I would like you to fly out for the new grand opening. It is time for you to move home to Chicago and become someone to, Edmond. Our Jewish parents didn't raise us to be two bit bums. It is time for you to get a real job and be part of the family again."

"I may not be a success in your eyes, Maxi, but I am in mine. I am a damn good private detective, and that is what I have always wanted to be. I don't need a large bank account or someone else's kids to make me happy. Now, get off my back."

"As I have told you before, Edmond, a successful, Jewish, private detective would own his own agency." She retorted, not backing down.

"This call isn't going anywhere, Maxi. I am what I am. I don't want Jen's kids in my life. You made a choice between me and her. I am not playing second fiddle to Jen in life or death, nor will I embrace and teach her little fiddlers to play."

"Grow up, Edmond. Grown men don't spend their whole lives belly aching over a skirt that got away when they were young. Jen moved on after college. You have sat around and moaned the blues. Just as I am a Lesbian, you are a gay man. I assume that is why Jen chose someone else, and her reason for calling you a dud."

"Is that what she told you?" I asked mad, moving my cell phone to my other ear.

"She asked me on her death bed to tell you that she was sorry for calling you a dud the day the two of you broke up."

"You are walking a fine line with me, Maxi. By all rights, I should slam this phone shut, and never talk to you again. I am not a gay man and Jen was, in my book, a conniving bitch who purposely hurt me in the most demeaning way. You are a bitch for trying to cram dead Jen and her kids down my throat. I once was passionately in love with Jen, now I hate her with just as much passion. I hope she rots in Hell, if there is such a place."

"We don't always make good decisions when we are young, Edmond. If I could go back to our college years, I would insist that Jen tell you the real reason she dumped you."

"Get a life, Maxi. Jen has brainwashed you, ever since the Christmas you went and got her and forced me to play

Santa for her kids. You chose her and I got the shaft as your brother."

"Okay, here it goes, whether or not you want to hear it. Jen was in love with me in college, not you."

"What?" I half yelled in a shocked voice.

"Jen dated you, so she could be near me. You proposed to Jen, and I found myself spending more time with you and her, as the two of you planned your wedding. In the middle of the wedding plans hoop-la, Jen snagged my attention and we became lovers. She never intended to go thru with the nuptials with you from the start. It was me she wanted, Edmond. Jen was a lesbian like me, only she was closeted. I only hung out with Jewish, on track, business types in college. She was working her way thru college and ran a register where I bought my coffee in the morning. I totally ignored her. She didn't run in my circle of friends. She used you to enter my world."

"She dated me for three years of college, in order to be near you?" I asked totally pissed.

"I am sorry, Edmond. When you first started dating her, I actually thought she was beneath you. That is why I didn't hang out with the two of you much, before the wedding plans."

"Jen always begged me to include you in whatever we did." I sputtered with a shattered soul.

"I was the reason Jen dumped you, not the fact that you were a dud. In return, I dumped her after the two of you broke up. I knew I could never flaunt her on my arm in front of you, even though I was in love with her. Being lovers with Jen in secret was one thing. Hurting you by dating her openly was another. She made a choice, and I made a choice. I chose you and your feelings, instead of spending a lifetime in the arms of someone I loved."

"You were in Jen's bed when I was engaged to marry her?" I sputtered.

"We don't always make good decisions when we are young, Edmond. I was in love with Jen and yes we were lovers the last three months of our senior year. I had a broken heart that was equal to yours. I just didn't let it show, for your sake."

"How could you have done that to me?" I asked totally flabbergasted. "Loving and losing Jen destroyed me."

"You think I wasn't destroyed?" She asked harshly. "I gave up the only woman I have ever loved, in order to maintain my sibling, joined at the hip, twin relationship with you. I broke Jen's heart and sent her running into the arms of a jerk who didn't give a damn about her. It was too late for her to return to you. You had flown off to California. Time heals old wounds, Edmond. It is time to put yours and mine behind us."

"Did you purposely invite Jen and her kids to the toy store, that Christmas Eve?"

"No, she told you the truth about needing her kids to see Santa and not having the money till the last minute to do so. It was fate giving her and me another chance. You told me, on that holiday visit, that you were glad Jen hadn't married you, in case you have forgotten."

"You saw my words as giving you permission to run after her, when she took her kids and fled the toy store in tears?"

"It was the first time I had seen her, since she dumped

you way back then, and I dumped her. My heart came alive again. Yes, I chased after her. You said you were no longer interested in her."

"You just took up where you left off with Jen?"

"Yes, Jen and I found each other again, and now she is gone."

"I can see why you came out of our mother's womb first. You have some serious Jewish balls." I huffed.

"Life is what it is, Edmond. It is time for you to let go of the past and the two of us be family again for my children's sake."

"Your children . . . ," I sputtered with my depressed mood worsening. "If you were a man, Maxi, I would be doing more than talking about this with you."

"I am a male, Edmond. I am a male stuck, living a lifetime in a woman's body. Had I been born in a male body like you, we could have resorted to a fight over Jen. Even though you see me as your sister, Edmond, I am a male just like you. I am your brother, not your sister, and we happened to fall in love with the same girl. I backed off years ago to keep from hurting you, even though I was madly in love with Jen. Fate let me find her again. Now, her kids are my kids. Biology doesn't make a father, Edmond, love does. I may be Maxi your sister to you. To them I am their adopted father."

"I suppose you want me to start calling you Max?" I retorted sarcastically, totally peeved at everything she had told me.

"Actually, I would like that very much. I would also like it, if you would accept these children as your nieces and nephews. Jen and I have lived as husband and wife since that Christmas when you played Santa for her kids. Now, she is dead and I have her children to rear. I want you to be a part of our lives."

"Is Jen and her snotty nosed little elves all you have called to talk to me about, Maxi?" I asked, struggling with the bombshell that had been dropped on me.

"Yes, Edmond . . . it is time for you and me to bury our pettiness and embrace what life has given us. It has given me children, and you nieces and nephews. Family and friends is all there is in life, Edmond. Everything else comes and goes. We buy a new car and discard it three years later. You buy a new suit, and then have to replace it a couple of years down the road. Things come and go. When we leave this life in death, only our friends and family will one day join us in the afterlife. Our suits, cars, and other nonsense items will not be waiting on the other side. Father and mother will be waiting for you and me. Jen will be waiting for me. When I cross over, I will wait with Jen for our children."

"I get your point," I replied totally irritated. "Just don't wait with Jen for me."

"You cannot have what is not yours to have, Edmond. Jen is my soul mate. She will be waiting for me and our children. Somewhere out there is a woman that is right for you. Let go of Jen. She was never yours to have."

"I love you, Max. However, that love does not include dead Jen's kids. Calling you is all that I am willing to do. I will not be making any Uncle Edmond visits."

"That is a starter! Thank you, Edmond."

"Was there anything else, Maxi?" I asked, wanting to end the conversation and crawl into some dark hole somewhere and never come out.

"In July I am going to have a special summer event called Christmas in July. I want you to fly out and play Santa Claus for the three day event. All of my old customers will expect to see you sitting in the big red sleigh. My two oldest children can play elves for you."

"I have got to go." I stated, not wanting to get sucked in again to play the Santa bit. Then, I flipped my cell phone closed and muttered, "The Christmas craziness in my life never ends."

Overhead, the airport speaker system announced our flight. Milky Way and I boarded.

CHAPTER TWENTY-ONE

MEETING MISS PANDORA

A few days before Passover, I was summoned by my boss to his office for a new assignment. I was sure it would be another mundane assignment following a bed bug (as Mr. Shepherd had once put it), cheating spouse. Rarely did anything truly interesting in the way of a case come along. However, I was happy being a detective, even if I was working for Zeke's rival.

Standing in front of my boss's door, I took a deep breath and then knocked. I had been up all night, and he had summoned me into the office with my having had only an hour or so of sleep. I did not look my best, and had a serious four o'clock shadow. I should have shaved, but I rarely met the agency's clients. My boss felt it was best that his detective's faces weren't high profile. Gathering my composure, I knocked and then stuck my head in.

"Come on in, Monty. I have someone I want you to meet." My boss stated, as I stepped inside his office.

A young woman sat with her back to me. She was well dressed and had shocking pink, four inch, open toed spike heels perched on the floor next to her bare feet. When she turned in her chair to greet me, I noticed something really unusual about her feet. I wanted to gawk, but I didn't. However, that didn't mean I didn't take a couple of good looks when she wasn't looking. Between her middle toes on both feet, were taped what looked like doctor's tongue depressor boards. Her two toes, next to her big one, were taped in a very straight, somewhat miserable fashion, with the tongue depressors for splints. There was no way she could have walked in my boss' office wearing the pink spikes, placed by her feet. Her toes on both feet were swollen and wrapped in a sea of bandaging. I assumed that she recently had some sort of surgery done on her toes.

"Monty Marsh, I want you to meet Miss Panda."

"Miss Panda, this is Monty Marsh the Detective I am assigning to your case."

"Hello." She stated, reaching out her hand to shake.

I returned her shake and then sat down in the chair next to her facing my boss' desk.

"You are too young to have a cheating spouse." I stated, glancing at her and grinning. She blushed.

Miss Panda was very young and cute as a button. I guessed her age to be sixteen or seventeen. She was well groomed and her nails, on both hands and feet, were perfectly painted.

"Miss Panda wants to hire us to follow her employer, Monty." My boss Charlie stated, smiling from ear to ear.

I knew something big was up. Charlie looked like he was the cat that had just spotted an unsuspecting canary and was about to eat it. He also looked like he was about to break out in uncontrollable laughter, but was doing his best to control it. I pulled out a little note pad from my shirt pocket and a pen to take notes on my new assignment. The girl was too young to have a real employer. She was probably ditsy in love with some teenage fast food crew chief that was dating one or two too many fast food register girls. Her feet, I couldn't fit into the equation.

"So, I gather from my boss that you want me to follow your employer, Miss Panda?" I asked opening up dialogue with her. "Tell me about him and your relationship."

"He is my man, and I am going to marry him someday, as soon as I catch him."

I looked up from my pad and grinned in unsuspected amusement at her reply saying she hadn't caught him yet. My boss couldn't contain himself. He let out a slight snort and then turned in his swivel desk chair and faced the wall away from us to control him-self.

"I see . . . ," I stated, biting my own lip for a moment, to keep from laughing. Apparently, my new client was a teen with a crush on her boss. She was probably jealous of some adult woman he was dating. I was definitely amused. "What has your boss been up to, that you feel the need to have him followed?"

I couldn't just come right out and ask her about her boss' sleeping partners. She was way too young, underage.

"My boss thinks I am a kid. He doesn't see me as a woman, his woman. I have done everything to please him, including having had my toes straightened." She replied in a serious voice pointing to her taped toes on both feet.

"You have straightened your toes to try to catch a man?" I asked in disbelief.

"Some girls straighten their kinky, curly hair to look more attractive. I had ugly toes. My middle two toes, on both of my feet, overlapped each other. They looked like long slugs, crawling all over the top of each other, trying to get away from salt being poured on them. I knew my boss thought my feet were less than desirable, compared to the other women who work for him. I had to do something to even the playing field. So . . . , I straightened them."

I could hear a second snort escape from my boss who was still turned from us, facing the wall. Speaking with his back to us, he interjected into our conversation, "You haven't heard the best part yet, Monty."

I thought about Jen. When we dated in college, she had very kinky, curly black hair. I recalled how she vainly went, once a month, to get it straightened. She always did look better afterwards.

"That sounds like a reasonable thing to do, considering the condition of your toes. However, you still haven't told me why you feel the need to have me follow your boss. If you are not dating him, he is not a cheater if he sees other women. Cheating spouses is our agency's expertise."

Once again, I heard my boss snort.

"He is a cheater. He just doesn't know it yet." She replied unsmiling. "Until he discovers that I am his woman, he doesn't know that he is playing around on me."

For a moment, I wondered if my boss was trying to stick me with his worst case for the year. I could just see myself hanging out in some teeny bopper fast food place, eating one too many bad hamburgers, and photographing pimple faced register girls who were standing a little too close to whom Miss Panda thought was her man. I was going to kill my boss.

"Tell me about your boss." I stated, playing along with whatever my boss was up to.

"My boss hires only women and he pays for our once a week pedicures. He says beautiful feet are part of his reputation."

"Boss pays for pedicure feet . . . ," I repeated, while pretending to write it down on my note pad. Surely she wasn't a teen hooker working for some pimp. She didn't seem the type. "Go on!"

"There are five women who work for my boss, besides me. All have crushes on him and there is a competition to see who can snag, catch, and marry him. I think one of the five has managed to lure him into going with her on a romantic jaunt to Lake Tahoe this weekend. I need to know who my serious competition is, so I can nip it in the bud. No one is spending a romantic weekend with him but me. I will do anything, including slipping in and rubbing down his motel sheets with Poison Ivy. He will get a rash from her he won't ever forget. She will get a rash that she won't want to repeat. If that doesn't work, I just might cut off his hot dog and make him a man that no woman but me will ever want."

Then I snorted and laughed. "Are you serious?"

"Damn right, I am!" She replied. "He is going to save his yang for me, or I am going to see that he doesn't have one."

At that point, Charlie broke out into laughter with his back to us. "Ask her who her boss is, Monty?"

"Alright, Miss Panda, let us get down to business. Give

me the name of your boss and where you work." I replied, a little annoyed at Charlie's unprofessional ism, laughing, and interruptions.

"His name is Zeke. He owns Zeke's Feet Detective Agency." She replied, as she reached down and caressed what must have been an aching toe.

"This is a pro-bono case coming out of my pocket, Monty." Charlie, my boss, threw out as he spun around in his office chair grinning from ear to ear. "She definitely needs our help, not to mention Jackie over at the Hollywood Beauty Spa."

My mouth dropped open. I knew what he was inferring. It was well known that Zeke only dated one woman, a beauty operator named Jackie who did the hair of the stars.

"Who is Jackie?" Pandora innocently asked.

"She cuts Zeke's hair." I threw in, giving my boss somewhat of a 'be quiet' look. Most detectives kept their families and girlfriends a secret, in fear of some pervert trying to get even. My boss was one of the few individuals that knew Zeke had a lady friend. Apparently, Pandora and Zeke's female detectives did not know about her.

"Oh . . . ," Pandora replied. "After I catch him, he will use a male barber."

Once again, my boss Charlie snorted. I wanted to laugh, but I tried to control myself. I knew my boss was enjoying e very crazy bit of this encounter with his new, special, pro bono client. Charlie and Zeke were golfing buddies. They got together every Wednesday morning. Detectives have a tendency to pal up and be friends, just as nurses, teachers, or other professionals do. This was my boss' chance to be the man, or number one in his friendship with Zeke. I could see that he was enjoying the surprise canary he was eating.

"What is in this for you?" I whispered to Charlie when Pandora leaned over to stroke what must have been aching toes. The splints between her toes did look uncomfortable.

"Jackie . . . ," He whispered back. "Zeke fools around with one of his female detectives and I move in and get his hair dresser girlfriend and all her star referrals. Sweet . . . !"

I bit my lip and shook my head. Pandora was still busy with her sore toes.

"Are you nuts?" I spit out in a whisper to my boss. "Zeke is the finest detective in this city. He will know if he is being followed."

"He is good isn't he . . . ," Pandora stated, as she sat back up in her chair, looking a little dreamy eyed like teenagers did when they had crushes.

"I have to ask you one last question, just for the file. It is important. Has Zeke been messing with you, behind the other's backs?" I asked, knowing she was under age.

"I wish . . . ," She retorted. "I haven't managed to get past his office door. There is always a line of his female detectives catering to his every whim. They even carry him the coffee that I go to the trouble to make for him. I am just the girl who answers the phones, to him. I am low man on the totem pole, as they say. My flat chest and ugly toes hasn't helped me. I just don't have the upstairs endowments the older girls do. My toes I have straightened, but I can't make my boobs grow. I have tried."

My mouth dropped open at her surprise, unnecessary, shared information. I then recalled when I was a teen boy wanting my chin hair to grow. One of my uncles had told me to rub garlic on it every day. I did it, wanting beard hair so bad to make me look older. Pandora had straightened her toes for love, and was trying to make her boobs grow. A little tiny piece of my heart opened up, and I felt compassion for her. As a rule, I did not let women in my life, for my own personal reasons.

Charlie took over the conversation.

"We know what you want, Miss Pandora. I personally know that your boss Zeke plans to go to Lake Tahoe this weekend. I will send Monty down with his camera. If your boss is romancing one of his female detectives, Monty will photograph them. You will know who your competition is. If Zeke has his zipper unzipped, or his pants down, he is fair game for our camera."

"Thank you, Mr. Charlie. A girl has to do what a girl has to do. At the moment, I have to see who Zeke is cheating on me with. He is my man, even if he doesn't know it yet."

"Now, don't worry about a thing, Miss Panda. On your way out, leave photos of the five female detectives with the receptionist. She will make up a folder for Monty. You are guaranteed that we will catch your cheater!" My boss stated, trying to act professional and above board with Miss Pandora?"

Thank you, Mr. Charlie." Panda replied. "However, there is one more thing I need help with."

"What is that?" Charlie asked all smiles.

"I am sure you run across all sorts of unusual people in your line of work. Do you know where I might find a legitimate psychic healer? My aura is all out of whack, due to my toe surgeries. I can't concentrate on making myself over in a gorgeous manner for Zeke, when all my waking moments are spent wishing the pain in my toes would go away."

In shock at her request, I glanced over at Charlie who was out of the line of vision of Pandora. He put his finger to his ear and did the twirling crazy gesture sign. I bit my lip and nodded.

"Monty will be happy to find you a psychic healer." Charlie then replied. "In fact, I believe he rents his loft apartment from one. You will fix her up with Milky Way at my expense. Won't you Monty?"

"Your wish is my command boss." I replied, raising an eyebrow at him. "I assume you are paying for my time doing so?"

"Absolutely," Charlie replied. "Whatever the future woman of Zeke wants from us is at my expense."

Then Pandora left, hobbling barefoot and carrying her hot pink, open toed spikes.

When she was gone, and my boss' office door was closed, Charlie broke out in uncontrollable belly laughter. I knew he was about to stick it to his golfing buddy best friend and rival detective, Zeke.

"By the way Charlie," I spit out when he quit laughing, "Why didn't you offer to fix her up with Milky Way? You go to see her every week for a reading."

"I don't want Milky Way to think I am an associate of the

dits that just walked out. Milky Way is one hot, no nonsense mama. My going for Tarot and palm readings is my song and dance getting her to notice me."

Then, I snorted and belly laughed.

CHAPTER TWENTY-TWO

A NEW FRIEND

After meeting Miss Pandora in my boss' office, I returned home to my loft apartment above Milky Way's palm reading business. Seeing that Milky Way did not have a client, I popped in for a short visit. If I didn't, she would make her way upstairs later and disturb my sleep. I was fast learning my new landlord's quirks.

"Is business slow today?" I asked, finding her standing and staring at her white reading room door. I thought she perhaps had ideas about painting it. She was looking at it from all angles.

"I just can't figure it out, Monty. You and I were both witnesses to this door changing and becoming a portal opening. There has to be a way to get it to happen again. I am thinking about going to see Miss Wanda, for a little professional input."

"Who in the heck is Miss Wanda?" I asked.

"She is a street woman downtown who speaks with the dead. Every evening, just as the sun starts to go down, she sets up shop on the third bench in the park. She is the one who taught me to read the Tarot, when I first arrived in this city."

I shook my head. Was I in some sort of limbo? Pandora wanted me to find her a legitimate psychic. Charlie wanted to date my palm reading landlady, and Milky Way was thinking of inquiring of a medium named Miss Wanda. All I needed was for my crazy world to come full circle and find Miss Wanda knocking on my door needing my services.

"What makes you think Miss Wanda can solve your problem?" I asked, going along with the flow of conversation.

"If she can't help me, no one can. She opens her portal door every evening at will. The dead never cease speaking with her. Ask Charlie, he knows her. He is a regular on her bench."

Caught off guard, I snorted. "He what . . . ?"

"You heard me. He visits Miss Wanda regularly. She is pulling in big bucks off of him."

"This is a shocker. I have never heard him speak of her." I replied.

"He has a thing for her, I think." Milky Way replied with a sigh. "She definitely rakes in the cash from him."

"I assume that you know Charlie is attracted to you?"

"I don't have time for egotistical jerks who think a woman is nothing more than a good lay and someone to do their dishes and laundry. Charlie has no true interest in me and my world of mystical doors and astral travel. He just likes the idea of chasing me. I like the idea that his chasing me costs him forty dollars a pop." She replied, smiling from ear to ear.

"You are a smart business woman, Milky Way. However,

you probably should flirt with him a little, or he might take his forty pops and start crossing Miss Wanda's palm with them."

"You don't have to worry about that, Monty. Miss Wanda is so homely that she couldn't catch a man if she wanted, in my opinion. I think she might be one of Charlie's snitches. He sits on her bench on a regular basis, handing her his greenbacks."

"I have never heard of him speaking of a snitch named Wanda. Do you think she might be black mailing Charlie for some reason?" I asked, knowing everyone had secrets of some sort. I was a detective.

"Go down town and ask her, if you dare." Milky Way replied with a snicker.

I was left wondering what my boss' secret was. However, I had no intentions of messing in my boss' affairs. It had taken me years to get on with a detective agency. I wasn't about to rock my boat and get fired for approaching one of his possible secret snitches.

"I think I will pass on visiting Miss Wanda on her bench. However, I have other business to take up with you. Charlie has asked me to make an appointment with you for one of his clients, a Miss Pandora. Charlie says for you to bill him for her reading. Miss Pandora thinks her aura is out of whack, whatever that means." I stated, as I was about to end our visit.

Milky Way grinned and then replied. "An aura is a ring of energy emitting from your body. It is sort of a full body halo. Holes or cracks appear in it when something is wrong or out of whack, as your Miss Pandora stated. For instance, your aura has a huge hole in it, at your center lower torso level. A girlfriend or a few hot nights with the right woman could cure it."

"I do not believe in such crap, and my sex life is not up for discussion, thank you." I replied a little annoyed.

~   ~   ~

Returning to my loft apartment, I stripped off naked and then sprawled across my bed to sleep. Daytime was the middle of my night. Cheaters did their thing mostly after work and late into the night. I was a detective who kept their hours. Being the middle of my night, I fell instantly asleep.

Suddenly, I found myself leaving my body and levitating. Then, I flew thru my ceiling and off into the skies of the land of dreams and nightmares. I shot like a jet past cities, forests, and farm land. I flew past strange gatherings of people with unfamiliar faces. Then, I found myself hovering on the porch of my 'fifty miles from nowhere' cabin. I peeped in the front window and saw that Kristina was busy cooking at the antiquated wood, cook stove. She was beautiful, as always. Once more, she looked younger like she was de-aging. My heart leaped inside me, just as it did every time when I saw her.

Turning from the window, I peered out at the mountainous landscape. There was no snow. It appeared to be spring time. Floating over to the cabin's door, I raised my hand and gave the plank door three firm knocks. No one came to the door. Disappointed, I gave the portal door a second round of firm knocks. Still the door didn't open. That annoyed me, because I had been very good at opening the door and letting strangers seeking shelter in years before. I wanted in. No one was making an effort to open the door for me.

A strange bench suddenly appeared on the cabin's porch, beneath the window. Along with the sudden appearance of the window seat, a strange being popped out of nowhere and into my presence. A troll of a little woman hovered next to me, as I studied the door and wondered why it would not open. I glanced down at the face of the ugly little woman, who was barely taller than my knee. I told myself that she had to be some distant relative of the dwarf Wise brothers, from my original cabin experience.

As I glanced down, I could see that the short female Troll was visibly angry, showing her silver capped teeth, and snarling at me. I was a little frightened, even though I was six feet and she was barely four. At the same time, I was amused with the sight of her. She had on a bathing suit with Florida scenes printed on it. Although she was short, she had the proverbial problem with cottage cheese thighs and aging, old hag wrinkles. On the tip of her nose, in an about to slip off my perch position, she was wearing sunglasses that had 4th of July red, white, and blue striped frames. On her head was a big floppy sun hat that had all colors of tropical birds and Tarot cards attached. I snorted, and then bit my lip to control my laughter. As a woman, she definitely was not eye candy. However, she did come across as being a character. You have heard the expression, concerning an ugly baby, 'Only their mother could love them'? In my opinion, she definitely fell in that category.

"What makes you think you can cross my bridge, or approach this portal?" The Troll of a little woman snarled.

"I gave up listening to the demands of short, snotty nosed

elves like you, years ago." I shot back in annoyance, thinking about all the Christmas crazy kids I had played Santa for, in prior years at Maxi's toy store. "What are you, a reject from my knee who didn't get what they wanted for Christmas? Did good old Protestant Santa disappoint you? Did the experience make you ugly and stunt your growth? Is your name now Shorty or Stumpy?"

"My name is Wanda, and you will address me respectfully." She stated, suddenly going for my knee, missing, but biting the crap out of my Jewish thigh.

I fought her off, and then backed up from her in shock. "Bite me again, and you will regret it. This bridge, as you call it, is just as much mine as yours. We are equal in our stance on it. However, I am about to throw you off." I spouted, from my backed up position in a corner, beyond the bench.

"You . . . equal with me . . . !" She snarled. "I am not a dimwit, dud of a giant cowering in a corner. Just try to throw me off this porch bridge. You have no power here. Do you want to know why?" She asked with a sadistic grin.

I was not smiling. She had dared to call me a dud. I felt freshly sliced open, just as I had felt the day Jen called me a dud, breaking off our engagement.

"Why?" I asked in a pissed off voice, fully knowing she was going to tell me anyway.

The ugly, little Troll of a woman reminded me of my dominating sister, Maxi. I had always been the shrinking violet, the cowering half in our relationship as twins. She said what she thought, and I was forced to listen, whether I wanted to or not.

"You have no power, because you are hiding in your California hole, like a frightened little run away dud of a rabbit with only three legs. Furthermore, this cabin's porch is my bridge, and you are not three legs hopping across it." She spit out.

"Watch me!" I stated, standing up in a flash from my cowering position. I stepped from the corner and darted in my birthday suit past her. Then, before she could react, I quickly gave the cabin's door three quick hard raps yelling, "Help . . . ! Let me in!"

Instantly, the cabin's door swung open in my dream. Just as quickly, the troll of a woman disappeared in a split second poof, taking with her the bench and cabin's porch out from under me. I fell to the dirty, grass less, rocky ground below, harshly scraping my naked knees and elbows. There was no snow to buffer my fall.

"I am sorry, Wanda!" I yelled, wanting the vicious, little woman troll to return the cabin's steps and porch. "I need the porch to access my cabin's door."

Suddenly, Kris stepped to the door, which was now above my head. She peered down at me and asked snidely in her feminine charming manner. "Do you always attend Christmas Eve gatherings in your birthday suit?"

Embarrassed at being naked, and remembering that I was a dud, I covered my male parts with my hands.

"I am sorry that I am naked." I yelled up at Kris. "I am not sure where my Santa suit is." Then I bit my lip and wondered why I had said that. I hated the years I donned the Santa suit, playing Maxi's toy store St. Nick.

"I am sorry that my heart is stripped naked." She replied.

"I do not know where my husband is."

It annoyed me that Kris always totally ignored the fact that I had feelings for her. Sometimes, the person you love, or think you love, can bring out the worst in you.

Realizing that my dream portal visitation with Kris could end as quickly as it had started, I blurted out. "Your perverted Santa husband has married another. He has traded you in for six dogs, three cats, a taxi, and a sexy second wife in Chicago. There is no need for you to wait for him in your Heaven. When he crosses over, he will be bringing his preferred second wife with him. He does not want you or your son. He has chosen a family of pedigree cats and dogs, instead. Your Santa husband sees you as genetically flawed and worthless. He refers to you and your son as 'throw backs.'"

Suddenly, starting to hover in a standing position on the ground beneath the cabin's door, I watched Kris burst into tears. There was no way I could rise and access the door to comfort her. There was some sort of force shield preventing me from doing so. My angry words (throw backs) had hurt her, just as Jen's word (dud) had hurt me years before. The door of the cabin started to fade. Then, 'poof' the cabin, with Kris in it, in my dream disappeared. I angrily yelled begging Kris not to leave me on the outside of her world looking in. She did not reappear or respond.

Just as the cabin door had disappeared in a flash, I suddenly whooshed into the astral, passing a sea of unfamiliar faces. Somehow, I knew the unfamiliar faces belonged to souls of deceased humans. I shot across the astral skies, naked as a Jay Bird. In just a matter of moments, I was hovering above the roof of my loft apartment. In a flash, I then shot down thru the roof and into my sleeping human form.

Waking from my dream, I realized that I was wringing wet with sweat. I ran my fingers thru my hair, punched my pillow, and they lay back down. Sleep would not come. How could I have been so cruel, using the words 'throw backs'? I was really disgusted with myself. Once more, I was sure that I had alienated Kris. I wanted so much for her to love me, not be annoyed with me. As I lay there sleepless, I thought about how she had once more appeared younger, seeming to have de-aged five or so years. I was pleased with her look. My displeasure was in myself, and my cutting words. Jen had sliced my heart into a thousand pieces with her word 'dud'. I had just sliced Kris open with mine.

Kris' ability to de-age fascinated me. However, I knew that Christmas crazy Kristina was trying to look better and younger for her husband, not me. I was obsessed with having what I could not have. I had also wanted Jen, once upon a time. Now, I was in a state of limbo wanting Kristina, and not willing to want someone new. A Christmas crazy, protestant, female ghost controlled the beating of my Jewish heart. I wanted to walk away from her and her memory. I just couldn't.

As I lay fighting my pillow, trying to force sleep to come, I considered Wanda the Troll's ugly predicament. How many rejections in life had she endured, to make her such a vicious little creature? I was sure that she was just as hopeless as I was, when it came to relationships. I was sure that Milky Way would have a field day reading her 'out of whack' aura.

~   ~   ~

My dream encounter with Kris left me in a depressed state. The only way I saw out of my blue state was to dive into my work as a detective. My love for my job was the only thing that kept me sane. Fighting depression, I decided it was time to back off from all mystical doors, palm readers, and ghosts. Sometimes, if you can't fix yourself, you have to just walk away from your problems in order to cope. Milky Way was a little disappointed in my sudden lack of interest in her mystical world. It caused a fork in the road of our friendship. Her path was leading her to further pursuit of doors and portals. My chosen path was leading me away from them. Our friendship cooled, at least on my part.

First on my immediate calendar was to follow Zeke for the weekend in Lake Tahoe. It proved to be a simple case of snapping a few photos of Zeke, publicly, with the woman he met there. The weekend away was good for me.

Miss Pandora was the youngest client I had ever done work for. Charlie had warned me not to take any overly sexy or nude bedroom shots, because of her age. This wasn't a divorce case. It was just a ditsy teen who wanted to know who her competition was. Secretly, I knew that Charlie hoped his golfing buddy was cheating on his hairdresser companion in Hollywood. Charlie's detective agency was second in the area. He wanted to be first. Zeke's Feet Agency occupied that spot. Charlie hoped a little scandalous dirt, on his golfing pal and fellow detective, might degrade Zeke to number two and upgrade him to first. It didn't turn out that way. Zeke's woman in Lake Tahoe turned out to be Jackie the hairdresser. Also, Zeke's parents from the East had flown in for the weekend. Zeke, Jackie, and his parents spent the weekend very publicly together. It was sort of a small, planned, family weekend reunion.

I was sure Miss Pandora would be pleased about Zeke not being with one of his hot female detectives. How she would feel about the hair dresser, I wasn't sure; or if she even knew about her. I was used to old women crying in our offices over photos of cheating husbands. I had learned to deal with it. However, I wasn't sure I wanted to listen to the drama tears of a teen. My lesbian sister Maxi, as a teenager, had driven me wild with her emotional outbursts and tears when straight skirts wouldn't give her the time of day. My sister never seemed to get it thru her head that straight girls were not attracted to her. I was sure that Miss Pandora was probably just as dense. There was no way that her boss Zeke would ever consider having a relationship with her. She was seventeen and he was in his thirties. Not only that, it was very evident in Lake Tahoe that he was very fond of his Hollywood hairdresser.

I returned to the city late on Sunday night and met Miss Panda on Monday evening at her job to give her the photos. Zeke and his detectives had left for the evening to do their thing, following cheaters. It was about six in the evening.

"Why are you staring at your desk drawer?" I asked, taking a chair across from her at her receptionist's desk, where she answered the phone. I had my packet of photos in hand to present her, of Zeke and the hairdresser.

"I think I may have taken one too many of my toe surgery pain pills." She replied, continuing to stare at her desk drawers. "My middle desk drawer became stuck earlier, right after I popped a couple of my pills. I hit the drawer hard three times, trying to loosen it. Then, I started seeing things. I may be a little higher than a kite, Mr. Monty."

"Do you want to close up the office and let me take you home?" I asked, seeing that she was a little fidgety, perspiring, and pale.

"Taking me to a psych ward might be more appropriate." She replied, pointing to her desk drawer which I could not see from my seated position the other side of her desk. "Come around to my side of this desk, and tell me that I am not seeing a ghost peeping at me from my desk drawer, which is now a house door with butterflies painted all over it."

"What?" I asked, dropping my packet of photos on her desk. I rose quickly and circled the desk. I arrived on her side, just in time to see a door fading. It wasn't my cabin door, but it was definitely a mystical door belonging to some unknown witch, seer, or medium. I was in shock.

"Did you see the ghost peeping at me?" She asked nervously in an excited voice of disbelief.

"Holy, Jewish sh . . . it," I replied, as I watched the door fade and disappear.

I had forgotten that I was in the presence of a woman. The foul expression had just fallen out of my mouth, due to shock. My devout Jewish mother, had she heard me speak so as a boy, would have taken me by the ear and marched me on tippee toes straight to the bathroom, where she would have soaped my Jewish mouth out. I would have been blowing bubbles out both ends for days.

"So, it isn't my pain pills causing me to see the butterfly door and ghost?" She asked, in a somewhat relieved voice.

"I didn't see your ghost, but I definitely saw your mystical butterfly door. How did you get it to appear?"

Once more, my safe haven world in California was being invaded by portal doors and ghosts. It was like I didn't have the choice to walk away.

"The phone was ringing off the hook, and I had run out of room in my phone message log. I needed a new phone log pad from that middle drawer. It was stuck and wouldn't open. With three incoming calls waiting, I was in a panic. I gave the drawer's handle some hard shaking. It remained stuck. Then, I stood and gave it a couple of serious kicks. It didn't budge. In desperation, I stooped and pounded on the drawer as hard as I could with my fist. That was when I heard voices inside the drawer. There might be a bugging device in the desk. I figured the little thing was probably what was causing the drawer to stick. I was angry, thinking Zeke was keeping tabs on me, when he wasn't in the office. I gave the drawer three more hard pounds with my fist. I was determined to get that device. Instantly, the drawer turned into the butterfly door you saw. I think I have taken an overdose of my pain pills, Mr. Monty. You won't tell Zeke that I may be a druggy, will you? I promise to clean up my act as soon as my toes are well."

"If you are suffering a pain pill hallucination, Miss Pandora, so am I." I replied.

"Are you taking pills too?" She asked naively.

At that point, I was totally amused with her. She was young, gullible, and had the most 'ditsy' sense of humor. I liked her. It was a pity she wasn't older. I was over thirty and she was just seventeen.

"I only saw the fading door. Maybe, had I taken one of your special toe pills, I might have also seen the ghost." I replied chuckling. "Demonstrate to me exactly what you did to get the butterfly door to appear? I need to document it for Charlie, just in case it is some sort of a virtual reality bugging device."

Stooping beside her, as she sat on the edge of her office chair, I took a good look at the three wooden desk drawers. I tried pulling open the middle drawer. It was stuck.

Miss Panda stooped down beside me, gave me a young, know it all female grin, and then knocked three times on the door with her knuckles yelling, "I need in."

Then, to my shock, the drawer started to become misty, like a cloud. Then in a 'poof' moment, it turned into the white door with butterflies painted all over it.

"Oh my Jewish God . . . You have figured out the secret to opening some other seer or medium's antiquated portal between worlds. How long has Zeke had this desk and where did he get it?"

"Zeke purchased my desk from a man who inherited a rundown mansion in Los Angeles, when he first went into business. He didn't have the funds for a new one." She replied, eyeing the butterfly door that was once more looming mystically in our sight. "The man told Zeke the desk talked, and he wanted it gone. Zeke laughed thinking he was crazy, and paid the man twenty dollars for it. I guess, I am the one the desk talks to now." She added with big eyes. "I am throwing my bottle of toe pills away, as soon as I can."

I turned to her, put my arm around her and hugged her,

excitedly. "You are wonderful, Miss Pandora. My Jewish mother would love you, if she were alive."

Pandora looked into my eyes sheepishly and grinned, with her little wire framed glasses sliding to the end of her nose. Then a familiar voice began to speak, interrupting our moment. I glanced at the butterfly door which was now open. Standing in its doorway was my deceased Jewish mother, who was holding a bar of soap.

"What do you mean, Edmond, if I were alive? I am very much alive, and heard you speaking of your Jewish excrement earlier. When you cross over here to my paradise, expect a good mouth washing. I am ashamed of you for speaking in such a manner in front of a female you barely know. Do you want our Jewish God to be angry with me for not raising you properly?"

At that point I fell to my knees in shock. I felt Pandora put her arm around my shoulders, steadying me. My dead Jewish mother was chewing me out for using foul language. What next? On my knees, and totally at a loss for words to reply, I watched as my mother faded from the feet up, and then the butterfly door do the same.

Regaining my composure, I stood with help from Miss Pandora.

"What do we do about our shared hallucination?" Miss Pandora asked.

"I won't tell anyone about what we have seen, if you don't. We definitely do not want your boss Zeke thinking you are hooked on toe drugs, or my boss Charlie thinking I have been nipping the bottle." I replied.

Turning my face toward Pandora, I noticed that she was

giving me the funniest look.

"Is something wrong?" I asked.

"Earlier, you said I was wonderful. Did you mean that Mr. Monty, or was it just the alcoholic in you talking?"

Chuckling and ignoring the alcoholic innuendo, I replied. "Miss Panda, it takes a special person to walk between worlds and open portal doors. I only know two people that can do it. You are one of the two. Yes, you are wonderful, and I am lucky to know you. It isn't every day that a guy meets a Protestant woman who can put a Jewish man on his knees. That was my mother beyond the door. You, Miss Pandora, are a Heavens Walker."

"My religion only speaks of one Heaven and Hell." She replied big eyed. "My church pastor has never spoken about other heavens, where ghosts and Jewish mothers exist."

God . . . I loved her craziness. If I were Zeke, I would dump the hairdresser in a heartbeat for Miss Pandora. I snorted at her remark and then grinned. Miss Pandora was pretty, psychic, odd, and ditsy funny. I could see myself asking her out in a few months, after she turned eighteen. I was ready to love again. Then a familiar voice spoke in my head.

"You are a dud!" Jen stated. "No woman wants a man who cannot father children."

My own voice followed in my head telling me, "Forget asking her out. Quit fantasizing. Miss Pandora will want a man who can give her children."

I immediately dismissed the thought of ever considering her more, than a detective agency client.

"Do you know anything about psychics or mediums, Miss Pandora?" I asked, wanting to give her some insight into what was happening to her.

"I am a good Baptist. I don't believe in such things. Psychics and mediums talk to the dead. They are devil worshipers and cursed in the eyes of God. You won't catch me within ten feet of one, or a Tarot Reader. I am born again and going to Heaven." She quickly replied, pulling out a little gold cross on a chain, and displaying it for me. "Psychics and mediums are human tools of the devil."

"Well, Miss Panda, I hate to burst your religious bubble." I stated, trying to control my amusement with her. "You may be a good, Bible thumping Baptist. However, you are also a medium. You have the gift of opening doors between worlds and speaking with the dead. The ghost in your drawer was my deceased mother."

"The ghost, speaking of soap, was your mother?" She asked in shock.

"It was definitely my mother, and she definitely was not a good old Baptist." I replied, grinning from ear to ear. It had been hard for me to admit over the years, that those of other religious faiths crossed over and lived in paradise. I had always been taught that anyone not Jewish was doomed.

"I knew I would be in trouble, if I didn't put my tithes in the Baptist's Sunday morning offering plates last year. I thought God would understand that I needed every penny I could get a hold of, to pay for straightening my toes. Now, I am cursed by my Baptist God for not paying tithes. I am not into abusive relationships. I may need to divorce him and choose another. Is your Jewish God easy to get along with? Maybe he will let me sit on his pew, if I promise not to hold back my tithes anymore."

I laughed. She was naïvely ditsy, but so utterly wonderful. I even liked the thick lens, wire rimmed eye glasses she wore. Without her glasses, she was probably blind as a bat in the physical world. However, she could see between worlds with no problem. That made her unique. I liked unique. Jen, my former fiancé, had a crazy head of curly, black, ringlet hair. That was what had made her unique.

After discussing seers, witches, psychics, and mediums with Miss Pandora, I informed her that Zeke had gone to Lake Tahoe to spend time with his visiting parents from the East Coast. I then carefully told her that Zeke did have a woman on his arm, but the female wasn't one of his detectives. She seemed relieved that it was a hair dresser named Jackie from Hollywood that he was seeing. I gave my young client a photo of the hair dresser on Zeke's arm.

"Are you okay?" I asked, as Pandora stared at the photo.

"Well . . . the hair dresser has him just two days on the weekend. I have him five days during the week. I have the upper hand, and newly straightened toes. " She replied with a serious tone in her voice. "Give me a little time, and she will be history. My five days will overcome her two."

I admired the fact that she was totally committed to loving and snagging Zeke, although I was a bit jealous. I wondered what it would be like to have a woman love you so much, that she would have her toes straightened for you. Zeke was one lucky man, even if he didn't know it.

~   ~   ~

Weeks passed and I didn't see any more of Pandora, not

that I didn't want to call her. She was underage and I knew better. It was Easter time in the Protestant's world. I had been on a grueling two week case that had just ended. Tired to the bone, I had crashed in the nude on my loft apartment bed. It was a warm spring day. I had opened the window before lying down, to let in the warm spring breeze. My sleep was suddenly disturbed by someone sitting down on the side of my bed. Alarmed, I turned over and quickly reached for my handgun which I kept beneath the edge of my mattress. Detectives have enemies. Ex-spouses, photographed for cheating, were top of the list. In an instant, I was sitting up in my birthday suit, with gun aimed.

"Don't shoot me, don't shoot . . . , it is me, Miss Pandora."

I lowered my gun and stuck it back beneath my mattress. "How did you get in?" I asked, half asleep. Then I quickly grabbed for the edge of the top sheet to cover myself. A woman dropping in unannounced had not been a consideration when I crashed on top of my sheets in the nude.

"Zeke fired me!" Miss Panda stated sniffling. She then instantly burst into tears.

I watched as she pulled her feet, in her four inch open toed, pink spikes, upon the bed and fold her arms around them. Then she rocked back and forth like a little girl, as her tears fell like waterfalls.

"He what . . . ?" I asked, trying to get fully awake, while at the same time wondering why she had made her way to me.

Sitting up, dragging the sheet with me, I scooted over to the side of the bed and put my arm around her shoulders to comfort her. Tears and snot were definitely flow-ing. My Miss Pandora, in her little wire rimmed glasses, was not a pretty picture at the moment. However, her hot pink painted toe nails were very eye catching. The wooden splints and tape were gone from between her toes. I liked what I saw. However, I knew what adult and children boundaries were. Treating her like a little sister was as far as I could go. I was sure she wasn't eighteen yet. Besides, I was not a man. She wouldn't want me, if she knew I was a dud.

"He fired me for the photo you took and a note I wrote." She replied thru sniffles.

"What kind of note?" I asked, hugging her shoulders to me and snuggling my four o'clock shadowed, Jewish face next to her pale ivory one.

"I wrote his hair dresser in Hollywood, staking my claim for Zeke. You would think I started World War III. All I did was ask her to back off, telling her that Zeke was my man. I did not know that she was the main source for Zeke's rich Hollywood clients. Zeke was furious. He yelled at me, saying that she was more important to him, than I was."Pandora stated, bursting into a second round of tears and running snot.

"I am sorry, Pandora." I replied simply. "In my opinion, you are far prettier than the hairdresser I saw him with. Not only that, she looked like she had size thirteen feet in her hi-heels. You are one up on her, Mss Pandora. You have pretty dainty feet."

"Thank you, Mr. Monty." She stated, wiping her nose on the sleeve of her blouse.

I reached for a tissue from a box on my nightstand, and

handed it to her.

"She puts her spikes on, just like me." She stated as she blew her nose. "She might be Zeke's source for rich and famous clients. However, it is me that answers the phones and sets him up with appointments from the yellow book ones. I am just as important as she is."

I wanted to laugh, but I didn't dare. I bit my lip for a moment and then waded into conversation.

"I dare say your newly straightened toes have walked a little heavy on Zeke's financial egg shells." I stated, trying not to laugh. I was sure that my boss Charlie was laughing his head off at the idea of Zeke trying to explain Miss Pandora to Jackie, the Hollywood hairdresser.

"I may have walked on his eggshells, but he has stomped all over my heart. Did you know that hearts are like egg shells, Mr. Monty?" She asked thru sniffles.

"Yes, Miss Pandora, I definitely know how fragile the heart can be." I replied, thinking about Jen and Kristina. They had both trampled on my fragile heart. Both had dumped me for someone else. "May I ask why you have chosen to make your way here to me?"

"I don't have anywhere to go, Mr. Monty. I secretly lived and slept in a sleeping bag in the back stockroom of Zeke's offices for the last year. I saved and spent all of my wages, for the last year, having my toes straightened. Would you let me stay with you for a day or so, till I figure out what to do? I don't have a family to go home to. I am now homeless."

I bit my lip. How could I turn her down? I knew what it was like to have a broken heart, and to have to walk away and leave all that was familiar. I had abandoned Maxi, my Jewish temple, and Chicago when Jen hurt me. California had become my safe haven. Now Miss Panda needed my apartment for her safe haven, till she found her balance again.

"Yes, you can stay with me, till you figure out what to do. I sleep days. You can have the bed nights." I replied, secretly thrilled to have someone in my world. "Make yourself at home. This is the middle of my night, and I am going back to sleep."

"Thank you, Mr. Monty. I won't forget this. I am devoted to those who are loyal to me. Is there anything about me that you want me to change? Zeke saw my toes as less than desirable. I will change for you."

"There is not one thing I would change about you, Miss Pandora. In my book, you are just perfect. To mess with your uniqueness, would be like taking scissors to a Picasso masterpiece." I replied removing my arm from around her shoulders.

"Really . . . you think I am perfect?"

"Yes, Miss Pandora, you are a number ten in my book, a gorgeous goddess."

Just as quickly as she had burst into tears, she quit her sniffling and beamed. I could see that she needed me, just as much as I needed her.

Pandora and I become roommates. Knowing she was young, I respected her and did not make any moves on her. I was twice her age. Milky Way and Pandora became friends. My landlady taught Pandora to read the Tarot cards, and then hired her as a part time assistant. Pandora became a new person, and started dressing like a gypsy. She wore lots of gold bangle bracelets and flat sandals that tied up her legs. Watching her change and evolve was fascinating.

After her initial moment of tears in my arms for comfort, she never mentioned Zeke again, even though we lived next door to his agency. Pandora's total clamming up about Zeke worried me. I wondered if she had internalized Zeke's words, inferring she was unimportant, like I had Jen's calling me a dud. Pandora and I were both locked Pandora boxes. Both of us had secret hurts.

Charlie did enjoy gloating over getting to stick it to his friend, Zeke. In doing so, he lost his golfing buddy.

After a week or so, Zeke sent Pandora a bouquet of pink roses, apologizing for his temper and asking her to come back to work for him. Pandora threw the roses and the unopened note in the trash. There are some hurts in life that flowers and words cannot make go away. Even if it meant never getting on with Zeke's Feet, I decided to stand by Pandora, no matter what. I knew what she was going thru. She had loved a man, who had chosen someone besides her. His firing her and telling her she was not important to him had cut her to the bone. It had taken me over ten years to halfway get over Jen's words calling me a dud. I wondered if it would take my Miss Pandora as long.

CHAPTER TWENTY-THREE

PANDORA'S DOOR

It was the end of June. Fourth of July weekend was approaching. Maxi had insisted that I fly back home to Chicago and play Santa for her Christmas in July, grand re-opening of her toy store. I was reluctant, but I did have one consolation; Jen was dead. No human should hate someone so much that they wish them dead. However, my emotional state embraced that feeling. I was glad Jen was gone. At the same time, I was dreading interacting with her children, whom my sister had adopted. I was unlit fireworks, wrapped in a human body. I feared going off on Maxi, who seemed to be oblivious to the fact that Jen had almost destroyed me as a man.

Life is full of choices. Sometimes, we have to suck up who we are for the best of everyone concerned, if we love them. I was trying to make peace with my dominating sister Maxi, who was actually a brother stuck in a girl's body. The easiest way to do so was to play Santa for her. I planned to take a week of vacation time over the fourth to fly home. I had my ticket purchased, but felt the need for a little emotional support. I asked Pandora to fly with me to Chicago. She declined my invitation, much to my disappointment. She stated simply that she had already made plans.

It was the Eve of Independence Day. I was packed and ready to board a late day flight at six P.M. Having worked the night before, following a cheating spouse, I was sleeping my usual daytime hours. Awaking from a sound day sleep, about three in the afternoon, I expected to hear Pandora rattling about in the kitchen. However, the apartment was eerily quiet. Sitting up, I glanced about as I rubbed the sleep from my eyes. Then, my eyes focused in on a pile of familiar clothes, stacked on top of my trash can. I jumped up in a panic, recognizing that the clothes belonged to Pandora.

"Pandora . . . ?" I yelled. There was no answer.

Hurrying to the trash can, I checked to see if the pile of clothing articles were just discarded worn out ones. In shock, I realized that all of her new gypsy costumes, shoes, jewelry, and the clothing she had originally showed up at my apartment with, were there. I really panicked when I saw that her purse, wallet, money, and identification were also discarded there.

"Oh God . . . , please no!" I stated, making a run for the bathroom and flinging open the door in expectation of discovering that she had committed suicide in some fashion, while I was asleep. Pandora wasn't in there.

I knew how fragile Pandora's emotional state was, since Zeke had made her feel less than his Hollywood lady friend. No woman discarded all of their personal possessions for any reason other than suicide. Entering the bathroom, I quickly flung open the tiny door to the medicine cabinet. All of my items were there, including a prescription sleeper. However, Pandora's shelf was cleaned out. I glanced down at the trash can. All her personal items, including her toothbrush, deodorant, and nail polish, were discarded there. There was no mistaking that Pandora had snapped.

Returning to the one main room of my loft apartment, I quickly thumbed thru her clothing, spikes, and purse, on top of the trash can. I decided that she had left wearing her favorite pair of gypsy sandals and her first Gypsy costume, the one Milky Way had given her. She had chosen what I felt was the clothing she wanted to leave her Earth life in. I scanned the apartment for any sign of where she might be heading. That is when I spotted a handwritten note on the fridge front, held there by a butterfly magnet. Pandora loved butterflies. I grabbed the note quickly and started reading.

Dearest Monty,

Thank you for taking me in when I didn't have anywhere to go. You have stood by me! Thank you, for being my friend. I have tried to move on and forget about loving Zeke. I just cannot seem to do so! For my own sanity, I feel it is necessary to put some serious space between him and I. Milky Way does not know how to open her portal door between worlds. I do, and have secretly done so, making a trial run yesterday. While Milky Way is gone this morning, for a reading with Miss Wanda downtown, I plan to open the door, step thru it, and not return. My only regret in making this decision is leaving you behind. If it weren't for Zeke, I could fall madly in love with you. Thank you for seeing me as perfect, even though I know that I am not. Zeke's words, making me feel less of a woman than his hairdresser, gnaws at me. I know that I am a flawed reject that no man will ever want.

I will have crossed over to the other side by the time you read this. I will be taking my human body with me. You are a Jewish man, a religious one down deep. In your Bible, the Old Testament, one of your prophets was caught up to God in human form and did not taste of death. He was a portal walker, Monty, just like you and I. Special ones can walk physically between worlds. I am choosing to walk thru Milky Way's portal and dwell in the parallel world that humans, without our uniqueness, call Heaven. I have already been to Hell, loving Zeke.

Love, Pandora

P.S. When I opened the portal yesterday, a woman in a red pantsuit confronted me, asking me to beg you to look for her live son and care for him. She called him Snicker Doodle. She wants you to be Santa to him.

I sat down on the end of my unmade bed and ran my fingers thru my hair. Pandora was a female version of me. I saw myself as a dud, and she saw herself as a reject. Now, she was gone. Just as I had once fled to California, after Jen dumped me, Pandora had just fled to the in-between world of ghosts, her California. I wondered how many other deeply wounded individuals like Pandora existed on Earth.

Pissed over losing Pandora, I ignored the message from Kris. Pandora had been the only good thing in my life for years. I had secretly fought myself to keep from falling in love with her.

~   ~   ~

I knew Pandora was never returning. I showed Milky Way her discarded clothing and items, before boxing them and storing them in Milky Way's attic. In grief over losing Pandora, I cancelled my plane reservation and stood my sister up. She was not happy with me.

Six months passed and it was once more Christmas Eve. Maxi and I were not speaking again. I had no great plans for the Protestant's holiday. It seemed odd to me, that my Catholic boss Charlie would give me a holiday off that I did not celebrate. I was Jewish. Christmas Eve and Christmas Day meant nothing to me, other than reminding me of my cabin experience so many years before, and the years I reluctantly played Santa for Maxi in her toy store.

About four in the afternoon on Christmas Eve, my phone rang. I started not to answer it. However, after checking the phone number of who was calling, I answered. It was my boss Charlie.

"In case you have forgotten, I am officially off for the holidays." I blurted out, ignoring the hellos and pleasantries most phone calls started out with.

"I realize that, Monty. However, I have a favor to ask of you. I need you to deliver a little gift for me. I am tied up here in the office with back to back clients till at least seven tonight. Afterward, I am attending three back to back Christmas Eve parties, and then midnight mass."

"You want me to deliver a Christmas present?" I asked in disbelief. "You know that I am Jewish."

"Don't get your Jewish holy feathers ruffled." He huffed harshly, slightly raising his voice. "It isn't like I am asking you to deliver a red bowed, Santa paper wrapped box. It is just an envelope of cash."

"If it is a charity gift you are sending to the army or some other protestant organization, the answer is no. There are some boundaries I won't cross as a Jew. My Jewish God could strike me dead for supporting some gentile charity."

"Well, I am sure that my Catholic God and your Jewish God are going to be one and the same when we meet him someday. The only difference between Catholic me and Jewish you is that I confess in a booth and you confess and wail at a wall." Charlie retorted. "Besides, who has ever seen God? I haven't and neither have you. He could be a fairy tale like Santa Claus."

I bit my lip. His reference to Santa pushed all my faith's buttons. At the same time, I had to admit that my Jewish God of wrath had never actually spoken or appeared to me. Only mystical doors and ghosts seemed to have an interest in me.

"Okay . . . okay!" I huffed. "When and where do you want me to pick up the money, and where does it go?"

"Come here to the office. Millie will have the envelope of money ready. She will tell you how to find the person it is to be delivered to. It will be an easy, quick drop."

"How much money are we talking about?" I asked, thinking that Charlie was dealing in something illegal, or was possibly being blackmailed.

"Just a couple of hundred . . . to get a woman I know downtown thru the holidays."

"Oh . . . ," I stated, thinking that Charlie possibly had a secret lover stashed somewhere downtown. Maybe Milky Way wasn't the only woman he was chasing. "Is she a hot dish that you have stashed, to prevent me and your other detectives from hitting on her?"

"Yes, I have kept her a secret from you and my staff. However, I guarantee you that you won't be hitting on her, if you want to keep your yang."

"What is she; a police woman or possibly a Marshall Arts teacher?"

"I think Lion Tamer would come closer to describing her. She makes me jump thru hoops at times."

"A woman makes you jump thru hoops? She must be something." I laughed.

"You will understand when you meet her. She will be sitting on the third bench on the left path going into the downtown park. Just toss her the envelope of money and then get out of there."

"Just toss her the money and get out of there." I repeated.

"She has a nasty temper, not to mention being a little crazy. You don't want to mess with her." Charlie replied.

"What do you mean by crazy? Is she likely to pull a gun or knife on me?"

"She is not that kind of crazy, Monty. She hears voices, and can't hold down a job. So, I help her out now and then."

"Okay . . . , I will do it."

"Great! Forget my receptionist Millie. I will stick the envelope of money in your locker here at the office. Wanda will be waiting on the bench. She is expecting me, but I just can't make it." Charlie stated. Then he hung up.

Suddenly, it dawned on me who my boss was speaking about. It had to be the Miss Wanda who taught Milky Way to read the Tarot. Milky Way had spoke of a Wanda setting up shop on a bench. I did wonder what Charlie's relationship with Wanda was all about. Maybe she was one of his snitches, and he was trying to make me think she was a schizophrenic charity case.

~   ~   ~

With nothing better to do on Christmas Eve, I headed down to the detective agency where an envelope with Wanda's name on it, was taped to the inside of my locker door. Afterward, I rode my bicycle downtown, thinking I might enjoy a little ride in the park after delivering the cash. It was a sunny day and the temperature was in the upper seventies. The national weather report earlier, had said it was snowing in Chicago. There were some things I missed about Chicago winters. Snow was one of them. When we were kids, Maxi and I played for hours in the white stuff building forts, having snowball fights, and making snow men. I missed snow, Chicago, and Maxi. However, Maxi had chosen Jen and her children over me. I couldn't get past that betrayal.

As I bicycled into the downtown park, I pulled Charlie's envelope of cash from my back pocket. I intended to just ask whoever was sitting on the third bench if they were Wanda, pass the envelope to her, and go on with my evening. Entering the park, I headed left toward a bench area where individuals were throwing food to ducks. As I neared the benches, I counted. A street person was asleep on the first bench. I pedaled on. On the second bench was a pair of Goth teenagers necking. I pushed on. The next bench was about a hundred feet further. When I bicycled to a stop at the end of the third bench, a very tiny female figure was seated with her back to me. Her hat looked really familiar to me. I couldn't recall being acquainted with a little girl that was in the habit of wearing a floppy hat with birds on it. For a moment, I felt I had somehow missed the woman that Charlie referred to as Wanda. Maybe she hadn't arrived yet. Then the little figure turned around, and I backed up my bicycle in a frightened frenzy. It was not a child sitting on the bench. It was the ugly female Troll that I had encountered in my dream, the one who had collapsed the porch of my cabin, causing me to fall and injure myself. I was terrified.

The little Troll of a woman jumped down from the bench, put her hands on her hips, and gave me one of the harshest 'do not mess with me' frightening looks that I had ever experienced.

"Charlie sent me!" I yelled in fear of her flattening the tires on my bike, or making the earth beneath my feet disappear.

As a detective, I carried a handgun. However, a firearm was of no use when confronting a ghost, or a being not human. I was sure that Wanda was not human. She was a wrinkled, vicious, ugly, little dwarf of a woman, whose age I could not guess. I did recall Milky Way telling me that she had met Wanda when she was fifteen and had first come to California. The female Troll had to be at least ten years older than Milky Way, possibly near or a little older than me. I was in my thirties.

"Run . . . , run as fast as you can. I just might turn out to be your boogie man!" She snarled, as I continued to roll my bicycle backwards. I needed room to turn and cycle away from her. There were bushes on either side of the walk.

I knew I was no match for Wanda the Troll, as well as

knowing my Jewish God rained wrath on those fraternizing with seers, trolls, and witches. I was walking a Jewish tightrope.

"I will run like lightening, as soon as I get this bike turned around." I yelled, tossing her the envelope. " I am just Charlie's delivery boy."

"You are more than that, you Jewish giant. I have not forgotten that you dared to defy me and run across my bridge in the in-between world without permission. No man runs past me in defiance, and gets by with it. Maybe I will make the earth disappear under your feet, and then let you drop into the flames of the Protestant's hell. Maybe you deserve to experience their hell, fire, and damnation."

"Are you Protestant?" I spit out asking, thinking of nothing better to say in my moment of fear.

"Hell no . . . ," She replied looking me up and down.

"Are you Catholic like Charlie?" I asked, trying to keep her fuse under control, as I backed up further looking for an opening in the bushes to turn around in.

"Do I look like some wimpy, hymn singing, kiss the preacher's backside girl?" She asked in a disgusted voice, while removing her floppy hat and tossing it on the bench. That wasn't a good sign. She looked like she was about to go to war with me.

"Definitely not . . . ," I quickly replied. "Are you Hindu?" I asked, trying to buy a little time. I just couldn't get my bike to back up or turn around. I was in an unexpected predicament. The path thru the park was one way, and it looked like I was going to have to ride by her to rid myself of her.

"What are you, a dimwit giant?" She asked, stopping to pick up the envelope of cash which had fallen off the bench onto the ground. "Where in the hell did Charlie find you, in some big nosed 'I hate trolls' cult somewhere. I can read your mind. I don't like being called an ugly troll. Don't even think about trying to take out your prejudices and rage on me. I don't take persecution well?"

"Me . . . persecute you?" I inquired, letting out a fearful, nervous, snort and laugh.

Had I sat down in Charlie's office and fell asleep? He had interrupted my sleep pattern to run this errand for him. I had to be dreaming.

"Why are you laughing, dimwit giant?" She asked, giving me an evil eye. Her red, white, and blue sunglasses were pushed up, and resting in her hair above her forehead, like they were a head band.

"I am laughing because I think I am sleeping. I dreamed of you once before. You prevented me from entering my cabin door, 'fifty miles from nowhere.'"

"You were dimwit and powerless then, and you are the same now. It was sheer luck that you made it past me in your dream. I was distracted by your nakedness. I don't, as a rule, find naked dimwit giants trying to cross my bridge."

"You looked at my nakedness?" I asked blushing, and hoping she did not know that I was a dud.

"You dimwit giants go to strip clubs and look at naked girls. What is the difference?" She replied with a weird half grin on her face. "I am human just like you. I know a good looking naked man when I see one. However, in your Jay Bird state you were a little too hairy for my taste. If you were my dimwit giant, I would have to spend a fortune in wax and razors cleaning you up."

I blushed. As a Jewish man, I was quite hairy.

"You just inferred I was a dimwit, hairy, giant, Jay Bird. What do those of your world refer to you as? I have my doubts that you are human." I spit out, losing my cool.

"I am human. Dense, dimwit men, like you, call me a schizophrenic. What does the dense minded in your world call you, Dimwit?"

"A dud . . . ," I retorted without thinking. Then, I turned red and hoped she did not know what I was referring to. .

"Giants are often dud dimwits." She replied, sticking the envelope of cash down inside the front of her blouse into her high pocket. "You can't help being a dud, anymore than I can help being me. I guard a portal between parallel worlds. A door keeper is a lowly job, but necessary in the grand scheme of all things. You could learn the way of seers and mystics from me, if you are willing. Milky Way was willing. Voices tell me you know her."

"I think I will pass on instructions." I replied, as I found a hole in the bushes to make a turn in. "No one can teach a dimwit or a human not to be a dud."

"That is where you are wrong, you egotistical dimwit. Biology doesn't make a father. Love does." She retorted with a look that said she was receiving information from a world of voices that I could not hear.

Thinking she was referring to Jen's children, I replied, "I don't want to love or father children that are the products of a lifetime nightmare. If it is Jen speaking to you from beyond the grave, tell her so."

"Your sister's adopted children are not yours to have, just as Jen, Kris, and Pandora was not yours to have." Wanda the troll spit out in disgust, after pausing to listen to voices I could not hear.

I was totally annoyed with her reference to the three women I had once had feelings for. Suddenly, Wanda's face turned a bright red. She immediately turned from me, gathered up her belongings from her bench, and walked away as fast as she could go. I wondered what her red face was all about. Had one of her voices said something to embarrass her?

As she walked away, I took a good look at the swaying, ankle length skirt she had on, with Florida beach scenes printed all over it, as well as her floppy hat with Tarot cards and birds attached. She was unique. However, she was one wrinkled, little prune of a woman that I never wished to encounter again. Charlie had pulled a fast one on me, getting me to deliver his pay off to her, for who knew what.

After she had disappeared from sight and I was cycling out of the park, I was disgusted with myself. Why hadn't I asked if Pandora was well and happy in the mystical land beyond the portals?

CHAPTER TWENTY-FOUR

SNOWING ON THE CARPET

The Protestant's Christmas season once more faded into history. I concentrated on my detective work, and tried not to think about my secret life of being haunted by ghosts and mystical doors. Charlie didn't ask me to make any more money deliveries to Wanda. When he asked if everything went well, I acted like nothing was out of the ordinary. I wasn't about to admit that his Wanda snitch had scared the crap out of me twice.

Easter came and went without any visitations or portal openings. Then, Memorial Day weekend rolled around. I didn't have any plans for the weekend, and was looking forward to just a couple days of sleeping in late and some beach time. I needed a little sun. I moved around so much at night in my occupation, that I was a little on the Lily White side.

I had just put on my swim trunks and was preparing to head for the beach, when a knock sounded on my loft apartment's door. I wondered who it was. Milky Way had stopped making regular visits when I didn't pursue with her an interest in opening portals. Slipping my feet in my beach flip-flops, I headed for my entry door to see who it was. Opening it, I was surprised to see Milky Way standing there. It wasn't rent day.

"What is up?" I asked.

"It is snowing downstairs on my carpet. You know what that means." She replied with a disgruntled look on her face. "Pandora may be trying to return to us."

I know my face lit up like a light bulb. I made a dash past her and down the outside stairs, where I entered Milky Way's back door. She was hot on my heels. I quickly made my way to her inside reading room door. Once there, I watched as her door slowly turned into my 'fifty miles from nowhere' cabin door. As it changed, a fierce blizzard dumped snow on Milky Way's carpet. Immediately, I started shivering, having stepped from Sunny California temps into zero weather. Standing in my swimsuit and flip flops, with snow swirling around me, I put my hand on the door handle in an effort to open it. It would not budge.

"I can't get in," I called out to Milky Way.

"I managed to get the door to appear, but I cannot get it to open, either." She replied, as falling snowflakes started to turn her hair white. She began to shiver and rub her bare arms.

"How did you manage to get the snow and door to appear?" I asked in excitement, thinking I might be able to figure out a way to enter the in-between worlds and find Pandora. She was the only woman since Jen that I had happy moments with. Secretly, I wanted her to return to me.

"I knew that there had to be a key or set of steps to gain access. Today, I recalled about all your ghosts knocking and needing shelter. I knocked on my reading room door three hard raps with my knuckles. I then yelled that I was cold and needed shelter. This is the results." She replied excitedly, thru chattering teeth.

"Oh . . . ," I replied, stepping back for a moment staring at the door.

Then I recalled Pandora and what she had said about her mystical desk drawer portal. She said she had yelled to be let in, and then had pounded three times.

"I think I know the key sequence, Milky Way. Pandora discovered it the day before she left us."

"Give all the credit to Pandora." Milky Way huffed. "She gets the gypsy mystic of the year award."

I turned and looked at Milky Way for a moment. I could see jealousy in her eyes. I refrained from making any more references to Pandora. I had always thought that Milky Way and Pandora were friends. Something had caused their relationship to go sour. I wasn't sure what.

"The strangers at my door years ago in my cabin 'fifty miles from nowhere', were on this side like you and I are now. A person on the inside, or the other side of the door, must do the opening. Someone, whom I thought was a wild animal scurrying, opened the door originally for me. Knocking three times and asking to be let in is our part of the key sequence. The other part is performed on the other side of the door." I quickly relayed, knowing the mystical door could disappear at a moment's notice. We have not been able to open it, because whoever exists on the other side of the door is either not there, or doesn't wish to interact or socialize with us. Sometimes, I don't answer my loft apartment door upstairs, if it is in the middle of my sleeping hours."

"Pandora was young, needy, and naïve. They let her in because of it." Milky Way replied, suddenly big eyed. "I have been used. She needed access to me, in order to have access to her door. I can't open this door, because it is not mine."

I turned back to the door and gave it three sharp knocks. Then, I yelled, "Pandora . . . I know what your hidden secret is, your love for someone that did not love you. I have peeped into your box, your soul. Open up and let me find shelter with you. Your secret is my secret, and my secret is your secret."

Suddenly, the door creaked open and a pair of familiar eyes peeped out at me, thru little wire rimmed glasses containing very thick lens.

"I know your secret, Monty?" She asked curiously, standing in the door preventing me from stepping inside with her.

"Zeke hurt you with his words, making you feel like you were not woman enough for him. My college fiancé hurt me with her words, making me feel like I was not man enough for her." I spit out, trying to avoid using the word dud. "We are alike."

Pandora opened the door wider and stood barefoot in her red gypsy skirt and white blouse, staring at me. She was no longer seventeen, but appeared to be in her late twenties. She had aged. I glanced down at her toes which were no longer straightened. Her toes looked like new born kittens or puppies lying on top of each other to stay warm. I realized in that moment, that we could not take to the other side man-made alterations to ourselves. I stared into her blue eyes. My heart was doing some serious palpitations. I so wanted to be loved. I was willing to step thru the door, if she would love me.

Knowing that portal doors never stayed open long, I sputtered, "I like you just the way you are, Pandora. Don't change for anyone. Glue the shattered pieces of your heart back together again and fly out of your box to love again. I want you to fall in love with me. I need you."

Pandora's face suddenly beamed. "Thank you for seeing me as special. However, I know that I am a reject. Needing someone and loving someone are two different things."

Immediately, Pandora started to fade from the feet up.

"I am a dud." I yelled, not wanting her to go.

"I am a reject." She yelled back sadly. "No man should settle for a woman, whose heart belongs to another, because he is a reject like me. This Pandora's box is closing."

"Don't go, Pandora." I begged, as I shivered, standing in ankle deep snow, ignoring Milky Way. "I love you."

'Poof' . . . Pandora disappeared. Then the door faded and 'poof' it was gone. Then the snow disappeared. In distraught, I turned to Milky Way, expecting comfort from her.

"What does Pandora have that I don't?"

"What?" I asked, tuning into her disgruntled demeanor.

"You are an unbelievable Jewish ass hole." Milky Way sputtered. "Has it ever occurred to you that I might have feelings for you? You are an asshole declaring your love for Pandora in front of me. Get out of my shop and my life forever." She yelled.

"I . . . I am sorry!" I stated, as she practically pushed me out the back door of her shop. "I didn't know."

"Well, you know now, you Jewish ass hole. Now, find yourself somewhere else to live. I am not renewing your lease next month. You want Pandora, you have got Pandora. A missing woman doesn't make a warm bed partner."

~   ~   ~

Milky Way kept her word. She did not renew my lease. I had to move from my loft apartment a month later. I put my stuff in storage and moved in temporarily with Charlie, my boss, who was willing to put up with me till I could find another suitable place.

CHAPTER TWENTY-FIVE

TAMING CHARLIE'S CHIHUAHUA

Independence Day rolled around. Charlie had a slew of company coming to spend the Fourth of July with him. He planned to van them all up to a rented cabin in Lake Tahoe for the holiday. I agreed to give up my bedroom for one night, while his relatives arrived by plane, bus, and auto. I agreed to sleep in a sleeping bag on the balcony till the gathering was complete and they all left. Charlie's Fourth of July celebration was a planned, small family reunion.

All families have one member that doesn't get along with the others, or is just such an idiot that they drive everyone crazy with their self-centeredness. Charlie warned me ahead of time that he had one of such. He told me that he had an odd sister, but didn't elaborate on what odd was. My sister Maxi was different. Perhaps Charlie's sister was Lesbian like her. Maybe Charlie's arriving house guests were homophobic. The only thing Charlie volunteered about his sister was that I had met her once. He did not tell me where. I figured that I had possibly bumped into her at the agency, and spoke briefly, thinking she was a client. We averaged a hundred clients a month. After awhile, one client just looked like another. It was the cheaters I remembered, because I stalked and photographed them in their insane moments.

Being a temporary, free loading roommate of Charlie, I agreed to blend into the wallpaper and do what I could to make his guests comfortable for the one night. His one big request was for me to run interference, keeping his guests from killing his sister, and her from antagonizing them. He asked me to keep his odd sister busy and out of everyone's cross hairs. I agreed, not wanting to rock my boat. Besides, it was not like my little black book was overflowing with numbers. I didn't date.

One by one, Charlie's guests started to arrive. It wasn't long before Charlie's place was a mad house. Three snotty nosed brats were running amuck, getting into everything and seeing just how much noise they could make. Their mother, who claimed to have a migraine, was ignoring them. My boss' two brothers and a couple of cousins were sitting out on the balcony drinking beer and flipping cigarettes over the railing. In the kitchen, three middle aged women were swapping childbirth stories and other family gossip. Behind the couch, on the carpet, some older uncle was asleep and snoring. He had arrived by bus, having spent two days and nights on it. In the hall bathroom, two teen girls were sitting on the lavatory counter, talking on cell phones. It was a mad house, and in hindsight, I wished I had rented a motel room for the night. Being a good sport, I smiled and tried to stay out of the way, as I waited for my charge, Charlie's odd sister, to arrive.

Then the door bell rang.

"I'll get it!" I yelled at Charlie, who had one little snotty nosed kid under his arm, having just rescued him from his two siblings who had tried to color his skin green with permanent magic markers. The kid was a leprechaun green mess and his mother was hysterical.

Making my way to the door, I opened it wide, expecting to see a thirty ish Lesbian to be standing there, possibly sporting tattoos and a man's haircut. In shock, I gasped and jumped back. My nightmare, Wanda the Troll, was standing there. She was wearing the same clothing I had seen her in back on Christmas Eve when I had delivered the envelope of cash. She had on the Florida scene skirt, patriotic sunglasses, and the floppy hat with the colorful birds and Tarot cards on it.

"I am not on your bridge," I sputtered, at a loss for words.

"No . . . , and you will never cross my bridge again, if I have anything to say about it, you dimwit giant." She retorted, stepping past me after giving me a little push. I obligingly backed up. "What is your name, anyway?"

"I am Monty, one of Charlie's detectives. Who are you, one of Charlie's snitches?"

"I have been called a lot of names, but never a snitch." She retorted, pushing her sunglasses to the end of her nose, and looking over the top of them at me. "Where is Charlie?"

"He is in the kitchen trying to wash permanent green marker off of a kid." I replied, almost flattening myself against a wall in the entry way in fear of her. This wasn't a good time for the ghost world to be haunting me. Also, I wasn't sure how Charlie would feel about one of his snitches showing up at his house door.

"Mess with me, giant, and it will be permanent outhouse crap that Charlie will be trying to wash off of you." Wanda replied, as she peeped in the living room door, to see who was gathered there.

Taking a deep breath, I replied. "You don't have to worry about me messing with you. I am waiting for Charlie's sister to join me on my bridge. Charlie has assigned her to me, to keep track of for the day. I will definitely stay out of your way, and off whatever you say is your bridge."

"Charlie has assigned you to keep track of me for the day?" She sputtered, turning red in the face.

"You are Charlie's sister?" I asked in a gasp.

"My brother is always trying to fix me up with some dimwit, loser detective of his." She replied, pushing her sun glasses back up in position. "Forget about me, dimwit. You go hang out with the snotty nosed kid who has green marker on his face. He is probably your speed."

"I am going to kill Charlie," I muttered, following her to the kitchen. She headed straight for the kid who had a green face and hugged him. She ignored completely the others present, as well as the other two wild little brats who were out of control.

"Where is my brother?" She asked in a cold voice, turning and scanning the room.

It was strange. Everyone in the room seemed to rise slowly and move as far away from Wanda as they could get. I was of the opinion that they all had been on Wanda's bridge, at some point, and had been violently thrown off. I could tell they all seemed to fear her. I didn't blame them.

"Charlie is in the hall bathroom looking for something

that might remove permanent marker." One of the women replied.

Wanda left the room. I followed her into the hall. I kept what distance I could.

Halfway down the hall, the little Troll of a woman spun about and peered at me, putting her hands defiantly on her hips.

"Why are you following me, you big nosed dimwit?" She demanded harshly.

In reaction, I immediately took my hand and touched my nose with my fingers. I did have a big nose and was at times somewhat self-conscious about it. It annoyed me that she had made reference to my facial flaw.

"Charlie has assigned me to hang out with you. I am not following you. I . . . I am sort of your baby sitter for the day." I retorted, suddenly regretting my use of the word 'baby sitter'.

In a flash, Wanda flew into my leg and started biting my thigh, just above the knee cap. In pain, I began to yell and kick, trying to free myself. Charlie and everyone imme- diately came running. I couldn't get free of her fangs. As I yelled in pain, Charlie pulled her off of me, grinning.

"I see you have met my sister," Charlie stated, smiling from ear to ear and holding his sister, Wanda the Troll, back from me. He was holding her by the neck of her blouse. She was kicking and snarling.

"Your sister just bit me, like a dog." I sputtered.

Then all of Charlie's house guests started to laugh. I think it was in relief that it wasn't one of them that she had affixed her rage on.

"Wanda, be nice." Charlie demanded, as he stooped down and stared her in the eyes, not letting go of her blouse. "Monty is single, as well as being one of my best detectives. You should feel lucky to have him to hang with for the day. Women chase him like he is a god. He doesn't have to spend time with you. He can date any woman he wants. Hanging with you to day, is him doing me a favor. Now, cool it."

I was in total shock. For one thing, I didn't have women chasing me. Charlie was lying to his sister to control her.

"Sorry, Monty . . . ," Charlie stated turning to me. "She needs a strong armed man to put her on the end of a short dog leash and walk her. I think she must be constipated."

"For your information, I have a man." Wanda spit out with Charlie still holding her back. "As far as constipation goes, you and the family are what make me so. Just maybe I should eliminate all of you."

There was a chorus of gasps that fell from the mouths of Charlie's guests.

"You had a man, Wanda. Gold is dead. Not only that, he had a restraining order placed on you, before his demise." Charlie retorted.

"Who is Gold?" I asked, rolling the name over my tongue slowly.

"Gold was a circus performer who lived in Florida, before dying in a plane crash. He dumped Wanda for a trapeze girl, who had the figure of a model, and a face that wasn't a prune."

In amusement, I snorted. My hat was tipped to Gold for putting a restraining order on her. I might have to do so myself, before the day was over.

"Laugh at me, you dim witted giant, and you will regret it." Wanda snarled.

I now knew what Wanda and my shared interest in the cabin was all about. Gold was a ghost behind my portal door, the cabin door. She was stalking him in the astral when she made the cabin's porch disappear beneath my feet. Gold was one of the three Wise brothers.

Biting my lip for a moment, I stooped to her level and extended my hand, "Truce for the day, for Charlie's sake? I understand loving someone so much you can't let them go. I now understand why your bench was beneath the window at my cabin, in my dream. You were using it to stand on and peep in."

"What bench . . . what window?" She huffed, eyeing Charlie.

Somehow, I knew Wanda didn't want Charlie to know about the event. I backed off.

"You are right. I have mistaken you for someone else." I replied. "Besides, girls that stalk me are tall, gorgeous, model types. I am a god."

"You, dimwit, are far from being a god. In my book you are a three legged, hopping rabbit. You couldn't catch a normal female rabbit if you wanted to; much less, a pedigreed and pedicured one. You are a dud to normal women, just as I am flawed in my brother's eyes."

"I bit my lip, when she used the word dud. That was the key to opening up all of my old wounds."

"Cool it, Wanda!" Charlie demanded, releasing his hold on the back neck portion of her blouse. "Monty is not the one who dumped you for a model. Gold was. Furthermore, you are what you are, a schizophrenic dwarf. You have got to learn to deal with it. Who knows, Monty here could be your soul mate." He stated and then winked at me.

"That is insulting." Wanda replied putting her hands on her hips and looking Charlie straight in the eye. He was still stooped down to her level. "Dimwit giants don't appeal to me, besides, how would a girl ever get around his big nose to kiss? He has a disgusting, monstrous, nose; not to mention that most giants are duds."

At that point, I was self conscious about my nose, as well as being insulted.

"Take it from me," I huffed, finding my backbone. "I have no intentions of ever letting you try to maneuver around my Jewish nose and kiss me. I prefer a well mannered, gorgeous, tall female who doesn't bite and bark like a bratty little Chihuahua dog."

"You just dared to call me a dog, you dimwit giant." She stated, shaking her dwarf fist at me, and then trying to kick me on the ankle. I jumped back.

I then reached down and snatched her Tarot and bird hat from her head and held it out of her reach. I then opened the front door and threw it outside. Then I reclosed the door. "Hats off in this house," I stated in a harsh voice.

Charlie got distracted by one of his three guest brats running by us with a dripping ice cream on a stick. He ran after him. Charlie's carpet was new.

Wanda quit lunging at me and grinned from ear to ear

with all of her teeth showing.

"If it is hat off for me, it is clothes off for you. You dimwit giant."

Then I watched as Wanda raised her hand to eye level, pointed her stubby finger at me, and waved her finger in a circle like it was a wand, placing a curse on me.

Instantly, she quit twirling her finger wand and my clothes went 'poof'. I stood in shock and Jay Bird naked in a house filled with strangers. Immediately, I covered my manhood with my cupped hands and made a run for the hall bathroom.

Wanda yelled after me, "Don't cross me, or my bridge, dimwit."

Luckily, the teens had vacated the bathroom. I ran in , locked the door, and then proceeded to dig in the clothes hamper there, for clothes to put on. In my thinking, dirty clothes were better than no clothes.

~   ~   ~

I stayed clear of Wanda till after lunch, as did most of her relatives. If she seated herself on one side of the room, her family moved to the other. If she crossed over and went to sit with them on their new side, they would one by one excuse themselves and leave her presence. I felt sorry for her, but at the same time, I was afraid of her. I knew she was more than just human. She was a portal keeper. She had special powers that common humans didn't have, or weren't aware of having. Stripping me of my clothing was a power I didn't want her to use on me again. It was embarrassing to be a grown man, a gun toting detective, who was vulnerable to a four foot nothing troll of a woman, who scared the pee out of you.

Two or three hours after the marker event and Wanda's arrival, Charlie had a chance to grab a beer and join me on his balcony for a quick breath of fresh air. He was unaware that Wanda had earlier made a naked Jay Bird out of me.

"Are you aware that your sister is head strong and tries to intimidate your relatives, as well as me?" I asked, as we stood leaning on his outside railing. There was no way I was going to admit to him that I was frightened out of my gourd in her presence.

"My sister is a nutcase, Monty. She is a schizophrenic who thinks she has powers that enable her to speak with the dead and travel to in-between worlds. She is thirty-five years old, never held down a job, and is a spoiled pain in my ass. I give her money and check on her, only out of respect to my dead mother who, on her death bed, asked me to keep an eye on her.

Neither Charlie, nor I, saw Wanda step out onto the balcony behind us as we discussed her.

"I am not a schizophrenic and I do work." Wanda yelled, interrupting us.

We instantly spun around. I instantly wondered if I should jump from the balcony for my own safety, as Charlie choked on a mouthful of beer. I knew that Wanda had collapsed a porch beneath my feet in my first encounter with her.

After regaining his composure, Charlie spoke. "Our parents kept you constantly on a psychiatrist's couch, when we were kids. You know as well as I do, that schizophrenia is your diagnosis."

"Our partners were dimwits and I do support myself, I will have you know. Your handouts have always been unwanted on my part. I have accepted them, in order to let you feel good about avoiding me. You were never a brother to me when we were little, and you still aren't. I can read you like a book. You weren't able to not invite me for this family gathering. However, down deep you have wished I wouldn't come, as have the others. Do you know what it is like to be unloved and unwanted?"

Charlie didn't reply. Suddenly, I was aware that Wanda was somewhat like me. I was unloved, due to being a dud. Wanda was unloved, because her family didn't see her uniqueness.

Biting my lip, I spit out, "Milky Way has told me how much money you make reading the Tarot, and how good you are at it. How about a truce between us?"

"You want a truce . . . ?" She asked in a sputter. I could see in her eyes that she didn't trust me. "Okay, dimwit, as long as you stay off of my bridge."

"I think you have met your match, a Jewish giant who can tolerate you." Charlie stated, while taking a drink from an almost full can of beer.

Wanda turned toward him. In an angry flash, she raised her hand and did a little twirling thing with one extended finger. Instantly, the beer can exploded; drenching her brother.

"Can a schizophrenic do that, Charlie?" Wanda asked in a very ticked off voice.

"Only you can do that." I replied, walking over and taking a stance next to her. "This giant wants to stand with you.

I don't want to be sprayed with beer, nor have my clothes disappear again."

Wanda looked up at me, and I thought I saw a sparkle in her eye, that had not been there before. As frightened as I was of her and her powers, I felt she needed me. Her human body wasn't much to look at, but the Wanda inside of that vehicle was a force to be dealt with. She was able to walk between Earth and the heavens, not lying her human body down. I now understood Old Testament prophets who were caught up to God, not tasting death. They, like Wanda, were portal walkers.

~   ~   ~

Charlie, in a sour mood, pushed past us and entered his place to go wash the beer off of himself. I glanced down at Wanda with a grin. She smiled back. Her smile was definitely nicer to look at than her snarl.

"This dimwit giant is going to take a walk to get some fresh air. I will probably end up down at the corner convenience store, where I plan to grab a soda and a candy bar. Would you like to walk with me? I am buying."

"Why are you asking me?" She inquired, suddenly blushing.

I wasn't sure why she always seemed to be blushing and turning red in my presence. I decided she had to have high blood pressure and that was causing it.

"Well, for one thing, it is a relief not to have a woman hitting on me. Three of the women in the kitchen have already made suggestions to me, as well as one of the teen girls. Since you find me a dimwit, and definitely beneath you and not desirable, I figure I will be safe with you." I stated, winking at her.

"Have you got a sty or something in your eye, dimwit?" She asked, raising one eyebrow at me. Then, she winked at me.

"Do you also have a sty or something in your eye?" I replied, knowing she was warming up to me.

"I definitely have something in my eye." She replied, blushing. "I think it is your big nose that is making my eye twitch. Perhaps, I am allergic to you."

At that point, we left Charlie's place and proceeded to take a walk. Wanda's legs were shorter than mine. I walked slowly, so she could keep up with me. I felt a bond forming between us, as we shared small talk. We discussed my cabin dream and her world of reading for individuals who were trying to contact the souls of their deceased loved ones and friends. Her ability to receive and relay messages from those crossed over fascinated me. Wanda was a medium. Her Tarot card readings were for individuals who were just seeking guidance.

By the time we reached the convenience store, we had sort of become friends. After purchasing sodas and candy bars, we started our slow walk back to Charlie's place. As we sauntered along, I got up the nerve to approach Wanda about contacting Pandora for me. I was lonely, and I wanted her to return to me.

"Suppose, I have a deceased girlfriend or soul mate living in the in-between worlds . . .," I spit out, wading in to conversation. "Is it possible for you to contact and speak with her, just for the heck of it? Can you call forth and chat with individuals, like one girlfriend calling another on the phone?"

"Why are you asking?" She asked, ripping the wrapper off of her candy bar, and taking a bite.

"I had a fiancé named Jen, when I was in my early twenties, that I was madly in love with. She dumped me, because I discovered that I had a medical problem."

"Go on . . . I know that you are a dud."

I glanced at her for a moment in horror. I had tried to hide my secret of not being able to father children from all women. I realized that there was nothing I could hide from Wanda. She was a psychic know-it-all. I continued.

"I was devastated when Jen called me a 'dud'. She wanted children more than she wanted me. Within weeks, she married a man who could get her pregnant. She destroyed a piece of my psychological balance that I can't reclaim. After her, I met and fell in love with a married woman who chose her abusive husband over me. I spent at least ten years trying to convince her that she should love and be with me, not him. I was just getting over her, when Pandora entered my life last year. I opened up, and was developing feelings for her. She chose to enter a portal and cross over to the other side. I would like to send a message to each of these women!" I stated.

"You cannot have what is not yours to have, dimwit giant." She retorted, stuffing the last bite of her candy into her mouth, and sticking the wrapper in her skirt pocket.

"I have told myself that. However, telling the human heart that is another thing." I replied.

Wanda looked up not smiling at me. "What is the message you wish to send them?"

"I would like to tell Jen how much I hate her for destroying my self-esteem and image of myself as a man." I spit out, biting my lip for a moment.

"Go on . . .," She replied.

"I would like to tell Kris that she hurt me, not loving me. She is always sending me a message asking me to look for her son. I want you to tell her no. I am not doing any detective favors for a woman that just wants to use me, not love me."

"That is probably a smart decision, dimwit. I don't do pro-bono readings and you shouldn't let yourself be used for free detective work. We do have to support ourselves." She replied with a slight smile. "Go on . . . !"

"When I met Pandora last year, I wouldn't ask her out for two reasons. Number one was the fact that I felt she was too young for me. Secondly, she was in her child bearing years. I feared she wanted children. I didn't want to be hurt again, by a woman calling me a dud and dumping me again. Pandora was vulnerable and needed me, for reasons I can't go into. I feel I failed her."

"Self preservation is not a bad thing. I watch my backside with Charlie and my family. All of them would like to see me institutionalized." She replied, and then took a sip from her soda straw. "What message do you wish to send to Pandora? Do you wish her to find someone her own age in the land of beyond?"

"I would like to tell her that I am ready to love again. Would you tell her that I would like to pursue a relationship with her?" I spit out, and then turned red knowing how much older I was than Pandora.

"You are an ass hole, you dimwit giant." Wanda retorted, with a hint of rage in her voice.

I quickly backed up a bit from Wanda, wondering what I had said to antagonize her. She was livid and seriously red in the face.

"What did I say to offend you?" I blurted out.

"You are an unbelievable dimwit, you want what is not yours to have, and don't see what is right before you. Just like all other human giants with big noses and brains in their yangs, you choose young things and pretty faces. It is an insult, to ask me to play cupid. This walk has been a ploy on your part. You want to use me to get even with your past lovers, and land you a young thing in the present." She sputtered loudly, while raising her hand and extending a finger in a pointed position at me. I knew if she twirled it, I was in serious trouble.

"Er . . . Uh . . . ," I sputtered, wondering if she were going to make the Earth disappear beneath my feet, or cause my clothes to disappear again. I could tell by the look in her eyes that I was on her crap list.

After a moment of pointing her finger at me, and my almost crapping in my jeans, Wanda turned and walked in a rage to the nearest tree. I watched in fear, as she knocked three times on its bark. Immediately, a door appeared and she stepped thru it. Turning, she yelled at me, "I hope you rot unloved in the Protestant's Hell!" Then the door went 'poof'.

I was left standing with my mouth agape, wondering why she was angry, but thankful she hadn't taken out her wrath on me. Maybe Charlie was right. Even though she was a portal keeper, maybe she was a certifiable nut case. I gave her soda cup on the sidewalk a good kick. She had thrown it down when she walked away from me and knocked on the tree. After kicking the cup, I proceeded to pick it up. I was not a person who littered.

Suddenly, I felt very sleepy. I could not explain my overwhelming urge to nap. I sat down and leaned against the tree that Wanda had knocked on. I could feel myself dozing off. Dealing with Wanda the prune faced troll had zapped my energy. I needed to sleep. I knew I would not be able to take a siesta back in Charlie's apartment. His three snotty nosed, elf nephews were there, continuously screaming their lungs out and causing havoc.

CHAPTER TWENTY-SIX

CHRISTMAS COMES KNOCKING

I was startled from my nap by a loud pounding. I opened one eye slowly, and then the other. Afterward, I blinked a couple of times and shaded my eyes with my hand, in an effort to get my eyes to focus on whomever it was interrupting my sleep. To my surprise, I was looking out a driver's side window of a vehicle. A parking officer was pounding on the side of my driver's door. I set up straight, rubbing my face with one hand, while rolling down the glass with the other. Where in the hell was I?

"You have been parked here too long, buddy. You have got to move it. Let some other joker with a kid wanting to see Santa, have this spot. I have already given you three parking tickets. You have been parked here three, going on four hours. Now move it, or I am going to have your vehicle towed, with you in it." The female parking cop stated harshly, in her Chicago accent.

"Have you seen a little troll of a woman, named Wanda?" I asked in confusion.

"This isn't St. Patrick's day. Now, move it or I am going to send for the paddy wagon and have you locked up for public drunkenness? I have been pretty lenient, letting you sit here and sober up. It is the Christmas season, and I am trying to be nice."

I glanced about and realized that I was parked in front of Maxi's toy store.

"What did you say today is?" I asked, suddenly realizing that I was in the four wheel drive that I had rented over ten years before to drive to the mountain cabin.

"It is December 23rd, buddy. Tomorrow is Christmas Eve. Now get the lead out and move on, before I lose my Christmas patience with you."

Yawning, I took a good look at the face of the female parking cop. Then, I gasped. She was the door knocker who forced everyone to read her Kingdom literature. "Toilet paper, we used your writings for toilet paper . . . !" I muttered, still trying to make sense of my situation

"Use my parking tickets for toilet paper if you want. I am sure the judge will be thrilled to hear about your lack of respect for me."

"No . . . No . . . I didn't mean that the way it sounded. I will move. Just give me a minute or two to get my wits about me. I was in California having a soda with Wanda the Troll, just before you knocked."

Then, the traffic cop snickered, apparently amused with me. "She wasn't one of Santa's elves, was she?"

"I am Jewish. Santa isn't embraced by me, or my religion." I quickly retorted, putting my hands on the steering wheel. That is when I noticed hands they were ten years younger and white from washing dishes and food prep at the fast food place I first worked at in California. Was I in some sort of limbo?

"I know you. Why are you wearing a cop's uniform and where are your Witness pamphlets?" I asked the female cop, as I turned the key and started the rented vehicle's engine. "Your name is Angelica."

"People in this area of the city, are always confusing me with my door knocking twin sister. Right now, she is on her way with a Kingdom Hall group to the mountains to knock on doors. We are identical twins. She rents an apartment from the owner of Maxi's Toy Store."

"You are kidding me!" I stated, still in total confusion as to how I was ten years younger. "I shared a mountain cabin with her and some friends!" I blurted out. "She provided us literature that we used for toilet paper."

"I doubt that." The cop replied, tearing off a 4th parking ticket and handing it to me. "I know for a fact that you are the toy store's brother. I have brought my kid to sit on your lap for the last three years. That is the reason I am going easy on you. I plan to bring my kid tomorrow on Christmas Eve to sit on your lap and give you his list for Santa. You arrive by plane, and catch a taxi here every year on the 23rd. On Christmas Eve you set up shop in Maxi's big, red, fake sleigh. I have kept an eye on you all day, knowing who you are. If I were guessing, you probably had one too many shots of something potent on the plane flying here. You have been mumbling off and on all day, something about being a dud."

"I have been asleep?" I asked slowly, still confused.

"Yes, bud, you have been sleeping a serious drunk off sitting here, or a serious case of jet-lag."

I rubbed my face and eyes once more. Then I looked at the palms and backs of my hands. I was in my early twenties. Then, I broke out in laughter. I realized that I had been dreaming. I must have met Angelica, at one time or another, when she was paying Maxi her rent. Clumsily, I put the vehicle in drive and slowly pulled away from the curb. Down the street, and around the corner, I found another parking spot. I immediately got out and fed the meter.

Unsure of my still sleepy state, I took the array of parking tickets from the windshield and looked them over. They were real. Then reality set in. Pandora, Kris, and Charlie were characters in a crazy Christmas dream. As I started up the sidewalk, heading for the toy shop, I pulled my coat about me. It was icy cold and the wind was blowing fiercely. There was every possibility that the protestant's holiday season in Chicago was going to be a white one. Spotting a bench, a few feet from my Sister's shop, I sat down and rested my head in my hands.

As I sat there, I stuck one hand in my jacket pocket, to warm it. I felt a crinkled piece of paper and pulled it out. On it was written a California phone number, the name Wanda, and directions to the cabin 'fifty miles from nowhere. I tore off the part that had the directions to the cabin 'fifty miles from nowhere', and discarded it. I kept the part having Wanda's telephone number on it. Life suddenly made sense. Swallowing hard, I decided to suck up my pride and tell Maxi that it was okay for her to pursue a relationship with Jen. I could not have what was not mine to have. The dream had taught me that I could not have what was not mine to have. The dream was wisdom and instructions being passed to me from someone in the in-between world. I was no longer afraid of not being a man, or the wrath of my Jewish God.

I thought about Wanda and smiled. When I returned to California, I had new plans for my future. The first thing on my agenda was to bicycle to the downtown park, to the third bench, and hopefully find Wanda waiting for me. I was indeed a dimwit, for not seeing she was the one I had been making my way to in the dream. I now somehow knew she was the other half of me, my eternal soul mate.

For every man there is one woman, the other half of him. For every woman there is one man, the other half of her. Settling for one that is not yours to have, will only bring you misery.

Shalom to you in your Christmas dream or nightmare!

~   ~   ~

THE END

Update

The dream did lead me to Wanda. After returning to California, I bicycled to the park and she was sitting on the third bench reading Tarot Cards. I stood nervously at a distance and proposed to her in a yell. Suprisingly, she did not make the ground disappear beneath my feet, or strip me naked. Instead, she yelled back, "Who in the heck are you, dimwit?"

Six months after the proposal, Wanda and I married. I am Jewish. My wife is Wiccan. Our adopted son is a Christmas crazy Protestant. Our special son made his way to us from the North Woods, after having lost his mother in a snow mobile accident. He once flew a red, snowmobile plane with ironing board wings. Now, in sunny California, he rides a Harley with wings. At Christmas, we string balls of Christmas lights (runway lights) up the sidewalk, so Santa Claus can find his way to us. Snicker Doodle knows he is adopted and that his real dad is Santa Claus.

Other Books Available In The Zeke's Feet Detective Series

By Jo Hammers

Book One - SILENT WINGS – The story of a window peeper, named Zeke, who grows up and becomes a detective. It is a rag to riches story about a kid, from a white trash drug dealing family, who overcomes life's difficulties and becomes the owner of Zeke's Feet Detective Agency. His best friend Jack is a girl living in a boy's physical body. Zeke accepts those in his life for who they are, because he knows what it is like to be looked down on. He is from a white trash family, and has been judged his whole life by their meth making and drug dealing.

Book Two - TEST THE GODS – This is the tale of a boy named Chester who wants to escape his low class, garbage truck driving, dump family. He dreams of running away and becoming a detective who works for Zeke's Feet Detective Agency in California. In pursuing his goal to escape his garbage hauling and dump life existence, he accidentally discovers a sociopath's killing field. Chester, a lily white skinned teen falls in love with an ebony black skinned girl who is older than him. His stepfather, an extremely prejudiced member of the white sheets, is not pleased with Chet's interracial relationship and seeks revenge on his stepson for costing him a promotion in the white sheet society. Women disappear and voices cry in the night, as the stench of death insults the noses of those living outside the gates of a garbage dump named Gardenia.

Book Three - CHRISTMAS COMES KNOCKING.

Book Four - SIZZLE - Coming Fall 2014.

www.ingramcontent.com/pod-product-compliance
Lightning Source LLC
Chambersburg PA
CBHW071049250626
47159CB00002B/411